Una-Mary Parker lives in Knightsbridge, London. Drawing extensively on her background as a former social editor of *Tatler* and a prominent member of the social scene, Una-Mary Parker has written a dramatic and compulsive novel of suspense. Her previous international bestsellers, *Riches*, *Scandals*, *Temptations*, *Enticements*, *The Palace Affair*, *Forbidden Feelings*, *Only The Best* and *A Guilty Pleasure* are all available from Headline and have been extensively praised:

'A compulsive romantic thriller' *Sunday Express*

'Deliciously entertaining' *Sunday Telegraph*

'Scandal . . . saucy sex and suspense' *Daily Express*

'This novel has everything – intrigue, romance, ambition, lust' *Daily Mail*

'Blue-blood glitz at its best' *Prima*

'Will keep you glued to the page' *Daily Express*

'The characters ring true and the tension mounts nicely' *Sunday Express*

Also by Una-Mary Parker

Riches
Scandals
Temptations
Enticements
The Palace Affair
Forbidden Feelings
Only The Best
A Guilty Pleasure

False Promises

Una-Mary Parker

HEADLINE

First published in 1995
by HEADLINE BOOK PUBLISHING

First published in paperback in 1995
by HEADLINE BOOK PUBLISHING

10 9 8 7 6 5 4 3 2 1

All characters in this publication are fictitious and any resemblance to real persons, living or dead, is purely coincidental.

ISBN 0 7472 4874 5

Typeset by Keyboard Services, Luton, Beds

Printed and bound in Great Britain
by BPC Paperbacks Ltd
A member of The British Printing Company Ltd

HEADLINE BOOK PUBLISHING
A division of Hodder Headline PLC
338 Euston Road
London NW1 3BH

This is for my mother,
Laura Nepean-Gubbins,
a star in her own right.

God said take what you want and pay for it.

St Thomas Aquinas
c. 1225–74

AUTHOR'S NOTE

Whilst this novel was inspired by reports of recent events at Lloyd's of London it is a work of complete fiction; all characters and institutions are imaginary and their actions bear no relation whatsoever to those in real life except by coincidence. Nevertheless, I would like to thank the many people who so kindly helped me with my research into the subject.

Chapter One

London, 1991

Liza did not realise her husband was missing until two uniformed police officers knocked on her door one afternoon, asking if she knew of his whereabouts or if she thought he was likely to have committed suicide.

She stared at them, blankly. 'What are you talking about?'

The chief constable drew a notebook from his back pocket and flipped it open. 'This *is* the home of Mr Toby Hamcroft?' He glanced at the brass numbers screwed to the smart black front door. 'This *is* twenty-two Holland Park Walk, isn't it?'

Liza nodded. A creeping numbness was crawling up her spine and her heart was being stabbed by icy shards of fear. Something had happened to Toby, she was sure of it.

'Has . . . has there been an accident?'

'Not that we know of, ma'am.'

'Then what's happened?'

'May we come in for a moment, ma'am?'

She stood aside to let them enter. The hall was full of luggage: Liza, her three children and the au pair had only just returned to London from the country. She led them into a large, airy drawing room. French windows opened out on to the garden at the back of the early Edwardian house.

Suddenly, from the depths of a sofa, a velvety face looked up, dark eyes gleaming with shining expectation. Then a bolt of amber-coloured silk hurled itself joyfully forward, to greet them with exuberant delight.

'Down, Lottie!' It was no use. The Cavalier King Charles spaniel quivered with excitement, tail wagging, mouth grinning, and barked ecstatically.

'Quiet, girl! Down!' Liza's voice was stern now. Lottie gave another defiant wriggle before leaping back on to the sofa, where she scrabbled herself into a comfortable position once more, looking at them between golden tufted paws.

In silence, the policemen looked around, taking in the expensive clutter of a rich man's home. They'd been told Toby Hamcroft had made a packet; now they were seeing how he'd spent it. The large pale yellow and green room was arranged into several seating areas, divided by small tables on which stood large orchid plants, their blooms as delicate-looking as finely carved jade. Pale pink and sky-blue silk covered some of the chairs and sofas with surprisingly good effect, preventing the room looking bland. Amid the fine French antique furniture were the modern gadgets associated with wealth; state-of-the-art adult toys. Also to be seen were the toys of the rich man's child: two Gameboys and a stack of video cartoons. And among the arrangement of valuable trinkets, including a Fabergé box, stood a touching collection of pottery animals, painstakingly moulded by loving little hands. Trophies of achievement brought home from school for proud and doting parents.

Liza sat on the pink sofa, indicating two chairs that faced her.

'What's happened to my husband? Why are you here?' she asked anxiously.

The more senior of the two, Detective Inspector Robin Buck, consulted his notes. He was a sharp-featured man with piercing brown eyes and a blunt manner.

'Your husband's with an insurance company called Martin E. L. Hamcroft's, I believe?'

Liza nodded silently, wondering what on earth was coming next.

'And Mr Declan Connolly is a colleague of your husband's?'

'Yes. But I don't see . . .'

'Mr Connolly contacted Scotland Yard this morning, saying he has reason to believe your husband is missing. Mr Connolly has been trying to get hold of you since Saturday but he didn't know where you were either. He even phoned your parents in Scotland, and when they said they had no idea where you or your husband were, he became most concerned.'

'But this is absurd!' Liza exclaimed. 'No one's missing!

My husband is in New York on business, which I would have thought Declan would know, and the children and I have been staying with friends in the country. My husband certainly knew where I was.'

'But no one knows where your husband is, Mrs Hamcroft,' Buck pointed out. 'When did you last have any contact with him?'

Liza's heart started to pound uncomfortably. 'Last Thursday,' she replied.

'Nearly a week ago?'

Nearly a week ago! Oh, God! If only she'd swallowed her stupid pride and instead of waiting for him to ring and apologise, why hadn't she phoned him first? Now she felt dreadful, and it had been such a silly argument they'd had too. How could she have got so heated over something like how much they should spend on the children's birthday presents? Toby had said he wasn't having his children spoilt by giving them gifts that cost hundreds of pounds; she had said to give children something that made them happy wasn't the same as spoiling them. Because it was late and they'd both been tired, what had started as a fairly petty row had blown out of all proportion.

'I'll see you next week,' Toby had said curtly, as he'd left the next morning. Liza hadn't answered because she'd still felt so cross. And he hadn't phoned in the meantime ... and she was damned if she was going to ring him first.

Guilt made Liza blush.

'Yes, nearly a week ago,' she admitted.

'What time did your husband leave here last Thursday?'

'He left at about seven in the morning. He had to catch a flight to New York. I don't understand what's happening? Why are you here?'

The atmosphere in the room was tense.

Buck spoke again. 'Do you know for certain he flew to the States, Mrs Hamcroft?'

Liza looked at him in disbelief. '*Of course* he flew to the States! He had a lot of business to do in New York. I don't understand what you're saying. Are you sure you've got the right person?' It couldn't be Toby, she assured herself. There had been some terrible mix-up.

'Isn't it strange that you haven't talked to each other on the phone in that time?' Buck asked.

Liza hedged and then decided to be honest. 'Toby usually rings me when he lands, but we'd had a stupid quarrel ... and I decided I wouldn't ring him. I don't understand any of this. What's going on?' Fear now hammered in her head alongside bewilderment.

'Mr Declan Connolly has reported your husband as missing, Mrs Hamcroft. If you can tell us where he is, we won't trouble you any further. But it's our job to follow up reports of this kind.'

Liza got to her feet. 'But this is madness! I tell you Toby isn't missing! He's working in New York!'

Buck sat stiffly, looking up at her as she stood with her back to the fireplace, her hands clenched by her side.

'We've checked with the hotel, and the airline, but although he was booked on the New York flight, he did not go to New York. In fact, we've been unable to confirm he has even left the country.'

'Dear God!' She turned her face to look out of the window, as if she would find the answer among the sun-dappled leaves of their paved garden. Then she turned sharply to Buck again.

'Are you *sure*? Millions of people must fly abroad every day... There are so many airlines. Surely you can't have checked them all?'

'We're certain he never left the country,' Buck replied. 'Unless he used an assumed name and a false passport. From our enquiries, no one seems to have seen him since last Wednesday evening, with the exception of yourself. You say you saw him Thursday morning.'

Liza flopped down on to the sofa again, as if the strength had drained away from her legs.

'I don't believe this is happening,' she said desperately. 'There's *got* to be an explanation.' She was scared now. Declan wouldn't have contacted the police unless he thought something was seriously wrong. Toby had known Declan Connolly for fifteen years; he was a reliable friend and colleague. But why hadn't he told her Toby had failed to turn up in New York before reporting it to the police? Then she remembered she'd been visiting her old schoolfriend, Emma; he wouldn't know where she lived, now she was married.

'We were hoping,' Buck began, breaking into her

thoughts, 'that you might be able to give us a lead? Tell us where you think your husband might have gone?'

Liza looked at him miserably, her eyes deeply troubled. 'I don't know! I've no idea! There has to be some ghastly mistake.'

Buck's partner spoke for the first time. He was a much younger man, keen and open-looking.

'Your husband has a private helicopter, I believe?' he remarked, almost with eagerness.

She shook her head. 'Not any more. He sold it. Because his business trips are all in the States, he wasn't getting enough use out of it.'

'But you still have a yacht?' Buck intervened.

'Yes. *Morning Glory*. She's moored in Monte Carlo; that is when we don't hire her out for charter.'

The two men exchanged looks. Buck's expression seemed to say, *Nice for some*. The younger man looked impressed.

'Oh, I wish to God I knew what was happening!' Liza exclaimed, suddenly on the edge of tears. 'I don't believe Toby's missing. It's not possible, unless he's had an accident and no one knows who he is.' The thought terrified her. Supposing he was lying unconscious in some hospital having lost identifying papers? Maybe he'd even lost his memory?

'Tell me, Mrs Hamcroft,' Buck spoke as if he were picking his words with care, 'does your husband have any business worries? His syndicate is in Lloyd's of London, isn't it? Is he in financial difficulties?'

Liza looked incredulous. 'Toby with money worries?'

If the situation hadn't been so serious, she'd have laughed.

'He certainly doesn't have money worries,' she protested. 'He's a very successful businessman. He's been at Lloyd's for over twenty years,' she added, 'in a syndicate started by his father.'

At that moment, howls broke out in the hall outside the drawing room; children's voices high-pitched and angry.

'I did *not* use your paints!'

'Yes, you did! You used them without asking . . . and you haven't put the tops back on the tubes . . . and now they're *ruined!*'

'Don't lie! They're *not* ruined!'

'They are!' Sobs filled the air.

Liza jumped to her feet and hurried towards the hall. 'Tilly! Thomas! Stop that at once, Tom.' She scolded her nine-year-old son as he executed a well-placed kick on his sister's shin.

'Mummy . . . Tom took my new paints,' wept Tilly, who at eleven already showed signs of being a beauty when she grew up, but at this moment looked quite plain, with her face flushed and her hair dishevelled.

'We don't tell tales,' Liza said firmly. 'Give me that box of paints and go down to the kitchen and have your tea.'

'What are you going to do with the paints?' Thomas asked suspiciously. 'I only *borrowed* them for a minute.'

'I'm going to look after them for now,' Liza replied, giving him a warning look. He was an expert at winding up his sister, and Tilly always fell for it.

'You didn't borrow them, you took them,' Tilly said shrilly, determined to have the last word.

'That's enough. Off you go. Ingrid will give you tea.'

'Who are you talking to, Mummy?' Thomas asked, as he swung on the banister rail.

'Some policemen,' Liza replied lightly. 'Where's Sarah?'

'Having tea. Why are you talking to the policemen, Mummy?'

'I'll tell you later; now run along or Sarah will eat all the biscuits.' Her four-year-old daughter had a prodigious appetite and, when given the chance, stuffed food into her mouth with relentless determination.

Tilly spoke. 'I want to know why the policemen are here, Mummy. What do they want?'

'They're just asking some questions,' Liza replied evasively. 'Now do hurry up.' She gave them a gentle push in the direction of the stairs that led to the basement kitchen. 'If you're good you can watch television for half an hour before you go to bed.' She hurried back into the drawing room.

'You'll have to excuse me,' she told Buck and his colleague. 'I'm afraid I can't help you. There's obviously been a hideous mistake. I don't believe my husband is really missing at all. He's a most reliable man. If he'd changed his plans, he'd have let me know.' Even if we had quarrelled, she thought. Aloud she said: 'I'm certain there's been a mix-up somewhere along the line.'

Buck handed her what looked like a business card. 'If

you hear anything, will you call me immediately at this number?' he asked.

Liza took the card. 'My husband's due back tomorrow evening; why don't you give us a ring then, and you can ask him yourself where he's been?'

Down in the warm and comfortable pine kitchen, there was temporary silence as the children ate bread and honey sandwiches made by Ingrid, the Norwegian au pair. She looked up as Liza entered. She was a striking-looking girl, with blonde hair cut in a fringe and a wide smile that showed even teeth.

'You like a cup of tea, Mrs Hamcroft?' she enquired.

Liza sank on to one of the pine chairs. 'Yes, please, Ingrid.'

'Hello, Mummy!' Sarah crowed, clapping her hands with delight, her small mouth rimmed with honeyed crumbs.

Liza smiled vaguely, too worried to pay much attention. She felt totally stunned, as if she'd had all the breath squeezed out of her body. And terribly guilty too. She and Toby had never parted on a row, in all their married life; supposing something dreadful had happened to him?

'Mummy, I want Coke for tea,' Thomas complained. 'I *hate* milk.'

'You know you're not allowed anything but milk for tea,' Liza replied automatically.

'Can I have a chocolate milkshake, then?' His tone was querulous.

'Yes, OK.' Anything for a bit of peace and quiet, she thought.

Tilly looked at her half-empty cup of milk. 'Can I have a milkshake, too?'

'You've already drunk most of your milk,' Liza pointed out.

'But it's not fair that he should have a milkshake if I can't,' Tilly whined.

'Can you make them both chocolate milkshakes, Ingrid, and then get them into the bath?' Liza said in desperation, knowing they were manipulating her, but too anxious about Toby to care.

Ingrid nodded.

'Do I have to have a bath?' asked Sarah.

'Yes. And your hair has to be washed, too.'

'No way, José,' she replied cheerfully. She was always picking up Tom's catchphrases.

Liza rose, taking her cup of tea with her. 'Can you manage, Ingrid? I've got to make some urgent phone-calls.'

'Of course, Mrs Hamcroft. It no problem.'

Upstairs, in the cosy privacy of her sitting room which led off the drawing room, she dialled the familiar number of Martin E. L. Hamcroft's.

'Can I speak to Declan Connolly, please?' she asked the girl on the switchboard.

'Hold on, please.' There was a pause and then she came back on the line.

'I'm afraid Mr Connolly is in a meeting.' Her voice was high-pitched and sing-song. 'Can I get him to call you back?'

'Could you ask him to phone Mrs Hamcroft, please? It's very urgent.'

'I'll do that.' There was a click and she was gone.

'Damn!' Liza swore. She dialled the number again and got the same telephonist. 'You cut me off,' she complained. 'I want to speak to Mr Charles Bryer, please.' He was Toby's boss and chairman of Martin E. L. Hamcroft's, appointed by Toby's father before he'd retired.

'Sorry, Mrs Hamcroft,' she trilled, not sounding sorry at all. 'I'm afraid Mr Bryer has left for the day.'

What the hell was going on? The police turn up at her house and tell her Toby had been listed as missing, and she can't even get hold of anyone in his office to find out what was happening.

'Mr Bryer has left already?' she asked. 'Are you sure?'

'Well, it is half past six. We're all going home in a minute!' The girl sounded quite offended.

Liza hadn't realised it was so late. All she could do now was wait for Declan to return her call.

The house was silent, the children asleep on the top floor, and Lottie curled up on her bean-bag in the corner. Ingrid had gone out for the evening, and Liza, not bothering to cook herself anything, sat at her desk going through the pages of her address book for the umpteenth time. Declan had never returned her call and when she tried his home there was no reply. There was no reply from Charles Bryer's home number either. It was now eight o'clock and a dreadful thought had just struck her. It swooped out from nowhere with black wings of fear that enshrouded her, smothered her, made her go cold with horror and her heart stand still. No, it couldn't be that! Not in a million years! She and Toby were so happily married. He'd never looked at anyone else in the thirteen years they'd been together ... and yet the thought persisted. Supposing Toby had run away with another woman? It hadn't occurred to her until she came across the name Victoria Burchfield in her address book, and she remembered how Victoria had been the last person to know her husband was having an affair with his secretary, until the day he walked out saying he wasn't coming back.

Liza drew a deep, frightened breath. *Had* Toby gone off with another woman? Was that why he hadn't phoned her all week? Perhaps he'd even engineered their quarrel, knowing her pride would make it hard for her to make the first move?

For a long time she sat gazing into space, wondering what to do, unable to bear the thought that he might have left her. Then it occurred to her that Declan surely wouldn't have phoned the police to say Toby was missing ... unless of course Declan had no idea either? Liza racked her brains, wondering who Toby might be having an affair with? When could it have started? Had he changed towards her in the last few months? Had he been coming home late, saying he was working? Panic made her mind spin in increasingly demented circles. Was it all her fault?

Liza got up from the desk and started pacing the room in her stockinged feet. Lottie glanced up but then, deciding there was nothing exciting in the offing like a biscuit or a walk, settled again with her head resting on her paws.

'Toby ... Toby.' Weeping now, Liza repeated his name, saying it aloud, as if she could conjure him up. 'Oh, Toby! What's happening?' She was shaking all over, her breath catching in sobs. He couldn't have found someone else, could he?

Liza awoke after a restless night. The minute she opened her eyes, the most appalling sense of anxiety washed over her again. She looked at the bedside clock. Half-past seven. On the floor above she could hear Ingrid getting the children ready for breakfast. There were yells from Tilly as Ingrid tried to brush the knots out of her long fair hair, and then came Thomas's voice, loudly complaining, 'I can't find my shoes.'

Oh, God! she thought. Another day. Toby is supposed to be coming home this evening... She pulled herself into an upright position. She stretched out her hand, knowing his side of the bed would be cold.

'Oh, Toby!' she whispered, looking round the blue and white bedroom they'd shared for so many years. She tried to control the fear that filled her heart.

'Toby, you *must* come home... God, what'll I do if...'

It didn't bear thinking about. Her breath caught in a sob and she jumped out of bed and pulled on her jeans and a sweater. Then she hurried down to the kitchen to make herself a cup of coffee, wanting to get to her desk before the children came downstairs, bombarding her with their usual early-morning racket, which never failed to include wails of dismay at unfinished homework, mislaid school uniforms, and Tilly fussing over her hair.

As soon as she'd let Lottie into the garden, she hurried up to the ground floor again and, slipping into her little sitting room, shut the door and went to the phone. A minute later the phone rang and it was Declan Connolly.

'Liza! Christ! Where have you been? I've been trying to get hold of you all week.' He sounded agitated. 'I tried to call you last night, but your phone was engaged all the time. In the end, Maxine and I had to go out, and we didn't get back until three o'clock this morning; I didn't like to ring you then. What's happening?'

'I took the children to Surrey, to stay with Emma Turnbull. Declan, what's going on? Why have you reported Toby as missing?'

'Oh, Jesus!' He sounded dismayed. 'The police have contacted you, have they? I'd hoped to be able to speak to you first, but we're really worried about Toby. No one's heard from him for a week now. He never turned up in the States; have you any idea where he is?'

'No idea at all, Declan. I'm frantic with worry. I don't

understand what's happening.' Liza couldn't bring herself to voice her fear that she thought perhaps another woman might be involved.

'He was due to call us on Monday,' Declan's voice was filled with anxiety, 'to tell us how things were going, but we haven't heard from him at all, and frankly, Liza, I'm worried sick. I talked to Charles Bryer before calling the police, and he agreed we should report Toby as missing.'

'I tried to get hold of you and Charles last night, but there was no reply from either of you,' said Liza.

'Oh, I'm sorry. Charles has gone to New York to see to things that end. Liza, have you any idea where Toby is? It's so unlike him to vanish like this.' He sounded strained. 'I'm afraid something's dreadfully wrong.'

'I know, that's what scares me.' Liza's voice broke.

'You've no idea where he could be?'

'None.' She paused. 'We had a fight before he left, and it blew up in the most ridiculous way, and we were hardly talking. Oh! It was all so silly, but he didn't phone me as usual and...' her voice broke. 'Declan... Could he have run off with another woman?'

'Liza!' Declan sounded shocked. 'How can you even *think* such a thing? You know Toby wouldn't even look at anyone else; he adores you.'

'How can you be so sure?' she said, fighting back tears. 'Toby is a very attractive man, and the wife is always the last to know if a husband is playing around.'

'Listen, Liza, put the idea right out of your mind. You're crazy to think Toby's left you. Not in a million years would he do such a thing: you must know that.'

Liza sighed. It wasn't that she didn't trust Toby. To her knowledge, he'd never looked at anyone else, but what other explanation was there? The alternatives of him committing suicide or having been killed in an accident were even worse.

'What shall I do, Declan?' she asked, helplessly.

'Nothing for the time being,' Declan advised, 'and let's keep this quiet. Don't tell anyone Toby's missing. The last thing we want is for it to get into the newspapers. I've already told the police that on no account must the story be leaked.'

Liza felt stunned. 'Why on earth not?'

'Because people will start asking questions.'

'What sort of questions?'

'It will draw attention to the syndicate, and Lloyd's, and we don't want that.'

'Why the hell not? Listen, Declan, I want to know what's happened to Toby. If he hasn't run off with someone else, then we've got to find out what's going on. Anything could have happened.'

'I realise how worried and upset you are; we all are. But you must be brave, Liza, and pretend to the outside world that Toby's still away on business. It's vital no one knows anything's wrong.' There was a veiled threat in his voice.

'What are you saying, Declan?' She was angry now, frustrated by his desire for secrecy.

'Think of the alternatives, Liza. Do you want banner headlines in all the newspapers, and great splashes on the TV news, declaring LLOYD'S UNDERWRITER VANISHES?

Do you want the media camping on your doorstep? Questioning you and your children? Following your every move and exposing your whole private life to the world?' He sounded furious now, and she burst into tears.

'I don't care what happens as long as he's found,' she wept. 'I'm desperate, Declan. We've got to do everything we can to find him.'

'Believe me, between the police and Interpol he'll be found without the media getting in on the act.' His tone was more soothing now. 'You see,' he continued, 'we must handle this in the right way or it could be devastating for us.'

'What do you mean by "us"?'

'The syndicate. Martin E. L. Hamcroft's, of course.'

'I don't understand.'

'Liza, it doesn't do for a company to be associated with a scandal and, let's face it, Toby has a high profile in Lloyd's.'

'What are you suggesting? What do you think's happened?'

There was silence on the line.

'You know something, don't you, Declan?' she said with sudden intuition.

'We've got to talk.' He sounded immensely tired. 'I'll be with you in half an hour.'

Then he hung up without another word.

Chapter Two

London, 1976–1990

Liza would always remember the summer of '76, because the weather was endlessly wonderful, with blisteringly hot days and long, languid, balmy nights. More importantly it was the summer she met Toby Hamcroft.

Sharing a flat in Chelsea with her old school friend, Emma, her life was an endless round of parties, interrupted only by the various courses she had been taking since leaving school. Having been a débutante, she was now, at twenty-one, proficient in typing, arranging flowers, cordon-bleu cooking and was currently learning the art of curtain-making. Emma, who was more ambitious, had become a journalist, and had recently got a job on the *Evening Standard*, having worked on a provincial newspaper for the two previous years.

'Why don't we give a party?' Emma said one evening. 'Nothing grand, you know. Just wine and dead bits on toast.'

Liza surveyed their living room. They had a flat on

the top floor of a converted house; its low ceilings and small windows were almost level with the treetops of the central garden of Paulton Square.

'We could do,' she replied, 'if we can put all the furniture in the bedroom, but it will still be a squash.'

'Who shall we invite?' said Emma, getting excited at the prospect.

They drew up a list.

'How many is that?' Liza asked, sitting cross-legged on the floor. She wore a pair of old flared white trousers reminiscent of the sixties, and one of her brother's shirts, pinched from him the last time she'd been up to her home in Scotland. In the heat, her fair skin looked pink and flushed. She ran her hand up the back of her damp neck, lifting her long blonde hair out of the way.

'Twenty-six,' Emma replied. 'Of course they won't all come.'

Liza studied the list, her blue eyes scanning her friend's scrawled handwriting. 'We've got too many girls; don't we know any more men?'

Emma sat bolt upright from her lounging position on the sofa.

'I know! Let's ask Toby Hamcroft.'

'Who's Toby Hamcroft? I've never heard of him.'

Emma laughed. 'He's . . . the older man.'

'What older man?' Liza asked suspiciously. Emma's taste in men could be really way-out, and was definitely suspect. 'We don't know any older men.'

'I met Toby skiing in February. He's quite amazing.' Emma added seriously; 'Sadly, not my type, though.'

'What do you mean by old?'

Emma pushed her almost black hair behind her ears, and looked at Liza with dancing black eyes. 'Oh, about forty-something, I suppose,' she said casually.

'What?' Liza's eyes widened. 'You can't be serious.'

Her friend laughed again. 'You should see your face! No, I'm only joking. I'd say he was about thirty, actually.'

'What does he do?'

'I think he's in Lloyd's. You'll like him. He's really dishy, full of energy, quite a high-flyer.'

Liza laughed. 'Then get busy with your invitation to this Toby whatever-his-name-is!'

On the night of the party, the girls greeted their guests in the little hallway of their flat, where they'd set up the kitchen table as a bar for dispensing red and white wine. In no time at all the place was crowded, cut-glass voices drowning out all other sounds, cigarette smoke turning the air blue.

Liza was at the far end of the living room, refilling people's glasses, when she looked over to the doorway and saw that Toby Hamcroft had arrived. There was no mistaking who it must be: he stood out from all the other men like a sophisticated adult among a group of teenagers.

She was also aware that there was something incredibly charismatic about him, a powerful sexuality in the way he stood, hand in pocket, other hand holding a glass of wine; his eyes, too, very dark and penetrating, seemed to be regarding the assembled company with mild amusement, and his full mouth hovered on the edge of a smile. Then he caught Liza's eye and, as she returned his stare, something deep inside her tugged with excitement. He moved towards her and the smile deepened, broke, revealing attractively crooked teeth.

'You must be Liza Mortimer. Emma's told me all about you. I gather you both went to Tudor Hall?' He spoke with an easy charm, as if they were already old friends.

'That's right,' Liza replied, suddenly shy.

'What are you doing with yourself now?

'I think I'm fast falling into the category of being an eternal student,' she admitted. 'I'm doing a course on curtain-making at the moment.'

He didn't laugh, as she'd expected. He looked interested, but their conversation was interrupted as Emma came up with some new arrivals. It wasn't until near the end of the party that they found themselves face to face again.

'Hi, there!' he said chummily. 'Great party! Have you managed to enjoy it?'

'I have, actually,' she replied.

'What are you doing afterwards?'

'The washing-up, I expect.'

'Oh, come on! Let me take you out to dinner. I can't let you turn into Cinderella as soon as everyone's gone home. What sort of food do you like? French? Italian? Indian?'

Laughing, Liza accepted, realising he'd taken it for

granted she'd agree anyway. Suddenly and unaccountably, she felt very feminine and protected; it was a sensation she discovered she liked.

In the weeks that followed, they became increasingly close. Liza had never imagined that falling in love could be so wonderful. There was not a single thing about Toby that she didn't admire and adore, from the way he looked to the way he spoke. He was athletic, playing tennis, skiing off-piste and riding, and he loved country pursuits such as shooting and fishing.

'He's everything I ever dreamed of,' Liza confided to Emma one evening as they got ready for bed.

Emma nodded wisely. 'I told you, didn't I? And he also loves London, and being sociable, like you. You're made for each other.'

Liza's parents flew down from Scotland to meet this paragon of virtue their only daughter kept talking about.

'We'll be staying at the Berkeley; why don't you bring him to dinner?' her mother, Lady Mortimer, suggested.

'That'll look a bit obvious, won't it?' Liza pointed out. 'Why don't you come to the flat for a drink, so that you bump into him "accidentally"?'

'Why can't we meet him "on purpose"?'

'Well . . .' Liza hesitated. 'I don't want to make it look obvious . . . like I hope he's going to ask me to marry him.'

There was a stunned silence.

'It's as serious as that, is it, darling?' Lady Mortimer's

voice sounded hollow. 'You're only twenty-one, Liza. Do you really want to get married so soon?'

'Oh, yes! If he asks me I'll say yes, at once.'

When Toby heard her parents were in London, he took the matter out of their hands by inviting them all to dine with him at the Connaught.

'I just hope he doesn't break Liza's heart,' General Sir George Mortimer said worriedly to his wife. 'We don't really know anything about him or his family. I hope to God he's not some rich, flashy philanderer.'

'He sounds all right,' his wife, Helen, replied.

'At least he's in Lloyd's so that's something.' Lloyd's was more like a club for the élite than an insurance institution: as far as George was concerned, the right public school, the right club, and being a member of Lloyd's were the credentials of a gentleman.

'His father was in Lloyd's, too, but he's retired. He founded his own syndicate, Martin E. L. Hamcroft's.'

'How did you find that out?' Sir George asked.

'Liza told me. That's why Toby joined the firm ten years ago, and why he's destined for great things, according to Liza.'

Sir George smiled in approval. 'Ah, yes. The old-boy network. It never fails.'

'Not just "old boys" now; women can become members too,' Lady Mortimer pointed out mildly.

Her husband shuddered. 'Unbelievable!' he snorted. Then he added: 'This Hamcroft chap sounds fairly suitable. Pity Liza is quite so young. I'd have liked to have seen her kicking up her heels for a bit longer!'

'She's not one of your horses, George,' Lady Mortimer reminded him. 'As to whether she'll ever marry Toby, we'll just have to wait and see.'

They didn't have long to wait. Six months later, Liza and Toby were married in the small kirk adjoining her father's estate in Scotland, and Emma was one of the bridesmaids.

Freddy, Liza's twenty-two-year-old brother, was very impressed with his new brother-in-law.

'He's good news,' he told his best friend, Archie Cummings, who'd been at Eton with Freddy, and who was equally in awe of Toby.

'He's so *rich*!' Archie commented. 'And yet he's so *nice*!'

'I've a good mind to join Lloyd's myself,' Freddy commented. It was the day after the wedding and they were travelling back to Oxford where they were both reading English and Philosophy.

'You'd hate working in an office!' Archie said, 'and do you want to live in London?'

'I wouldn't necessarily have to work in Lloyd's if I became a Name.'

'How do you make that out? What exactly does being a Name mean?'

'A Name is a person who puts up money to become a member of several syndicates, where insurance policies are underwritten. Let's say you have a boat, and you want to insure it. You'd give the business to a broker in Lloyd's, and he in turn would go to a syndicate to place your policy. If, at the end of a year, your boat is still OK, I, as a member of the syndicate, get a share of the profits. If, on the other hand, the boat sinks, I've made an agreement to compensate you up to an agreed figure.'

'So I can replace my boat?'

'Yes.'

'But you'd have to work in an office, wouldn't you?' Archie pointed out.

Freddy's smile was slightly smug. 'That's just where you're wrong. There are such things as "Outside Names". That means I don't work in an insurance company, I merely put my money at their disposal.'

'How much?' Archie asked, intrigued.

'Toby said seventy-five thousand pounds.'

Archie burst out laughing. 'And where are you going to get that sort of money?'

Freddy looked thoughtful. 'It could be worked ... I think.'

'I'd like to know how. You've either got seventy-five thousand, or you haven't.'

'Yes, but I wouldn't actually have to produce all the money. I'd merely have to show assets to the value of that amount.'

'Same thing,' Archie pointed out. 'What assets have you got that're worth seventy-five thousand? You haven't even got a car! And you live on an allowance from your father.'

'I know.' Freddy felt impatient with his friend for being so negative. He had the whole thing worked out in his head, and he was sure it was possible. 'My idea,' he continued, 'is that Dad should make over Balnabreck to me now, instead of my inheriting it when he dies, in which case—'

Archie looked appalled. 'Why should he do that? It's his and your mother's home! You can't expect him to give it to you lock, stock and barrel, now?'

'Oh, I don't!' Freddy looked equally shocked at the idea. 'Nothing like that. I mean he should make the deeds over to me, which would be advantageous in two respects.'

'I don't see how,' Archie said doubtfully.

'Firstly, it would save having to pay death duties on the property, providing Dad doesn't die within the next seven years, which he's not likely to; in the meantime – and this is what makes the proposition so attractive – I only have to *show* assets worth seventy-five thousand. I don't have to produce the actual cash. Even if I had seventy-five thousand pounds in the bank, I wouldn't have to hand it over to Lloyd's; I could use it to invest elsewhere at the same time! That means a double income from the same amount of capital – I think it's incredible!'

'It sounds almost too good to be true,' Archie queried. 'If, as you say, you don't even have to hand over the capital to Lloyd's, just let them see you have it, why don't more people become "Outside Names"? I might try and get hold of some money and do it myself!'

'Because you have to be invited – or have family links, to get in. It's like a club, Archie. But Toby has advised me to do it soon if I'm going to, because soon it's going to cost a hundred thousand pounds to join as an "Outside Name".'

Archie was making mental calculations, muttering under his breath. At last he spoke. 'Forgive me for playing the devil's advocate, but what happens if a lot of people put in claims at the same time? Isn't it possible that Lloyd's might ask for your actual *money*? To pay the claims?'

Freddy laughed uproariously. 'Not a chance, mate! One would, individually speaking, spread one's money over several different syndicates. Toby called it "spreading one's losses", so you *can't* be wiped out! Don't forget there's reinsurance, too. I'd be able to insure against losses. Toby says Lloyd's is as safe as houses. Look at how much money he's made!'

Liza and Toby returned from their honeymoon in Jamaica, tanned and with the flushed look of supreme happiness.

'It was glorious,' Liza told Emma, when they met a few days later for lunch. 'I can't tell you how wonderful married life is.' Liza was limpid-eyed and dazed from a surfeit of passionate sex and blazing sun. 'I never dreamed that life could be so fantastic,' she added in a reverent voice.

Emma, snatching an hour between covering a fashion show and interviewing the designer for an *Evening Standard* feature, grinned with delight.

'As good as that?' she enquired.

'Even better,' breathed Liza. In the days when they'd

both been virgins, they'd discussed sex, wondering what 'it' would be like; now that it had happened to both of them they no longer went into the details. It was too private, too sacred, to be shared except in the broadest terms.

'I'm so pleased,' said Emma. 'Aren't you glad I introduced you to Toby?'

Liza closed her eyes rapturously. 'My God, supposing you hadn't? I'll never be able to thank you enough, Em. It was fate; you meeting him skiing, and then asking him to the party so that I could meet him. It was destiny. I just know it.'

Emma looked at her friend affectionately. 'How is the new house?'

'I love it. Holland Park is a fantastic area, and as soon as the decorators have finished you must come to dinner.'

'I'd love to,' Emma grinned. 'Actually, I wanted to ask you . . . Do you think Toby would introduce me to some people at Lloyd's? I want to do a piece on it.'

'Well, it's a huge place. But it would be the underwriters and the brokers you'd want to meet, wouldn't it? They're the only ones who actually work in "The Room", as it's called.'

'Is that what it's called? "The Room"? Could you fix it for me, Liza? There's so much mystique surrounding Lloyd's, it would be a great coup for me if I could get an exclusive for the *Standard*.' Emma had cheered up visibly at the thought of a good story.

'I'll see what I can do. Toby hasn't taken *me* around

the place yet; I have a feeling that women, especially glamorous women, are not encouraged,' she added with a laugh.

'How typical of men! Why on earth do they keep on behaving as if they were still at prep school?' Emma demanded.

After she'd left Emma, Liza did some shopping before returning home. She hadn't exaggerated when she'd told her friend how blissful life was with Toby. For the first time in her life she awoke each morning filled with excited anticipation. Sometimes she just lay still, looking at Toby as he slept, his face young and smooth in repose, his dark hair ruffled at the back, glossy as a raven's feathers. Other times she'd move closer to him, moulding her body to fit against his, breathing deeply of the warm, sweet smell of his skin.

'Morning, sweetheart,' he'd say sleepily, and she'd snuggle closer still, hot with sudden desire, wanting him with fierce urgency. As if he sensed her need, he'd put his arms around her, kissing first her neck, then the soft skin just below her ear, and then her mouth, which was soft and responsive and pink like a child's.

'Oh, I love you...' she'd gasp, arching her back, spreading her legs, hands stroking his back, her warm breath soft on his cheek. 'I love you so much I could die.'

Quickly aroused, excited by the sight of her smoothly

rounded breasts and the curved line of her hips, Toby took her hand and placed it where he wanted her to touch him, stroke him, bring him nearer to the moment when he'd ease himself gently into her young body.

Then she'd cry out, the delicate edge between pleasure and pain leaving her balanced for a precarious moment between heaven and hell, and then finding it was paradise all the way, her cries became rapturous, fervent, desperate for him to bring her to the crest of the wave that would curve and then crash gloriously, overwhelming them both in undulating ripples, until they lay spent on the shore.

When she heard Toby's groan of exquisite pleasure in that vulnerable moment when he gave himself to her, when he was defenceless and drained of the juices of life, it was then she loved him most of all. She would hold him close, nurture him until his strength returned, press her head against his and tell him softly that he was the most wonderful man in the world.

Liza, with Toby standing on one side and Emma on the other, gazed with amazement at the vast marble-pillared ground-floor room in the Lloyd's building. It reminded her of one of the display rooms in the Victoria and Albert Museum, except that there was nothing still and silent about this place. The Room, as it is known, was crowded by well-turned-out dark-suited men, of all ages; some dashing from one point to another, but most wandering languidly about, stopping occasionally to chat to a friend. Hundreds of oak desks, with wooden benches placed on either side, divided the room into dozens of small sections, each desk having wood partitions down the centre holding stacks of files. It gave the desks a cubby-hole feel, and had earned them the name of 'boxes'.

'The underwriters sit in the boxes,' Toby explained, 'and when a broker such as myself wants to place an insurance policy, or maybe wants to renew a policy for a client for another year, we take the slips to an underwriter. If he wishes to take a line, he'll stamp and sign the agreed percentage he'll take.'

'Hey, wait a minute, you've lost me!' Emma said. 'What's a "slip"?'

'A "slip" is a white card, folded three times. It's about the same size as a business envelope, and it's got the name and address of the person wanting insurance, plus the details. Hopefully the underwriter will be satisfied with the person's track record and, if no claims have been made in the past year, he will take a line.'

'And what's a "line"?'

'A line is a percentage of the amount requiring to be covered. A small syndicate might only want to be responsible for, say, point three of a per cent, while another might go as high as ten per cent. Then it's my job as a broker to go on queueing up at the various boxes until I get enough lines to cover the whole policy.'

Emma was looking fascinated. 'Let me get this right,' she said, still hoping she'd be granted permission to write a feature on the most famous insurance institution in the world. 'Are you saying, Toby, that not one of those chaps sitting in their little boxes – syndicates you call them, don't you? – is prepared to insure the whole policy? If I wanted to insure, say, my house, would my policy be spread over all these syndicates?'

'Yes, but at the same time, your policy would be dealt with by someone in a company like Martin E. L. Hamcroft's; we'd be the ones picking up all the various "lines" for you; so if you put in a claim, we'd collect up all the money and send you your cheque.'

'Yes, I see,' Emma said slowly.

'There are non-marine and marine syndicates, too. Horses for courses, you might say. Some syndicates specialise in insuring ships or oil-rigs or aeroplanes, others play it safer by covering houses or cars, or maybe jewellery, providing it's kept in the vault of a bank! The important thing, from my point of view as a broker, is to know which is which, and to strike up a good friendship with them all; you never know when you might need a favour.'

As he talked, Toby led them round the room. The atmosphere was surprisingly relaxed, considering that people were gambling with billions of pounds, even if it was in a controlled and organised way.

Standing on a central podium talking into a microphone, was a very tall man. He wore a scarlet coat which reached down to his knees and had wide black cuffs and collar. With it he wore black trousers and a black silk top hat trimmed with a wide gilt band with a buckle in the front. On his hands were immaculate white gloves.

'What is that commissionaire doing?' Liza asked Toby in a low voice. He reminded her of one of the grand figures at the Mansion House.

Toby looked amused. 'He's known as a "waiter". He's paging someone.'

'Is that what the loudspeaker is doing?' She giggled. 'Any minute I expect to hear, "The train standing at platform three is for Axminster"!'

'I admit it's a rather antiquated system in this day and age, but Lloyd's loves tradition. The top boys lunch in The Captain's Room: that's the holy of holies; the room was brought lock, stock and barrel from a country mansion. It was designed by Robert Adam; plasterwork, pillars, chandeliers, the lot.'

'How extraordinary,' Emma said. 'And how would you actually describe Lloyd's?' she asked Toby. 'People talk about "being in Lloyd's", but what does that actually mean?'

'Lloyd's is an insurance market made up of underwriters, brokers and members' agents. We all have offices of our own nearby; collectively though, we are *all* a part of Lloyd's, and it's here, in the Room, that we carry out our transactions. The Room is like a marketplace where we come to get the best deals; where we try to give a service to the general public by insuring their goods, and where we hope to make some money for ourselves.' Toby looked round the crowded room with pride. 'The money we make is what I call "Happy Money", too. We make a profit simply from collecting premiums and renewing policies. As long as nothing happens to whatever is insured, we make a profit.' He turned to look at her, dark eyes earnest. 'If we suffer a loss,' he said quietly, 'then it means someone else has made an even greater loss, in emotional *and* material terms.'

'My God, isn't it fascinating?' Emma said, awestruck. 'There's something so glamorous about this place.' She glanced up at the large bell, famous the world over, suspended from a wooden frame.

'I presume that's the Lutine bell?'

Toby nodded. 'It belonged to the British frigate HMS *Lutine*, which sank in 1799 off the coast of Holland. It's struck once when there's a disaster at sea and twice when a missing ship comes safely back. They say the tradition is going to stop soon.'

'Oh, what a shame! Why do people constantly want to change things, just for the sake of change? Toby, can't you get me permission to write about all this?' She gestured to the room with a swing of her arm. 'It would make a fascinating feature; it really would,' she begged.

He smiled at her ruefully, understanding her fascination. 'I don't think it will be possible, Emma. Lloyd's hates any sort of publicity.' Then he stopped as if deep in thought.

'What is it?' Liza asked.

'I've had an idea.' He looked at Emma again. 'I could probably get permission for you to write about the Nelson Collection.'

'What's that?'

'Isn't it a collection of memorabilia? Letters to and

from Nelson and Lady Hamilton; silver, jewellery, that sort of thing? I remember you telling me about it,' Liza exclaimed.

Emma looked wistfully around the Room that had started as a coffee-house, growing and growing as Edward Lloyd had persuaded more and more merchants and shipowners to carry out their insurance transactions over a cup of coffee...

'There's so much history here,' she said.

Toby looked as if he too were visualising something of the past, then he gave a quick sigh. 'I don't think we're going to be in this building for ever, either,' he said regretfully.

Both Liza and Emma looked startled.

'Why not? Where would you go? ... Unless you took over the Albert Hall on a permanent basis!' she joked.

'There's a rumour that we're going to have a new Lloyd's building. The present chairman is desperately keen, even though it's going to cost about a hundred million pounds, they say. Richard Rogers has been asked to design it.'

At that moment Toby, recognising a colleague, hailed him with a friendly wave before introducing him to Liza and Emma.

'This is Declan Connolly,' he said. 'Declan is a broker with Martin E. L. Hamcroft's.'

Liza found herself shaking hands with a slightly younger man than Toby; she'd have put him at around twenty-seven. He was of medium height, although his square body and sturdy legs made him seem stocky.

Eager grey eyes looked into hers; his handshake was very strong.

'Nice to meet you,' he said briskly. 'Is this your first visit to Lloyd's?'

'Yes,' Liza replied. 'We've been hearing a new building might be built in the future, and we were thinking it was rather a shame.'

The grin broadened, and Declan turned to look at Emma, as if he liked what he saw. 'Do you think it would be a shame?' he asked.

'It depends what they replace it with,' she replied, sensibly.

'Why don't we go and have lunch now,' Toby suggested, looking at his watch. 'Ha! It's twelve-thirty; I thought my stomach was trying to tell me something!'

'How about that little Italian restaurant near St Mary Axe?' Declan suggested.

'Good idea.'

With Toby and Liza leading the way, Emma followed with Declan; they were soon deep in conversation. Liza raised her eyebrows as she caught Toby's eye.

'Suitable?' she mouthed.

Toby's eyes widened comically and he made a tiny grimace.

'What's wrong?' Liza whispered.

'He's married. Tell her to watch it.'

Declan Connolly liked women. He also liked fine houses, fast cars, vintage champagne and handmade Savile Row suits. Although he came from the North of

England he'd soon found his way around the high spots of London with remarkable speed and ease. Few knew that it was Charles Bryer who had given him a job as a broker in Martin E. L. Hamcroft's, because that was something Charles wished to keep private. Even fewer people knew that his parents were still alive. He never mentioned them and his smart new friends got the impression that they were dead. Declan wanted to join the ranks of the rich upper classes, and so far he had done very well. He had a house in Kensington, reckoning it to be an area inhabited by well-to-do professional classes into which he fitted comfortably. He'd also married a very pretty French girl, called Maxine, with whom he felt at ease; her background was similar to his own in that her father owned a small restaurant on the outskirts of Paris.

There was another advantage, quickly taken into account; it was impossible to judge her background from her broken English: a great asset, Declan realised, in a country where your accent exposes your class quicker than anything else.

Maxine was small, dark and luscious-looking. She made her own clothes, quickly learning what English upper-class women wore, and she was fast overshadowing the very women she'd striven to emulate. She studied *House and Garden* avidly, and then proceeded to decorate their Scarsdale Villa house, copying ideas as she went along. Declan's colleagues, whom he sometimes invited to drinks, were soon proclaiming at Maxine's exquisite taste.

They had decided not to have children; both were too keen to acquire the best of everything. To occupy herself once she'd finished doing up the house, Maxine became immersed in charity work, knowing that was the way to meet the right class of person, particularly if you were careful enough to choose the smart charities, like the British Red Cross or the Royal National Lifeboat Institution.

When Declan made useful contacts in Lloyd's, he asked them to dinner, while Maxine invited her new charity friends, and so a system of networking began for them both, and they worked in complete harmony for the betterment of themselves. Except that Declan was a heavy flirt, sometimes going further than mere flirting. The relationships never got serious, though, and, being French, Maxine pretended not to notice. She was the wife. That was what mattered.

'Can I see the Nelson Collection this afternoon?' Emma asked as they sat in the crowded restaurant, eating pasta.

'I don't see why not!' Declan declared breezily. 'You could fix it for them, couldn't you, Toby?'

'I'll see what I can do.'

'What's the problem?' Liza asked.

'It's housed in a strongroom, designed on the lines of a captain's cabin. We'll have to get permission and someone will have to open it up for us.'

'How fantastic!' Emma exclaimed. 'Oh, I do hope they let us see it.'

* * *

Later that afternoon, the four of them were looking at the collection, which included silver-gilt wine-coolers, a magnificent soup tureen, and a lock of Lord Nelson's hair contained in a pearl brooch that had once belonged to Lady Hamilton.

'Your namesake, Emma,' Declan pointed out, sliding his arm round her waist.

'And that's where the similarity ends,' she observed tartly, moving away from him. 'Look, Liza!' She turned to her. 'Here's a log-book, written at the time, describing the Battle of Trafalgar.'

Liza stood beside Emma, blocking Declan's way. 'God, isn't that amazing?'

'Have you noticed the painted pennants round the cornices?' Toby pointed up to the ceiling. 'Do you know there is no flag for the word "duty" and so it had to be spelt out in full?'

'As in: "England expects every man this day will do his duty"?' said Liza.

'Exactly,' Toby agreed. 'Ugly old buzzard, wasn't he?'

They all looked at the portrait of Nelson. It hung on the wall above his collar of the Order of the Bath, which was displayed in a large, velvet-lined case.

'I think he's quite sexy,' said Emma, her head on one side as she regarded the painting.

'I think he's more powerful than sexy,' Liza pointed out.

'Isn't that the same thing?' Declan asked. 'Powerful men are always supposed to be attractive to women.'

'Are they?' Emma looked doubtful, but Liza shot Toby an intimate look.

'Oh, yes, definitely,' she said, smiling wickedly.

'Do you know what I want for us?' Toby asked her after their first wedding anniversary. They were lying in bed, having been out for a celebratory dinner.

Liza turned to look at him. Six months pregnant now, she wondered what more she could expect from life. She had Toby, a beautiful house in a part of London she loved, and they were expecting their first child.

'What do you want?' she asked softly.

He turned to look directly into her eyes and, as always happened when he did that, her heart gave a little lurch of excitement. Although she knew him as well as she knew herself, his sexuality still had the power to thrill her. There was something about Toby that was dominantly attractive, and she knew others were affected by his charm, too. When he entered a crowded room, people stopped talking to turn and look at him; his presence seemed to fill the room. He had an animal magnetism which seemed to affect both men and women; a power to draw people towards him and to make them like him. To be loved by Toby was like basking in the glorious warmth of the sun, she thought.

'What I want us to have,' he was saying, 'is a house in the country.'

'And leave London?' she asked, startled.

Toby shook his head, reaching for her hand as he did so. 'No, I'd like to keep this house, but buy a beautiful old farmhouse, in Hampshire or Wiltshire. With a few acres of land, and ponies for the children...'

'Children?' Liza cut in, laughing. 'Give me a chance, sweetheart. I haven't even had the first one yet.'

Toby's smile was deeply contented. 'We'll have more babies in time,' he said complacently. 'I want you to have a marvellous life, sweetheart.'

'But I have a marvellous life now,' she pointed out, smiling. 'I don't think there's anything else I want.'

'One always wants more than one has, Liza. A better house, and a better car, a place in the country and a place somewhere in the sun. Bigger and better jewellery for you, a helicopter for me; one never has enough of anything in this world.'

'That's like saying that greed breeds greed.'

'No. It's just once you get your eye in, for top-quality goods, or a certain type of lifestyle, then there's a continual seeking for even greater perfection. One becomes a connoisseur of excellence in all things.'

Liza burst out laughing. 'That's the best excuse I've ever heard for having a good time and living the life of Riley! And the most pompous!'

Toby chuckled. 'I enjoy spending money,' he admitted, 'but I also enjoy making it, too.'

'Which is just as well, or you'd have to start robbing banks to put your plans into operation.'

Toby was brilliant, though, and she knew it. People had told her he had inherited his flair from his father, Martin. Certainly Hamcroft's was now one of the largest companies in Lloyd's, incorporating twelve syndicates with a combined premium income of over five hundred million pounds. The name Hamcroft carried with it a reputation for honesty, integrity, and shrewd-though-daring underwriting. One day Toby would be chairman, but meanwhile Charles Bryer held the post, and Toby was a broker, and the chief executive in charge of the Hamcroft's Members' Agencies, which looked after all the Outside Names.

From the beginning Liza knew she'd do anything to help him realise his dreams. As it was, in the year since they'd been married, they'd given an average of one dinner party every week – her cooking skills were always praised; and they'd also held a large drinks party just before Christmas for everyone in Hamcroft's, including the cleaners who looked after the floor of offices they occupied in Fenchurch Street. In fact, all their entertaining was business-orientated now, but Liza did not mind. Toby's life was her life too, and if it helped to have boring people to the house from time to time, then that was a small price to pay in return for the greatest happiness she'd ever imagined.

'Is there anything I can do to help you make these millions?' she asked, nuzzling into his neck. Toby hugged her close, his eyes tender.

'Just go on being your usual smiling self,' he said softly. 'That's all I need: you. I don't know what I'd do without you.' Then he kissed her lips very slowly and gently.

Liza looked at him, her eyes teasing. 'You'd soon find someone else to look after you if I wasn't here! I bet there's a queue of women forming outside the front door right now. You'd be spoilt for choice.'

Toby laughed but his eyes were serious. 'No. Only you know how to handle me in the right way. Only you sense what I need.'

'Really?'

He nodded. 'Why do you think I didn't get married before? I was waiting for the right person to come along. We were made for each other.'

'I know we were.' Liza stroked his face with gentle fingertips, tracing the line of his black eyebrows and the curve of his jaw. His full-lipped mouth, in repose, was strong but gentle, and she ran her forefinger along the curved line of his upper lip.

'I love your mouth,' she said, and kissed him.

'And I love all of you, my sweetheart, and I intend to give you the world. One day.'

'We're dining with Toby Hamcroft and his wife next Wednesday,' Lady Rosemary Davenport pointed out, a tall elegant figure in cashmere and pearls. 'I told you, Humphrey, when we were first invited. I don't see how you can go shooting that day. You'll never get back from High Wycombe in time.'

Tall, balding and pink-skinned, Sir Humphrey blinked pale eyelashes at his wife and looked perplexed.

'But I promised old Johnnie I'd go shooting,' he said fretfully. 'Who are the Hamcrofts?'

'You know perfectly well who they are. He's the chap who's in Lloyd's; you told me he might be able to make me an Outside Name. Remember? You said he was one of the nicest people you'd met in years. They live in Holland Park.'

Humphrey stood in front of the log fire that was the focal point of the large drawing room of their stately home, Cavenham Court in Suffolk, jingling the small change in his trouser pocket; it was an unconscious habit that drove his wife mad.

'I sort of remember him,' he said vaguely, 'but do let's say we can't go. You know how I enjoy shooting, Ros.'

Lady Rosemary Davenport, the former Lady Rosemary Fortescue, only child of the late Earl of Whittlesey, looked at her husband with irritation. They'd been married for thirteen and a half years, which at times seemed to her like thirteen years too long. The trouble with Humphrey, she realised, was that, although he could be quite sweet, he was also deeply stupid. He only became clear-thinking when he was involved in hunting or shooting. They were his passions in life, equalled only by his adoration foı Phoebe, Melody, Belinda and Zelda; not their daughters, but his four black labrador gun dogs.

'I've already accepted the Hamcrofts,' she said firmly. 'If you go shooting that day you'll just have to leave early.'

'That's a poor show,' he grumbled, reaching to stroke Phoebe's head. 'Isn't that a poor show, Phoebs?' The dog thwacked the floor with her tail and looked up at him in adoration. 'Poor Phoebs! We won't be able to stay long that day.' He leaned forward to stroke her back, and immediately the other dogs clustered around, begging attention.

Lady Rosemary sighed inwardly. Really, Humphrey cared for the dogs more than he did for Laura and Richard. Certainly more than he did for her. He fussed over them and babied them in a way she found quite ridiculous, but then she'd lived in the country all her life, while he'd always lived in London, and so her attitude towards animals was quite different. Especially gun dogs. They were working dogs, and she'd insisted they be sent away to be properly trained. But whilst he admired their instant obedience when they came home, he also undid a lot of the good by petting them and feeding them delicious morsels, turning them into pets.

'I'm going to see to the packing,' she announced, rising from the elegant Louis XIV sofa that faced the fireplace. Her pale aquiline features regarded him with a touch of scorn. How could she have married anyone so hopeless.

'All right,' he replied. 'I suppose we'd better leave early to avoid the traffic going into London; unless we leave very late?' he added hopefully, 'or even tomorrow morning?'

Lady Rosemary shook her head. 'We can't do that, Humphrey. The children have school tomorrow, and you know how bad-tempered they get when they're tired.' Laura was eight and Richard five, and were at a day-school in London. Unless they had a good night's sleep, they became impossible.

'It's a pity we have to go up to town at all,' he mumbled

unhappily. Sir Humphrey loved Cavenham Court, set in its twenty acres of prime Suffolk countryside, which in fact belonged to his wife, bequeathed to her by her late father. He'd be happy to live there all the time, but Rosemary preferred being in London, which she considered to be the arts capital of the world. During the week, therefore, they lived in a spacious flat in Eaton Place that she'd bought when they'd got married.

Humphrey was right, of course, when he pointed out during arguments that 'it was all hers'. It was. Everything belonged to her, and Humphrey only had a few thousand pounds left him by his father, a directorship of a small company on to the board of which he'd been invited because of his title, and no property at all. At first he hadn't minded, but gradually over the years, her wealth had eroded their relationship, making him feel inadequate at times. Then he remembered. It was Toby Hamcroft, going on about Lloyd's and how rich one could get that had prompted him to say, 'Get in touch. I might be very interested in our becoming Outside Names.'

He'd forgotten all about it. Humphrey wrinkled his forehead in concentration. Dimwit he might be, he thought, but Toby Hamcroft had assured him that, if he joined Lloyd's, he wouldn't have to do anything except sit back waiting for the profits. The idea suited him down to the ground.

During the next few years, Toby began to see his dreams coming true. There had been a boom in the financial world during the seventies, which carried on through to the eighties. Everyone was making money, and Lloyd's was no exception. As a broker, placing insurance policies with a wide variety of successful syndicates, Toby was making a fortune. Soon, he and others like him were buying and furnishing grand houses, gliding around in Rolls-Royces, buying jewellery for their wives and Impressionist paintings for themselves. Those whom Toby invited to become Outside Names were also making excellent profits, because Toby placed their business with the most successful syndicates, including his own, Martin E. L. Hamcroft's. It was not all United Kingdom business, either. Toby was becoming accustomed to broking policies from the four corners of the world, and especially North America. New Outside Names were joining every day, so that Lloyd's became less like an insurance institution and more like a marketplace for the élite. The former coffee-house now boasted 30,000 members and a turnover of hundreds of millions of pounds, insuring anything from a film star's legs to the QEII.

In 1986, Lloyd's moved into their revolutionary new building. No one in Britain had ever seen anything to compare with the tall tubular steel-and-glass construction. Toby loved it, describing it as 'state-of-the-architecture'; Liza hated it, and liked retelling the current joke that it was the first time anyone had put the plumbing on the outside of a building and the arse-holes inside. But as long as the money came rattling in, no one cared. Life was good, lunches were long, and the pickings were rich; and there was no reason why the halcyon days should not continue for ever.

Liza had given birth to Tilly fifteen months after their marriage, and Tom arrived eighteen months later. As Toby had promised, they bought an old farmhouse in Hampshire and spent a hundred thousand pounds doing it up, and for a further hundred thousand pounds had added a top floor to their Holland Park house for the children's bedrooms. Next came the helicopter so Toby could hop around the country in minutes instead of hours, and for Liza new jewellery. To go with the diamond engagement ring and earrings he'd given her, he added a diamond bracelet and a beautiful necklace, with a large drop-pearl forming a pendant.

When their third child, Sarah, was born, they were both delighted. To celebrate, Toby bought *Morning Glory*, a yacht which, he assured everyone, would pay for itself by being chartered to his rich American clients who wanted to cruise around the Mediterranean. He also added to Liza's jewellery collection by giving her a rope of perfectly matched pearls with an emerald clasp. Since their marriage nine years before they had become the epitome of a rich, successful and sublimely happily married couple. They were also extremely popular, and belonged to an ever-widening circle of friends, many of whom Toby had made Outside Names at Lloyd's.

On their tenth wedding anniversary, Toby and Liza gave a party for a hundred guests at Annabel's, Mark Birley allowing them to take over the club for the night.

'I don't care what it costs,' Toby said. 'It's to tell the world how blissfully happy we are, and if we're going to do it at all, let's do it in style!' He hadn't been nicknamed the 'Broker Baron', by this time, for nothing.

Engraved invitations were sent out, and Toby planned the evening with meticulous care. He was determined it was going to be the best party of the year and an unforgettable night for Liza.

Almost everyone accepted and, in the semi-dark of London's smartest nightclub, the guests were seated at intimate tables decorated with white flowers and candles, while in the background romantic music played evocatively.

It reminded Liza of their wedding, when everyone had quaffed vintage Bollinger champagne, and drunk a toast to their health. Only this time, Toby had ordered an exquisite dinner to be served, with salmon from Scotland, truffles flown from France that morning, tiny wild strawberries from Italy, and to serve with the coffee and liqueurs, handmade chocolates from Switzerland.

After dinner, Toby and Liza were the first on to the dance floor, which had been transformed into a bower of greenery and flowers for the night. Within minutes, everyone was getting up to dance, too, clinging to each other in the old-fashioned way, as the music Toby had chosen dictated. The party went on until a rosy dawn stole over the trees of Berkeley Square and, when the guests began to drift home in laughing, languid groups, Toby and Liza lingered on amidst the sweet-smelling flowers and guttering candles, holding hands and having a last glass of champagne together.

Toby was right about one thing: not only had he given Liza a night to remember, but everyone else as well.

Chapter Three

1991

Liza replaced the receiver slowly and looked at her wristwatch. Declan had said he'd be with her in half an hour; her mind wandered to banal trivialities. Half an hour to shower and dress and do her face. Half an hour before the children left for school. *Half an hour before you know what has happened to your husband*, said the voice in her head. That was the bottom line, she thought, the realisation hitting her like a blow. That was what she had to face; where was Toby?

Down in the kitchen she could hear Tilly and Thomas squabbling over who got to sit on the red-cushioned chair; they were supposed to take it in turns, but every morning they argued about it. Liza hurried back up to her bedroom, leaving Ingrid to deal with them. She'd skip breakfast this morning. She hadn't an appetite, anyway.

At exactly eight-thirty the front door bell rang. Lottie charged, barking hysterically, and pranced about the hall with manic excitement, followed by the children who always wanted to know who was at the door. It was Ingrid who let Declan in as Liza came hurrying down the stairs. One glance at his face made her draw in her breath sharply. He looked grey and strained; his eyes flickered nervously around the hall.

'Hello, Liza,' he said quietly.

'Come in, Declan.' She led the way into the drawing room.

'How are you?' She spoke from habit and scarcely heard the answer.

'OK.' He placed his briefcase, which was bulky and heavy-looking, on the floor by the side of one of the armchairs. Then, straightening up, he looked searchingly into her eyes.

'How are *you*, Liza?'

She gave a sigh of frustration. 'I don't *know* how I am, Declan. I want to know what's going on.' She faced him challengingly, a slender figure in a cream cashmere skirt and a navy-blue blouse. Behind her, the morning sun slanted with golden beams through the french windows, creating a halo effect round her shoulder-length fair hair.

'Do you know where Toby is?'

He met her gaze steadily. 'No. I must be honest and say I've no idea.' He ran a hand over the lower half of his face, as if checking he'd shaved that morning. Liza could tell he was nervous, his usual *savoir faire* lacking.

'But you know something about his disappearance?'

'I wish I could say I do, but I haven't got a bloody clue.'

Liza looked stunned. 'Then what...?' Not to know was better than knowing – if the news was bad. To know could mean the end of everything she held dear.

'You think he may be all right?' she asked hopefully.

Declan eased himself into a chair as if he ached all over. He spread his hands in a gesture of helplessness. 'If anything had happened to him, I'm sure we'd have heard by now,' he said slowly. 'If there'd been an accident, or he'd been taken ill, then we'd have been informed. Having said that, of course, you've been away yourself for the past week, haven't you? Did anyone know where you were? I couldn't get hold of you anywhere. You should have left your forwarding address with someone.'

Liza bristled. He made it sound as if she'd been irresponsible. 'Odete, my daily cleaner, had my phone number in case of emergencies.'

'I suppose I must have phoned when this house was empty. Not that it's made any difference. I had hoped, though, that you'd be able to throw some light on the situation. We've had dozens of angry calls from the States, from people Toby was supposed to meet. It's been awfully awkward.'

'I thought you had something to tell me, Declan. I got the impression that you were keeping something back on the phone just now.'

'How much does Toby discuss business with you, Liza?' Declan leaned forward, arms resting on his splayed knees, expression intent. His cufflinks, she noticed, were gold, and so was his watch. On his left hand he wore a gold signet ring engraved with a ram, his birth sign under Aries. He'd got the idea from Toby's ring, not realising that the lion engraved on it was a family crest rather than the sign of the zodiac for Leo.

'Not much ... well, I suppose hardly at all,' Liza admitted. 'We're always so busy with the children, or entertaining, or making plans for the weekends at Chalklands; we've got an unspoken arrangement that I look after all the domestic side of our lives, and Toby looks after the business end.'

'What I mean is, do you know if Toby is keeping things from you? Business problems or worries? New developments in Hamcroft's, for example?'

A cold wave, like a dark, foreboding shadow swept over her; what had the police said yesterday? 'Does your husband have business worries?'

'Is Toby in some kind of trouble, Declan?' she asked sharply.

Suddenly he reached forward and laid his hand on her arm. 'I want you to remember that everything Toby has done has been for the sake of you and the children. He wanted you to have the best of everything. He's worked his guts out for the past fifteen years to build up the syndicate; to enlarge the members' agencies; to get into the North American market. Apart from making money for himself, he's enabled a lot of people to make their money work for them too, and to bring them a nice amount of extra income which they would not otherwise have had. Sometimes it has meant underwriting high-risk business. Up to the mid-eighties everything was booming…' He paused, letting what he'd said sink in.

Liza's brow was furrowed. As if Lottie could sense something was wrong, she snuggled against Liza, pressing herself close in affectionate and silent devotion. Absently, Liza stroked the amber silk ears. 'I don't think I understand what you're getting at, Declan,' she said finally.

He gave a quick sigh. 'It's a very complicated business, Liza, especially trying to explain it to someone who doesn't actually work in Lloyd's.'

Her voice was tense. 'Try me.'

He suddenly looked flustered. 'Well,' he began hesitantly, 'you have to understand that as early as the seventies, Charles Bryer was encouraging us to introduce new Outside Names. Both Toby and I were told that it must be done discreetly, because the whole mystique of Lloyd's is based on its élitism. If anyone could join, there'd be no cachet, so we had to be subtle about it.'

'But anyone *could* join, if they had the right kind of assets,' Liza pointed out. 'Including women.'

'Of course, only it mustn't be made to look so easy. Toby had a lot of success, though. With his charm and personality – and of course you to help wine and dine these prospective new members – he found it easy. His knack of inspiring people helped, and when they saw how well you both lived – well, it made some of them very greedy.'

'Declan, get to the point.'

'The Piper Alpha oil-rig disaster in 1988 was one of the first calamities to hit Lloyd's, in more ways than one; the losses were astronomical.'

Liza nodded. 'Followed by the Exxon Valdez and the millions of gallons of oil it spilled into the sea, and then Hurricane Hugo, and the San Francisco earthquake ... Toby told me that many of the members would suffer and that they couldn't expect the sort of profits they'd been used to. I also know he was very worried about the massive claims from asbestosis sufferers: the American courts have been awarding huge amounts in compensation against the claims, haven't they?'

'You *are* well informed about what's happening, aren't you?' Declan sounded surprised. 'And I also suppose you know that financial losses don't show up for three years, because that's how long it takes for the accounts to be done.'

Liza nodded. 'I know. The 1988 figures only came out quite recently. Toby said the accounts for 1989 are going to be even worse. I think everyone is aware of this, Declan. What are you trying to tell me? Are you trying to say that Toby and I have lost everything? That we're wiped out?'

'To my knowledge, Liza, you probably haven't suffered any losses, but of course I can't be sure. Toby never discussed his personal finances with me.'

'So, what are you saying?' Liza felt angry at Declan's seeming reluctance to come to the point. She scarcely cared whether they had lost their money or not; all that mattered was that Toby should be all right.

'I'm merely saying that a lot of people have lost money and they're not too happy about it.'

'Nobody likes losing money, but what has this got to do with Toby's disappearance?' Liza demanded. 'Toby's not the sort of person who would run away like a coward just because there was trouble, if that's what you're suggesting.'

Declan rose and started pacing around the drawing room, hands dug deep into the pockets of his beautifully cut dark-blue suit.

'I understand how you feel, Liza. Knowing Toby as well as I do, I know he wouldn't turn his back on his friends, but he *has* been very worried about the state of things on the Hamcroft syndicate. We have over three thousand members now – that's enormous by some standards. And Toby knows and I know that they're in for an almighty shock. It's meant we've been able to increase our underwriting capacity to hundreds of millions of pounds, but we may soon see the day of reckoning. The losses are phenomenal – worse than in Lloyd's' entire history.'

Liza was scared. Toby had told her things were bad, but not as bad as this.

'But world catastrophes, such as hurricanes and earthquakes, are hardly any one individual's fault! No one could blame Toby . . . !'

'But haven't you thought that the worry might have triggered a nervous breakdown?' Declan asked.

'I'd have *known* if he was having a breakdown,' she said, distressed. But *would* she have known? she asked herself. Weren't both she and Toby so wrapped up in their busy lives, he in the City, she with the children and the two houses, that in spite of the great love they felt for each other, there was never time to really talk?

Declan looked at her searchingly. 'It's possible Toby didn't even realise himself how near the edge he may have been.'

'Oh, God! I feel dreadful!' She was shaking all over now, consumed with anxiety and guilt. 'What are we going to do, Declan?'

'Sit tight, for the time being,' he said grimly, coming to stand before her.

Liza looked up at him, startled. 'What do you mean? You've told the police, haven't you? Now we must get it into the newspapers, and on the television news . . .'

'. . . *No!*'

She broke off, startled by his vehemence. 'What do you mean?'

'The last thing we need is this getting out. People on the syndicate will start to panic.'

'This is my husband we're talking about! I don't give a damn what other people think; we must find Toby. He may be ill . . .' Her voice drifted off. A great feeling of helplessness seemed to drain her of strength as she looked up at him. And it struck her in that moment that Declan had always seemed to be lurking in Toby's shadow, trying to emulate Toby, copying his style of dress, struggling to keep up with him at Lloyd's, but never quite succeeding. As she looked at him now she realised he was a pale imitation of Toby; without substance, lacking in charisma, unable to draw people to himself because his charm wasn't genuine. It was an act. He simply didn't have the magic which Toby exuded.

'Toby's disappearance *mustn't* get into the newspapers,' he was insisting. 'What are people going to think?'

Liza felt wild now, with anger and fear and frustration. 'For God's sake, Declan!' All he seemed to care about was the reputation of the syndicate, while Toby might be—

Declan gripped her shoulders. 'Listen to me, Liza. Do you want people thinking he's run off with funds? Charles Bryer gave me the strictest instructions that I was to inform the police only, and make sure they didn't leak anything to the media. Do you think Toby would want the syndicate that his father founded involved in anything that would cause a loss of confidence? Most of the people who work in Hamcroft's aren't even aware Toby hasn't been seen for a week. It could cause a panic at Lloyd's. Toby has a very high profile there; one day he may even be the chairman. How's that going to look if there are headlines in all the tabloids, LLOYD'S BROKER VANISHES? When for all we know he may be resting in some clinic, being treated for nervous exhaustion?'

Liza moved impatiently from Declan's grip. 'If Toby hasn't returned by this evening, which is when he was due to come home, then I don't care what you or Charles Bryer says; I'm telling everyone. I want Toby found.'

Alone in the house, while the children were at school and Ingrid did the shopping, Liza sat at her desk making a series of telephone calls. The first one was to her father in Scotland.

Sir George Mortimer sounded deeply concerned. 'I wish to God Declan had told me why he wanted to know where you were staying. Do you mean to tell me Toby's been missing for a week and no one has done anything about it until yesterday morning? Christ! The man might be...' He broke off, his voice gruff with anxiety. 'I'll fly down right away on the shuttle; you shouldn't be alone at a time like this.'

'Oh, Daddy, would you really? I feel so helpless. I don't know where to start. I'm so scared something has happened to him! It's not like Toby to be unreliable.'

'Mummy says to tell you she's coming with me. We should be in London some time after lunch,' he added.

Next, Liza rang her brother. Freddy was married now, to a girl called Melissa who worked on a fashion magazine; he had been at Sotheby's for the past ten years, and was now recognised as an expert in the field of Old Masters.

'Freddy? It's me,' Liza said as soon as she was put through to his office. 'You haven't forgotten you're coming to dinner tonight? I need to see you.'

'Liza.' His voice sounded hollow and strained. 'This must be telepathy.'

'What do you mean?' she asked. 'What are you talking about, Freddy?'

'Lloyd's, of course. I had a letter this morning. God, Liza, what am I going to do?' Freddy sounded desperate.

'What letter? What's wrong?'

'Haven't you heard? Christ, I daren't tell Dad; he'll do his nut. Lloyd's have asked me for one hundred and seventy thousand pounds, to be paid now. It's to cover the losses incurred in 1988, and someone has just told me they'll demand even more from me next year! I'll be ruined, Liza. Balnabreck will have to go ... and what are Mum and Dad going to do then? I'm not even allowed to resign from Lloyd's! I'm stuck with an "unlimited liability" clause, which means they can demand as much money as they want and I haven't got a leg to stand on. Oh, God! Liza, what am I going to do?' His voice quavered, cracked, and then fell silent.

'Oh, Freddy,' Liza gasped. 'I'd no idea ...'

'Isn't that why you phoned?' he asked.

'No,' Liza said slowly. 'No, it isn't.'

'Then what is it? You sound funny ... have you and Toby suffered terrible losses, too?'

'I don't know,' she said honestly. 'I phoned you to say that Toby's been missing for a week.'

The cicadas were the only noise disrupting the silence that hung heavy and hot over the pale sapphire-blue swimming pool in the garden of the large white villa. In the shade of the veranda, grouped hospitably in a circle, were garden seats and low tables, comfortable turquoise and white striped cushions and an array of fluffy white towels, spread to dry over the blinding white stucco of a garden wall which divided the pool area from the terraced garden. Overhead, unrelenting and unchanging, a sky as blue as the pool seemed to press down on Nina's head, giving her a headache, as it always did.

Martin and Nina Hamcroft had gone to live in Spain – his choice, not hers – when he retired from Lloyd's. Here, in magnificent isolation and comfort, they had lived for the past fourteen years. Martin had bought several hectares of land, far enough away from Jerez to be remote, but not too far to drive into town for the necessities of their very luxurious lifestyle. They entertained frequently and lavishly, in the large house built to Martin's design, which had huge white airy rooms, cool marble floors, elegant bedrooms furnished with taste and style, and balconies overlooking the garden. Here, iced sherry was served by Maria, who, with her husband José, looked after the house and the garden. Later, on the lantern-lit terrace, on a marble-topped table, traditional Spanish dishes were served for lunch and dinner, accompanied by the local wines.

It was an idyllic existence, in an unspoilt and uncommercialised part of Spain, and Martin felt he deserved every moment of the contentment he felt. He'd worked hard all his life to arrive at this exact moment, secure in the knowledge that his son, Toby, would one day become chairman of the insurance company Martin had founded. Meanwhile, the long, lazy days under the relentless sun continued; with Nina by his side he was a happy man.

When the phone rang on this still, hot morning, no one was in any hurry to answer it. Martin was dozing by the pool after his swim, and Nina was absorbed in a novel. Presently, Maria picked up the receiver gingerly and held it to her ear.

''Ullo? 'Ullo?' she demanded. There was a pause and then she nodded. 'Plis to wait?' Out by the pool, Martin awoke and reached for the mobile phone.

'Who is it, Maria?' he called out as she appeared in the veranda doorway.

'Meeses 'Amcroft.'

'Thanks, Maria.'

Nina looked up from her book. It must be Toby, she reflected; Liza rarely called them, knowing that in their heart of hearts it was their son they really wanted to talk to.

'Hello? Ah, Liza! How are you?' Martin was saying. 'Children well? It'll soon be the holidays, won't it? We're looking forward to having you all out here for a couple of weeks! . . . What's that, Liza?'

Nina watched as her husband suddenly sat bolt upright, his bathing towel dropping to the ground, his face growing pale even through his deep, permanent tan.

'A *week*! Good God Almighty!' Martin exclaimed, shocked, and then he spoke abruptly.

'Nina and I will fly over at once. I think there's a flight

this afternoon. Yes. Yes, *of course* you must notify the media. Pay no attention to what Charles Bryer or anyone else says. We'll see you later.' He switched off the phone, pushed the aerial down, and looked at his wife with a stunned expression.

As they packed, Martin told her what had happened. 'I don't like the sound of it at all,' he said. 'Why should Toby vanish at the exact time the syndicate has had to announce these calamitous losses?'

Next Liza phoned her old friend, Emma. Emma was now married to a Tory MP, and had three small children. She'd given up full-time journalism, but still wrote freelance articles for magazines. Her husband, Anthony Turnbull, was one of the people Toby had encouraged to become an Outside Name.

'How was your trip home?' Emma asked, before Liza could say anything. 'It was jolly nice having you down here, and didn't all the children get on well together? We must do it more often, although I suppose you feel you have to go to Chalklands every weekend.'

'Emma . . .' Liza began.

'What is it?' Her friend had lost none of her intuitive sensitivity. 'What's wrong?'

'Toby's missing.'

'What do you mean?'

'He never went to New York. No one has seen him since he left here a week ago; I don't know where he is.'

'I don't believe it!' In all the years she'd known her,

Emma had never heard Liza sound so desperate. 'What's going on?'

Briefly Liza repeated what she'd told her parents and her in-laws. The more she explained what had happened, the more extreme it seemed. At any moment she expected to awake and find the whole thing was a nightmare. 'I don't know what to do, Em.'

'Do you want me to help you issue a press release tonight?'

'Would you really?'

'Of course, though I think it should have been done a week ago. Nevertheless, I'll handle that side of it for you. I've still got all my contacts ... In fact, I'll drive up to London and stay at the flat tonight, so I can be on the spot.'

'What about the children?'

Emma sounded as capable as ever. 'The two au pairs can look after them. Anyway, Anthony has a late sitting; he quite likes me to be at the flat when he gets home in the middle of the night,' she chuckled. 'Don't worry about a thing, Liza. I'll come to you as soon as I arrive in town. Can you look out some head-and-shoulder photographs of Toby?'

Liza's heart seemed to miss a beat. 'For ... for identification purposes, you mean?' she said falteringly.

'News desks like pictures to go with a lead story,' Emma said matter-of-factly. 'Don't panic, Liza. I'm sure there's a perfectly simple explanation. Toby's much too sensible to let anything happen to him.'

'There's something else, Emma ...' Liza hesitated.

'Yes?'

'Have you or Anthony heard from the Hamcroft syndicate in the past twenty-four hours?' She waited in dread for Emma's answer.

'No? Were we supposed to have done?'

'I don't know, but Freddy's had a letter, and they're demanding one hundred and seventy thousand pounds . . .'

'What? Freddy?' Emma spoke incredulously.

'Yes. He's in a terrible state. It's all these losses the syndicate has suffered; asbestosis, environmental pollution claims, hurricanes . . . Oh, I knew there had been a lot of disasters and that most of them were going to affect Lloyd's, but I thought the family firm was all right.'

There was a long pause.

'Christ,' Emma said softly. 'That's all Anthony needs at the moment.'

'I'd like to speak to Mr Toby Hamcroft, please.' The voice was aristocratic, but at this moment also agitated. 'It's very urgent.'

'Who is that calling, please?' asked the operator on Martin E. L. Hamcroft's switchboard.

'This is Sir Humphrey Davenport.'

'I'm afraid Mr Hamcroft is unavailable.'

'When can I speak to him? Will he be long?'

'I'm afraid Mr Hamcroft's away on business. Can I take a message, sir?'

'Do you know when he'll be back?'

'I believe he's returning tomorrow. Shall I get him to call you?'

Sir Humphrey spoke with finality. 'Don't worry. I'll leave a message at his home.'

When he'd rung off, the switchboard girl turned to one of her colleagues.

'That must be the tenth call I've had this morning for Toby Hamcroft!'

The second girl looked bored. 'So what?'

'Something's up. I'm sure of it.'

Her companion examined her long, pink-varnished nails. 'D'you mean he's got another woman?'

'No. It's something more interesting than that. Money. A lot of money. Millions, I wouldn't be surprised.'

'What are you talking about? All them insurance claims? There'll be heavy losses!'

'That's what I'm talking about. Funny, isn't it, a lot of people are suffering losses on the Hamcroft syndicate, and then everyone's ringing up wanting to talk to Toby Hamcroft himself!'

'This nail varnish don't half chip easily,' observed the second girl. 'I'm more interested in what's happening with Declan Connolly.' Her smile was sly. 'I overheard him on the phone just now talking to a woman. It wasn't his French wife, neither. I wonder what he's up to?'

'I could ring Liza,' Lady Rosemary Davenport suggested, 'although I don't think she really knows what is going on in Lloyd's.'

Sir Humphrey blinked rapidly, his expression riven with anxiety.

'It wouldn't look very good, would it? Not very businesslike, eh?'

Lady Rosemary was also anxious, but she was managing to stay calm.

'Humphrey,' she said, endeavouring to sound reasonable. 'My family home, my fortune, and everything I possess is in danger, thanks to our believing that becoming a member of Lloyd's was a perfectly safe way of making money . . . What was it Toby Hamcroft said? "It'll never happen, of course, but you are liable down to your last pair of cufflinks." So, this demand for over half a million pounds may only be the first instalment in meeting insurance claims. I don't know about your cufflinks, but I'd better hang on to my diamond earrings very tightly, because I may not have them for much longer.'

'Oh, Rosemary, what have we done?' He looked at her in appalled anguish, aware it was he who had in fact persuaded Rosemary to become an Outside Name.

'There's no point in getting in a state,' Rosemary said, going over to him and laying her hand on his shoulder. 'Maybe this will be the worst year, or maybe next year will. I can't believe we'll make these sorts of losses every year. It's never happened before; I'm sure Toby will have taken care of us. Remember how he talked about reinsurance, and spreading ourselves over several good syndicates? Let's wait until he comes back and we'll talk to him then.'

Humphrey looked up at her, his expression like that of one of his labradors when they were about to be punished. 'I'm so sorry . . .' He bit his underlip. 'It's most frightfully worrying, isn't it, old gel?'

Surprisingly, having got over her initial shock, Rosemary felt tenderly disposed towards him. It wasn't entirely Humphrey's fault. She should never have let Toby talk them into taking a risk with the family inheritance, but it hadn't seemed at all like a risk at the time. She had thought of it as a considered and wise investment, from which their children would, in years to come, benefit.

The first question Sir George Mortimer asked Liza, as they sat down to discuss Toby's disappearance, was:

'How did Toby travel to Heathrow on that last morning you saw him?'

'Hire car,' Liza replied immediately. 'He never takes our car to the airport, because it's such a drag putting it in a parking lot, so we have an account with Première Cars. They're very reliable and the drivers are nice. We use them when we go out in the evening so that Toby can drink.'

Sir George's eyes lit up. 'I suppose the police have interviewed the driver? Was he one you knew? Had he driven Toby before?'

Liza thought about it. 'To be honest, I don't remember . . .' Her voice broke momentarily, thinking how they'd parted without making up their quarrel.

Ingrid had made some coffee before going to collect

the children from school. Liza busied herself pouring the hot, fragrant liquid into the chunky dark green coffee-cups she and Toby had bought on their last trip to France. As she tried to regain her composure and quell the panic she felt, her mother spoke.

'I'm sure the police will have checked with the car hire firm; I mean, Toby must have got to Heathrow, or else the driver would have said something, wouldn't he?' Helen Mortimer reasoned.

Liza nodded. 'Oh, God, wouldn't it be wonderful if he just walked in here tonight, as if nothing had happened.'

'Oh, darling, this is so awful for you. Have the children any idea what's going on?' Helen dropped her voice even though they weren't in the house.

'No. They've no idea,' Liza replied. 'Tilly and Tom think he's coming back tonight, although I've told them he's been delayed by business, but Sarah has no idea.'

Sir George rose, a dapper-looking man who'd retained his military bearing. 'I'd like to talk to the police, Liza. The ones that came to see you yesterday.'

Opening her handbag, she handed him the card Detective Inspector Robin Buck had given her. He regarded it, holding it at arm's length. Too vain to wear glasses, he couldn't read anything unless it was two feet away.

'Humph,' he mumbled, frowning. 'I may know someone a bit higher up in the force who might be helpful.'

'Anything, Daddy. Oh, and Toby's parents are flying over from Spain. They should be here by this evening.'

'Martin and Nina?' said Lady Mortimer. 'Oh, it will be

nice to see them again. Now, is there anything I can do to help, darling? You don't need the work and worry of a house full of people at a time like this.'

'Thanks, Mum, but the bedrooms are all ready, and Ingrid has done most of the shopping, and what she couldn't get, Harrods are delivering,' Liza replied. 'Thank God you *are* all here; I wouldn't want to be alone.'

Her parents exchanged looks.

'Can I use the phone in the little sitting room to make some calls, Liza?' Sir George asked.

'Daddy, help yourself to anything you need. Just help me find where Toby is.'

[illegible] see them again. They've been [illegible] school. Darling! You don't need [illegible] work. You're [illegible] [illegible] a girl like this.'

'Thanks, Mum, but [illegible] are already [illegible] has done most of the shopping. And what else [illegible] Honestly [illegible] I [illegible] and [illegible] I wouldn't want to be [illegible]'

Her parents exchanged looks.

'[illegible] the [illegible] little [illegible] some [illegible]' Tig George asked.

'Teddy, help yourself [illegible] you [illegible] and [illegible] me [illegible]'

Chapter Four

By six o'clock, everyone had arrived at the Hamcrofts' home in Holland Park Walk. Martin and Nina were unpacking in the second-floor guest room, trying to acclimatise themselves to the coolness of an English summer's day after the scorching heat of Spain, and wondering if they'd brought enough warm clothing. Sir George was still in the little sitting room making phone calls, while in the kitchen, Lady Mortimer helped Ingrid give the children their supper. Liza, with Emma, was sorting through the drawers of her bureau, searching for suitable photographs of Toby.

When the phone rang just after six, Sir George answered it immediately. His manner was crisp.

'Hello?'

'Has . . . er-um . . . has Toby Hamcroft returned yet?' a male voice, diffident and nervous, enquired.

'Who is that?'

'This is . . . er-um . . . Humphrey Davenport here.'

'I'm afraid Toby's not here. This is his father-in-law speaking. Can I help you?'

'Is Liza there, I wonder?' The voice sounded anxious now.

'Wait a moment, will you please? I'll go and see.'

Rising, Sir George stomped into the drawing room, where Liza was gazing wistfully at a snapshot of her and Toby with the children, taken a few months previously in the grounds of Chalklands.

'There's someone calling himself Davenport on the phone,' he said, as if he were delivering a military communiqué. 'Do you want to speak to him?'

'Humphrey Davenport? Oh, Daddy, can you take a message for me?' she asked.

'Of course, my dear.'

A few minutes later he returned. 'Wouldn't leave a message. Said he'd call Toby at the office tomorrow. Don't know what it's about.'

Liza knew. Humphrey and Rosemary would probably have received the same sort of letter as Freddy. As her father retreated once more to the sitting room, Liza looked at Emma knowingly. Neither said anything at that moment, but Liza was only too aware that Emma and her husband Anthony could soon find themselves in the same position.

'If you're thinking what I'm thinking,' Emma remarked after a pause, 'I want you to know that Anthony and I would never blame Toby. I know he acted in good faith, and I know he had our interests at heart when he suggested Anthony become a member of Lloyd's.'

Liza looked down at the photographs miserably. 'I know, Em. If something's gone dreadfully wrong, I know it won't be his fault, but God, isn't it going to be embarrassing? He introduced nearly *all* our friends to Lloyd's. Because we were doing so well, everyone was clamouring to join. What are they going to say now?'

'Nobody was forced at gun-point,' Emma retorted. 'We're all grown-up, too. Nobody can blame Toby for giving us the chance to do well. We were also warned we were taking on an unlimited liability when we joined.' She lowered her voice. 'I'm wondering how your father-in-law's going to take it; the company is even *called* Martin E. L. Hamcroft, isn't it? Won't that be an embarrassment if the balloon goes up?'

Liza spoke *sotto voce*. 'I haven't had time to talk to him about anything except Toby's disappearance; I suppose he knows what's happening? He's been away from the City for fourteen years now. I'm not even sure he gets the English newspapers.'

'But he's still a member?'

'Oh, yes! My God, I suppose he and Nina could face ruin, too!'

They looked at each other again, round-eyed with dismay.

'Let's face it, we may all end up in the poor-house!' Emma said with an attempt at joviality.

A moment later, Martin and Nina appeared, tanned and ill at ease in formal town clothes after years of dressing casually.

They made a final decision about which photographs

to release of Toby and, while Liza put the others back in the drawer of her bureau, she indicated the drinks tray by the doorway.

'Please help yourselves,' she said. 'I've invited Freddy and Melissa to dinner, but they won't be here for a while yet.'

Martin regarded the heavy silver tray set with cut-crystal decanters and glasses. There was gin, vodka, whisky, sherry; Toby always kept a well-stocked bar, but then everything he did was carried out with flair and verve, Martin reflected. Suddenly the glittering crystal blurred as he fought for control, saying a silent prayer for his son.

In due course, Sir George emerged from the sitting room looking exhausted. The children had come up with Nina from the kitchen: if they hadn't all been looking so serious and talking so earnestly, Liza realised, it could have looked like a family reunion. Martin and Nina hardly ever came over from Spain, and it took a lot to persuade her parents to come down from their beloved Balnabreck to endure the 'filthy fumes' of London. Yet here they were, and her friend, Emma, all rallying round and being supportive at a time when she desperately needed them. It only needed the rattle of a taxi drawing up in the street outside now, and the sound of feet charging up the front steps, then the key in the lock, and...

The pain Liza felt in her heart was physical. A hurting ache that made her feel like weeping. Yet she couldn't. Her hands shook as she sipped her Perrier water and stroked Lottie's ears. All she wanted in the world this moment was for Toby to come home.

Martin came over to her, his deeply lined face like polished leather, his dark eyes – so like Toby's – sympathetic.

'I'm sure he's all right, you know, Liza,' he said softly. 'Think about it. If anything had happened to him, *anything*—' he emphasised the word again – 'then we'd have heard.'

'But people do go missing . . . hundreds of people every year,' she replied. 'Most of them are never seen or heard of again.'

'But not people like Toby. Not middle-aged men in his position. Everyone in the City knows him, you know. He's the "Broker Baron" of the eighties,' he added with a touch of pride.

'This is the nineties.' Her tone was dry.

'Nevertheless, Toby is a very prominent man in Lloyd's. I'm afraid the people who go missing are the young, poverty-stricken boys and girls who run away from home and get into trouble.' He shook his head. 'They're the ones who slip through the net and are never heard of again.'

'But what do you imagine has happened to him?'

At that moment, Thomas leaned over her shoulder from behind her chair, twisting his neck to look into her face. 'Is Daddy lost? Isn't he coming home tonight?' he queried.

'Daddy's been delayed,' Liza said, giving him a quick kiss on his firm baby-soft cheek.

'Is that why Grampy and Grandma and Grandpa and Granny are here? To look for Daddy? Can I look too?' His voice was clear and fluted. His headmaster had told her he should have singing lessons.

Liza smiled. 'Daddy will come back when he's finished his business,' she said.

'But if he's lost, we must look for him,' Thomas insisted. Then he raised his voice. 'Daddy's lost, Tilly! Are you going to help us look for him?'

Tilly looked alarmed. A miniature version of Liza, with her fine features and long fair hair, her blue eyes were shadowed with fear. 'Is Daddy really lost, Mummy? Is he lost in America?'

Sarah too was looking anxiously at her mother. Liza took a deep breath and lifted her on to her lap.

'Listen, children,' she began. 'Daddy may not be lost at all. We don't know where he is, that's the problem, and so of course we're all a bit worried. He said he'd be home tonight, and he may be,' she added, though without much conviction. 'But if he's not, then we're going to tell the newspapers so that they can help us find where he's gone.'

'Wouldn't the police be better?' Tilly suggested helpfully.

'The police already know,' Nina Hamcroft said, wrapping her arms around her elder granddaughter and hugging her. 'We're sure there is nothing to worry about. I expect your Daddy is so busy, he's forgotten what day of the week it is!'

Thomas gave her a scathing look. 'Daddy wouldn't do that! Mummy, where can we look for him?'

'The police and the newspapers can do a better job than us,' Liza pointed out. 'Because they'll know where to look.'

'Will Daddy being lost be on the telly?' Thomas asked, wide-eyed.

'Maybe.'

'Wow! Tilly, did you hear that? Dad may be on the telly!'

Melissa spread out the fabric samples for the nursery curtains and surveyed them with a pleasure that was almost sensual. Should she choose the chintz patterned with the letters of the alphabet and nursery-rhyme figures? Or the white-sprigged muslin? Doing up their little home was giving her intense delight, and it was addictive, too. She pored over *House and Garden* for hours looking for ideas, and hardly a day passed when she didn't pop along to Peter Jones to buy fabric or braid, roped tassels for tying back curtains, or a selection of tapestry cushions. It was all a sheer delight, and she never wanted the house to be finished.

'You'll be gilding the lily if you add anything else,' her mother said in a critical voice during one of her frequent visits. 'You'll make the whole place look too fussy.'

But Melissa was not to be deterred, and anyway, Freddy loved it even if he did have to sleep under a rose-patterned canopy edged with pink frills.

Tonight they were dining with Liza and Toby, and

Melissa looked forward to the evening with mixed feelings. The trouble was her sister-in-law was so damnably rich. She and Toby had the best of everything, from the fine linen on the beds to the crystal and silver on the table. Sometimes Melissa felt an ache of longing for all the beautiful things Liza could afford. If the house in Holland Park Walk had belonged to Freddy . . . ! Melissa sighed with deep hankering. What she could have done to that grand house if it had been hers! Maybe one day Freddy would be as rich as Toby; until then she would turn their modest three-bedroom terrace house into a miniature haven of perfect taste. Melissa turned back to examining the fabric; the baby was due in two months and there was still a lot to do.

When Freddy got back from Sotheby's at half past six, she was so absorbed she didn't notice his face was a stunned mask of anxiety.

'Had a good day, sweetie?' he asked, automatically kissing the top of her head. Unlike Liza, who had become finer-featured and more beautiful over the years, Freddy had grown plump and pink, with thinning blond hair and faded blue eyes.

She smiled up at him quickly and absently. 'Lovely, darling. Tell me, do you think this wallpaper will go with a pale blue carpet?'

'What was that?' Freddy slumped on to the sofa, as if his legs were suddenly weak. 'Yes, I'm sure it will be lovely,' he replied without looking.

Melissa glanced at him curiously. 'Are you all right, Freddy?'

'I'm fine,' he replied a shade too quickly. 'Just tired.'

'Do you want to cancel going to Liza's tonight?'

'No, she needs to see us. Ma and Pa are going to be there, too.'

'What? They're down from Scotland?'

Briefly he told her about Toby being missing, glad of an excuse for his worried demeanour, because he hadn't yet summoned up the courage to tell her about Lloyd's.

Whilst the children were being put unwillingly to bed, and the dinner prepared, Sir George and Martin Hamcroft found themselves on their own, each nursing a large whisky and soda.

'I don't suppose you've got any theories about Toby's disappearance, have you?' Sir George asked hopefully. He'd had a disappointing afternoon on the phone, and he wasn't quite sure what to do next. He'd spoken to a friend who was in a high position at Scotland Yard, but he'd been told the police were being hampered by the embargo Declan Connolly had imposed. Without media coverage, looking for Toby Hamcroft was like searching for a diamond on a beach of pebbles.

'Did you have any luck with the car hire firm?' Martin asked.

Sir George shook his head before taking a swig of his drink. 'The driver who took Toby to Heathrow is out on a job in the country, and can't be contacted for the time being. I left a message; I hope he'll call me back later.'

'Not that he'll be able to tell you more than he told the police,' Martin observed.

'Maybe not, but I'd like to know how Toby was that morning, whether he said anything to the driver that might give us a clue.'

'You're thinking he might have fallen into a depression, or something like that?'

Sir George shrugged. 'Obviously you know your own son better than I do. One reads in the newspapers that Lloyd's isn't having too good a time; who knows? He may be worried about business. Has he said anything to you?'

'Not a great deal. I've been away from the City for a long time now, George, and whilst I know we've had some massive claims, I'm sure the syndicate can stand it. We reinsure ourselves to the hilt. "Excess of Loss" reinsurance, we call it. If we didn't do that, even a big syndicate like ours would go out of business. We also have large reserves, you know, because we insist on our members leaving some of the profits in the company, so we have a bit put aside for a rainy day; it's as simple as that.'

He drained his glass, looked into its empty cut-crystal depths and said, 'I'm going to help myself to another drink. How about you?'

'Yes. Thanks.'

At seven-thirty, with everyone back in the drawing room, and the fragrant aroma of roasting lamb emanating from the kitchen, Freddy and Melissa arrived.

The atmosphere was tense and troubled; everyone

spoke in low voices, and with an urgency that was coupled with impotency; no one knew what to do, and yet everyone felt something should be done, and quickly.

For Liza, this had been the longest day in her life, and she felt now as if it was reaching crisis point. By nine o'clock Toby would either be home . . . She couldn't think of the alternative. She glanced nervously at the gold wristwatch he'd given her many years before, and her feelings of despair deepened. As she went to check with Ingrid that the dinner was nearly ready, Freddy followed her into the hall.

'Does Dad know about the letter I had?' he whispered nervously. He was clutching his gin and tonic so tightly that she was half afraid he'd break the glass.

'No, not as far as I know. I haven't mentioned it. Why don't you have a word with Martin first? He might be able to reassure you about future years, which would help when you tell Dad,' she suggested.

Freddy looked stricken, eyes almost popping. 'But I've heard that future years are going to be *worse*! 1989 and 1990 are dreadful, with flooding, hurricanes, forest fires, pollution . . . and claims for this goddamn asbestosis, that goes back to 1962! There's no end to it, Liza. It's a devastating situation. If I've been asked to stump up one hundred and seventy thousand pounds now, what the hell will they want next year and the year after? I'll . . . we'll be wiped out! And the worst of it is I'll have to wait three years just to find out how ruined I am!'

She laid her hand sympathetically on his arm. 'Try not to worry too much. I'm sure Toby will have looked after you and made sure you're on safe, low-risk syndicates.'

'Christ! But where is Toby?' Freddy looked searchingly into his sister's eyes, as if seeking comfort. Suddenly she understood his acute anxiety.

'You haven't told Melissa yet, have you?' she asked intuitively.

'Oh, God, no! With the baby coming and everything ... and she's so extravagant, Liza. She likes to have the best of everything ... This will kill her! She'll go mad!'

'I think you'll find Melissa is a little more resilient than you're giving her credit for,' Liza said drily. 'You'll have to tell her, Freddy. And you'll have to tell Dad.'

Freddy rubbed the crown of his head with the palm of his hand, a panicky gesture Liza remembered from childhood. They were in the dining room now, and she was lighting the candles on the table.

'Listen, Freddy – oh, help me light these bloody candles, will you? – no one's going to blame you for joining Lloyd's. It's been a great investment until recently: the good times will come back again. Dad's not going to be angry with you, for God's sake!'

Freddy struck a match and lit the candles as if in a dream, but aware that, even in crises, his sister always liked standards upheld and everything beautifully done.

'Dad needed some persuading, though,' he pointed

out. 'Toby had to tell him it was a good idea. What if Balnabreck has to go? Where will they live? Where are Melissa and I going to live, now? We could all go bankrupt.'

For once Liza looked at him severely. 'Pull yourself together, Freddy. You're being bloody selfish! Here am I, worried *sick* about Toby, imagining him lying somewhere – ill, injured, dead even – wondering if I'll ever see him again ... and all you can think about are your bloody syndicate losses.' She covered her face with her hands, her control going. 'Fuck your money!' she stormed tearfully. 'And stop thinking about yourself all the time!'

Instantly he looked contrite and, going over to her, put his arm around her shoulders. 'Oh, Liza ... I'm sorry, pet ... Of course I'm worried about Toby.'

'Suppose I never see him again?' she wept, looking up at her brother with a tear-stained face.

'What's going on?' asked a sprightly voice, and they turned to see Melissa standing in the doorway, watching them suspiciously.

Neither Liza nor Freddy said anything, but Liza quickly wiped her cheeks and Freddy moved away, almost guiltily.

'I'm sure Toby will be all right, Liza.' Melissa, trying to sound kind, merely sounded patronising. 'I don't know what all the fuss is about. Shall I tell the others that dinner is ready? I think the men are getting hungry.' She gave a light, tinkling laugh as she turned back to the drawing room.

Liza blew her nose and spoke. 'Let's have dinner before we say anything to anybody. Who knows? A miracle may yet happen and Toby might return.'

'Yes,' Freddy replied dolefully, 'and we might all win the pools!'

The hands of the grandmother clock in the dining room moved slowly forward. No one had much of an appetite, but the wine flowed freely, dulling the edge of their apprehension. Conversation was stilted and there were long silences, as if they were all stranded on the shore of unreality, with the tide going steadily out.

'I can't stand this any more,' Liza suddenly burst out, putting down her knife and fork. Her plate was virtually untouched. 'Toby isn't going to turn up, you know,' she continued despairingly. 'I was mad to think he might.'

Emma looked questioningly at her. 'OK. Shall we get started? We've missed the first editions but if I call Associated Press and Reuters straight away, we'll make the second.'

Liza nodded.

'You can use the phone in the sitting room. You won't be disturbed there,' Sir George commented, rising in his courteous manner to pull back her chair.

Emma's smile was enigmatic. 'Thanks, but I brought my own.' From her large leather shoulder-bag she drew out a mobile phone, a Filofax and a notepad. She strode off in the direction of the sitting room with a purposeful expression on her face. Liza followed her more slowly.

'So,' remarked Sir George, sitting down again and

pouring himself another glass of wine, 'all hell should break loose as soon as the press gets wind of this. About time, too. I don't know what the hell Charles Bryer and Declan Connolly thought they were trying to achieve by keeping his disappearance secret. Mad, if you ask me.'

'I agree,' said Martin, 'but I do realise they probably thought it would avoid a lot of unpleasant publicity at Lloyd's. No doubt Charles and Declan thought they were protecting Toby from unwanted speculation.' In the candlelight, his skin was dark as mahogany and more dry-looking than ever.

'Unless you're in Lloyd's,' he continued, 'it's difficult to understand what a secretive place it is. Any form of publicity is abhorred. I have to admit it's outdated in many ways, but for three hundred years it has been the most exclusive institution in the City of London – or anywhere else for that matter – and, quite frankly, at any hint of trouble, we close ranks instantly.'

Sir George, who had been listening intently, looked up. 'But why,' he asked argumentatively, 'should Lloyd's, collectively speaking, be so secretive about its affairs and its members if it has nothing to hide?'

Liza had come back into the room and resumed her seat. She looked at her father and her father-in-law. Suddenly the atmosphere seemed to be bristling with hostility.

'Surely you, as a military man, must know what loyalty to your regiment means? Loyalty to Queen and country?' Martin said almost angrily.

'Yes,' Sir George countered swiftly, 'but if one of our

ranks breaks the rules, we don't sweep the matter under the carpet! He's court-martialled and punished! Men who break the rules are drummed out of the regiment! They don't have friends who help them escape to some tax haven from where they can't be extradited! I remember the Lloyd's scandal that *did* get into the newspapers a few years ago. A chap had salted hundreds of thousands of pounds of members' money into an offshore company before he did a bunk!' Sir George was heated now, his voice low with fury. 'He was never brought back to this country to face punishment, and when last heard of, was working for an insurance company in America, having financially ruined a lot a people in this country! No wonder you don't like the press sniffing around!'

There was a stunned silence, broken suddenly by Liza's sobs. 'Will you both stop it!' she shouted. 'Is *none* of you worried about Toby?'

Everyone started talking at once.

'Oh, darling, we *are* worried,' Helen Mortimer exclaimed, jumping up to rush round the table to comfort her daughter, but not before she'd given her husband a filthy look.

'Liza, I'm sorry,' Martin Hamcroft said with sincerity. 'God knows we're worried about Toby. I was just explaining . . .'

'Well, we don't need your explaining,' Nina Hamcroft cut in crossly. 'You men are all the same!' She, too, rushed to comfort her daughter-in-law.

'Sorry, pet,' said Freddy, giving her a rueful smile,

although he hadn't said anything. Only Melissa looked unconcerned.

'Why on earth are you all in such a state?' she remarked. 'Just because it seems Toby didn't fly to the States when he was supposed to, you all go berserk! He's probably fine! I expect he just wanted to get away from everything for a few days.' She eyed the tearful Liza and said no more.

At that moment they heard the sitting-room phone ring.

Liza looked up, frozen for a moment, and then she jumped up and ran out of the room.

'Oh, please God let it be Toby,' she prayed, slipping on the polished parquet floor and almost falling. She hurtled into the cosy little room, where Emma was talking on her mobile phone, and grabbed the receiver. At that moment she would have given everything she possessed to hear Toby's voice saying, 'Hiya, sweetheart!' the way he always did.

Of course it wasn't Toby. It was a man's voice she didn't recognise, and he was asking to speak to her.

'This is Liza Hamcroft speaking,' she replied, heart thudding in her ears.

'This is Gerry Shalto, from B-Sky-B Television News.' The voice was warm and encouraging, and very friendly. 'We've just been informed that your husband, Toby Hamcroft, has been reported missing. I wonder if you could tell us...'

Emma's labours, as she sat with her mobile phone opposite Liza, were already beginning to bear fruit.

* * *

An hour later, in a corner of the drawing room in one of the artfully created sitting areas, Freddy sat facing his father while he plucked up the courage to tell him the news. They were not alone in the room. Martin and Nina Hamcroft and Helen Mortimer sat on the sofa, deep in conversation, while Melissa, looking bored, sat nearby, flipping through the pages of a book on French interior design, wondering if ruched blinds wouldn't look prettier in the bathroom than roman blinds.

'Dad,' Freddy began wretchedly. 'I know we're all uptight at the moment about Toby, but I had some very bad news this morning, and I have to tell you about it.'

Sir George straightened his back and squared his shoulders. 'I thought something had happened as soon as I saw you,' he replied. 'What is it? Heavy losses?'

Freddy nodded. 'Dreadful losses,' he said in a stage whisper. 'I haven't told Melissa yet, but Liza knows. I got a letter this morning,' When he told his father the amount they were demanding, Sir George's jaw dropped, and his skin, suddenly putty-coloured, seemed drawn taut over his prominent cheekbones.

'God Almighty!' His voice was hoarse too.

'I'm told it's going to get worse as well,' Freddy said.

'I'd heard that too, but I didn't think it would happen to us; not to people on the Hamcroft syndicate.'

'I wish I'd never joined. I feel so guilty now, Dad.'

'Too late for regrets, m'boy.' Suddenly Sir George's eyes sparked with barely suppressed anger again. 'I thought Toby was supposed to be looking after the Outside Names: he's the members' agent for Hamcroft's, isn't he?'

'He hasn't been the members' agent for years, Dad. Toby's entirely involved on the broking end of the business now. It's his job to place policies all around The Room, on all the syndicates.'

'Then who's the members' agent?'

'Declan Connolly.'

'Ah, yes.' Sir George thought about this for a moment.

'I'm sure none of this is Toby's fault,' Freddy pointed out. 'And I don't think it's got anything to do with his disappearance, either. If he'd screwed up, he's the sort of person who would stay and face the music.'

'Yes, I know,' his father replied, looking across the room as his beloved Liza entered with Emma. 'I know Toby's not a coward,' he added *sotto voce*, 'which makes his disappearance all the more worrying.'

The two men sat in silence, gazing bleakly at the carpet, bonded by blood but otherwise not resembling each other at all: Sir George dark-haired and dapper, Freddy fair-skinned and blond and rather rumpled-looking.

'Balnabreck will probably have to go . . . in time,' Sir George said at last. 'Sad that. I'd hoped you and your children would live there one day.'

'Oh, God, Dad . . .' Freddy groaned quietly. 'What can I do? How can I get out of this mess? Melissa's going to go crazy! Is there any way I can get out of Lloyd's, do you think?'

'This is one occasion when you can't say "I don't want

to play any more." Lloyd's have got you by the short and curlies, m'boy. There's no get-out clause.'

Freddy flushed deeply with misery and mortification. 'Christ! It's like a prison sentence.'

'Pretty well. Don't think I'm blaming you, though. When I made the deeds of Balnabreck over to you thirteen years ago, I knew what I was doing. At the time it seemed like a sound idea. But we were wrong. End of story.'

'But everyone has always made money in Lloyd's,' Freddy protested, looking round the exquisitely furnished and decorated room on which Liza and Toby had lavished money, as if to make his point. 'So what's happened to us? Why should we be about to lose everything?'

It was a question Sir George would very much like answered too, but first they had to find out what had happened to Toby.

Chapter Five

As Liza joined Sir George and Freddy, they were still deep in conversation.

'Daddy, there's a call for you. A man called Colin Henson. He says he runs Première Cars.'

Her father rose creakily; for the first time she realised he was beginning to grow old.

'I left a message for them to ring me back. Thanks, darling.'

Liza watched him walk slowly into the next room before joining her mother and Nina Hamcroft on the sofa. He looked as if he'd aged ten years in the last half hour.

'How are you feeling?' Nina asked her sympathetically. 'This is all terrible for you.'

Liza reached out to take her mother-in-law's hand. 'It's just as bad for you. It's the not knowing that's so awful,' she added. 'My mind is going round in circles and I'm imagining the most awful things.'

'I'm sure,' the older woman pointed out, 'that once the

news is made public, Toby will be found. He's got to be somewhere.' The fine lines etched in her tanned face were like dark furrows. The sun, Liza reflected inwardly, had robbed her mother-in-law of all the luscious bloom that should belong even to a woman of a certain age, leaving a wizened, crêpe-like husk in its place. Funny, she'd never noticed it when they'd stayed with Nina and Martin in Spain. Only here, in the pallor of the English light, did the damage show.

'Sky TV are going to televise a newsflash every few hours throughout the night and tomorrow,' Liza told her.

'That should help. Emma's a wonderful friend, isn't she?' Nina observed.

'The best,' Liza enthused. 'Her husband is coming by to collect her later on. You'll like him, too. He's a really lovely man and Toby and I are very fond of him.' Then she winced. The 'Toby and I' had slipped out so naturally, so easily; her breath caught at the thought that there might not be any 'Toby and I' in the future.

Nina was patting her arm. 'He'll be all right, my dear,' she said gently, knowing what Liza was thinking.

At the far end of the room, Freddy was whispering to Melissa. From his earnest expression and her shocked gaze, Liza guessed he was telling her about Lloyd's. Suddenly Melissa's face went very white and she gave a cry, like the yelp of a small dog. 'How could you let this happen?' she said loudly and shrilly.

'But Melissa ...'

'What are we going to do now . . . ?' she shrieked.

At that moment Sir George came back into the sitting room. 'I've had the *most* interesting conversation with the chap who runs Première Cars,' he announced, looking pleased with himself.

'The one who drove Toby to Heathrow?' Liza said.

'No. This chap is the owner. The driver who took Toby is a middle-aged man called Henry Granville. He's only been with Première Cars for a few months. It's a sad story really.'

The others looked at Sir George with interest.

'What's sad about him?' Martin asked.

'He used to have his own business. A property company. Did very well, had a big house, a high standard of living, a wife; all the trimmings, you know. Then the bomb dropped.'

'What bomb?' Liza asked, knowing her father was leading up to something.

Sir George drew in a deep breath. 'He was an Outside Name at Lloyd's. On the Martin E. L. Hamcroft agency. His losses have practically wiped him out. All he has left is his car. He and his wife now live in a couple of rooms in very reduced circumstances.'

Liza's hand flew to her mouth, and she gave a little gasp, guessing what was coming. Her father looked at her.

'Now he drives his own vehicle for Première Cars as a means of eking out a living,' said Sir George.

There was a stunned silence. Then Liza spoke, tentatively.

'So he was the last person to see Toby?'

Martin Hamcroft had been trying to get hold of Charles Bryer on the phone, but without success. At last the receptionist at the Plaza Hotel told him Mr Bryer was out for the evening, and not expected back until later.

'Damn and blast!' Martin cursed, looking at his wristwatch. It was midnight, which meant it was only seven o'clock in the evening in New York. He couldn't expect Charles to be back for at least another three hours.

'You can't sit up all night!' Nina protested. 'Call him in the morning, for heaven's sake! We've been up since dawn, we've flown from Spain, and now I think it's time we went to bed.' She leaned back against the sofa cushions and closed her eyes.

'I've got to talk to him,' said Martin. His voice had an urgency about it, though he sounded hoarse from exhaustion.

Liza looked at them with concern. They were older than her parents, and years of lying about in the sun seemed to have softened them, and drained them of vitality. Her own parents, hardy Scots, accustomed to walking for miles up and down the mountains surrounding Balnabreck, seemed much stronger and fitter by comparison.

'I think you should all go to bed,' she said tactfully. 'Emma and I are going to wait for Anthony, but it's silly our all staying up.'

Angry whispering, like the hissing of snakes, could be

heard from the far end of the room where Freddy was once again facing an almost hysterical Melissa.

'I will *not* live in a poky little flat!' Liza heard her say with furious passion.

'We may *have* to!' Freddy shot back furiously.

Sir George raised his eyebrows and with a measured tread walked over to where they sat.

'There's no point fighting over it,' he said mildly. They both looked up at him, startled.

Melissa burst into noisy tears. 'How can I be expected to manage with no money? You seem to forget I'm having a baby! We need a house, with a nursery and a bit of a garden ... and ... and ... Christ! How could you have been so *stupid*?' she raged at Freddy.

Martin and Nina looked at Liza, mystified. In a low voice she told them the reason for the fracas.

'Oh, my God. That's serious.' Martin looked deeply shaken. 'I've got to get hold of Charles. I didn't know anything about this. What the hell's going on? Have you and Toby suffered losses?'

'I don't know,' Liza replied honestly.

'I don't know whether we have either,' Emma remarked, 'but as we're all with Hamcroft's, I suppose we're all in the same bloody boat.' Suddenly realising she was talking to the founder himself, she blushed. 'I'm sorry ... I didn't mean ...'

He gave a tired smile. 'I know you didn't, my dear.'

At last Liza managed to persuade Freddy to take Melissa home. Then the two older couples went up to bed, leaving her alone with Emma, to wait for Anthony.

'What an evening,' Liza sighed, collapsing on to a sofa and putting her feet up. 'All we needed was Melissa making that scene.'

Emma yawned. 'She's a spoilt cow, I think.'

They sat in silence, each deep in their own thoughts, Emma wondering nervously if she and Anthony were going to face financial ruin, too. Would all their lives be changed, their dreams dashed, their hopes ruined?

Suddenly Liza sat upright, breaking into Emma's thoughts.

'What's the matter?' Emma asked, alarmed.

'I haven't warned Declan that I'm making Toby's disappearance public!' she exclaimed in dismay.

'I thought you told him you were going to do it when he was here this morning?'

'I threatened . . . but I'm not sure he took me seriously. He's going to be furious that I haven't told him what we're doing.'

Emma shrugged. 'I think he's behaved irresponsibly by keeping it a secret! God, do you realise, he's been putting Lloyd's before Toby? What sort of a friend is that? Don't worry about it, Liza. When I told your Detective Inspector on the phone earlier, that we've told the media, the whole of Scotland Yard practically cheered!'

'It will help, won't it, Em? Oh, please God let it help find Toby,' she said, clasping her hands tightly together.

'Yes, of course it will help.' Emma reached for the notepad she'd left on the table beside the coffee-tray. 'Listen. I've been on to Associated Press, Reuters, the

Press Association, *every* national daily newspaper, and my old stamping-ground, the *Evening Standard*, plus every television and radio station. Couriers have been coming here, as you know, for the past three hours, to collect pictures of Toby which will make the second edition if not the first ... My God, Liza, by lunchtime tomorrow, there won't be a person in the land who won't know Toby Hamcroft has gone missing. We're talking front page, lead story. You do realise you'll have to give interviews tomorrow, don't you?'

Liza agreed reluctantly. 'I suppose so. What am I going to say?'

'Tell them the truth; everything. You've nothing to hide. Stress that Toby is an utterly reliable man and that you're desperate to know where he is and what's happened. Wear something simple and plain, too. Don't put on too much lipstick, and hold your hair back with combs at each side; that style really suits you.'

'God, Emma! I'm not doing an audition! Why do I have to do all that?'

Emma spoke in a no-nonsense voice. 'Because you don't want to come over looking like a rich middle-class housewife, do you? You've got to look serious and dignified and very much in control of yourself.'

In spite of how she felt, Liza smiled affectionately. 'Good old Em. Still bossing me about.'

When Anthony arrived an hour later, he hugged Emma and kissed Liza on the cheek. 'Liza, I'm terribly sorry to hear about all this,' he said as she poured him a drink. 'You must be frantic.'

'I can't believe it's happening. It's all totally unreal.' She shook her head, and he saw how white her face was, a sick, translucent white, her blue eyes silvery-grey, almost as if she were bloodless.

Anthony paused for a moment before saying cautiously, 'I think there's something brewing at Lloyd's. Even before Emma told me on the phone earlier that Toby had disappeared, there were rumours circulating around the House. You know, there are several members of the Cabinet who are Outside Names, not to mention dozens of MPs, like myself.'

'What sort of rumours?' Emma asked curiously, her journalistic instincts sending humming messages to her brain.

'There's talk of heavy losses. Maybe in the region of a hundred and fifty million in total. Some say more.'

Liza and Emma looked at him, stunned.

'But *why*?' demanded Liza.

'I think we're just seeing the tip of the iceberg,' Anthony continued. 'Something's gone very wrong with the "Excess of Loss" reinsurance, and the fact that it's spiralled out of control. Too many risky policies have been insured and then reinsured, and then reinsured again and again, and passed on and on, in smaller and smaller units. It's being likened to a game of pass-the-parcel. Now the buck has finally come to rest, it seems. It's time to pay up. All these world disasters were insured and reinsured at Lloyd's, and the balloon's about to burst!' He took an appreciative sip of his drink and gazed fondly at his wife. He was a large, rangy-looking man, untidy and slightly crumpled at this time of night.

Emma returned his look with a smile. They'd been married nine years and were devoted to each other.

'How serious is it going to be, Ant?' she asked.

'Probably as serious as they come,' he replied.

'So what happens next?' Emma asked.

Anthony made an expressive gesture with his hand. 'Some syndicates will suffer total meltdown. People on those syndicates will go bankrupt. It's even possible the unbelievable will happen and Lloyd's will run out of money. Questions are going to be asked as to how in hell's name things have been allowed to get into such a terrible state in the first place.'

Liza looked at Anthony, her eyes glazed and her expression blankly stunned.

It was Emma who put into words what they were all thinking. 'Do you know something?' she said slowly. 'I think Toby's disappearance is linked to something much bigger than any of us imagines.'

At last the house was silent, as if it had folded up within itself while the occupants slumbered: the children peacefully, the adults restlessly.

Martin Hamcroft was the only one who couldn't sleep at all. He knew that something was dreadfully wrong as far as Toby was concerned. He could feel it in his bones. Lloyd's had been Martin's life ever since he'd joined at the end of World War II. By 1954 he was a working

Name and, ten years later, he'd started his own underwriting syndicate. The company grew and prospered, and he'd expanded into bigger offices in Fenchurch Street, starting a members' agency at the same time. When he retired in 1976, a year before Toby married Liza, Martin E. L. Hamcroft's was one of the largest and most highly respected insurance companies within the framework of Lloyd's. That famous phrase he so loved, 'Individually we are part of an insurance company, collectively we are Lloyd's', was as dear to him as if it had been his personal family motto. People looked up to those in Lloyd's. Members had a right to hold their heads high, he reflected, because, throughout the world, Lloyd's was synonymous with all that was truly British, decent and absolutely honourable. Or was it? Had some new element infiltrated the previously upright honest brokers and underwriters of yesteryear? Had it flung its doors too wide for the sake of profits, allowed in all and sundry, people who had no sense of tradition?

It was four o'clock in the morning; he knew he would never get to sleep. Better to get up and slip quietly out of the room so as not to disturb Nina. It would be eleven o'clock in New York now: surely Charles Bryer would have returned from dining out.

'There's no crisis!' Charles Bryer said firmly. 'I'm not saying we haven't had some problems, but so have insurance companies all over the world! Munich Re, in Germany, have had their ups and downs too, but both they and Lloyd's are handling around five billion pounds in premium income annually, so there's really no cause for alarm. We're in a deep recession, my dear Martin. Other insurance companies in Europe aren't exactly happy, either, but it's swings and roundabouts. That's what it is, Martin, swings and roundabouts.'

It struck Martin that, if nothing else, Charles Bryer had enjoyed a very good dinner. And, although Charles was more than aware that Toby had been missing for over a week now, he seemed more interested in denying there were financial problems in Lloyd's than in worrying about what may have happened to Toby.

'When are you returning to England?' Martin asked abruptly.

Charles seemed to hesitate. 'There are a lot of loose ends here which Toby was supposed to have tied up. Now I have to see to them, so I suppose it will be another few days at least.'

'I'd like us to have a meeting. There are things which are worrying me.'

Charles sounded surprised. 'Apart from finding out what's happened to Toby, what is there to talk about, Martin?'

'I may have retired, but I'm still a Name, and I did start the company,' he protested. 'We're staying with Liza. I'll give you a call as soon as you're back, and we'll have lunch.' He spoke with a touch of imperiousness. If it hadn't been for him, Charles probably wouldn't be where he was today, he reflected.

'Fine.' Charles didn't sound pleased. 'I hope Toby turns up soon. His vanishing like this has made things very awkward here, but I think I've got it all under control.'

'I don't suppose he did it on purpose,' Martin replied tartly. 'I'll see you.' Having rung off, Martin felt more disturbed than ever. Talking to Charles Bryer seemed to have posed more questions than it had answered.

Wandering into the drawing room, he went to the long french windows and pulled back the heavy curtains. The paved garden was a melancholy blue, with the cold light of an English dawn. He'd forgotten how lonely and desolate the start of each day was here. Dawns in Spain were swift, hazily bright, the stillness disturbed by the *pfit-pfit* of the automatic hose, which their gardener turned on when he arrived at six o'clock to water the coarse-bladed grass. Soon the sun would be riding high in a spotless blue sky, the bougainvillaea would hang motionless from dazzling white archways, and the stone beneath his feet would be blisteringly hot.

Martin looked up at this English sky, and saw with surprise a sliver of transparent moon still hovering, as if reluctant to leave. A blackbird shrilled loudly in the yew tree at the far end of the garden, and then a London sparrow flew chirpily down from the honeysuckle, picking the ground for insects.

How different from my new home, he thought. And how glad I am that I don't live here any more. Subject to depression caused by lack of sunlight, he also knew he could never come back. Not on a permanent basis. Not at his age, either.

* * *

Declan Connolly, across the park in his house in Kensington, hadn't slept well either. He'd been to a dinner party with Maxine, in the roof-restaurant of the Park Lane Hilton, and he'd rather overdone his intake of champagne. And lobster mornay. And fillet steak with vegetables. And a chocolate gateau laced with white rum and cream. Then there was the cheese and biscuits. Then marrons glacés with the coffee, and a few brandies to keep the Monte Cristo cigar company. By three o'clock his heart was pounding as heavily as his head, and while Maxine slept the sleep of the dieting self-righteous, he felt as if his whole system was collapsing.

At six o'clock he got up, ready to try anything that might make him feel better. In the bathroom cupboard he found some Alka-Seltzer. In the kitchen he made himself a cup of coffee, and because he couldn't bear the silence of his own company, switched on the small portable television set that stood on the counter.

A moment later, hangover vanished, he was standing in shock as the face of Toby Hamcroft looked smilingly at him from the small screen.

'... A leading Lloyd's broker, Toby Hamcroft, has been reported missing for the past week ...' The newscaster's voice, cool and impersonal, announced the bare facts. That was all. It was a brief news item, sandwiched between an IRA incident in Belfast, and the closing of another coal pit in Wales. Declan sank heavily on to one of the kitchen chairs and switched over to the other channels to see if they were carrying the same story. They were. By the time he'd had his second cup of coffee, he knew Toby's disappearance would feature in every headline throughout the country.

The effect in The Room at Lloyd's was going to be electrifying. It would be the talk of every broker's queue and underwriter's box, and speculation, rumour and gossip would be rife. Especially as he knew a lot of people on the Hamcroft agency had just received letters announcing the losses and demanding immediate payment. Most of the worst hit were the Outside Names – and Declan thanked God for that – but nevertheless, a lot of questions were going to be asked. And wasn't there a risk, he reflected, that the losses and the disappearance of Toby might well be linked together?

There was a crowd of journalists, photographers and television crews outside the house by the time Liza awoke. She looked carefully through a gap in her bedroom curtains so as not to be spotted, and saw them milling around on the pavement and road outside, some looking up at the house with curiosity, others huddled in groups, talking to each other. They were all hung about with cameras and recording equipment and trailing cables.

She felt besieged and panicky. Any minute now she guessed they'd start ringing the front door bell, and Ingrid, if she was up, wouldn't know what to do. Then they might start questioning the children ... Liza hurried up the flight of stairs to where her parents were sleeping in one of the guest rooms, and rapped on the door.

'Come in.' Her mother sounded alert. Liza found her sitting up in bed, looking anxious.

'What's happening, darling?'

'There are dozens of press people ... Oh!' She gave a small gasp as she heard the front door bell ring. 'What shall I do? I'm not even dressed. I didn't think they'd arrive so early.'

Sir George sat up in bed, his grey hair ruffled from sleep but looking as alert as his wife. Throwing back the bedding, he got out of bed and reached for his thick tartan dressing-gown.

'How long will it take you to make yourself presentable, Liza?' he asked, combing his hair quickly.

'Half an hour, I suppose ... I mean ...' She felt disorganised, caught on the hop.

'Fine. I'll tell them to come back in forty-five minutes.' He marched out of the room as if he were about to give orders to a battalion.

Liza looked at her mother. She was shaking. 'There are so *many* of them,' she said appalled. 'I'm really scared.'

Helen Mortimer was clambering out of bed too. 'I'll go and make some tea while you get dressed. Just keep calm, Liza. After all, neither you nor Toby has done anything wrong. They'll probably only ask you damn silly questions like "How do you feel about your husband being missing?" or stupider still, "Are you worried?"'

She snorted with contempt. 'The press are far too intrusive for my liking.'

'But we have as good as invited them to do something. We need them to publicise Toby's disappearance, Mummy. Oh, I hope Daddy isn't being rude!' Liza hurried out of her parents' room and met Ingrid on the landing.

Quickly explaining to her what was happening, she told Ingrid that the children must stay at home today. 'I don't want the school disrupted, Ingrid, or the children pestered. Keep them away from the front door and windows, too.'

Ingrid looked wide-eyed and fascinated. 'I do that, Mrs Hamcroft,' she promised.

Liza grabbed clothes from her wardrobe; a suit, shoes, a silk shirt. Clumsily she tried to get dressed, but she felt as if she was at the bottom of a swimming pool with the weight of the water on her head. She could scarcely do up the buttons of her shirt because her hands were trembling like an old woman's. Then the phone rang, making her jump.

It was answered before she got to it. A few minutes later, Martin Hamcroft, already dressed, came hurrying up the stairs from the hall.

'That was Emma on the phone,' he informed her breathlessly. 'She's coming round now, to help you sort out that lot in the street. Your father's told them they'll have to wait before they see you, but they're acting like a pack of hungry wolves.'

'Thanks, Martin.' Liza flew down the stairs, trying to

keep a grip on herself. At least something was being done to help find Toby. She could sense the positive atmosphere in the house, with everyone pulling together. Maybe by tonight, tomorrow...? She didn't dare let herself think ahead. There were the next few hours to get through first, and she couldn't afford to break down.

In the kitchen, her mother, still in her dressing-gown, was dispensing tea to her father and the Hamcrofts. The children, she hoped, were still asleep. But not for long. The bell ringing again and then the banging of the brass front door knocker was enough to arouse the whole street.

'It's OK,' said Liza, putting down her untouched cup of tea. 'I'll just go and tell them that I'll talk to them as soon as Emma arrives to organise everything.'

As she left the kitchen, Sir George said quietly, 'I think that's a mistake. They're going to recognise Emma and look upon her as a rival journalist who's been given an exclusive interview.'

Liza opened the front door, then stepped back appalled, as if she'd been hit by an invisible tidal wave. Dozens of eager faces stared at her, flashbulbs half blinded her with their dazzling light, and then voices, urgent and aggressive, filled the air like a swarm of angry bees.

'Oh, God!' she gasped, trying to shut the door, but a foot was already jammed against it. The hungry pack pressed closer and she knew a moment of panic.

'What do you think has happened to your husband, Mrs Hamcroft?'

'When did you last see him?'

'Are you worried about his disappearance, Mrs Hamcroft?'

'Have you any idea where he might have gone?'

Liza raised her hand and looked pleadingly at the motley collection of faces. Then a single voice came louder than the others, an authoritative voice from a serious-looking reporter with glasses.

'Is there any truth in the rumour, Mrs Hamcroft,' he asked, 'that because of the financial difficulties at Lloyd's, your husband may have faked his own death?'

Chapter Six

Liza looked at Emma, stricken. 'That was horrible!'

Emma nodded sympathetically. 'That's why I said I'd come round to give you a hand. Weed out the reputable journalists from the hack-pack.'

They were sitting in the drawing room, Liza recovering from her doorstep encounter. Luckily Emma had arrived in time to rescue Liza from her ordeal by cutting a swathe through the press, getting to the front door and slamming it shut before they realised what was happening.

'What shall we do now?'

'I'll go and talk to them. I think the best thing is for you to make a statement.'

'What shall I say?' Liza asked, stupid from shock. 'Did you hear one of them ask me if Toby faked his own death in order to escape some financial scandal? How could they say a thing like that?'

Emma rose. 'Leave it to me. I'll go and tell them you'll make a prepared statement in fifteen minutes. You'll answer no questions. It's too much to expect you, at this time, to give individual interviews.'

'OK.'

'I must say I'm pleased with the result of last night's work, though. With all this hype going on, we're sure to find out what's happened very quickly now,' Emma added, swinging briskly out of the room.

I think that's what I'm afraid of, Liza thought as she sat alone for a few moments. Her regret at not phoning him to heal the rift still tormented her. Something had gone terribly wrong, and now she might never even get the chance to say goodbye. But he couldn't be dead. If he was she'd feel it in her bones, she'd know the savage pain of abandonment, a part of her would have died, too. Yet what could have happened?

Liza kept going over those last few minutes before he'd left the house for Heathrow, looking for clues that with hindsight might help her understand what could have happened.

She remembered him standing in the hall, ignoring her as he got ready to leave. 'Passport, tickets, itinerary, Filofax . . .' He rattled off the usual things, as he always did before he left on a business trip. 'Money . . . plastic . . . files . . . de-dah, de-dah, de-dah . . .' Satisfied, he shut the case with a snap. His luggage was already by the front door. A moment later he was gone, with only a cool: 'Goodbye.' Now she didn't even know where he was or what had happened. With a surge of despair she wondered if she'd ever see him again.

'Oh, darling, try not to upset yourself,' said her

mother coming into the room at that moment. 'I know it's hard.'

Liza tried to stem the flow of tears, but they plopped unchecked on to the lapels of her pale yellow suit. 'I'm ... I'm so frightened,' she sobbed. 'What can have happened to him?'

Helen Mortimer hugged her, patting her back as if she were still a child.

'That driver from Première Cars; the one who lost his money in Lloyd's,' Liza said brokenly. 'I forgot to ask: did he get Toby to Heathrow? Does he know anything, or was it just a coincidence that it was Toby he was driving that morning?'

'Just a coincidence, I think. Your father said the driver – Henry Granville was his name, wasn't it? – had made a statement to the police saying he'd never driven Toby before and didn't know who he was, but that he took him to Terminal Three and saw him enter the building.'

Liza blew her nose. 'And that's all?' Her mother nodded.

Emma came back into the room at that moment, and took in the situation at a glance. 'Would you like me to draft a few words for you to read out?' she suggested softly.

Liza looked grateful. 'Would you, Em? I'd be terribly grateful. I'm sorry, I'm being really hopeless.' She straightened her back and gave a final sniff.

'I'll get you both a cup of coffee while you work out what to say,' Helen remarked. She tightened the sash of her Japanese cotton kimono. 'If I don't get dressed soon, everyone will think I'm a slut,' she said, forcing her voice to be jokey.

Liza managed a wobbly smile.

'Let's get to work then,' said Emma briskly. 'Those chaps are not going to doorstep all day.'

It was exactly what Liza needed. 'I'd like to begin by saying...' she told Emma, who had begun to make notes; ten minutes later the statement was ready.

'OK, then?'

Liza looked at herself in the mirror, powdered her pink-tipped nose and nodded. 'I'm ready.' Emma, looking at her, marvelled at her apparent composure.

The woman who faced the formidable phalanx of reporters and photographers that morning was a very different person to the startled wife who had opened the door and then fled half an hour before. As if inspired, Liza stood at the top of the steps outside her front door, a slim and vulnerable-looking woman, yet one who spoke with such dignity and confidence that there was instant and attentive silence.

'I'd like to thank you all for coming here today in response to my request to have it made publicly known that my husband, Toby Hamcroft, disappeared a week ago and has not been heard of or seen since,' Liza began. She looked up from her notes, her blue eyes sweeping over them all with such an expression of pain that they watched her, mesmerised, microphones thrust forward, camera lenses zooming in for a close-up.

'Contrary to the sort of rumours I believe are circulating about his disappearance, I would like to make it absolutely clear that he is in no way involved in financial difficulties of either a personal nature, or in connection with Lloyd's of London. My husband is a man of honour and he would never be party to any wrongdoing. I would appeal to anyone who may have seen him or has any news of his whereabouts to contact the police immediately. His absence is of grave concern to me and my family, and we would be grateful for any information. Thank you.'

After a moment's silence, and before she could get back in the house, the clamouring questions started again, as if the journalists had been reactivated.

'What d'you think happened to him?'

'Have you a message for him . . . ?'

'Do you believe he's still alive, Mrs Hamcroft?'

Liza swung round to face them again, one hand on the door-frame.

'I *have* to believe he's alive, for my sake and for the sake of our three children, and I will go on believing he's alive until it is proved otherwise,' she said firmly.

She paused and swallowed before adding, 'Please. Help me to find him.' Then the black front door was shut quietly and she was gone.

In the hall, away from prying eyes, Emma hugged her. 'Well done! You were brilliant! Oh, Liza, Toby will be so proud of you.'

'You think? Was it all right?'

'It was perfect! You had them eating out of your hand.

Now we must watch the lunchtime news on television. I bet they transmit your whole statement.'

'Which, thanks to you, wasn't too long,' Liza remarked. 'What do we do now?' Her confidence had returned and she felt on a high, capable of moving mountains if necessary in her search for Toby.

'I think I should stay and handle all phone calls,' Emma suggested. 'This is going to be a frantic day, I can tell you, and you don't want to talk to all and sundry.'

The meeting took place at dawn in a derelict barn, on the outskirts of Bodmin Moor. Reached by a dirt track, the procession of cars that arrived could not be seen from the A30; secrecy was of paramount importance. There were eight men and two women and they sat in a circle on a variety of camp stools and upturned crates. The youngest was thirty-eight, an ex-SAS officer who had been invalided out of the army a few years ago after suffering head injuries sustained in combat. His training and tough, ruthless personality had made him an obvious choice as leader. The oldest, a widow, was thin and nervous-looking, her claw-like hands bare of even a wedding ring. Next to her sat a middle-aged teacher. The others were undistinguished-looking retired businessmen, with the exception of a man in his sixties with sparse silvery hair and piercing eyes. On his knee he held a briefcase, so stuffed with papers it would not shut.

'Are we all here?' barked the SAS officer.

'You can see we are,' ventured the widow, querulously. She was ignored. The meeting began. It lasted two hours and at times was heated. They were reminded by their leader that the stakes were high but the rewards were great. The old man patted his briefcase.

'There are so many . . . so many,' he murmured, and there was a glint of a tear in his eyes.

'Are we agreed on phase two of our plan? We should put it into operation within two days, allowing us all time to get back to our homes first?'

The others agreed. It was time to go. Some left in pairs. The widow and the schoolteacher. A retired army officer and the farmer. The oldest member of the group and a retired businessman. The others left singly, and the ex-SAS officer last of all. He wanted to make sure they'd left no evidence of their being there. He kicked to one side the wooden crates, adjusted the holster strapped to his body in which rested a revolver, and took a last look round.

It was now time to proceed with the rest of the operation.

Declan arrived to see Liza shortly after noon. The house seemed to be swarming with people and, to his shock, Martin Hamcroft was there, on his way out.

'Good to see you, Declan,' he said, shaking the younger man's hand.

'Good morning, sir. How are you?'

'Worried about Toby, of course.' Martin turned to

Liza. 'I'm off to the bank,' he explained. 'I'll only be about an hour.'

Liza nodded in understanding. Then she led Declan into the drawing room. 'Any news?' she asked.

'No. Nothing. Has his father come over from Spain because Toby's missing?' he asked curiously.

'Of course. Nina, too. We're all desperately worried, Declan. Have you heard anything at all?'

Declan, wandering restlessly about the room, hands in pockets, seemed reluctant to answer at first. Then he took a deep breath.

'I have to be frank with you, Liza, but the word is out that Toby has skipped the country, having robbed many of the Outside Names of their money, which they say he'd placed in an offshore company.'

Liza felt sick. 'That's the most terrible thing I've ever heard! You don't believe it, do you?'

He hesitated for a moment before answering. 'I'm not saying I believe it, but things don't look good. Lloyd's, in general, is in a bad way, mostly through mismanagement, but also because corruption on a massive scale has been practised by certain individuals. Not just on the Hamcroft syndicate, but others, too.'

Liza's face stung red with anger. 'But Toby hasn't done anything wrong, Declan! Are you accusing him of embezzlement, for God's sake?'

Declan shook his head vigorously. 'Of course I'm not, but he is, unfortunately, in the hot seat. He has a very high profile at Lloyd's.'

'But he'd never do anything *wrong*,' Liza insisted.

'I'm not saying he would.' Declan looked longingly over at the tray of drinks. 'Can I help myself, Liza?'

'Of course,' she said in surprise. She knew him to be a very light drinker, especially in the middle of the day.

'Can I get you anything?'

'No thanks, Declan. I want to keep a clear head. I want you to tell me what the hell is going on in Lloyd's.'

He sighed. 'So much has happened concerning the business of reinsurance over the past ten years. Reinsurance premiums from "baby syndicates" have been transferred abroad, for tax reasons, and the interest invested.'

'Isn't that illegal?' she asked, aghast.

'No. There's been nothing to stop the formation of offshore companies and to buy land, and build properties; it's perfectly legal,' he explained, 'as long as the Names agree.'

'Then what are "baby syndicates"? I don't think I've ever heard the term.'

'They're an offshoot of the parent company. Toby's probably on the "baby syndicate" of Hamcroft's!' Declan took a swig of his gin and tonic as if he really needed it.

'What's wrong with that?' Liza asked, confused. 'Many companies have offshoots.'

'Yes, they do, but things haven't been as straightforward as that.'

'I don't understand what you mean.' There was an

edge of coldness in her voice, and she was looking at him sharply.

'What I'm saying,' Declan explained slowly, as if he were talking to a child, 'is that the baby syndicate should not cream off the best of the business, leaving high-risk business with the parent company. I don't know, mind you, but Toby may well be in the embarrassing position of having made a fortune for himself by putting his own money into the low-risk baby syndicate, while his friends find themselves wiped out because they were on the parent company's syndicate. Do you understand what I'm saying? The Martin E. L. Hamcroft syndicate has incurred losses of over one hundred million pounds, and there's not enough in the way of reserves to meet those claims.'

Liza's head was reeling; confusion, bewilderment and fear clamoured to be topmost in her mind.

'I don't believe I'm hearing this! Declan, what are you saying?'

Declan finished his drink, and rose as if to refill his glass. 'The crux of the matter is that now big claims have come in, there isn't the money in the syndicate to pay them! That's why Names are being asked to ante up! If there hadn't been any baby syndicates, there would probably have been sufficient money. As it is, those who invested in the low-risk baby syndicates are now sitting with their bum in the butter, while the other poor sods have lost their shirts on the parent syndicate.'

Liza looked horrified, as a dawning realisation of the

implications sent shock waves through her brain. 'But that's dreadful! That's like insider trading! Having special knowledge of what's going to make money ... and what isn't!'

'You're right.' For the second time in two days he was impressed by her quick comprehension. 'We, and many other companies, are in the same boat.'

Realisation of a deeper kind dawned on Liza.

'So you're saying, Declan, that the working Names looked after themselves, putting their own investment on the low-risk syndicates, while the *Outside* Names were placed on high-risk syndicates?'

He looked at her, and slowly he nodded. 'Got it in one,' he remarked, 'we have to look after ourselves. It goes with the territory.'

'Then...?' Her hand flew to her mouth. 'But Toby wouldn't do a thing like that. Does he even know such a system exists?'

'He knows all right. He and Charles Bryer have had many meetings about it. It's not illegal. What is more worrying is that many people believe Lloyd's itself is on the verge of bankruptcy. Collectively we may be in debt for billions of pounds.'

'Have any of the Working Names been asked for money?' she asked.

'Oh, yes. Everyone's been affected, some more than others, because of a string of disasters. There have never been so many claims in past years, and if there have they've never been on such a big scale.'

'Dear God.' Liza sat stunned, her breath taken away

by the enormity of the situation, and by how thoroughly Toby had shielded her from all that had been happening.

Declan spoke again. 'All this doesn't mean you and Toby are broke, you know.'

Liza looked at him through a veil of pain. 'I don't care about that,' she said distantly. 'All I want is to have Toby back.' Then she seemed to rouse herself. 'But of course we must be broke, if Freddy is, and I believe the Davenports ... maybe Emma and her husband too ... How could we have escaped?'

'As I said the other day, I'm not *au fait* with Toby's personal financial affairs, but being as bright as he is, I very much doubt he's lost a penny.'

'Are you saying that to reassure me? Or do you believe it?' Liza asked him directly. 'If people are going around accusing Toby of being involved in some financial scandal, I must know exactly what has happened, so that I can set the record straight. Prove his innocence until he is here to defend himself.'

Tears, never far away, brimmed in her eyes, and she looked hastily away so that Declan should not see them. In the past hour she had come to wonder if he was really her and Toby's friend after all. Would a friend point the finger of suspicion? Would a friend even *suggest* that a husband had been involved in some chicanery?

Declan remained silent, as if he were unwilling to say more. Perhaps, she thought, he realises he may have already said too much.

Emma, who had been on the phone in the little sitting

room that she now referred to as the 'headquarters', bounded into the drawing room. 'The news is about to start on BBC1,' she announced.

Liza turned on the television. The screen flickered, blossoming into colour, and a moment later she was looking at herself and hearing her appeal for news of Toby.

'Terrific!' Emma announced, when the piece came to an end.

Liza looked doubtful. It had been strange watching herself. 'Was it all right?'

'Perfect,' Emma assured her, while Declan nodded in agreement.

'I'd better be getting back,' he said after a few minutes, 'although I'd much rather stay here. It's been hell in The Room this morning, though I was rather expecting it to be.'

'Everyone asking you questions, I suppose?' Emma observed. 'Tell me, Declan, are you facing severe losses too?'

'Not that I know of! Should I?' He sounded wary.

'Oh, good,' Emma replied, pretending not to notice the change in his manner. 'Maybe Anthony and I will be lucky, too.'

Declan said nothing. He kissed Liza lightly on the cheek and, with a slight swagger of the shoulders, strode into the hall.

'Keep in touch, Liza!' he said. 'Let me know the *instant* you hear anything about Toby, and I'll do the same.'

'Thanks, Declan.'

When he had gone, Emma looked at her curiously. 'Do you actually like Declan?' she asked.

'I'm not sure,' Liza replied. 'Sometimes I think it's a bit tiresome, the way he tries to emulate Toby in everything he does; I suppose it's because he admires him. I'm not sure I trust him, actually.'

'Umm.' Emma looked thoughtful. 'I've always thought of him as a bit of an upstart, myself.'

Sir Humphrey looked at his wife with a stupefied expression. He blinked rapidly. 'What does it mean?'

Lady Rosemary was still watching the television screen as if she was expecting some further announcement.

'I don't believe it,' she said at last. 'Toby Hamcroft would never run off with other people's money.'

'Then why did Liza say all that on the box, just now? Isn't it odd that he's disappeared? Just as Lloyd's ask us for all that money?' His brow was puckered. 'I think I need a sherry,' he added.

They were in the library at Cavenham Court, and had been watching the one o'clock news while waiting for Masters to serve lunch.

'You can pour me one, too,' Lady Rosemary said. 'This is really the most dreadful shock.'

It was the second, though not the worst, shock she'd had that day. The first had been the letter she'd received from the bank manager, advising her to sell Cavenham Court. Funds were going to be needed to cover both her past and possibly her future losses, which in his opinion could eventually reach over three million pounds. To lose Cavenham Court, her family home for the past three hundred years, was as painful as the prospect of having a limb amputated, but she could think of no alternative.

'Couldn't we get a mortgage on the place?' Sir Humphrey suggested. 'Or a bank loan?'

'When could we ever pay it back?' Lady Rosemary reasoned. 'I wonder if we could sell some of the paintings? The most valuable ones might even raise enough to cover the losses. I think I'll get Sotheby's to value them.'

Meanwhile she phoned Mr Smythe of Coutts & Co., bankers to her family ever since they had started in Fleet Street over three hundred years before. He was gloomy as he forecast her financial future.

'This is a tragic situation, Lady Rosemary, and we have many clients in the same situation as yourself. We will, of course, be happy to set up a loan account, to cover your immediate losses, which I believe have to be paid by the twelfth of the month, using Cavenham Court as collateral, but that won't solve the problem in the long run. The interest will be heavy and what happens next year? And the year after?'

'It would help if I could have a loan for the time being whilst I get our paintings valued. Maybe we could clear all the losses by putting my grandfather's art collection into an auction?' she suggested, a note of desperation creeping into her voice.

'Why, certainly, Lady Rosemary. That will be no

problem. I will arrange matters right away.' Mr Smythe bid her a polite goodbye, in a tone similar to their letters which always ended with the words 'from your obedient servant'.

'That might do the trick,' Sir Humphrey said when she told him what she'd arranged.

'Anything to keep this place,' she replied wistfully, as she gazed out of the long library windows at the stretches of parkland that surrounded Cavenham Court.

Later that day she phoned Sotheby's, and it was arranged that someone from their art department would come down to do a valuation in two days' time.

'Freddy Mortimer will be with you by noon,' she was informed.

The police phoned Liza during the afternoon to tell her they'd set up an incident room at New Scotland Yard and that, although they'd had no definite news of Toby yet, they were hopeful of knowing more before the day was over.

Liza's heart lifted in a dizzy rush. 'You'll find him by tonight?'

There was a momentary pause. 'We can't be sure we'll *find* him by tonight,' the officer in charge said carefully, 'but we hope we'll have some news of him or his whereabouts.'

'That's wonderful,' she said, grateful. 'Oh, God, that's so wonderful.'

The officer cleared his throat. 'Mrs Hamcroft, I think maybe, perhaps . . .' he hesitated.

'Yes?'

'I think perhaps you should prepare yourself, you know, just in case . . .'

She scarcely dared ask. 'For what?'

'Well, I think it only right to warn you that, after this length of time – eight days, isn't it? – your husband, he may not still be alive.'

'Oh-h-h-h!' The sound escaped her in a moan of desolation. In her worst moments she'd thought of nothing other than this possibility, but somehow the officer's words made it seem suddenly more likely. She couldn't speak, and her mother and father, watching, stiffened with concern.

'Shall I take over, darling?' Sir George asked gently.

Liza nodded dumbly, handing him the phone with a shaking hand. While he talked, Helen Mortimer put her arms around Liza.

'They think he may be dead,' she told her mother.

'Surely not, my darling . . .' Helen wrapped her arms around her daughter, wishing desperately she could do more to help her.

The day dragged on slowly, nobody knowing quite what they were supposed to do. Emma and Sir George stayed near the phone, dealing with a variety of enquiries from the media, friends who had watched Liza's television appearance and more reporters requesting an interview. Mostly they tried to keep the line clear, in case the police had any news of Toby. Outside, on the pavement, a small group of pressmen still loitered, hoping Liza would come out.

Martin Hamcroft, anxious to find out what was happening at Lloyd's, arranged to meet an old friend who had been an underwriter for twenty years.

'We're having lunch at Boodles. I'll be back around teatime,' he told Nina.

Meanwhile, Nina and Helen entertained their three grandchildren, spoiling them for the sake of peace. Liza was too distracted to do anything but give them a hug when she saw them.

Then, just as Ingrid was getting tea, Sir George called Liza to the phone.

'Who is it?' she asked.

'A woman called Rachael Clarke. She says she's a personal friend.'

Liza looked nonplussed. The name meant nothing to her. Shrugging, she took the receiver from her father.

'This is Liza Hamcroft speaking. Can I help you?'

'*I hope your husband rots in hell!*' the caller shouted in a shrill, high-pitched voice.

Liza froze, too stunned to say anything.

'Thanks to your bloody husband, I'm a widow now! A widow with no money. I'm going to lose my house, everything I've got, thanks to Toby Hamcroft!' The voice edged near hysteria, and was frightening in its piercing quality.

'I . . . I'm sorry . . .' Liza faltered, aghast.

'You *will* be sorry! I hope your husband's dead, like

mine is! Dead because he was ruined by Lloyd's, dead because they demanded hundreds of thousands of pounds from him *which he didn't have*. Which I don't have ... but even if I did I wouldn't let the buggers have it. Do you realise, Mrs Hamcroft, that *my husband committed suicide* because your husband got him into Lloyd's?'

Appalled, Liza listened as the woman started sobbing: great, tearing sobs that sounded as if she was going mad. Then she became calmer.

'He ... he shot himself! They wanted everything! You don't know how I've suffered ... seeing a good man lose everything he'd spent a lifetime working for, seeing him being dragged down with despair and worry ...' She broke off again and with another sob she hung up.

'Oh my God!' Horrified, Liza told her father and Emma what the woman had told her.

'Do you know her?' Sir George asked.

'No. I don't know who she is. Rachael Clarke ...?' Deeply shaken, Liza tried to recall the name, but it meant nothing to her. 'I must ask Declan if he knows her. Her husband must have been on the Hamcroft syndicate, though why she should blame Toby ...' Liza's voice drifted off. 'If Declan can find out who her husband was, perhaps we can do something; do you really think it's true that he killed himself because of the losses?' she added.

'There may be more to it than that,' Sir George tried to sound comforting.

'But why blame Toby?'

Emma leaned forward, chin cupped in the palm of her

hand, eyes staring down at the carpet in concentration. 'Someone is trying to put the blame on Toby. We have to find Toby as quickly as we can so he can defend himself, otherwise his reputation will be in ruins,' she said.

'It seems it already is,' Sir George commented grimly.

Sir Humphrey, awakened as if from a long sleep by the turbulent events that threatened their whole future, looked at his wife with a determined air, when she told him the bank would arrange a temporary loan.

'Why do we have to take this lying down?' he protested. 'What can Lloyd's do to us if we refuse to pay?'

'I dare say they could sue,' Lady Rosemary replied sadly.

'But it's iniquitous!' He blinked rapidly, his fair eyelashes reminding her of a moth's wings, batting for survival. 'Absolutely nobody warned us this could happen. That can't be right, Rosie, can it?'

'We're not the only people to suffer,' she pointed out gently.

'We can at least get out now, can't we? Resign or something? I mean, dammit, your family have hung on to this place for seven generations; we can't let a bunch of City boys take everything away from us now.' He plonked himself unhappily behind the vast desk, at which he never normally sat, and with a clenched fist banged on the antique leather blotter which bore the family crest in silver.

Lady Rosemary looked thoughtful. 'I suppose we could go and see Richard Brooks and ask his advice.'

'Good idea. You go and see him, m'dear. You're much better at this sort of thing than I am. Tell the fellow it's impossible for us to raise this money without parting with historical family heirlooms.'

In London the next morning, Lady Rosemary sat looking across the cluttered expanse of her solicitor's desk and saw in his expression her own downfall.

'Unlimited liability.' She repeated his words; they rang out like a doom-laden forecast of what was to come.

'Did no one explain that to you?' asked Richard Brooks of Stafford, Brooks and Gardener, solicitors at Lincoln's Inn.

'A friend of ours, Toby Hamcroft, seemed to explain it very well . . . he may have mentioned we were liable for an unlimited amount, but, well, everyone makes money in Lloyd's; it seemed as safe as houses . . . I suppose I never stopped to think,' she replied.

The eyebrows in the otherwise implacable face shot up, and the eyes quickened with interest. 'The Toby Hamcroft who's been reported missing?' he asked.

When she nodded he leaned back in his chair and regarded her thoughtfully. 'Oh dear,' he said. Then he sighed gustily. At fifty-seven, Richard Brooks had seen a great deal in his life. Being a solicitor wasn't all fusty document-filled rooms, laden with dust and the traditions of hundreds of years; it was about drama and dying, divorces and division of property and money; he saw life as it really was; people stripped of their veneer.

Pretences went out of the window when reality came in at the door.

'Oh dear,' he said again.

'Is there no way I can get out of paying future years? Can't Humphrey and I resign now?' she asked desperately. Lady Rosemary handed him the letter she'd received from Lloyd's. His eyes briefly took in the salient points.

'. . . I am afraid you have sustained a loss,' he read, 'of five hundred and twenty-one thousand, four hundred and eight pounds and six pence for the year 1988. I would be pleased if you would forward a cheque for the above amount by the twelfth of July. We are advised by our managing agents that any amount still outstanding after the fifteenth of July will be subject to interest.'

'Have they the right to do this?' she asked.

'Indeed they have, I'm afraid. You invested in Lloyd's because you hoped to make a profit. Unfortunately, as in all forms of gambling, you can also lose. You lost,' he added bluntly.

'So we could go on getting demands like this, year after year, with no get-out clause, until everything's gone?'

'I'm very much afraid you could, Lady Rosemary. As you probably know you are not alone. Several members of the royal family are suffering, including Prince and Princess Michael of Kent, the Duchess of Kent, Princess Alexandra . . . the list is endless. Some people have already lost hundreds of thousands of pounds; more will follow.'

'But I had an underwriting limit of five hundred thousand pounds, so I don't understand why there's a risk of my being asked for *more* than that amount?'

'You won't be asked for more than that amount in any *one year*, Lady Rosemary. This is for losses incurred in 1988. Who knows what the picture is for 1989, 1990, and so on?'

'I've heard they were even worse years,' she said desperately, seeing her whole life blown away. It was like being a helpless passenger on an endless helter-skelter.

Richard Brooks tried to sound cheerful. 'But maybe the years after that will be good. There may not be any more massive claims, and then you'll make a profit from all the premiums people had paid. Those premiums will be higher than previously, too, because of the losses. In the long run, you could make up your losses and be in profit again.'

She looked at him doubtfully. 'If I wait about a hundred years,' she said flatly. Then she rose, gathering up pale kid gloves, a handbag and a long, elegant umbrella.

'Thank you for seeing me. I suppose, as my late father used to say, I must put up and shut up.'

The solicitor's face was filled with compassion. 'I'm dreadfully sorry, Lady Rosemary. I wish there was something I could do.'

As Lady Rosemary walked through Lincoln's Inn Fields, she thought about Toby Hamcroft, and cursed the day Humphrey had said he was such a nice, trustworthy sort of fellow. At that moment she caught sight of an *Evening Standard* poster on a street newsstand. Scrawled in heavy black lettering were the words: LLOYD'S BROKER VANISHES WITH MILLIONS.

As she bought a copy of the paper, she wondered just how much his wife Liza knew about Toby's activities.

Chapter Seven

Liza read the newspapers the next morning with growing dismay.

'I thought those journalists were on my side! Look what they've written. How dare they suggest Toby's disappearance has anything to do with the losses!' she exclaimed, flinging one of the tabloids down on the kitchen table. She pointed to a headline: LLOYD'S MAN MISSING – SO ARE MILLIONS!

'Isn't this libellous? How can they get away with accusations like this?'

Martin Hamcroft looked up from an article he was reading in *The Times*, his expression troubled.

'It's a very hostile press, I must say. In my day no editor would have allowed this sort of thing. It even says "Why should we sympathise with the rich if they lose their money?" Damned cheek! Has this paper gone left-wing?'

The others, clustered round the table, reading avidly, didn't answer. Then Nina Hamcroft gave an outraged cry.

'Look at this!' she exclaimed. 'It says here that people who became members of Lloyd's did so out of greed! I don't think it's greedy to invest in something you believe in. We were only interested in making a living, weren't we, Martin?'

'You always get this sort of thing when anything in the Establishment runs into trouble,' Martin replied. 'It's partly envy, but a lot of it is gloating that someone else has skidded on a banana skin. There are bound to be people who will say: "Wasn't he lucky to have all that money in the first place?"'

Liza looked up, indignation bringing pink patches to her cheek. 'I hope no one is going to say that about us. I really thought the press would be sympathetic. Toby worked so hard to make sure the children and I had everything. There's no crime in that, is there? And here they are, reporting him as missing, but with a very obvious subtext that says, "He's probably run off with millions of pounds!" It's so unfair.' Angry tears sparkled in her eyes.

Sir George put a comforting arm round her shoulders and held her close to his side. 'Try not to take it to heart, Liza. The downfall of the mighty always produces glee amongst the less fortunate. It's the there-but-for-the-grace-of-God-go-I syndrome.'

'But instead of concentrating on finding Toby, all they're interested in is stirring up what they hope is a scandal! Who said there is any money missing in the first place?' She'd spent another sleepless night praying for news, and now she had to contend with these press insinuations.

'Why don't you go back to bed and rest after breakfast,' her mother suggested. 'You look worn out, and there's nothing you can do.'

'And that's the most exhausting thing of all. It's the waiting that's killing me,' Liza declared. 'I don't want to go to bed. I want to stay...' Her voice trailed off poignantly. She sank on to one of the pine kitchen chairs and covered her face with her hands. 'All I want is Toby back,' she wept.

Freddy turned over in bed to look at Melissa; his emotions were mixed. He felt partly filled with disquiet but also partly relieved at what she had just told him. Nevertheless he had a gut feeling it was a bad idea.

'But if Mummy pays our losses for this year, it means we won't have to leave here, doesn't it?' she protested almost tearfully. Freddy would never know how much this house meant to her. It wasn't just bricks and mortar, a roof over their heads, a place to make pretty. It was her first home, a place that belonged to her and Freddy, a sign of a growing independence, away from the home of her childhood, and her mother. Freddy was partly aware of this; he couldn't stand Eileen Blagdon and the way she dominated everyone and that was why he was reluctant to accept her offer. On the other hand...

'Please, Freddy,' she begged. 'Maybe by next year

we'll have enough money to pay the losses ourselves? Perhaps I could get a better job after I've had the baby. You might get a rise. Our losses might not be so bad next time.'

Freddy leaned back against the pillows, hands clasped behind his head, schoolboy-type striped pyjamas unbuttoned at the neck.

'I thought you wanted to get away from your mother,' he pointed out; knowing it was time to get up, but too comfortable to move.

'I do,' she nodded in agreement. 'But I don't want us to leave here, especially with the baby coming. I've worked so hard to make this house beautiful . . . it will break my heart if we have to leave.' Her voice rose to a thin wail of distress.

'Well, it's your mother,' he conceded. 'I can't ask my parents for help because I know they can't offer it. Dad has his army pension and Mum has a tiny private income, but otherwise there's just Balnabreck, and Dad's already realised it will probably have to go.'

'Maybe not. Maybe things will get better.' Melissa jumped in eagerly. 'Perhaps we can ride out the storm.'

Freddy didn't argue any more. It was bad for Melissa to get upset so far on in her pregnancy, and it would certainly be a boon if Eileen Blagdon took care of this year's losses. But at what price? asked a small voice in his head. She was a possessive widow who hadn't been keen on Melissa marrying him in the first place, having set her sights on someone with a title and a lot of money.

'I'm going up to Cavenham Court next week,' he said, in order to change the topic of conversation.

'What for?'

'The Davenports want me to value their art collection. We're not the only people in trouble, Melissa.'

When the phone rang for the umpteenth time at four o'clock that afternoon, Liza paid little attention. She was reading to Sarah, while Sir George handled all the incoming calls. Emma had returned to the country because one of her children was unwell, and so her father had taken full command of the situation. She didn't even look up when he came into the room.

'Liza?'

Something in his voice made her look up, and when she saw his face, she jumped to her feet in a heart-stopping moment.

'What is it? Is it . . . ?'

He rested his hand on her shoulder. 'Don't get excited,' he said quietly. 'It's not Toby.'

'Then who . . . ?' She could tell by his expression that the call was important.

'It's the chairman of Lloyd's. He says he wants to see you urgently; and privately.'

Liza had only met Malcolm Blackwell once before, at a City dinner, not long after his appointment as chairman. Toby had filled her in briefly beforehand.

'He's an Old Harrovian; he joined Lloyd's as a broker over thirty years ago. He's a very sociable chap.' Now, as she picked up the phone with shaking hands, she tried to visualise him: tall, grey-haired, with an easy, smiling manner, full of *bonhomie*. Toby had never liked him much.

'I have to see you . . . about this business.' He sounded strange, almost vague. 'You'd better not come up here,' he continued, 'nor do I think I should come to your house. Where can we meet, away from prying eyes? I have to talk to you in the strictest confidence.'

'About Toby?' she breathed. 'Have you heard from him?'

'I can't talk on the phone,' came the abrupt reply.

Her mind raced in wild circles, wondering what he wanted, wondering where they could meet, and why secretly?

'I have a friend who runs the Hotel Inter-Continental at Hyde Park Corner,' she said. 'He could probably arrange for us to have one of the small reception rooms. If we arrived separately . . .'

'Fine! Fix it, will you? Give me the name of your friend, and I'll ask for him when I arrive. Shall we say at six-thirty?'

'I'll arrange it,' Liza promised.

'You understand no one must know we're meeting,' Malcolm Blackwell insisted. 'I know the hotel. I'll get my chauffeur to take me to the underground car-park. I'll come up in the lift instead of using the main entrance. The press may follow you, and we mustn't be seen together.' There was a click and she realised he'd hung up.

Liza turned and looked at her father, her eyes wide with amazement. 'That was *extraordinary*!' she said.

'I gather he has some information about Toby?' Sir George tried to keep the excitement out of his voice. 'What did he say?'

'He wants to meet me secretly. Why on earth does it have to be so cloak-and-dagger? It was as if he was terrified we'd be seen together.' She shook her head, puzzled.

'Why couldn't he talk to you on the phone?'

'He sounded as if he were afraid someone might be listening in. God! I wonder what it means?'

Sir George looked at her steadily, his dark eyes like bright buttons. 'It could mean anything, but it looks as if he must know something. That's a start, isn't it?'

'Oh, Daddy! I don't know what to think ... Malcolm Blackwell said I mustn't tell anyone I'm meeting him, but it will be OK for Martin and Nina to know, won't it?'

Her father hesitated. 'I wouldn't if I were you,' he said at last.

She looked shocked. 'Don't you trust them?'

'It's not that, but it might raise their hopes, and then they could be bitterly disappointed. If you come home with good news, then that's a different matter.'

Liza nodded in agreement.

At six o'clock, the car she'd ordered from Première Cars arrived to pick her up. A group of reporters and photographers still hung around outside the house but with her father's help, she hurried past them and climbed quickly into the back of the BMW, evading their questions. As far as the Hamcrofts and the children were concerned, she'd told them she had to go to a radio interview at the BBC studios. It was a white lie, done for their protection, but she still felt badly about it.

Liza had never seen the driver before. With a pang she realised she'd half hoped it might be the one who had driven Toby to Heathrow that fateful morning, but she remembered now that he'd been a much older man. This one was in his twenties, broad-shouldered and robust-looking. He grinned at her over his shoulder, showing perfect white teeth.

'You've been on the telly, haven't you?' he asked immediately in a chummy Australian accent. 'Any news of your old man yet?'

Liza shook her head, disinclined to talk. She felt tense, apprehensive about her meeting with Malcolm Blackwell. The driver was not abashed.

'Bad show, your old man vanishing like that! What d'you think he's doing? Sunning himself on Bondi Beach, perhaps?' He chuckled, and she looked at the gold-streaked hair and bronzed neck with distaste.

'He went to Heathrow that morning in one of our cars, I gather,' he continued.

Liza nodded.

'So what d'you reckon's happened to him?'

'I don't know and I'd rather not talk about it,' she said sharply.

'Have it your own way, lady! But if I'd been left behind

and my partner had made off with all the lolly, I'd be mighty pissed off!' He shook his head knowingly. They'd just pulled up at the traffic lights in the Bayswater Road. Without a word, Liza opened the back door of the car and stepped out.

'Hey, lady! Whattya doing?' he shouted, alarmed.

'I think I'd prefer to walk than have you for company,' she replied with ill-concealed fury as she slammed the car door shut. Glad to have the chance to walk after two days' confinement in the house, Liza quickly mingled with the rush-hour crowds. It would only take her ten minutes to walk to the Inter-Continental if she cut through Hyde Park. The exercise would do her good, too.

The room she was shown to was perfect; a small sitting room with a sofa, armchairs, and a low coffee-table. It was at the end of a corridor on the first floor, and the large windows were curtained in white voile. Below, the swirl of traffic going round Hyde Park Corner provided a never-ending kaleidoscope of moving shapes and colour.

For a moment, Liza stood looking out, envying the people as they hurried to and fro, going about their business with seemingly not a care in the world. It seemed like two years, not two days, since she'd felt carefree and happy. What if he never returned . . . ? The thought was unbearable. Without Toby she didn't know how she'd survive.

'Hello,' said a voice behind her; startled, she spun round and found herself face to face with the mighty chairman of Lloyd's himself. He was stockily built and of medium height; his pugnacious face, folded into untidy lines of weariness, was in juxtaposition to his smoothly groomed grey hair and exquisitely cut pin-stripe suit. Today he was not smiling.

'Hello,' Liza replied, searching his eyes for some clue that might tell her why he wanted to see her. They shook hands, but his expression gave nothing away.

The hotel manager hovered in the background. 'What can I get you to drink, madam? Sir?' he asked.

'I'll have whisky and soda,' Malcolm Blackwell said.

'And a gin and tonic for me, please,' Liza added.

A few minutes later they were alone, sitting facing each other, the drinks on the table between them, the silence leaden with tension.

'Have you heard from Toby?' Liza tried to keep her voice steady.

'I regret not,' Malcolm Blackwell replied. 'Everything has taken on a most serious twist in the past few hours, and now we have to be extremely careful what we say and do, for fear of making the position worse.'

For the first time Liza felt frightened. 'I don't understand.'

'Let me show you something.' He reached into the inner pocket of his jacket and withdrew a thin sheet of paper on which a letter had been typed.

'What is it?' she asked as he handed it to her across the table.

'Read it for yourself. As you will see, your husband's life could be in jeopardy.'

'Oh, God!' She was trembling all over now, the words

jumping and skipping about the page, and she felt too dizzy to make sense of it and saw only, 'central fund', 'compensation', 'brink of bankruptcy' and 'Outside Names' before she started to feel sick.

'Kidnap.' Malcolm Blackwell said heavily. 'That's the gist of it.'

'*Toby's been kidnapped?*' Liza looked at him incredulously. 'Kidnapped?' she repeated. 'I don't believe it.' Thoughts of Beirut hostages being held for years flashed through her mind, but *this was London*. That sort of thing didn't happen in England.

'I'm afraid it's true,' she heard the chairman say. 'Who else would know that Lloyd's holds several million pounds in a central fund? I think it is an inside job carried out by Outside Names.'

'Wait a minute . . .' She wanted a few moments to read the letter, to digest the pale computer printout, for the letter was not typed as she'd first thought.

Chairman
We have Toby Hamcroft. His release will only be secured if we are compensated for the gross losses we have suffered at the hands of Lloyd's. We demand every penny held in the central fund, to save us, and others like us, from bankruptcy.

You are not to inform the police or the press of this letter, or to announce the abduction of our prisoner. To do so will mean you will never hear from Toby Hamcroft again. We will contact you in due course, but only if you remain silent.

Liza's mind cleared slowly, like fog dispersing, as she assimilated the contents. A part of her rejoiced to know Toby was at least still alive; another part of her, though, feared for him and the mental anguish she knew he must be going through, away from his family, wondering what was happening.

'What do we do now?' she asked.

'We must wait for them to make the next move. That is why it's essential we don't say anything. No one must know; you can see what will happen if it gets out.' He sighed heavily. 'I just wish I knew who was behind this.'

'How much is in the central fund?'

'I can't tell you at the moment,' he replied. 'You're going to have to leave things in my hands, I'm afraid, but I'll keep you posted as much as I can.'

'But we can't just sit and wait,' Liza protested. 'We must do something.'

'You can see from the letter what will happen if we do.'

'Even so ... and why Toby? Why him, for God's sake?' she demanded. 'Why is everyone blaming Toby? Other people must have been involved! Can't you make a public statement to that effect? They'll listen to you. Do you know I had a phone call...' With her voice choked with emotion she told him about the call she'd had from the woman whose husband had committed suicide.

He listened attentively, nodding sympathetically from time to time. 'That's terribly sad,' he agreed. 'Look,

Liza, we'll do everything we can. I suspect he was kidnapped because he has a fairly high profile in the City. They knew it would attract attention to their plight. The "Broker Baron", they call him, don't they?' The smile was gentle but the eyes were stony; in that moment Liza realised he didn't approve of Toby's 'high profile'.

'If they wanted a well-known person, why didn't they kidnap you?' she asked, eyes flashing.

'It isn't my syndicate that's sustained the worst losses,' he explained. 'I'd say these people—' his hand with its heavy gold signet ring waved towards the letter that now lay between them on the table – 'are all with the Hamcroft syndicate, or else on the Hamcroft agency. They've obviously got a grudge and, as Toby is the son of the original founder, they've decided to try and blackmail us for money by abducting him.'

'But they're blaming *him* for their losses; him personally! World catastrophes are no one's fault!' Liza argued. She paused, then said, 'Have you seen today's newspapers? They all suggest Toby has run off with the funds.' She leaned forward, not caring any more if she was blunt or even rude. Toby had to be found and brought home safely. The chairman, and Lloyd's, and the whole City of London could go to hell for all she cared, as long as Toby was found.

'You *must* refute these rumours,' she continued fiercely. 'It can't be good for Lloyd's to have one of their head brokers accused by the gutter press of absconding with members' money! And if you were to deny there was any truth in it, surely the kidnappers would realise they'd got the wrong man?' It seemed so simple and straightforward to her but, as she looked into Malcolm Blackwell's crumpled-looking face, she knew she'd met a ruthless operator.

'The committee and I are in the middle of investigating the Hamcroft syndicate,' he said smoothly. 'The people who have lost a great deal of money may well have a rightful grudge against the syndicate, if not against Toby personally. There certainly seems to have been gross mismanagement, both within the agency and on the underwriting side; time alone will tell what has been going on.'

The silence in the room was smothering, and for a moment Liza wondered illogically why she couldn't hear the traffic outside, until she remembered that all the windows were double-glazed and sealed. They stared at each other; time seemed endless.

'You will pay whatever they ask for Toby's release, won't you?' She knew she looked and sounded much braver than she felt.

'My dear Liza, you can be assured we will do all in our power to secure Toby's release,' he said. He rose as if to leave. 'Try not to worry,' he continued. 'Whatever you do, don't tell anyone what has happened; we must keep up the act that we have no idea where he has gone. I think we can believe them when they say we won't hear from Toby again unless we do.'

Liza shuddered involuntarily. 'And we can't even tell the police?'

'Especially not the police. If you want Toby back, we must play it their way.'

She walked with him to the door. 'How long do you think it will be before . . . ?'

'. . . We hear again?' He shrugged. 'God knows. But I promise to keep you posted.'

'Thank you.' She felt weak and suddenly tearful. If only she could be sure Malcolm Blackwell was really on her side. Her fear was that everyone in Lloyd's clung together, hushing up any scandal that might cast a blot on their reputation; it was all for one and one for all; as bonded as a Welsh miners' union, as secretive as a Freemason's Lodge.

And what would they do to one of their members if he brought disgrace upon their heads? Toby was innocent, on that Liza would stake her life, but supposing a scapegoat was just what they were looking for; someone – anyone – to blame for the mess it was said they were in?

Would they cast Toby to the wolves to save their own skins?

On the way home, Liza sat in the taxi wondering how much she should tell her parents and Martin and Nina. The children needn't know, obviously, or Ingrid. In the end she decided to tell them everything; after all, they had a right to know, and at least it would assure them that Toby was still alive.

'Daddy?' Liza called out, letting herself into the hall. The aroma of roasting chicken drifted up from the kitchen, and it struck her as incongruous that, no matter what happened, people still went on cooking and eating. With six adults and three children in the house, they were getting through a monumental amount of food, and she supposed it was the comfort that nourishment brought that encouraged them to eat three times a day.

Sir George appeared from the little sitting room, a glass of whisky and soda in his hand.

'Any news?' he asked. At that moment, hearing the front door close, Martin and Nina emerged from the drawing room and Helen came hurrying down the stairs. They all looked at her expectantly.

With a finger to her lips, because she could hear the children in the kitchen having their supper, she indicated they should go into the drawing room. Once inside she closed the door quietly, and her voice was soft.

'No one must hear this.'

Her mother frowned. 'What's happened?'

'Toby's been kidnapped.'

They all stared at her in stunned disbelief.

She nodded confirmation. 'I've seen the ransom note. They're demanding the central fund, to reimburse them for their losses.'

Martin Hamcroft looked at her as if she'd gone raving mad. 'What is this, Liza? Who's been filling your head with nonsense? How do you know Toby's been kidnapped in the first place? Where did you get this cock-and-bull story from?'

She looked him straight in the eye. 'From the chairman of Lloyd's, Malcolm Blackwell.'

Martin's jaw dropped. Sir George leaned forward, his expression more hopeful and positive than it had been for days.

'At least it means Toby is alive,' he said, 'and thank God for that. How did your meeting go?'

Martin came back to life with a gulp. 'What meeting?'

'I was summonsed to a secret meeting with the chairman,' Liza explained. 'He made me promise not to tell anyone, because the note said Toby's life would be in jeopardy if this gets out.' Briefly, she told them the gist of the letter. 'Malcolm Blackwell thinks it's the work of some Outside Names, who are angry that they've lost money on the syndicate.'

'*Which syndicate?*' Martin's voice cut through the air like a knife through butter. Liza faced him, looking braver than she felt.

'The Martin E. L. Hamcroft syndicate, I'm afraid,' she said in a low voice. 'He told me that he and the committee are looking into the affairs of the syndicate, and the agency. He said these people might have a real grudge to bear, and because Toby is a Hamcroft, and he has a high profile, they're using him as a hostage.'

'I don't believe a word of it.' Martin sounded huffy, as if he'd been personally insulted.

His wife looked at him curiously. 'Why are you so sure it isn't true, Martin? It would explain everything.' She turned to Liza, her eyes shocked with sudden recollection. 'Do you think the driver from Première Cars had anything to do with it? We heard he'd lost all his money at Lloyd's, so he had a grudge, as well as the opportunity.'

'You're right,' Sir George said thoughtfully. 'We'll get on to the police so they can interview him again. In spite of what the police have been told, maybe he never took Toby to Heathrow at all, but went straight to wherever they're keeping him.'

'Oh, my God!' Nina said brokenly. 'How will they be treating him, d'you suppose?'

'This is absurd! You've all been watching too many Bond films,' Martin snapped testily, stomping over to the drinks tray.

'We can't tell the police,' Liza pointed out. 'That was the one thing Malcolm Blackwell impressed on me. *No one* must know what's happened. He said he'll keep me posted, but for the time being we can't do anything. If we do . . .'

'He's right,' Sir George agreed. 'We'll have to sit tight and wait for them to make the first move. Christ, you'd never think a thing like this would happen in England, would you?' He turned to Martin, who was pouring himself a stiff drink.

'How much money does the central fund hold?' he asked.

'Around five hundred million pounds.'

Sir George looked shaken. 'So much?'

Martin looked arrogant. 'We operate on a very large scale,' he said scathingly. 'Our assets are around eighteen billion.'

Helen Mortimer looked astonished. 'I'd no idea! But why do you keep so much in the fund? What's it for?'

'It's to enable us to pay out urgent claims in the short term, should the syndicates involved have insufficient funds to meet the amount required at the time,' Martin replied. 'But it's not there to bail out members' losses, unless it's on a very temporary basis while money is being raised.'

'So it's set up from surplus profits, for emergencies,' Sir George commented.

'Exactly.'

'They can't hope to get five hundred million pounds! It's an absurd demand,' Liza exclaimed. 'If only we knew where they'd taken Toby.' It was unbearable to think of him locked up. Somehow they had to get hold of the Première Cars driver, without letting him know they realised what had happened to Toby.

As if she knew what her daughter was thinking, Helen spoke. 'I know it's hard for you to sit here doing nothing, but I think Malcolm Blackwell's right. We must carry on as if we knew nothing. Hopefully he'll hear again from the kidnappers soon, and then negotiations can begin.'

'I wonder how much they'd settle for?' Nina said, fretfully. 'Oh, my poor Toby! I can't bear to think what he must be going through.'

Then, as if he'd been struck by an idea, Martin looked hopefully at Liza. 'I suppose you've no idea if Toby took out a personal policy to cover K and R?'

'What's K and R?' she asked blankly.

'Kidnap and Ransom insurance . . . No, I don't suppose he'd see the need, but several Lloyd's syndicates specialise in it. It's mostly used by pop stars, or people of enormous wealth who fear their children are going to be abducted.'

'Good Lord!' Helen exclaimed. 'Whatever will people think of next?'

'So what are we going to do?' Liza asked miserably. She was twisting her rings round and round on her finger, rubbing her thumb over the cluster of diamonds Toby had given her when they'd got engaged.

'Let's just be thankful he's alive, Liza. This time yesterday we weren't even sure of that,' Sir George reminded her.

'Your father's right, darling. He knows about these things. We'll just have to sit tight and see what happens.'

Suddenly Liza looked at her father. Yes, he did know about these things: he'd been in army Intelligence, hadn't he? A plan was beginning to form in her head; an amazing idea. She'd have to think it through, though, before she put it forward, because the risks could be great.

Chapter Eight

If there was one person in the world Liza could trust, it was Emma. Their friendship had spanned the last twenty years; never once in that time had Emma let her down.

Early the next morning, after another sleepless night, tortured by the visions her imagination threw up on to the screen of her mind, she dialled the familiar number of Emma's home near Godalming, in Surrey. Emma answered immediately.

'It's me,' Liza said, knowing her friend always recognised her voice.

'Liza, how are things with you?'

'I've got to talk to you, Em. Can I drive down and see you right away?'

There was a surprised silence before Emma spoke again. 'Of course you can come here, but can't you tell me on the phone what it's about? You've heard something about Toby?'

'I can't talk. That's why I have to see you,' Liza replied guardedly.

As always, Emma took everything in her stride. 'Come right away, then. I'm here all day; stay the night, if you like.'

'Thanks, Em. I'll be with you in a couple of hours.'

It wasn't as easy to get away from the house as Liza had thought. The children were in a whining mood, demanding to know why they couldn't go with her. Her parents, backed up by Toby's mother and father, were curious to know how Emma could help her.

'I just need to talk to her,' Liza replied vaguely. She went up to the top of the house, where they'd built an extension eight years ago for the children's bedrooms and playroom. Tommy and Tilly were lying on their stomachs on the floor, doing a jigsaw puzzle, while Sarah, in a frilly apron over her tiny denim skirt, was 'cooking' at the toy stove she'd been given the previous Christmas.

'Mummy!' She squealed with pleasure and launched herself into Liza's arms. Liza gathered her up and held her close. Then she sat in a chair near the others. They were all looking at her with bright hope in their little faces.

'Is Daddy coming home soon?' Thomas asked.

'Are you going to meet him?' Tilly asked.

'I hope Daddy will be coming home soon,' Liza replied with honesty. 'But we're going to have to be very patient, because it may take a little while yet.'

'Why?' Thomas demanded.

'There's business to be seen to first,' said Liza, knowing that was partly true.

'Why?' wailed Tilly. 'Why can't he do his business at the office and come home every night like he used to?'

Liza leaned forward to stroke her back and kiss her peach-soft cheek. 'Because it's not up to Daddy, but I know he'll be back just as soon as he can. I'm going out now. There's something I may be able to do that will help Daddy get home sooner, so I want you all to be very good, and help look after Grampy and Grandma, and Grandpa and Granny, and see they have a nice time. Will you do that?'

Tilly looked dismayed. 'You *are* coming back, aren't you, Mummy?'

Liza hugged her. 'Of course, my sweetheart. I'll be back later on today.'

'You promise?' Thomas asked solemnly.

She drew him towards her too, and held him close.

Eventually Liza rose slowly, gently disentangling the children, giving the crowns of their heads a quick kiss as she did so.

'I'll be back before you've had time to turn round,' she said lightly.

Thomas spun round on his heels.

'Ha!' he said triumphantly. 'I've turned round *twice* and you haven't even gone!'

At that moment Helen came into the playroom.

'Now then! What are we going to play?' she asked them brightly. 'How about a game of snakes and ladders?'

'Thanks, Ma,' Liza whispered, slipping out past her. 'I'll be home before dinner.'

In the street outside, a fresh shift of journalists and photographers had replaced yesterday's group of weary ones.

'Can you tell us anything, Mrs Hamcroft?' one of them asked.

'Any news of your husband?' demanded another.

Liza walked briskly past them to where her car was parked, keeping her eyes down and her lips pressed together. It wasn't easy to ignore the snapping lenses and persistent questioning, but she started the engine and set off down the road, glancing in the rearview mirror as she did so, and feeling a pang of compassion for the disconsolate huddle who were gazing at her retreating vehicle.

The drive to the picturesque village of Shere, a few miles outside Guildford, took an hour and a half, and as Liza found herself surrounded by the lushly fertile countryside, some of the anxiety began to slip away from her, leaving her feeling more relaxed than she'd done in days. It was a beautiful summer's day, offering up, as only England can, a gentle breeze to soften the air and a hot, hazy sky to mellow the landscape. Emma lived in a large red-brick Georgian house on the outskirts of the village, at the top of a steep incline, so that from the windows the countryside seemed spread out like a flowered patchwork quilt. The white-painted front door was flung wide, even before Liza had brought the car to a stop on the gravel drive, and there was Emma to greet her, surrounded by children and dogs.

'You look better, Liza,' she commented as she kissed her in greeting. 'Come in and tell me everything.'

The children, two boys and a girl, together with a dachshund, golden labrador, spaniel and a small white terrier called Snowball, once released from the confines of the house, spread out like a scattering of butterflies as they ran all over the garden, dodging with a ball, laughing, chasing and, in the case of Emma's younger son, hanging on to a silver helium-filled balloon and squawking at the top of his voice.

The sheer *joie de vivre* of the children and animals was so infectious that Liza couldn't help smiling as they cavorted about.

'I already *feel* better,' she informed Emma as she was led into the house.

'Now,' said Emma, with her usual charming bossiness; 'you're to sit down while I make you a stiff gin and tonic, and then we'll have a quiet lunch, sans the brats and the animals, and you'll tell me everything.'

'What would I do without you, Em?' Liza said gratefully as she sank into a chintz armchair plumped up with cushions. She looked around at the casually comfortable living room, and wondered why she found it more relaxing than her beautiful London drawing room.

'Now. Tell!' Emma commanded, handing her a drink and closing the door so they wouldn't be disturbed.

'What about the children?' Liza queried, hearing gales of laughter coming from the garden.

Emma was unperturbed. 'I've got a couple of Swedish au pairs, who are absolutely marvellous, and because there are two of them, they never get lonely, so it's a perfect arrangement, and the children adore them. Now, for goodness' sake, Liza, tell me what's *happened*? I'm dying to know. It can't be anything too terrible, because you look quite cheerful.'

'I'm hopeful,' Liza admitted. 'I had a meeting with the chairman of Lloyd's yesterday. Top secret.'

'You did?' Emma looked impressed.

'Toby's been kidnapped and is being held for ransom.'

'*What?*'

Liza nodded. Briefly she explained what had happened.

'God, Liza!' Emma was astounded. 'Talk about shocks! This is incredible! You mean they snatched Toby on his way to Heathrow, and they're holding him until they get the money from the Lloyd's central fund? What an extraordinary story.' She shook her head in amazement. 'What happens now?'

'I had an idea, but I don't know if it's possible or not; that's why I thought I'd discuss it with you first. You know that Daddy was in military Intelligence? And that he's kept up many of his old contacts?'

Emma nodded. 'So?' she asked, drawing out the word curiously.

'Because we can't tell anyone about Toby being kidnapped, I was wondering if I could get Intelligence – MI5 or MI6 or whatever they're called these days – to find out where Toby has been taken.'

'Yes?' said Emma after a pause. She looked at Liza with interest. 'Then what?'

'When we know where Toby is, we could get a rescue operation mounted with the help of the SAS!' she concluded triumphantly.

'Are you serious?' Emma looked astonished. 'I don't think they'd be allowed to get involved in a non-diplomatic civilian incident.'

Liza looked crushed. 'Don't you?'

Her friend looked at her sympathetically. 'I know how you feel,' she said understandingly, 'but this is real life, Liza.'

'I know, but I've got to get him back. I've got no guarantee that Lloyd's will pay the ransom; I mean we're talking about five hundred million pounds. *That's* unrealistic for a start.'

'They'll negotiate, though,' Emma pointed out. 'I'm sure they referred to the money in the central fund in general terms. They may not even know how much there is.'

Liza brightened. 'That's true, especially if they're Outside Names. Even so, I'm desperately worried; and the awful thing is that Toby will be worried sick too about me and the children. If only I could get a message to him to let him know we're all right, and that we're trying to do something to get him released. Oh, God, this is a nightmare. How long is it going to go on for?' She shook her head in despair.

'It doesn't seem to occur to you that Toby may be able to escape by himself?' Emma pointed out. 'He will if he can, I'm sure.'

Liza nodded, eyes brimming, her face flushed with unshed tears. 'I'm so frightened for him.'

'This thing has to be worked out very carefully, Liza, and I think for the time being we should wait to see what happens. It's going to be like a game of chess. Every move must be strategically planned, step by step. One false move, and . . . well . . .' She paused, looking sober.

'You're right,' Liza agreed. 'It's just that I feel so helpless.'

Back in London that evening, Liza was disappointed to find that nothing more had happened. She longed to phone Malcolm Blackwell, but her father said it was a bad idea, especially from a security point of view.

'His phones may be bugged,' Sir George said, 'and that's why he had to meet you secretly. No doubt he'll be receiving another anonymous letter setting out the demands in detail. How did you get on with Emma?'

Liza told him the idea she'd had, and that Emma had quashed it.

Her father looked at her strangely. 'Why didn't you ask me in the first place?'

'I knew you'd say you couldn't involve Intelligence, but I hoped she'd think of a way round it. Surely MI5 can tap any phone in the country? Aren't they able to find out things without anyone realising? They've got much more power than the police, haven't they? I hoped we could get them to help us find Toby's kidnappers, and perhaps where they'd taken him,' she added earnestly.

'I think you're getting confused between national security and civilian criminology, sweetheart,' he told her gently. 'If Toby had been abducted by Iranian or Palestinian rebels, then that would be an entirely different matter. You're thinking of the Iranian embassy affair in London, aren't you, when the SAS were able to blast their way into the building and rescue everyone.'

Liza nodded eagerly. 'Yes. That's exactly what I thought.'

'No can do, I'm afraid, darling,' he said regretfully. 'We're going to have to play this one by civilian rules.'

'I don't think I can bear it.' She was silent for a moment, her brow furrowed in concentration. At last she looked over to where her father was sitting reading the newspapers.

'There's nothing to stop me going to talk to Henry Granville, the man who drove Toby that morning, is there? I mean, we're allowed to say Toby is still missing.'

Sir George looked doubtful. 'Do you think it's such a good idea, sweetheart? He's already been interviewed by the police. I doubt if he knows any more than he's already told them.'

'Yes, but at the time they didn't know he was an Outside Name who had lost all his money. I'm sure I could get something out of him,' she said persistently.

'What are you going to say to him?'

'I'm going to ask him how Toby seemed. I'll pretend I'm worried because Toby had been depressed about business, which of course isn't true as far as I know, but he's not to know that. I'm going to ask him if Toby got a porter to help him with his luggage, all that sort of stuff, in the hopes that he might let something slip.'

Sir George looked thoughtful. 'Be very careful. You don't want him to get wind of the fact you think he may have helped kidnap Toby. I think it's too risky, myself.'

'I promise you I'll be careful. My God, I wouldn't do anything to jeopardise Toby's safety,' she added, almost fiercely.

Sir George left her to make the call. He was finding these days in London very long and stressful. It was the hanging around, not knowing what to do next that was a strain; he knew Martin felt the same, even though Martin was more used to a sedentary life. Nina and Helen seemed less fidgety: they enjoyed their time with the three grandchildren, and were able to sit and talk, whereas Sir George constantly felt, like Liza, that he should be *doing* something. He walked into the garden, finding the air of London solid and fume-filled compared to Scotland, where it seemed as clear as spring water, and as perfumed as the surrounding heather-clad mountains. How long was it going to be before Toby was released? One thing was certain; they couldn't leave Liza until it was all over. He was proud of the way she was bearing up but, sooner or later, if Toby didn't return, she was going to crack.

He wandered down the centre of the paved garden,

looking at the roses and the honeysuckle that straddled the wall down one side, wondering what would happen to all this if Toby had lost all his money, too. Liza and Toby had lived such a luxurious life in the last few years, with Chalklands to go to at the weekend, and the yacht in Monte Carlo if they felt like it. A wonderful life. Yet he knew his daughter would adapt to whatever happened: she'd never become spoiled by the material wealth her husband had heaped around her.

Sir George sighed. He was a man who would have done anything to have spared his son and daughter the trials and pain of life. At that moment he wished none of them had ever heard of Lloyd's.

'Daddy!' Liza's voice came floating into the garden from the drawing-room window. She was looking at him, her face white.

'What's the matter?' he called out, walking hurriedly back towards the house.

'I've been speaking to the man who runs Première Cars,' she said shakily, and he saw she was trembling.

'Yes?'

'He told me Henry Granville committed suicide yesterday.'

'That rules him out as having anything to do with Toby's abduction, doesn't it?' Martin Hamcroft observed, as they all sat down to discuss what to do next. It was mid-morning, and Liza was still deeply shaken by the suicide of Toby's driver. For the first time, their normally large Holland Park house seemed too small.

She began to notice how arrogant Martin was, and how her own mother fussed over the children to such an extent that they were becoming difficult and moody. Even her father was getting irritable as he turned to Martin.

'Henry Granville could still have had something to do with it,' he argued. 'Just because he kills himself, doesn't mean he wasn't involved. It might be a guilty conscience.'

'I think it's unlikely,' Martin replied stubbornly. 'If he'd thought he could recoup his losses through kidnapping, he'd have made sure he was around to do so.'

'Does it really matter?' Nina said. 'The poor man's dead, and that's that.'

'I want to go and see his widow,' Liza said suddenly. 'She may need help. If he's really bankrupt, she's probably penniless. What's going to happen to her now? I must see what I can do for her.' She rose, glad to have something to occupy her mind.

'I think that's most unwise,' Martin said. 'It could look like currying favour; making sure she won't sue her late husband's broker, or the syndicate. We mustn't have anything to do with her.'

Liza flushed hotly. 'That's a terrible thing to say. How can I ignore her? Of course I must go and see if there's anything I can do.'

'But you don't want to act as if you or Toby were responsible for her husband's financial state. The fool probably didn't know what Lloyd's is all about in the first place. It's not our fault if he got himself into a mess!'

Martin added angrily. Leaning forward to make his point, he reminded Liza of an old tortoise, with his small wrinkled brown face and long stringy neck rearing out of his collar.

Sir George had risen too, and was almost stuttering with anger.

'That's the most disgusting thing I've ever heard,' he barked. 'For Christ's sake, Martin! What have you got where your heart's supposed to be? A block of ice? I quite agree with Liza that we should see if the widow needs help.' He turned to Liza. 'I'll come with you, if you like.'

'Thanks, Daddy.'

'I'll find out where she lives, and we'll go straight away,' he continued, marching out of the room.

Nina sat looking embarrassed while her husband continued to speak his mind.

'We don't even know if he killed himself because he'd lost money! Maybe he suffered from depression. I sincerely hope it doesn't get into the newspapers that someone has committed suicide because of the Lloyd's losses,' he said bitterly.

'I think you have said enough,' Helen Mortimer pointed out quietly. 'We get your point, but I think you're being very hard.'

Martin was not to be silenced. 'If Liza goes to see this woman, especially with Toby missing, it makes it look as if she's accepting liability on behalf of Lloyd's for this man's downfall and death! The trouble with people who join Lloyd's as Outside Names is that they only like to win. Nobody should make themselves liable for more than they can afford to lose. That goes for any form of betting, Lloyd's included.'

'Then we personally haven't got a bigger stake in Lloyd's than we can afford to lose?' Nina asked.

Once more he shrugged, turning away so that she could not see his expression. 'Oh, I don't know,' he said with contrived carelessness. 'I was always a gambling man, myself.'

Sir Humphrey and Lady Rosemary were out walking the dogs when Freddy drew up outside the stately portals of Cavenham Court. Although he'd met the Davenports socially, he'd never seen their Gothic-style house, designed on the E-plan, and built of honey-coloured stone. He climbed out of his car and looked up at dormer windows and gabled roof, spiral chimney-stacks and finials. It was a superb example of sixteenth-century architecture and Freddy knew if the contents matched the building in excellence, Sotheby's would make a fortune if they were asked to handle the sale.

Masters, the butler, opened the front door before Freddy had even reached it, and ushered him into a hall hung with portraits of past generations. The scent of roses emanated from a large bowl of blooms on a central table.

'If you would care to wait in the library, sir, I will inform her ladyship that you are here.'

While he waited, Freddy looked at a large painting hanging above the deep stone fireplace. It was a family group, dated he imagined around 1775. It was pretty but not spectacular. Books lined the other walls from floor to ceiling.

After a few minutes Lady Rosemary came hurrying into the room, and Freddy got an impression of well-cut tweeds, soft beige cashmere, and a glowing aristocratic face.

'My dear Freddy, I've only just this moment realised it was you who was coming up from Sotheby's! How stupid of me. How are you? The last time we met was at one of Liza's splendid dinner parties, wasn't it?' Poised and charming, she indicated a chair where he might like to sit, asked Masters to bring in coffee, all the while chatting to Freddy with much-practised social grace. Sir Humphrey came bumbling affably into the room a few minutes later, surrounded by his collection of black labradors. 'Jolly good of you to come all this way, old chap,' he said, heartily.

Lady Rosemary had diplomatically avoided mentioning Toby's disappearance, but her husband lacked the finesse so beloved of the upper classes, of whitewashing over anything unpleasant.

'What's happening over Toby Hamcroft?' he asked, eyes blinking rapidly. 'Poor old Liza! Rather a bad show, isn't it?'

'We're all very worried,' Freddy replied earnestly. 'Liza's desperate; and have you seen the awful lies the newspapers have been printing about him?' He shook his head, cheeks pink with indignation. 'If I were Liza, I'd sue!'

'I think she should,' Lady Rosemary replied. 'It's

absurd to think someone like Toby would abscond with Lloyd's funds.'

Sir Humphrey left them to do a tour of the house, while he fed the dogs.

Lady Rosemary smiled as she remarked drily: 'He won't let anyone else prepare their food. It all has to be balanced and weighed; he never showed that sort of concern for the children!' Then she laughed indulgently. 'He loves those dogs so much.'

Making notes as he went, Freddy did a slow and thorough examination of the two hundred paintings that adorned the walls, from hall to dining room, and drawing room to upstairs landings.

'The Gainsboroughs and the Reynoldses are the most valuable, I imagine,' Lady Rosemary observed, looking at a portrait of her great-great-grandmother, which she'd admired ever since she'd been a little girl. 'Sad though it is, I'm afraid we're going to have to sell them, if we're going to keep the house. Have you any idea how much they would fetch at auction?'

Freddy gazed down at the notes he'd made, wondering how he was going to tell her. He decided to play for time.

'I'd like to go round again and have another look,' he said slowly. 'Have you had them examined in recent years for insurance purposes?'

She looked taken aback. 'Not examined, actually. The premiums seem to go up every year, but I imagine that's to be expected.'

Freddy set off on his own this time; he especially wanted to have a closer look at the Gainsboroughs and the Reynoldses. It would be the back of the canvases that would tell him whether his suspicions were right or not. Two hours later, hot and tired, he made his way back to the library, where tea was just about to be served.

The Davenports looked at him hopefully.

Freddy fumbled with the pages of his notepad, and his voice was shaky. 'I'm most awfully sorry . . . this sort of thing is not unknown . . . an ancestor wants to raise a bit of money, you know, without the rest of the family realising . . .'

'Just what are you trying to say?' Lady Rosemary asked sharply.

'I'm afraid,' said Freddy, turning red, 'that your Gainsboroughs and your Reynoldses are copies; not worth more than a few hundred pounds.'

The black Mercedes that Toby had given Liza for Christmas slid sleekly into a space outside an ugly red-brick and cream-stucco terrace house, twenty yards from Barons Court underground station. Liza and her father walked up the tiny stone-flagged front path and rang the bell by the side of a green-painted front door. As they waited, Liza looked up and down the street. It was drab and smelled of refined poverty; this was a place where people who had perhaps once held decent jobs retired to on a pension, trying to brighten their lives with gay little window-boxes and a coat of bright paint. Most concealed their private lives behind the protection of thick net or lace curtains.

When the front door opened, they knew that the widow of Henry Granville did not belong in these surroundings. Although tired-looking and tear-stained, she was a tall, elegant woman, dressed in a very expensive black skirt and silk shirt; her hands and well-kept nails showed that she'd hardly even washed a dish in her life.

'Good morning. I'm sorry to disturb you. My name is Mortimer. George Mortimer, and this is my daughter, Liza. Your husband was with the Martin E. L. Hamcroft agency, I gather?'

'Yes, that's right.' Her eyes opened wider and she looked nervous.

'We want to know whether we can do anything,' Liza said, gently.

Mrs Granville stared at her, a look of recognition filled her face. 'You were on the television...! Your husband's disappeared!' she exclaimed. Then she seemed to remember herself. 'I'm sorry. I didn't mean to be rude ... Do come in.' Mrs Granville had an educated and pleasant voice. 'I don't own this house ... We ... that is, *I*, just have a room in it, so please forgive the mess.'

She turned and led the way down a narrow passage in which a bicycle was propped against the wall, and then through a door at the far end. It was a small square room, with a hard-looking sofa that Liza presumed unfolded into a bed, a lumpy armchair and a small table. The furniture looked cheap and battered and the floor-covering worn. In a corner, an open cupboard door revealed a small cooker on which stood a couple of pans; on the shelf above were some plates and mugs. The only nice thing about the room was the windows which looked on to a very small patch of grass bordered by a few undernourished shrubs. She indicated the sofa, and Liza began to explain.

'My husband *is* missing,' she started. 'We're terribly worried about him, naturally, but there's absolutely no truth in the rumour that he's run off with a lot of money.'

Mrs Granville sat staring at the floor. 'It's an awful thing,' she said sadly, shaking her head.

'Your husband took Toby to Heathrow that last morning,' Liza continued.

'The last . . . ?' Startled grey eyes, red-rimmed and bleary-looking, stared at them. 'Oh, yes,' she said vaguely.

'Mrs Granville, I know this is a great intrusion, and I'm so sorry to have to ask you these questions, but did your husband mention anything at all to you about that trip to Heathrow?' Liza asked. 'Did they discuss Lloyd's, perhaps? Or your husband's losses?'

'I don't know. Henry never told me.'

'He didn't mention the severe losses he'd suffered? I thought that was why, perhaps . . . he took his own life?' Liza probed. She had a gut feeling that Mrs Granville knew a great deal more than she was admitting, or else she was heavily tranquillised: Liza couldn't tell which.

'Oh, all the money he lost, yes, I knew about that. We had to sell everything. The house, the furniture . . .

everything. All gone.' Mrs Granville's voice sank to a whisper.

Liza and her father exchanged looks. They were none the wiser than when they'd first arrived.

'I am very anxious to know where my husband is,' Liza said in desperation. 'Have you *any* idea what might have happened to him on that day when your husband drove him to Heathrow?'

The widow's mouth drooped at the corners, pulling her cheeks down into deep lines from her nose to her chin. 'Why should I have?' she asked listlessly.

Sir George was looking around the sparsely furnished and uncomfortable room. Then he spoke diffidently. 'Not to put too fine a point on it, Mrs Granville, I imagine you find yourself without funds, or any means of support?'

'I believe I can claim social security ... I don't know ... Maybe it's difficult for the widows of bankrupts,' she murmured. 'We only wanted what we'd lost returned to us,' she said, as if she were talking to herself. 'We weren't out for anything more ... but then Henry got disheartened; he said everything had been bungled, and now we'd not get anything. I told him to wait and see ... but he wouldn't.' Then she burst into despairing tears as great sobs racked her body. Distressed, Liza put her arms around the older woman, but her father was staring at Mrs Granville, a strange expression in his eyes.

'You hoped the central fund would reimburse your losses?' he said quietly.

'Yes . . . I mean, no . . .' She stumbled on her words, and then she shot him a haunted look. '*Yes*! All *right*!' She looked at him as if she now had nothing to lose. 'We thought that if we got Toby Hamcroft, Lloyd's would cough up from the central fund for his release!'

Chapter Nine

'I do not understand why you worry about Toby Hamcroft. It does not matter that he has vanished. You don't need him. Why are you upset?' Maxine Connolly's accent was still heavily French, as was her phraseology, although she'd lived in England for nearly twenty years. She turned to look at Declan as he drove their latest acquisition, a Rolls-Royce coupé, along Park Lane, stopping outside the ballroom entrance of Grosvenor House. Pudgy pink hands, the fingers tufted with dark hair, held the steering wheel lightly. His profile, she noticed, was becoming blurred with good living. His hair was thinning on the crown, though he strove to disguise it by combing his hair a certain way.

Declan glanced at Maxine, wishing at times she was slightly less intelligent. It was one thing to have a wife who understood your business life, quite another when she was one step ahead most of the time.

He didn't answer, but said instead, 'I hope they're going to park the car for me,' then climbed out, a chunky figure in a superbly cut dinner jacket that made him look powerful rather than plump, and waved the keys at the uniformed doorman.

'I'm sorry, sir. You'll have to find a parking place round the back. We're expecting several hundred cars tonight and I'm afraid you can't leave it here.'

Declan clicked his tongue in annoyance. Maxine was already standing on the pavement in four thousand pounds' worth of Bruce Oldfield black satin and chiffon, with a rash of dazzling diamonds.

'You'd better go ahead, Maxie,' Declan said sulkily. 'I'll meet you in the foyer.'

They'd bought tickets for one of the smarter charity balls of the London Season, and were joining a table hosted by Charles and Jane Bryer. Declan liked to be seen at this sort of function; he usually bumped into a few people he knew, many of whom he'd 'got into' Lloyd's. He reckoned it was good policy to let them see how prosperous he was. Even during a recession. Even with disaster and catastrophe closing in on Lloyd's, so that those on the high-risk syndicates had begun to topple like a row of dominoes, their fortunes wiped out, their houses sold. As long as he kept making money, the others could go fuck themselves, he reflected.

In the Ladies' cloakroom, Maxine went over to the mirrored dressing-table, as if to touch up her already perfect make-up, but in reality to give herself time to see who else was there. Satins and taffeta, fine lace and the gleam of valuable jewels caught her eye, and she was glad she'd worn her black tonight. With her cream skin and shining black hair drawn back into a chic chignon, it made her stand out dramatically against the profusion of pastel dresses and mouse-coloured hair of the English women. She regarded her reflection with pleasure; at thirty-nine she was as luscious-looking as a peach ready to be picked.

A cluster of women came bursting into the cloakroom, with little yelps of delighted amusement and a swish of silk. In their midst was a tall, slim woman of aristocratic bearing, wearing a deceptively elegant cream crêpe dress with several rows of pearls. Maxine instantly recognised her as Lady Rosemary Davenport. They'd met before, at one of Toby and Liza's cocktail parties, and so, unhesitatingly, she turned, smiling, and joined in the general chorus of praise.

'You look wonderful, Rosemary!'

'You must be exhausted. Being chairman of one of these "dos" is *such* hard work.'

'How do you do it, Rosemary? The ballroom looks like a dream!'

'My dear, you look fabulous! But then you always do! How many tickets have you sold tonight?'

Lady Rosemary smiled graciously although she looked pale and strained. The group drifted on past Maxine, leaving her with the hurt feelings of one who knows they are an outsider. The group clustered more closely round Lady Rosemary and then their voices dropped to a confidential whisper, excluding her totally. Only by moving closer to the hand-basins, where she let the warm water trickle over her fingertips, was Maxine able to hear the gist of what they were saying.

'... The most awful blow.'

'How much have you lost? ... Oh my God!'

'Have you heard that the Brodericks are wiped out ... bankrupt?'

'You mean you'll have to sell everything? ... *Everything?*'

'Oh, it's ghastly!'

'My husband's having a nervous breakdown ...'

'... someone else committed suicide ... Henry Granville. He hanged himself. That's the second suicide in two weeks ...'

'... But it's not only the natural disasters, my husband says ...'

'There's been fraudulence and cheating on a monumental scale ... !'

'I'm afraid this is only the tip of the iceberg!'

'... and I heard from a *very* reliable source that the losses will eventually reach twelve billion. That's an average of half a million per member.'

Maxine stood mesmerised, hardly able even to walk away. She felt numbed with shock and wondered why Declan had never told her things were so serious. In all the years she'd been in England, she'd never heard cloakroom chatter of this nature. Mostly the women gossiped and admired each other's dresses, grumbled about their husbands or enthused about their lovers; never before had she heard them openly moaning about the financial difficulties of themselves and their friends.

And all the time the name 'Lloyd's' was being passed from mouth to mouth with a hissing sound.

Maxine hurried away to find Declan. If they were to lose their money too...! It was too dreadful to think about. They'd both worked so hard to get where they were today, and she knew she could never go back to the poverty of her youth.

'I must talk to you,' she said urgently, pulling Declan away from the group of men he was talking to.

'What's the matter?'

In a rapid mixture of broken English and French, she told him what she'd heard.

'Are we going to have losses, too?' she demanded, her eyes like shining black olives as she gazed nervously at him.

'No,' he replied nonchalantly. He strolled over to the bar. 'Two vodka tonic – Absolut,' he ordered, flashing a fifty-pound note.

'How can you be so sure? Lady Rosemary Davenport was one of the women. She said something about enormous losses.'

Declan looked smug. 'A lot of people have lost money, but not yours truly!'

'But why not? Why should they...?' Maxine stopped suddenly, and she narrowed her eyes. 'Has the disappearance of Toby anything to do with the losses?'

'Not that I know of, but his going missing is bad for business. It's drawing attention to the Hamcroft syndicate, and that's the last thing we need right now.'

'Those women ... they seemed so shocked ... It frightened me.' She still looked shaken.

'I bet they were shocked.' He gave an amused chuckle. 'They are probably all married to Outside Names, who wouldn't have known anything was wrong until it hit them. The Lombards we call them. Now I *work* in the place; I know what's happening from hour to hour. A little bit of inside knowledge here and a careful spot of trading there ... and we're sitting pretty, Maxie.'

Maxine gratefully took her drink from the waiter and then sucked in a mouthful of the fiery Absolut through a chinking floe of crushed ice. 'What are Lombards, Declan? It is the name of the street near Lloyd's, is it that?'

Declan lowered his voice, looking around over his shoulder as he did so. 'LOMBARD stands for Loads Of Money But A Right Dick!' He chuckled, amused by his own wit. 'Remember, I have a friend in Charles. He'll always make sure nothing happens to my money. He's a good teacher, too. I've learned a great deal from Charles.' He nodded knowingly.

Maxine relaxed and started to enjoy the evening. She'd had a fright, but it had made her appreciate the good things in life even more; the things she could not live without, like couture clothes, exquisite jewellery, a marvellous house and a smart car. It also made her feel more kindly disposed towards the women in the cloak-room who had swept past her and then had snootily ignored her, excluding her from their conversation. After all, whilst they faced financial ruin, she would still be enjoying the lifestyle they all wanted. Somehow it made them seem more likeable.

Charles Bryer, having landed from New York that morning, looked remarkably fit; he introduced Maxine and Declan to his other guests. Jane, his wife, stood by his side all the time, a pale, insipid-looking woman in a beige lace dress, knowing that after thirty years of marriage she never got a chance of saying anything in her husband's presence, so that she no longer tried.

At the first opportunity, Charles drew Declan to one side. 'Any news of Toby?' he asked.

Declan shook his head. 'The newspapers are still going on about him being missing, and appealing to anyone who has seen him to come forward, but there's been nothing. I think he's probably abroad by now.'

'What makes you say that?'

'It's just a feeling. I believe if he'd been in the country he'd have been found by now; either dead or alive.'

'Have you been in touch with Liza?' Charles asked. 'I suppose I ought to phone her tomorrow.'

'I saw her a couple of days ago, and I've spoken to her on the phone. She seems quite composed, under the circumstances.'

Charles Bryer blew out his cigar smoke and shot Declan a look of curiosity. 'Do you think she knows what's happened to him?'

'She'd tell me if she did, I'm sure. She's a straightforward person; she'd never be able to keep anything secret. Let's hope the next few days bring some news; it's the talk of The Room, I can tell you.'

'Are the police doing everything they can? After all, it's twelve or thirteen days since he was last seen,' Charles pointed out.

'I last heard they're trying to get hold of the crew of *Morning Glory*. She's chartered to some rich Mexicans, and she's supposed to be somewhere off the coast of Spain.'

'Spain, eh?' Charles raised his thick white eyebrows. 'Toby's parents live in Spain, don't they? I wonder if there's any connection?'

Declan shrugged. 'You've heard about the other scandal affecting the company, I presume?'

'What's that?'

'Two of the Outside Names have topped themselves, because of their losses. Roger Clarke and Henry Granville. That's been in the newspapers too. People are going to think we're jinxed at this rate.'

Charles lowered his voice. 'Well, that's better than thinking anything else is going on, isn't it?'

Declan grinned knowingly. 'You can say that again.'

Dinner was announced and, like a sweeping tide, everyone walked down the wide stairs from the gallery to the large ballroom below.

At the top table, Lady Rosemary and Sir Humphrey were presiding with quiet dignity. They may have been about to lose all their money, but graciousness and style cost nothing, and they were determined to show the world they had a lot of that.

'At least we're not alone in this catastrophe,' Sir

Humphrey had said consolingly as they got ready for the ball earlier in the evening.

'We certainly aren't,' Lady Rosemary agreed. She was trying not to grieve over the loss of Cavenham Court and the whole way of life that went with it, but it wasn't easy. 'We must look upon this as an adventure, Humphrey. We'll get a flat with a garden for the dogs and I'm going to start working.'

Sir Humphrey's kind but stupid eyes looked into hers wonderingly. 'But what will you do?'

'I'm enrolling for a course on making curtains and covers and lampshades. Then I shall set myself up in business. I'll only need a room in wherever we live; I know I can make a lot of money. People are always hunting around for someone who can run up a pair of curtains or a chair-cover; especially if I start off by not charging too much.'

Meanwhile, she was chairman of tonight's ball, her last social obligation, taken on before the blow fell, and so she conversed with their other guests while Sir Humphrey became quite amusing as he wittily recounted incidents that had happened while out shooting.

At the next table, there were two empty seats. Toby and Liza Hamcroft had agreed a long time ago to take tickets and join Emma and Anthony Turnbull's party.

'Stupid of me to forget to tell the organisers they wouldn't be here,' Emma said lightly to her husband. He'd invited several other ministers and their wives to make up a table for a cause they all believed in, namely cancer research, and Emma knew the evening was important to him.

'Don't worry, darling,' he said. 'Everyone will understand. I suppose Liza's heard nothing?'

Emma averted her face, hating to lie to Anthony, even for Liza's sake.

'No, she hasn't heard from him,' she replied. That much was certainly true, she told herself.

Anthony looked worried. 'The longer he's missing, the more serious it gets,' he said, shaking his head. 'What the hell are the police doing, for God's sake?'

Emma shrugged her slim white shoulders, revealed by the pale blue chiffon dress she wore. 'I suppose it's like looking for a needle in a haystack,' she replied casually.

'I don't like it.'

She shot him a curious look; had he got wind of something? 'What do you mean?'

Anthony grimaced. 'As an MP I have to be careful; above suspicion. I wish now I'd never agreed to become an Outside Name at Lloyd's. If there's something funny going on, and Toby, who introduced me, is involved, it could be awkward to say the least,' he said in a low voice.

Emma's cheeks flushed with anger. 'How can you say such a thing? Liza and Toby are our best friends! Of course he's not...'

'Keep your voice down,' he murmured, angrily. 'For God's sake, Em!' He looked around at their guests with a false smile but to his relief they were all talking to each other. 'Let's get rid of these two places.' He waved and a white-gloved waiter was at his elbow immediately.

After the settings had been removed he nodded with approval.

'That's better! Those empty chairs were like spectres at the feast.'

Emma sat tight-lipped. Sometimes Anthony was inclined to put his political life before everything else.

There were only seven men and two women at the meeting. Their number had been depleted by the suicide of Henry Granville. The atmosphere was tense. Things were not going as planned. The women were openly frightened, as their leader sat staring at them with cold lifeless eyes, while he repeatedly slammed his bunched-up fist with a regular beat into the palm of his other hand. They'd only just realised this man was prone to violent outbreaks of fury. Then he would lash out, brandishing his revolver and saying he would kill them all if he didn't get what he wanted. Obsessed by the existence of the Lloyd's central fund, he threatened vengeance on anyone who might betray him. They were all in this together, he stormed, no backing out now. He threatened he would hunt down and kill anyone who did not obey him.

The oldest member of the group was the most distressed as he saw his altruistic plans being taken over by someone they now realised was a psychopath. The original idea had been so simple, too. Like thousands of others, he'd lost his life's savings at Lloyd's. Burning with the injustice of it he knew there were those who were older, weaker, more vulnerable and desperately in need of help. So why not kidnap one of the prominent Members and hold him for ransom? The money would then be dispersed amongst those who had suffered most. He couldn't do it alone, though. This was a big operation that would need all sorts of skills. Bit by bit, he had formed the group, taking into his confidence those he could trust. It had been Henry Granville, a friend of long standing, who had suggested they enrol the services of his nephew, an ex-SAS officer, who had also lost everything, to mastermind the operation. Henry Granville insisted on two conditions: no one was to get hurt and the plan must be carried out in a civilised manner. The old man was only slightly deterred when his sister called him a mad crank, who was obviously suffering from senile dementia. But now everything was going wrong.

At the same time a meeting was taking place between Charles Bryer and Martin Hamcroft, who faced each other across the little round glass-topped table of the American Bar at the Savoy Hotel. The atmosphere between them was cold and hostile.

'Let's order drinks before we talk business,' Charles suggested, playing for time. This wizened old creature, Martin Hamcroft, had demanded they meet, but from now on Charles determined to stay in control of the situation. Originally he may have owed his successful position to Martin, but for the past fourteen years he'd pegged his own route, thanks to no one but himself; if he had his way, Declan Connolly would succeed him as chairman of Hamcroft's, not Toby.

'I'm worried sick about Toby,' Martin declared. He looked older than ever today, shrivelled, as if the English climate was chilling him to the bone after the heat of Spain.

'What are you going to have?' Charles asked as he hailed a waiter.

'A dry Martini, please.'

'Two dry Martinis,' he ordered, 'with an olive and a twist of lemon.'

'Certainly, sir.' As the waiter sped away, Martin looked expectantly at Charles.

'Well? What's the position?' he demanded. 'If things have gone wrong in the company, why is Toby being blamed?'

Charles leaned forward, his voice lowered discreetly. 'He isn't being blamed by me. You know what the press are like. Everything is under control, actually. As you know, Declan acts on my instruction. He does exactly as I tell him. That's why I made him a members' agent, whose sole job it is to look after the Names' personal affairs.'

'Toby originally had that role in the firm,' Martin observed.

Charles nodded. 'But Toby did have some reservations and even objections to certain aspects of the job; did he not mention it to you?' Charles asked casually, but at the same time almost coaxingly.

'He may have done, I don't remember; I don't see that much of him, you know.' Martin sounded impatient, as if he were anxious for Charles to get to the point.

'Anyway, Toby's a brilliant broker and a highly successful one,' Charles continued warmly. 'His natural charm and ability to get on with people makes him a perfect middleman. He can get any underwriter in The Room to take a line on a policy, and he never lets anyone down. His commission on all the insurance policies he places has made him an enormous fortune!' Charles was nodding like a mandarin, his round chubby face and double chin bobbing up and down as if he were a puppet, pulled by invisible strings. Looking at him with an edge of revulsion, Martin imagined he must wine and dine twice a day without a thought for his health.

'I know all that,' Martin grumbled. 'I'm not here to listen to a dissertation on his ability. I want to know what's happening to the Outside Names. I've been abroad for the past thirteen years, you know. I never come back to this country if I can help it, and I don't like what I'm hearing.' He was careful not to mention Toby more than he had to. Charles obviously had no idea Toby had been abducted, or he'd have said something by now.

'What don't you like?' Charles asked, sounding mystified. 'We're in a deep recession, you know. Lloyd's is suffering like everyone else.'

Their drinks arrived. Charles drank his as if he were thirsty. Martin sipped his, feeling the fire of gin and vermouth streak down to his stomach in a gently explosive way.

Finally he spoke coldly. 'I don't give a damn about everyone else. I want to know whether I'm in the soup at Lloyd's or not!'

For a moment Charles held his glass half raised to his lips while he regarded Martin with astonishment. 'It sounds as if you are more worried about your money than your son,' he remarked.

'At the moment there's nothing I can do about my son; that's up to the police,' Martin retorted. 'I can, I hope, find out whether I've suffered losses like everyone else, or not. Tell me that, Charles.'

Charles's face became wreathed in smiles; he gave a short laugh that sounded like a bark.

'Haven't I just been telling you that Declan is a members' agent? And that he does as I instruct? Of course you haven't suffered any losses! I can always be relied upon to look after my friends, you know,' he added with mock humility. 'You are one of the people Declan has special instructions to look after. You're on our baby syndicate, high premiums and low risk being the order of the day, my dear Martin. You understand? You and I, and quite a few others have been getting the cream . . . ! *La crème de la crème!*' His voice rose with satisfaction. 'We look after our own, you know.'

A great weight seemed to fall away from Martin; even the deep lines in his face seemed to smooth out.

'Thank Christ for that!' he exclaimed. 'I'm more relieved than I can tell you.'

'You've been worrying unnecessarily. Let's have another drink.' Charles beamed benevolently; a grown-up's Father Christmas, tubby and twinkling, handing out the goodies to a grateful adult.

After a few minutes, and another round of drinks, Martin felt more mellow. Everything was going to be all right. The glow the Martini had given him assured him it would be so. But there was just one more thing he wanted to check with Charles.

'Presumably Toby's on the baby syndicate, too, so that he and Liza are all right?' he asked.

Something seemed to cloud Charles's face. He pursed his fleshy mouth and his white brows knotted together.

'Toby had strange notions about the baby syndicate,' he said shortly. 'Some sort of high-falutin idea that it was immoral. He wouldn't have anything to do with it. I've no idea which syndicates he's on, but he certainly isn't on the baby one.'

Liza had no idea either which syndicate Toby was on. It was the first thing Martin had asked her when he got back to Holland Park Walk. She looked at him blankly.

'I don't know. Does it matter?' Where *Toby* was mattered to her above all else now, not where his *money* was. She was feeling extremely tense after her meeting with Mrs Granville who, after her initial bombshell, had refused to divulge anything more about her husband's plan, sobbing and becoming incoherent when pressed. They left her after a while: it had been pointless to try and get any information while she was in that state. But now the thought haunted Liza that perhaps she didn't know anything more about it; that Henry Granville had taken the knowledge of Toby's whereabouts to the grave with him...

'Then you may have sustained large losses,' Martin was telling her.

'What?' She returned to the present and made a gesture of irritation with her hands. 'Who *cares*? It's only money!' she shouted, losing her temper.

Today had been the worst day so far. The shock of all that had happened had worn off, and so had the adrenaline lift she'd experienced after her televised appeal. Now she was stranded in limbo until either Mrs Granville came through with the information they needed, or Lloyd's met the kidnappers' demands.

There had been no word from the chairman, and when she'd phoned and asked to speak to him, his secretary had informed her he was in meetings all day, and probably wouldn't be able to return her call.

What did that mean? Liza asked herself. Who was he having meetings with?

When the police phoned to say there was nothing fresh to report, she felt an overwhelming desire to blurt out the truth. *Toby's been kidnapped... held for ransom ... Please find him before it's too late...* Just in time she stopped the flow of words, biting them back so that her throat ached and she felt as if she were suffocating.

'Are you there, Mrs Hamcroft?' Detective Inspector Robin Buck asked as she fought for control.

'Yes.' She felt like weeping with frustration. When he rang off, she wondered if she'd done the right thing.

Tilly, Thomas and Sarah had been argumentative and disobedient all day, too, leaving their toys and clothes all over the house, and answering back rudely when they were scolded.

'You'll be locked in your rooms if you don't behave,' Liza exclaimed, knowing she was overreacting, but driven crazy by the naughtiness and the noisy racket they were making.

Sarah burst into tears. 'I . . . o-only w-wanted to bring my dolls p-pram downstairs!' she sobbed. She looked beseechingly at her mother. 'It's not fair that Tommy can h-have his bike in the garden and I can't have my p-pram.'

Looking down at her, Liza saw all the heartbreak of the world scaled down in miniature on Sarah's face. Suddenly she felt a deep sense of guilt. It wasn't Sarah's fault, or Tilly and Thomas's either, that Toby had been kidnapped and that she was distraught: they were far too young to understand the seriousness of the situation. Liza dropped to her knees and held out her arms to Sarah, who rushed into them with a loud hiccuping sob.

'It's all right, sweetheart,' Liza comforted her. 'I'm sorry I was cross. I really didn't mean to upset you.' As Sarah continued to weep, so did Liza, too, and Thomas, who had been watching the scene with riveted interest, finally spoke.

'Shall I carry Sarah's dolls' pram into the garden for her, Mummy?' he asked, his face solemn.

'Thank you, darling. That's very kind. You're a good boy.' Then she whispered in Sarah's ear. A moment later Sarah spoke, too.

'Thank you, Thomas,' she said with a big sniff.

'That's all right.' With a manly swagger, he picked up the toy pram and walked into the garden with it.

When Martin returned to the house during the afternoon, smelling of brandy and cigar smoke and fussing about which syndicates Toby was on, something in Liza's head snapped.

'You're so bloody taken up with money!' she stormed. 'You'd think it was your precious money that had been kidnapped, not your son, the way you're going on.'

Martin looked at her stonily. 'There's no need to take that attitude, Liza. I know you're upset, but one has to be practical! If you've sustained heavy losses, like your brother Freddy, then you and Toby will have to try and take evasive action. You don't want to have to sell this house and Chalklands, do you? Or get rid of *Morning Glory*? Or take the children away from good schools?'

Liza ran her hands through her hair, her eyes wide with amazed anger.

'I don't believe I'm hearing this!' she exclaimed. 'Your son, your *only* son is being held for ransom – by a bunch of demented thugs, for all we know – and you're wondering if we'll be able to keep up the same standard of living! We can't even be sure they'll release Toby. They may torture him. They may even kill him. But oh, no! What's *really* important is that we can still afford two homes and a frigging yacht!' She sprang to her feet, her heart thundering in her ears. Nina came into the room at that moment; it was obvious she'd overheard what Liza had said.

'We do share your worry about Toby,' she pointed out, taking in the scene at a glance: Liza, hair tossed in anger, striding about the room, Martin standing rigidly in front of the fireplace, watching her emotional outburst with cold curiosity.

'But it is only natural that we should all be concerned about the financial situation after all the dreadful things we've heard since we arrived in England.' She turned to Martin. 'Did you see Charles for lunch?'

'Yes. We're OK. He made sure, through Declan, that we were on a baby syndicate; but he didn't know about Toby.'

Nina looked surprised. 'Do you know anything, Liza? Do you know which syndicates Toby is on?'

Martin cut in curtly, before Liza had time to reply.

'Don't ask, Nina. I asked her, and she bit my head off! Liza seems to think that it's a reflection on my feelings for Toby that I happen to be concerned about any financial losses he may have incurred.'

Nina looked at Liza sadly. 'Oh, darling. Martin wouldn't mean it like that. Try not to get too upset. I'm sure Toby will be released soon. I have the utmost faith in Malcolm Blackwell, you know.' She spoke earnestly. 'I'm *sure* he'll handle the kidnappers in the right way, and give them what they want to secure Toby's release.'

Liza looked at her mother-in-law almost pityingly. Was it the difference in generations? Or was Nina out of touch with the real world, having lived such a marvellously secluded and rarefied life in Spain for the past few years? Whatever it was, Liza thought her to be extremely naïve. She turned to Martin.

'Do you think Malcolm Blackwell will pay up?' she asked.

Martin looked at her long and hard, and then he looked down at the soft shades of pink, blue and green woven into the Aubusson tapestry carpet. The effect of the dry Martinis had worn off by now, and he no longer felt the euphoria he'd experienced when Charles had first told him his investment was safe. For a long moment he remained silent, not sure whether to say what was on his mind or not. When he spoke, it was obvious he was trying to tell her something as carefully as he could.

'You have to remember one thing, Liza. If kidnappers, or terrorists for that matter, have their demands granted, it will encourage others to think they can hold anyone to ransom to get what they want. Once we get a reputation for being a walk-over, we'll have company chairmen and directors being abducted and held for ransom all over the place, by people ranging from angry shareholders to downright cranks! In my opinion Malcolm Blackwell will *not* concede to the kidnappers' demands. If he did he'd be putting the security of other influential businessmen in jeopardy.'

Nina gave a gasping cry and collapsed on to the sofa,

clutching a handkerchief to her mouth. Liza's face was blank with shock and anguish, her eyes dark with pain.

'Yes. I see what you mean,' she said hollowly.

'But Lloyd's must pay up to get Toby released!' wailed Nina. 'They must, Martin! You must do something ... bring all your influence to bear.'

'I gave up being influential thirteen years ago,' he replied drily. 'There's nothing Malcolm Blackwell can do. I can assure you he's not going to hand over several hundred million pounds like a lamb and nor, I'm afraid to say, should he.'

'Oh, Martin! Our son! What are we going to do?' Nina looked at him beseechingly. 'We must get him back.'

He went over to where she sat, hunched in misery with her arms clasped round her ribs as if she were in pain. He put his hand on her shoulder. 'I'm sorry, my dear, but those are the facts.'

Liza sat, cold and stiff, wondering how soon her father would return. He'd gone on a mission, and if he'd failed, her immediate hope of finding where Toby had been taken would be gone.

This was Sir George's second visit in the past two days to the ugly little house in Barons Court. After he and Liza had seen Janet Granville on the first occasion, he'd said, 'I think, with careful handling, she'll tell us a lot more, providing we don't rush her.'

'Do you think her husband told her anything? He'd have to be certain she'd not tell a soul,' Liza pointed out.

'They sound as if they were a close couple; and, as you

can see, she's desperate for money. Now that her husband's dead, she may not feel the same sense of loyalty to the others.'

'What are you going to do?'

'I'm going to go and see her again, but on my own this time. I think she's a woman who has been used to being looked after by her husband, and I think she'd respond better to a man than she would to another woman. I'll go very gently, offer her financial help, which I'm quite prepared to do anyway, because I feel very sorry for her, and hope she'll spill the beans ... or a few of them anyway. Enough to give us a lead.'

'Are these old Intelligence tactics?' Liza asked.

Sir George gave a slight shrug. '"Needs must when the devil drives",' he quoted. 'I've no intention of conning her or anything like that. I'm going to offer her a straight deal: money for information. Only in her case, the deal is going to have to be prettied up a bit before she'll accept it, I reckon.'

The next day, at about the same time, he called at the house. This time the front door was opened by a boy of about fifteen in ripped jeans and a grubby T-shirt.

'Whaddya want?' he asked suspiciously.

'Might I see Mrs Henry Granville?' Sir George asked with exquisite politeness.

'Who?' He chewed gum, round and round his mouth, and his eyes were insolent.

'Mrs Granville? She has the room at the back . . .'

At that moment, Janet Granville opened her door. She stood in silhouette, with the window overlooking the tiny garden behind her. 'I thought I recognised your voice,' she began. She looked pleased to see him.

'Ah, my dear Mrs Granville.' Sir George strode past the youth, his hand extended. 'I hope you don't mind my calling around again so soon. I was coming this way and I thought I'd just drop in and say hello.'

As he entered her room, the youth stared after him as if he'd never heard or seen such a strange spectacle in his life.

Sir George placed a Marks & Spencer's bag on the floor in front of the cupboard which held the tiny cooker.

'I do hope you will accept these few odds and ends,' he said graciously. 'I happened to be passing M and S and, as I was sure you aren't taking care of yourself, or perhaps find it too stressful to go shopping at the moment, I got you some bits and pieces: cold chicken, some pâté, eggs, and a rather nice cheese. It's one of my favourites.'

Janet Granville's eyes instantly filled with tears. 'How kind . . .' she murmured falteringly. 'Do sit down. Would you like some coffee? It's instant, I'm afraid.'

'Yes, please.' Sir George smiled his broad, engaging smile, and while she boiled the kettle, he stood and looked out of the grimy window, keeping up a flow of idle chatter to make her relax. When she sat on the hard lumpy sofa, facing him, she was composed again.

'Thank you so much for coming today,' she said sweetly. 'I haven't quite got myself together yet. I'll have to get organised soon, though. I can't stay in this place for ever.'

'Have you a family?' he asked gently.

She shook her head. 'We never had any children, unfortunately, and my parents are dead. I have a sister, in New Zealand, but we've rather lost touch.'

Sir George was impressed by how much more talkative she was than on the previous day. He had the feeling she trusted him, that she trusted all men: she was that sort of woman. He was glad now that Liza hadn't come with him. He was going to be able to speak much more freely without her there.

After a few more minutes of exchanging information about their backgrounds, and finding that she'd had a Scottish grandmother, Sir George began very delicately to build up his case for her consideration.

'You've met my daughter, Liza, of course,' he said casually. 'She has three children. The boy, Thomas, is nine! A live wire, I can tell you. The youngest is only four.' He shook his head sorrowfully. 'Thank God they haven't so far realised that their father is missing. We can't keep it from the two older ones much longer, though. Tilly cries when she goes to bed these days: she senses something's wrong.'

Janet Granville nodded in understanding. 'They must all miss him.'

'*Dreadfully!*' Sir George pounced on the word. 'Most dreadfully; so does my daughter. She's distraught with worry. I'm really afraid she's going to crack up at any moment now. I'm quite sure your husband had no idea what he was getting into when he got involved in this business, you know. Toby is totally innocent of any financial duplicity. If these people have lost money and they have a real grudge against Lloyd's, they've got the wrong man.'

Janet Granville looked dubious. 'The others . . .' she paused, as if afraid she might say too much . . . 'they know what they're doing. They wouldn't pick just anyone from Lloyd's at random. There must be a reason why it was Toby Hamcroft.'

'Oh, yes, and we all know the reason. He's well known. Has good connections and what they call these days "a high profile". They *had* to kidnap someone well known, in order to get Lloyd's to pay any attention, and to take them seriously.'

She didn't answer but she still looked doubtful.

'I think,' Sir George continued relentlessly, 'that financial worry must have affected your husband's judgement. It's not surprising. When you consider all that he lost through Lloyd's, it's enough to turn anybody's mind.' He sighed heavily. 'I'm afraid it's about to happen to my wife and me, too. Our lovely old home in Scotland is going to have to be sold, sooner or later.'

'Oh, I'm sorry, I didn't know.'

'So many people have been affected, my dear Mrs Granville. But kidnapping my son-in-law isn't going to help the situation. Whoever thought up that idea is going to have a rude awakening. For the sake of those involved, we've got to mount a rescue operation.'

She looked alarmed.

He continued. 'They'll be found out, sooner or later, and then they'll *never* get any of their losses back.

Kidnapping is a serious offence. They could all go down for a long time. They must be mad to think they can get away with a thing like this.'

'The police don't know, do they?' Fear flickered behind her eyes.

'No,' he said shortly. Then he looked straight into her face and his voice was earnest.

'Do you realise, my dear Mrs Granville, that these men are the cause of your husband's suicide? I'm convinced that it was the stress of being involved in this crazy scheme that was the last straw for your husband. People can always get financial help when they're in a jam; but if they're involved in a criminal action, then they're really on the downward slope. You don't owe these men a jot of loyalty, you know. In fact, you should be thinking of ways to get even to seek revenge for your husband's death.'

'They aren't all men,' she said involuntarily, and then she raised her hand to her mouth, as if to prevent herself saying more.

Sir George raised his eyebrows in exaggerated surprise. 'Is that so? Well, of course, women could become Names just as easily as men. Oh, God.' He sighed gustily again. 'So many lives ruined. So much heartbreak, for you especially. And so much for my Liza and her children, if we can't find out where Toby is.'

Janet Granville didn't say anything. She sipped her coffee and stared at the floor.

'Have you thought of going to New Zealand? To be near your sister? Maybe start a new life for yourself over there. It's a wonderful country, I'm told. Great climate. Beautiful scenery.'

Her smile was faded. 'I couldn't even afford the fare to Heathrow.'

He said nothing for a moment, not wanting to rush her. Earlier, Liza had told him she'd pay anything for information about Toby.

'There's money in our joint bank account, Daddy,' she said. 'And I'll sell my jewellery. I could raise thousands, and I will if it gets Toby back.'

Sir George looked at Mrs Granville again. 'You'd like to go to New Zealand?' He was using his coaxing voice, a tactic that had often worked well during his career.

'Of course. My sister's a widow. She often suggested we go and live there, when Henry retired.'

He leaned forward and spoke as if he were talking to a child. 'I could make that dream come true for you, if you'll let me. I can give you enough money, in cash, to fly off to your sister's, and put all this terrible business, with all the unhappy memories it holds for you, right behind you. What do you say, Mrs Granville?'

The tears flowed silently down her cheeks, and she could hardly speak. When she did, all she said was: 'Please call me Janet.'

He smiled in understanding and, reaching out, laid his hand, strong and reassuring, on hers.

'You only have to say the word, Janet. I'm certain it's what your husband would want you to do, rather than stay here, living in poverty, with the kidnappers, whoever they are, languishing in jail! You won't even have any friends if you're known to have been associated with them. God, your life will be hell!'

'But I'm scared,' she whispered fearfully. 'And I have to tell you I don't know where they've taken your son-in-law. Henry never told me.'

'But you could find out, couldn't you? From one of the others?'

'I suppose I could,' she said, but she sounded doubtful.

'This could be a case of life or death, Janet. If we don't even know where they've taken Toby, there's not a chance of our being able to mount a rescue. I'm sure if your husband were here, and he realised what a devoted family man my son-in-law is, he'd realise that this is not the right way to seek compensation. Toby could end up losing his life and they could still not get a penny.'

Janet shuddered, twisting her hands in her lap. He could see she was wrestling with her feelings. Should she be disloyal to the group of people who had set out to obtain financial justice along with her husband? Or should she help set an innocent man free? The pawn in the game . . .

Sir George spoke again with gentle persistence.

'Contact the one you know best. Ask him what's going on. You've a right to know, as your husband's widow, you know. His share of any ransom money should go to you.' He purposely didn't ask who was in the group, that would come later. For the moment she must be lulled into thinking everyone could emerge from this situation unscathed.

'I'll come back tomorrow,' he continued. 'Find out

between now and then where Toby's being held. Be ready to leave, too. Pack what you want to take with you.'

She stared at him blankly, confused. 'Why?'

'Because you want to put the whole thing behind you, and get out of here. Start a new life. I'll come by car and I'll bring your flight ticket with me; luckily you don't need an entry visa for New Zealand. I'll also bring two thousand pounds in cash; that'll be enough to keep you going for a while. Remember to bring your passport. All right?' It reminded him of the briefings he carried out when he was in the army: he felt a shot of the old adrenaline, making him feel young and alive again.

Dazed, Janet Granville gazed at him, seeing, as if by the wave of a magic wand, a glorious future for herself and a new life beyond her wildest dreams. As long as she could find out where they'd taken Toby Hamcroft. Slowly and smilingly, she nodded in agreement.

On the third day Sir George arrived in Liza's Mercedes. There was a space right outside the house where Janet Granville lived. In his breast pocket he had her flight ticket, booked in the name of 'Mrs Harvey', and two thousand pounds in assorted notes. As he strode up the front path, he felt a pleasurable buzz of anticipation. Within a few minutes he hoped to know where Toby was being held, and the name of at least a few of the kidnappers. He rang the bell. The same boy, in the same ripped jeans and the same grubby T-shirt, opened the door.

'Yeah?' he asked.

'I've come to see Mrs Granville.'

'She ain't here.' He shifted the gum from one side of his mouth to the other.

Startled, Sir George stared at him. 'What do you mean, she isn't here? She's expecting me.'

'I tell you, she ain't here. Look in her frigging room if you don't believe me,' he added aggressively.

Sir George pushed past him, hurried down the corridor by the parked bicycle, and opened the door at the far end.

The place had been pulled apart. It looked as if a whirlwind had swooped around, tossing things about and destroying everything in its path. He turned to look accusingly at the youth.

'They came for her yesterday. I don't know nothing about it,' he said defensively.

'Who came for her?'

'Two men it was I saw. Took her off in a car they did. Me mum was bleedin' mad when I tells her. She owed two weeks' rent did Mrs Granville.'

Sir George felt icy cold. The next question was almost irrelevant, but he asked it all the same.

'Who made this mess?'

'They did. When they first came. Looked like they was looking for something.' The boy shrugged. 'I ain't going to clean up this fucking mess.'

'How did Mrs Granville seem?' Sir George steeled himself to ask.

'Whaddya mean?'

'Was she upset? Angry? Was she friendly towards

them?' Even as he said it he realised it was a ridiculous question.

The boy snorted derisively. ''Ere, 'oo do you think you are? I've already told the police I don't know nothing!' Then he grabbed the handlebars of the bicycle and manoeuvred it expertly backwards into the street, leaving Sir George standing helplessly looking at the wreckage of someone's life.

Chapter Ten

The chairman of Lloyd's received the second ransom note at six o'clock that evening. It was handed to him as he came down the steep main steps of the building by a helmeted courier dressed in black leathers, his eyes shielded by dark goggles. Taken aback by the speed with which the white envelope was thrust into his hand, Malcolm Blackwell gaped in confusion as the messenger roared off again on his bike. It had happened so quickly no one seemed to have noticed, except for Malcolm's chauffeur, who was waiting by the gleaming Daimler. He stepped forward anxiously.

'Are you all right, sir?' It was obvious from Malcolm Blackwell's expression that he was perturbed.

The chairman recovered himself quickly. 'I'm fine, Scott.'

It wasn't until Scott had manoeuvred the car into the heavy evening flow of traffic going west, that Malcolm Blackwell ripped open the envelope, knowing instinctively, before he even read it, that it was another message from the kidnappers. His eyes skimmed the computer printout, and he knew that his worst fears had materialised.

The contents made one thing clear: exactly what was required to secure the release of Toby Hamcroft. Listed were ten secret numbered accounts, spread between three banks in Geneva. The instructions were that £5 million was to be transferred from the Lloyd's central fund to each of the numbered accounts; only when that had been done would their hostage be set free. If Lloyd's refused, Toby Hamcroft would never be heard of again. The same would apply if the police became involved.

Slouched in silent shock, Malcolm Blackwell sat in the back of his car, wondering what the hell to do. He had a gut feeling now that these people would stop at nothing. The first missive he'd received might have been the work of a bunch of embittered cranks; this letter was quite different. Whoever was holding Toby Hamcroft as a hostage was well organised and highly professional. They had given Blackwell no room to negotiate, either. No opportunity to strike a deal. They were demanding a total of £50 million, and he reckoned that Toby Hamcroft was as good as dead if they didn't get it.

Not for the first time, Malcolm felt the terrible isolation of his position in Lloyd's. Whom could he turn to? Whom could he confide in and seek advice from? If Toby's safety and eventual release was to be accomplished, Malcolm mustn't make a false move; on the other hand it was ridiculous to imagine he could draft £50 million from the Lloyd's central fund to a string of numbered accounts in Switzerland.

The chauffeur drew up outside his gracious Belgravia house, its stucco-work painted pale cream, the front door a gleaming black. He and his wife were giving a small drinks party this evening, and he could see a few guests were already gathered in the chandelier-lit drawing room. Somehow he was going to have to act as if nothing was wrong. He clambered reluctantly out of the car, feeling as if the ransom note in his breast pocket were burning through to his heart. Abruptly he switched on his social smile. If anyone mentioned the disappearance of Toby Hamcroft, he would make a light-hearted joke about Lloyd's and the army being different; in Lloyd's you were allowed to go AWOL.

'Hello, dear.' His wife of forty-one years greeted him as she'd done all their married life, her hands placed on his shoulders, her face uplifted to his. 'There's a message for you, Malcolm. Someone called Sir George Mortimer phoned. He said it was urgent, wants you to call him back. I've put his number on the pad by the study phone.'

'Thank you, dear.'

The name meant nothing to him. If he had a sneaking hope that the caller was about to help solve his problems, those hopes were extinguished a minute later. Liza Hamcroft's father had phoned to let him know that Janet Granville had also been kidnapped.

* * *

'This is dreadful,' Liza exclaimed when her father told her what had happened. 'They must have feared she was going to talk. If only she'd told you more when you saw her.'

Sir George looked troubled. 'I feel badly at having put her in danger, too.' He also felt he'd bungled everything, acting in an amateurish way. Perhaps he was getting old. When he'd served in army Intelligence, he'd never have allowed a contact to be exposed to danger in this way. Now it was too late. Janet Granville's landlady had already told the police she'd been forcibly taken away; it was only a matter of time before they, and the media, put two and two together. Toby's disappearance, followed by Henry Granville's suicide because of his Lloyd's losses would appear very sinister when followed by the abduction of Mrs Granville. If no one guessed that kidnap was involved, they might jump to other conclusions. There might even be suggestions that Toby and Janet Granville had run off together with funds from Lloyd's, but had made it *look* as if she'd been abducted.

Sir George groaned inwardly. He felt deeply responsible for this latest débâcle, and he dreaded what the media would make of it.

Liza, on the contrary, didn't care what people thought. She only wanted to know where Toby was being held so that they could try and get him back.

'Oh, God! I wish we could tell the police what's really happened,' she burst out in frustration. 'They're going to look for clues in all the wrong places, and jump to the wrong conclusions. It could even be counter-productive to our getting Toby back.'

'Malcolm Blackwell implied on the phone just now that he's had another ransom note.'

Liza caught her breath. 'What does it say?'

'I'm on my way to go and see him now. He's got a drinks party and, as nobody will link him and me with you and Toby, he thought it would be a good opportunity for us to discuss the matter.'

'You mean I can't go, too?' Her mouth drooped in disappointment.

''Fraid not, my pet. Everyone knows what you look like. Absolute secrecy still has to be maintained; more than ever, in fact, if we're going to get Toby and Janet Granville out of this mess,' Sir George replied.

'What did the note say?'

'He wouldn't talk on the phone. That's why I'm going to see him. I'll get back as soon as I can and then I'll tell you everything.'

'Please do,' Liza begged. 'I don't know how much more of this I can stand.'

'Why don't we go down to Chalklands for the weekend?' He looked with sudden longing out of the window. 'It would do us all good to get a bit of country air.'

'Do you think we should leave London?'

'Why not? There's nothing we can do. We've just got to wait until something happens, so we might as well pass the time in the country as anywhere else. The children need to run wild for a bit, too. It's not good for them to be cooped up in this house all the time, frightened to go out in case a photographer pounces on them.'

Liza nodded. 'You're absolutely right, Daddy. We'll go down on Friday evening. I'll ring Bert and Margaret now and tell them to get the house ready. And I can always get back to London quickly if I have to, can't I?'

'Of course you can. I'll be off now. Tell your mother I've gone out, will you?'

'Yes. Where is Ma?'

'She's taken Lottie for a walk in Kensington Gardens. You know how she loves walking,' he replied, smiling. 'Lottie is as good an excuse as any.'

'Lucky Lottie! I don't think she's had so much exercise for years.'

'Martin and Nina are upstairs, resting, in case you want to know,' Sir George said. 'He didn't look too good at lunch.'

'I know. I'm worried about him. Nina says he's more upset about Toby than he's letting on.'

'Could be. Anyway, I'll be back as soon as I can.'

'All right.' Liza looked at him, the man who had loved and supported her since the day she was born. 'Thanks, Daddy. For everything,' she said gratefully.

Impulsively he took her in his arms and hugged her tightly.

'That's my girl,' he said gently. 'You'll be all right.'

'I know I will, Daddy. I've got to be, whatever happens, if only for the sake of the children.'

'For your own sake, too,' he reminded her gently.

'I want to make Toby proud of me. Whatever happens, I want that.'

Sir George cupped her face in his hands, wiping the sudden tears from her cheeks with his thumbs. 'Toby always has and always will be proud of you, darling,' he said tenderly. 'He couldn't be otherwise. I'm proud of you too; so is your mother. You're bearing up remarkably well under the strain.'

Liza blew her nose and gave him a watery smile. 'These damn tears. I wish I didn't keep crying. It's so babyish.'

'It's not at all babyish. It's a natural safety-valve: you should thank your lucky stars you can get it out of your system that way, instead of bottling everything up.'

When he'd left to go and see Malcolm Blackwell, Liza sat gazing out of the drawing-room window, her thoughts with Toby. She prayed inwardly at moments, trying to strike a bargain with God. *I'll never complain again if Toby comes home safely.*

Emma phoned her a few minutes later.

'I've got some really interesting news for you,' she said after they'd greeted each other. 'You're never going to believe this.'

Melissa was watching from the bedroom window for the return of Freddy. She could see along Quarrendon Street from this vantage point, watch him as he walked briskly along in his dark blue pinstripe suit, shining leather briefcase in hand, his eagerness to get home apparent in every line of his body. The one thing he looked forward to was getting home to Melissa every evening. Soon there would be a baby to go home to as well. The only dark cloud on his horizon was his Lloyd's losses. However, unlike the Davenports, their immediate problems had been solved by Eileen Blagdon. Maybe Melissa was right. Maybe they would be able to ride out the storm.

Something, telepathy perhaps, made him look up. He saw Melissa in their bedroom window, her bulk made larger-looking by the bright pink maternity smock she wore. He waved cheerily, and grinned up at her. She didn't wave back or even acknowledge him, but withdrew into the room abruptly, as if she'd not meant him to see her.

A moment later he was in the black and white tiled hallway of the little house, tossing his keys on to the silver salver on the hall table, calling out, 'Hi there, sweetheart.'

There was a stony response to his greeting.

'Are you all right?' he called out suddenly anxious. Supposing something was wrong with her? He hurried up the steep flight of stairs and charged into their room. She was sitting on the bed, her face averted.

'What's the matter, darling?' he enquired, going to put his arms around her.

Immediately she burst into tears, violent sobs shaking her shoulders, making her unable to speak.

Freddy had never seen her in such a state.

'Everything will be all right,' he assured her.

'How can it possibly be all right?' she demanded, her voice thick and choked. 'We stand to lose *everything*! If not this year, then next year and the year after. Mummy says we face ruin. She says Lloyd's itself may go under and take us with it ... like a ... like a sinking ship!'

'Then we'll just have to swim for land, won't we?' he replied flippantly, hoping to cheer her up. It wasn't the first time Eileen Blagdon had prophesied imminent disaster. When they'd first got married she'd assured all her friends that it wouldn't last a year.

'Oh!' Melissa seized one of the little white lace pillows that were heaped on their bed, and threw it at him. 'You're so *stupid*!' she wept. 'I've never known anyone so stupid as you. Don't you *care* that we're going to be penniless?'

'You're not telling me anything I don't already know.' He suddenly looked pink and flustered. 'But why are you taking it out on me? We're not the only ones in this predicament. I've been hearing of *hundreds* of people who have lost money – nearly all the syndicates have suffered. It's not my fault.'

'Why did you have to go into Lloyd's in the first place?'

Freddy recognised the work of Melissa's mother in her line of thinking. 'Now you're being stupid,' he said.

Melissa wiped her eyes with the back of her hand. 'No, I'm not. If you were going to become a Name you should have worked in the place, then you could have guarded our interests. At least Toby was there to make sure he was on the low-risk syndicates; no doubt he's been making a fortune . . . while we've lost every penny.'

Freddy regarded his wife of three years with a mixture of pity and panic. It sounded as if Eileen had really done a good job of brainwashing.

'How can you talk about Toby like that when we don't even know whether he's dead or alive and my sister is going out of her mind with worry?' he demanded. 'You're acting as if Toby let us rot in hell while he looked after himself.'

'It's true though, isn't it? Toby and Liza have everything, and next year we may not even have a roof over our heads – and we're having a baby, too. Why didn't Toby look after our interests? Liza is going to go on being seriously rich for the rest of her life, and you and I will have nothing, because Mummy can't afford to keep bailing us out, you know!'

'You're jealous, aren't you?' Freddy couldn't keep the shocked chill out of his voice. Melissa continued to cry and although he felt sorry for her, he was also deeply hurt by her attitude. Why did she let her mother influence her, he thought with irritation. Of course the mistake had been accepting her financial help. 'Come on, sweetheart,' he said coaxingly, putting an arm around her shoulder. 'Cheer up!'

'Leave me alone, Freddy,' she wept. 'Please.'

'OK.' He left the bedroom quietly, and went down to the kitchen where, as there was no sign of dinner, he made himself a cheese sandwich. He decided he must try and make allowances; after all she was young, pregnant and still under her mother's thumb.

A few minutes later he heard the front door slam.

'Melissa?' he called out. There was no answer. Dashing back up to their bedroom, he found a scribbled note on the pillow.

I've had enough and I'm going to my mother's. I don't think I can see you again.

M.

'I don't think we've met,' Amelia Blackwell said, as she greeted Sir George when he arrived at the house in Chapel Street. 'Are you an old business friend of Malcolm?'

'Er . . . no, not really,' he replied. 'But we have mutual friends.'

'How nice. Do have a drink.' Her bejewelled hand waved towards a butler who stood holding a silver tray, on which were set half a dozen cut-crystal glasses filled with champagne, the tiny bubbles rising like fragile stems to the top.

'Thank you.' He looked around, realising he had no idea what Malcolm Blackwell looked like, but hoping he himself would be noticed as an outsider amongst a group of friends. Then a thickset man in an exquisitely cut dark suit excused himself from the couple he was talking to, and made his way across the room, hand outstretched.

The first thing that struck Sir George was Malcolm

Blackwell's weary and battered-looking face, like a boxer after a few rounds; the puffy bulges under the eyes looked like bruises, and his mouth seemed to sag at the corners.

'Good evening,' Blackwell said, 'I'm glad you could come. Let's go into the study, where we can talk in private for a couple of minutes.' Turning to his wife, he said: 'There's a bit of business I have to discuss with my friend here. We won't be long.'

Amelia nodded, as if she were accustomed to her husband putting business before all else. Sir George noticed Malcolm hadn't called him by his name once.

The room next door was a surprisingly feminine-looking study, not what Sir George had expected at all. Brightly flowered chintz, shelves packed with paper-back novels, a scattering of needlepoint cushions, and a ginger cat who stood up and stretched languidly when they entered, completed a domesticated atmosphere. The only desk was a fine George III piece, its surface cluttered with papers.

'Take a seat,' Malcolm said, although standing himself with his back to the flower-filled fireplace.

'Did you know I'd had another ransom note this evening?' he asked, getting to the point immediately.

'I'd no idea. I phoned you because I thought you ought to know that Janet Granville has been kidnapped, too.'

'Tell me about this Mrs Granville. Who is she, exactly?'

Briefly, Sir George explained the situation.

Malcolm sipped his glass of champagne thoughtfully before speaking. 'They must have suspected that she was no longer on their side, and that she was going to help you by finding out where they'd taken Toby Hamcroft,' he said at last. 'Now both of them are incarcerated. You shouldn't have spoken to her, you know. I stressed to your daughter Liza that secrecy was vital in this matter.'

'You can't expect her to sit and wait for something to happen,' Sir George replied briskly. 'Mrs Granville was our only link through her late husband with the group who abducted Toby. Surely the answer is to find out where he's being held, and then to organise some sort of rescue operation? Rather than wait for the abductors to set the agenda?'

'I don't think it's going to be as simple as that. These people are highly organised and, it seems, well informed. Take a look at this.' Malcolm Blackwell handed him the latest ransom note.

Sir George read it through twice. His jawline hardened. 'What are you going to do?'

'Precisely nothing at this stage.' The bleary eyes closed for a second, as if he were too tired to keep them open.

'Then what?'

'If I don't respond to this, they'll get the message that I'm not playing their game.'

'And if you do?' Sir George's voice was hollow.

Malcolm Blackwell shrugged. 'I imagine they'll make their demand more realistic. Not that it alters the basic situation. Once we give in to this sort of thing, there'll be no end to it.'

'I know.' It was what Martin Hamcroft had warned them about the previous day. 'Then the only answer *is* to find out where they're holding Toby. Otherwise there is an impasse.'

'Quite.' Malcolm put his empty glass down and started walking to the door, as if to conclude their meeting.

'You realise,' Sir George pointed out as he followed Blackwell, 'that they may be very patient; time could be on their side. They may keep Toby as a hostage for weeks, even *months*,' he added, with growing disquiet. How would Liza bear it if Toby was held for a long time?

Malcolm Blackwell nodded. 'I know.'

'And you're prepared to let that happen?'

'What else do you suggest I do? I couldn't comply with their demands even if I wanted to: the Lloyd's Council would never sanction such an action in the first place. An institution like ours can't have a bunch of lunatics dictating to us! It's unthinkable.'

They were in the hall now. Through the door into the drawing room, Sir George could see more guests had arrived. Malcolm noticed it too.

'If you'll excuse me, I must get back to my guests,' he apologised.

'Of course, and I must be going.'

'Won't you have another drink?' Malcolm Blackwell was making an effort to sound sincere and hospitable, but Sir George could tell he wanted temporarily to erase all thoughts of Toby and the kidnappers while he socialised; Sir George's presence would be too much of a reminder.

'I want to get back to Liza,' he said diplomatically.

Malcolm could hardly disguise his relief. 'You'll give her my regards, won't you? Tell her I'm most awfully sorry about everything.'

'Yes, I will.' They shook hands. Two men with totally different priorities. One from Harrow, who'd entered the old-boy network of big business and wheeler-dealing in order to get rich; the other from Wellington and Sandhurst, an officer and a gentleman of honour whose thoughts had always been for Queen and country rather than personal gain.

But at this moment they had one thing in common: they both wanted to secure the release of Toby Hamcroft; though Sir George suspected they were about to handle the situation in very different ways.

Liza listened as Emma told her what had happened.

'Isn't it a coincidence?' Emma rattled on enthusiastically. 'When the editor of the *Globe* phoned me this afternoon and commissioned a series of articles about Lloyd's, I was dumbstruck! He'd no idea you were a friend, nor did he realise Anthony is an Outside Name.'

'What angle does he want you to take?'

'I'm to do an exposé! Reveal all the scams, being careful not to name names, of course – sorry for the pun!

I just wish Toby was home again, because that really *is* going to be a story when it comes out.'

'I know,' Liza said quietly.

'What's the matter, love?' Emma asked concerned.

'Well, of course I know you must do it; it's the type of journalism that's right up your street, but . . . I don't know . . .' Liza hesitated unhappily.

'Tell me.'

'I can't help feeling a sense of loyalty towards Lloyd's. I mean if there has been any fraudulence, I'm sure it's not widespread. There are always a few bad apples in every barrel.'

There was a long pause, and silence on the line. Then Emma spoke. 'I can understand how you feel, Liza. I'm not going to be writing a word until I've done a thorough investigation, either. Obviously I know damn all about the place right now, but I intend to find out, and I shall write as I find,' she added soberly.

'Oh, Em! I'm sorry . . . but I wish you didn't have to do it. Lloyd's have been good to us. Everything we've got is because we've done well at Lloyd's. Just because some crackpots are holding Toby hostage, doesn't mean the whole place is riddled with corruption.'

'I know it doesn't, Liza. It's obvious I've got to be careful what I write, too; I don't relish being sued! But it's you who is basically saying don't write terrible things about Lloyd's. What makes you think there's anything crooked going on in the first place? Why are you presuming I'm going to do a hatchet job? I may well end up concluding it's a perfect example of how the insurance market should be run! *Of course* there are fine, honest and honourable people working there, and the present situation may well just be the result of a combination of old-fashioned methods and unintentional mismanagement.'

'How are you going to set about it?' Liza asked.

'Knowing how secretive they all are, I'm just going to have to ferret around interviewing people and trying to make sense of all the facts and figures that are being quoted at the moment.'

'Why don't you talk to Martin? He'd be helpful, I'm sure, and at least he could fill you in on the background, and maybe tell you how things have changed since his day.'

'Brilliant! Thanks, Liza. Could you ask him for me? I plan to come up to London tomorrow to get this feature started; maybe I could come and see you. I want to know what's happening...'

'Yes. I can't talk on the phone, but there have been developments, and rather frightening ones, too,' Liza replied, cagily.

'Oh my God! Do you think, as a bona fide journalist, I could help, you know...? I've got an excuse now to ask questions and go to certain places, which maybe you can't without causing suspicion. Do you get my drift?' Emma replied with equal caution.

'I do. You're right. You could be enormously helpful. Talk to Daddy. He's being so wonderful and ... and it's such a pity...' Her voice drifted off as she thought of Mrs

Granville. He'd been within a hair's breadth of getting information out of her before it had all gone wrong. 'I'll tell you everything when I see you, Em. I can't talk now.'

'I'll see you tomorrow.' Emma replaced the phone thoughtfully. This could be the biggest journalistic coup of her life, but she also knew it could bring her into conflict with her best friend. Liza was a person who always thought the best of everyone and who was immensely loyal. She was grateful that Toby had given them such a wonderful life, and she wasn't going to believe anything was basically wrong with Lloyd's, even if the true facts jumped up and hit her. Having talked to Anthony, though, Emma was now convinced that, what had once been an honourable institution, had been infiltrated by an element of greed in its more virulent form. The research promised to be both exciting and revealing. Although it meant leaving her children behind for several days each week, she could hardly wait to start. As to what she was about to uncover, God alone knew what the outcome would be, but one potential scandal had already reached her ears. There was a rumour going around that the government was prepared to pay the losses of the fifty-one Members of Parliament who were Outside Names, because if those MPs, mostly in the Conservative Party, were made bankrupt, that would lead to by-elections, which might make many a Tory candidate lose his seat.

Emma found herself in an exquisite juxtaposition: if the taxpayer – because that is what it would amount to –

paid any losses Anthony might incur, she would consider it a godsend, but at the same time, an act of total immorality. It would be on a par with getting a charitable foundation to pay your betting losses.

She strolled into the kitchen where the children, scrubbed clean after their romp in the garden with the dogs, were having supper round the old pine table. A rush of dogs charged forward to greet her, and Barnaby, Robin and Rosie looked at her expectantly.

'Can we watch some telly before we go to bed?' Barnaby asked through a mouthful of baked beans.

'Can we, Mummy? Can we?'

Emma grinned indulgently, thankful for their sakes that they were still children, undisturbed and untroubled by the affairs of the adult world.

'Half an hour! No more.'

'Yeah!' The boys let out a robust yell of joy, but Rosie only smiled wanly.

'What's wrong, my Rosie-posie baby?' Emma asked, giving her a hug. 'Don't you want to watch some TV?'

'I don't want you to go away tomorrow,' Rosie replied in a choked voice. Rosie's problem was that she was only four, but looked at least six, so people always expected much more of her than she was capable of giving.

'But I'll be back the next day,' Emma said reassuringly. 'If you're a very good girl, I might bring you back something from London.'

'And me! And me!' chanted the boys. Rosie looked more cheerful.

'All of you,' Emma assured them. Something wistful tugged at her heart. Even though she knew she was on the verge of tackling the most important assignment of her career, she hated the thought of leaving the children behind.

Sir George let himself into the Holland Park Walk house, dreading having to tell Liza about his conversation with Malcolm Blackwell. She'd been showing signs of strain for the past few days that even she didn't seem aware of. She had a haunted look, and seemed to be a million miles away in a world of her own, where fear and doubt clouded her concentration, and a grim determination to remain strong and in control caused her to be unnaturally calm.

Sir George had seen these symptoms many times before in the army, when his men had been under stress; he knew if something wasn't done soon, Liza would have a nervous breakdown. He couldn't wait to get her down to Chalklands. The quietness of the countryside and lots of fresh air was what she needed. But first he had to tell her about the latest ransom note.

'Liza!' he called out. She came hurrying up from the kitchen, her face drawn, as if the skin had been stretched tightly over her cheekbones.

'What's happened? Did you see Malcolm Blackwell?'

He slipped his arm round her shoulder. 'Let's go and sit in the drawing room, and I'll tell you all about it,' he said soothingly.

'No!' She stood still, refusing to move. 'Tell me now. What is it?' Her eyes were beseeching and filled with pain. 'Tell me *now*,' she insisted.

Sir George sighed deeply. 'There's been another ransom note. They want fifty million pounds paid by bankers' draft to three Swiss banks, into numbered accounts, and they say they won't release Toby until the money's in those banks.'

Liza caught her breath. 'Fifty million . . . ! Oh my God, Lloyd's will never pay that much for his release.'

'Quite.' He spoke so low he was almost inaudible.

'Then . . . what happens?'

'He thinks they'll get the message and lower their sights.'

'Do you think they will? But even if they can't have fifty, they're going to want at least twenty or thirty million, aren't they?'

'Who knows? This has been a very well-planned operation. They mean business. The worry is that they may also be patient. We want Toby back, but they're obviously not in the same hurry as we are to settle the thing. They may, I'm afraid, be prepared to sit it out for weeks or even months, until they get what they want.'

'Oh-h-h!' Liza covered her face with her hands. 'I can't bear this, Daddy. I can't bear it. We've *got* to find a way of getting Toby home again. I suppose the note said nothing about Janet Granville?'

'Not a word. They won't be holding her for ransom, because there's no one who wants her back.' Sir George's voice was rough, as feelings of guilt swept over him.

Goddammit, he'd messed that one up, and now she, too, was no doubt living in fear and misery. In fact, he thought with growing horror, she was someone who was totally expendable. She only had a sister in New Zealand, who might not even have heard that Henry Granville had committed suicide. If Janet Granville became bothersome, she could be disposed of and no one would be the wiser.

Liza was watching him. 'What are you thinking about?'

'I wish to God we knew what sort of people we are dealing with,' he said. 'Are they common thugs? Hired assassins? Vengeful cranks? One thing is certain: I don't see how they can be a bunch of amateurs, because they're far too well organised.'

'We don't know how many are involved,' she pointed out. 'Maybe this is the work of one man? Or a small group?'

'I have a feeling there are quite a few people behind this, and I think Henry Granville was a small pawn in the game. Then he lost his nerve and became despairing.' His face suddenly looked alert, his dark eyes bright, as if he'd remembered something. Then he turned pale.

'What is it?' Liza questioned. She could always tell when something was wrong.

'We've only got the word of others that he committed suicide.'

'Yes?' Then her eyes widened too, appalled. 'You don't think . . . Oh, no! Surely not!'

Sir George nodded, wretchedly. 'It's a possibility he was murdered. Once he'd delivered Toby to them he'd be expendable, too, wouldn't he?'

'In which case,' Liza said slowly, 'Janet Granville may not just have been kidnapped, either.'

At dinner that night – a dreary, ritual affair only carried out because Helen Mortimer insisted they must all eat properly – Sir George was unusually quiet. While the others talked in a desultory fashion, he stared down at his plate, as if unaware there was anyone else in the room.

'Are you all right?' Liza asked him in a low voice. They were all concerned about Martin's health, and the strain he was under for a man of over seventy, but no one had given a thought to her own father, who was only three years younger.

As if he hadn't heard her, he laid down his knife and fork and turned to Martin.

'How do I get hold of a list of the Outside Names, especially those on the Hamcroft agency?' he asked.

At once Liza could see what he was getting at.

Martin looked up at Sir George, like a bleary-eyed old tortoise, his thin, stringy neck rearing out of his too-large white collar.

'I suppose you could ask Declan Connolly,' he replied, croakily. 'When I retired I left Toby in the position of members' agent, but it seems Charles Bryer saw fit to give the job to Declan.'

'Do you think he'd cooperate?' Sir George asked.

'It rather depends what you want it for.' Martin's reply was curt.

Liza and her mother exchanged covert glances, hoping the two men weren't going to engage in another argument.

Nina caught their glance and looked uncomfortable.

'I want to see the list because it strikes me that, if Henry Granville were on that list, his accomplices may be on it, too.'

'That will be like looking for the proverbial needle in a haystack,' Martin replied drily. 'What have you got to go on? With Mrs Granville out of the way, we don't even know who Henry Granville's friends were.'

'I'm aware of that,' Sir George said patiently. 'I still think it's worth a try. Something may ring a bell. I'm going to ask Première Cars where he lived before he lost everything, and was forced to move to that dreadful place in Barons Court. Maybe he had a neighbour who is on the Hamcroft syndicate and who is now involved.'

Martin looked flushed, his eyes blazing. 'Why do you keep supposing Toby's kidnappers have anything to do with the Hamcroft agency? Other syndicates have been hit just as hard as ours, you know. The people who are holding Toby for ransom could belong to a hundred other agencies!'

'I think,' Liza intervened, 'that it's only the Hamcroft agency which is being investigated by the chairman and the committee. Therefore I agree with Dad, that it's more likely the abductors were on the same agency as Henry Granville than any other.'

'Well, it's up to you, but you're wasting your time.'

'We must try everything,' Nina piped up in a small voice. 'The longer Toby is held hostage, the less likely we are to get him back.' She too, seemed to have aged years in the last few days. Her eyelids, scaly-looking with silvery blue eyeshadow, drooped sleepily.

'Surely that depends on the conditions he's being held in?' Helen Mortimer suggested. 'I can't believe anyone would be so uncivilised as to keep him locked up in some terrible place. What would be the point?'

'Security; so he can't escape,' Liza replied sombrely. 'Who knows where they've taken him? I hope to God they're not ill-treating him, but how can we be sure? The worst thing is he'll be so worried about *us*! If only we could get word to him somehow, that we're doing our best to find a way to get him freed.'

'We've got to get hold of that list from Declan,' Sir George said with renewed vigour.

'I suppose ...' Nina sounded tentative. The others looked at her. 'I suppose there's no way we can actually tell the police? Explain the position but say there must be a news blackout?'

'That's our very last resource, when everything else has failed,' said Sir George. 'At this stage, the kidnappers may think only Liza and I and Malcolm Blackwell are aware Toby has been abducted...'

'... They must be a very naïve bunch if they think we don't know,' Martin observed.

'Perhaps they're unaware you've come over from Spain,' Liza pointed out. 'Emma knows, but she's the soul of discretion. I'm praying she's going to be able to turn up something in the course of her research.'

'We've certainly got to do something very quickly. They're going to spin this whole business out until they get what they want, even, I fear, if it takes them months,' Sir George observed.

Liza shuddered, as if in physical pain.

'Therefore,' her father continued, 'we've got to get going; I don't think there's a minute to lose.'

Chapter Eleven

A nervous sense of pent-up energy pervaded the atmosphere the next morning. Liza was up first, making coffee, jotting down a list of arrangements to make for the coming weekend at Chalklands, wanting to talk to her father about contacting Declan. Her mother had awakened early too, and had started packing the clothes the children would need for the country. Then Martin and Nina appeared: he'd had a bad night and wondered if Liza had any aspirins. Soon Tilly and Thomas and Sarah were running around, still in their night-clothes, hunger and boredom causing them to be noisily excitable.

For a moment Liza wished they'd all shut up or go away: anything for a few minutes peace; anything to try and get her jangled thoughts in order and her confused state of mind quietened.

'Where's Daddy?' she asked her mother.

'Still in the shower,' Helen replied. 'Is there anything I can do for you, sweetheart? Shall I make a shopping list? The fridge is practically empty and so is the deep freeze.'

'Could you be an angel and stuff some breakfast cereal down the children's throats?'

'Of course.' Helen turned to her three grandchildren, who were jumping from sofa to chair around the drawing room, seeing if they could get round the room without touching the floor.

'Come on, my darlings! Time for breakfast! The first one to be sitting at the table gets a peach,' bribed Helen, in a falsely bright voice.

'I don't like peaches,' Thomas declared.

'Then you needn't have one,' she retorted, equally bright.

'Where on earth is Ingrid? She ought to be down by now,' Liza said in sudden irritation. This daily round of shopping and cooking, housework and chores was driving her crazy. Toby was out there, somewhere, incarcerated in God only knew what conditions, and her mother and mother-in-law were fussing about things like what they should have for lunch.

'Ingrid's asleep,' Tilly announced loftily as she pretended the sofa was a trampoline. 'Watch me, Tom! I bet you can't do this!' Then she hitched up her nightdress and, running into the hall, proceeded to do a handstand on the bottom step of the stairs. Her bare feet swayed dangerously near a large painting hanging on the staircase wall.

'Will you stop that!' Liza flared. 'It's dangerous. Go to the kitchen at once. Granny will very kindly give you breakfast, while I go and see what on earth Ingrid's doing.'

'It is only seven o'clock,' her mother pointed out mildly. 'It's all of us who are a bit early this morning, not Ingrid who is late.'

'Only seven . . . ?' Liza looked dismayed. 'Oh, God! This is going to be a long day.'

'Every day's a long day at the moment,' Helen replied with feeling. 'Come on, children.' She led them down the stairs to the kitchen in the basement. 'If you like I'll make you scrambled eggs!'

'I don't like scr—' Thomas began, but was silenced by a reproving look from Liza. 'Well, I suppose they're all right,' he added grudgingly.

Liza settled herself by the phone, her cup of strong black coffee beside her.

'Première Cars,' a man's voice announced when she got through. 'How can I help you?'

'This is Mrs Toby Hamcroft speaking. I don't want a car right now, but I wonder if you could give me some information regarding Henry Granville.'

'What is it you want to know? We're all very upset here that he took his own life. It's a terrible tragedy.' The telephonist had a chatty voice, and Liza's hopes rose. If she handled this call carefully, she reckoned she'd get the information she wanted.

'It is a tragedy,' Liza agreed. 'Can you tell me where he came from, originally? I have his Barons Court address, but I believe he lived in the country before he came back to work in London.'

'Just a moment, Mrs Hamcroft. We might have it.'

Liza could hear the soft tapping of the computer keyboard as the telephonist looked up Henry Granville.

'Here we are. The Moat House, Newbury, Berkshire. He and his wife left there some months ago, though. I think they sold it.'

Liza wrote down the address. 'Thanks very much.'

'Is there any news of your husband, Mrs Hamcroft? I haven't seen anything in the newspapers in the past couple of days. Does that mean he's home again?' The voice was pleasantly gossipy. Liza answered with care.

'He's not back yet,' she replied. 'Tell me, did Henry Granville often drive my husband about?'

The telephonist chuckled. 'It's funny you should ask. His first job with us was taking your husband to Gatwick, actually. He got a bit lost, never having done this sort of work before, and your husband was ever so kind. He told him how to get there, and suggested he buy himself a map, but in ever such a nice way. From then on, Henry Granville always asked if there were any jobs for Mr Hamcroft. It became quite a regular thing, especially on the Gatwick or Heathrow trips. He used to meet Mr Hamcroft with the car when he returned to England, too, and then bring him back to London.'

'Did he?' A cold tingle shot down Liza's spine. 'Was he booked to meet my husband on his return last time? On the Friday morning flight from New York?'

'Funny you should ask that,' the telephonist said again. 'Mr Hamcroft's secretary *had* booked the return pick-up, but Henry Granville called us after he'd dropped your husband off at Heathrow and said the booking had been cancelled. Mr Hamcroft had told him you'd be picking him up that morning, instead.'

'Oh, Christ,' Liza said softly to herself. Henry Granville had thought of everything, or else he'd been under meticulous instructions.

'What was that, Mrs Hamcroft?'

'Oh, nothing. Thank you for your help. I'm most grateful.'

As soon as she'd hung up, she dialled Declan's home number.

'Who ees that?' Maxine chirruped in her broken English.

'Liza Hamcroft. I'm dreadfully sorry to disturb you so early, but I wonder if I could have a word with Declan, please.'

'I get him. He ees still in the bath.'

Liza could imagine Maxine in high-heeled slippers and no doubt a satin and lace négligée, tottering through the over-furnished rooms of their house, an aura of Diorissima floating about her.

A moment later, and against the background of running water, Declan took her call on the bathroom phone.

'Morning, Liza. Any news of Toby?' he asked immediately.

'No, no news,' she replied, remembering just in time that he did not know Toby had been kidnapped.

'So, what's happening?'

'I'm just looking for clues,' she said truthfully, 'and I wonder if you could help me?'

'Sure. What can I do?' he replied. Then: 'Hang on a moment while I turn off the water.' There was a swishing sound. 'Yes, Liza. What is it?'

'Could you let me have a list of the names and addresses of all the Outside Names on the Hamcroft agency books? And also which syndicates they are on?'

There was a stunned silence. 'I don't think I can do that,' Declan said at length. 'What do you want it for?'

Liza thought frantically for a plausible explanation which would not give away the real reason.

'I hope there are some people on it who I know . . . and who might be able to tell me where Toby's gone,' she said, keeping as close to the truth as she dare.

'But this is confidential knowledge, Liza. We never reveal the names of our members, and certainly not which syndicates they're on. Surely you must know that? This is like asking a bank manager for his list of customers, and how much they have in their account.'

'Surely not, Declan.' Liza was so disappointed she felt crushed. 'Can't I at least have the list of members? That couldn't hurt.'

'I don't think so.' He sounded cagey. 'I can't see how it would help. A lot of them are yours and Toby's friends. Why don't you phone them direct, if you think they might know where he's gone?'

'But I don't know *which* of our friends has joined. I could be on the phone for days! Oh, come on, Declan. I'm terribly worried about Toby. Surely you could let me have the list? In confidence. So no one else would ever know,' she pleaded.

She heard Declan sigh noisily. 'I shouldn't really, Liza.'

'Just the names and addresses. I needn't know how much of an investment they've put up, or which syndicate they're on. I'd be eternally grateful, Declan.' She was begging now.

A great swishing woosh of water could be heard, as if Declan had risen and was climbing out of the bath.

'OK. I'll see what I can do. I'll try and organise a computer printout, although it won't be easy. When do you want it by?'

'Oh, as soon as possible. You've no idea how much this means to me, Declan.' Her voice broke with relief.

'I'll have it biked over to you later on today. Will that do?'

Liza longed to say: *Now! I can't wait!* But instead she controlled her voice.

'That would be wonderful. Thank you so much. I owe you one for this.'

'No probs, Liza!' He sounded more cheerful as he hung up.

As soon as Sir George appeared, in cavalry twill trousers and a dark blazer, although it was already a warm and sunny day, Liza told him what she'd done.

'If there's a member who lives near Newbury, I believe we'll be on our way to finding out who is behind this,' Liza said as she joined the rest of the family round the kitchen table.

'That list should prove fascinating reading,' Sir George observed. 'Pity he couldn't let you have a note of which syndicates they're all on, though.'

'I should damn well think he couldn't,' Martin Hamcroft snapped. 'He shouldn't even be giving you this list of Names.'

Sir George looked accusingly at him. 'I suppose you put the honour and reputation of Lloyd's before the safety of your son?' he demanded.

'There is such a thing as confidential information,' Martin replied scornfully. 'It is unethical to hand out the names and addresses, willy-nilly, of the members. I'm surprised Declan Connolly agreed.'

'Letting me see it is hardly handing it out willy-nilly,' Liza protested hotly. 'We're trying to secure the release of Toby – my husband and your son! I, for one, will go to any lengths, make use of any information I can lay my hands on, to get the information I need.'

Nina and Helen shifted uncomfortably in their seats, sensing a fight brewing.

'We're hardly talking classified information,' Sir George protested mildly. 'I don't know why you're objecting, Martin.'

Martin glared coldly at them, and for the first time Liza was seeing just how ruthless her father-in-law could be, beneath the charming exterior. It was no doubt that pitilessness and inflexibility that had enabled him to form one of the largest and most successful companies in Lloyd's but, from the bottom of her heart, Liza felt a sense of thankfulness that Toby was not like his father.

Liza felt a brief glow of pride in Toby. He was a man who cared passionately about what was right and what was wrong. He hadn't risked his friends' investments while making sure his own were safe. If Toby's code of ethics, she reflected, meant that they were to lose all their money, she would rather have it that way than if they remained rich, having cheated their friends.

Martin thumped the table. His face had turned puce and he spoke with barely controlled fury. 'I'm sick of everyone blaming Lloyd's for the trouble Toby's in! I spent all my working life in Lloyd's; I started the Hamcroft syndicate from nothing; everything I had went into making it a success, and it *has* been. I think Charles Bryer may have been a bit lax, but that's by the way. Lloyd's is a magnificent institution, world renowned, and I don't like the way everyone is knocking it now.' Martin turned to address Liza.

'It's provided a very nice standard of living for you and the children, hasn't it? You've nothing to grumble about,' he added.

Liza looked steadily back at him. 'I've never said a word against Lloyd's,' she replied calmly. 'And I'm very grateful for the wonderful life Toby has given me; no one is denying that, Martin.' There was a sharp edge to her voice now. 'All I want is for Toby to be set free. If, in doing that, we upset a few people, and unearth a few rotten elements, then that's just too damn bad.'

She rose from the table with dignity. In the last few

days, the pain she'd suffered had given her a mature confidence she'd never had before. It was as if something inside her was saying: *This is the worst thing that has happened to me ... But I'm still here surviving and keeping myself together*. That knowledge alone was giving her strength: she who had leaned on Toby for support for so many years; she who had looked to him to do everything he could to make her happy and to make their family life perfect. Now it was her turn to show that she, too, could be strong. She would hold this whole family together, somehow, until he returned. The time for tears and weakness was over. She was going to need every ounce of resolve and positive thinking to get herself and everyone else through this ordeal, and she would not let the petty squabbling with her father-in-law get her down.

'I'm going to phone Emma, to see if she's arrived in town,' she announced as she left the kitchen. Lottie, hoping she was being taken for a walk, ran ahead, wagging her tail joyously.

Before Liza could dial Emma's number, the phone rang and Freddy was on the line. He sounded distraught.

'She's left me, Liza! Gone back to her mother. Can you believe it?'

'What? Melissa's left you?' Stunned, Liza held the phone to her ear in disbelief. 'What do you mean?'

'Gone! Doesn't want to be poor. Couldn't face the idea of selling the house eventually. She walked out last night, after we'd had a fight.'

'Oh, for God's sake! I don't believe this. Are you sure this is not a form of prenatal blues, or something?'

'I don't know.' Freddy sounded lost and despondent. '*No*, I'm sure it's her mother, actually. I think she's trying to turn Melissa against me.'

'What are you going to do?' Liza asked. She'd always thought Melissa rather spoilt, although she'd never said so. 'I expect she'll soon be back, when she realises how silly she's being.'

'But what are we going to do, Liza? Nothing's going to alter the fact that we're going to be wiped out in the next two or three years. So are Mum and Dad, as far as Balnabreck is concerned. I don't mind for myself, but I feel terrible about the parents, and about Melissa, too. She expected such a comfortable life when she married me. I think she thought she'd end up having everything you have – you know, the lot – and of course she's terribly disappointed now. I think she's disappointed in me, too,' he added in a low voice.

'Then she's a bloody spoilt brat, who doesn't deserve someone like you,' Liza retorted with passion. 'Is that why she married you? To have the same lifestyle as Toby and me? Listen, Freddy. Money isn't what matters. I know that and, in your heart of hearts, so do you. All I want is Toby back. I don't care if we've lost everything! I don't care what happens as long as Toby is OK.'

'I know, sis. You two are so close you're sometimes like one person,' he said, almost wistfully.

'And you deserve better than this,' Liza continued.

'Let's give Melissa the benefit of the doubt for the moment. She's pregnant for the first time, she's probably feeling very vulnerable and frightened and disturbed, not that that's an excuse to behave in this way. But let her simmer for a while. I'm sure she'll come running back as soon as she realises what a fool she is.'

'But running back to what? A two-room flat in Balham?'

'Freddy, I'm sure you'll work something out. Would you like to come down to Chalklands with us for the weekend? I'd really like to see you.'

'Oh, Liza, here I am rattling on about my problems. Is there any news of Toby yet?'

'None, that's why I'd like to see you. To talk,' she spoke guardedly.

'Supposing Melissa comes back while I'm away?'

'That's why I think it's a good idea for you to come with us. *Not* finding you there might just give her the fright she needs.'

'Maybe.' He sounded doubtful.

'I can't really talk on the phone, Freddy, but I need to see you.' Liza had made up her mind to take her brother into her confidence. 'Leave a message to say where you are, if it makes you happier,' she added.

'Yeah. OK. Thanks. Shall we all go down together?'

'Why not? We'll take my car and yours, and between us we can fit in the others.'

Freddy sounded more cheerful. 'OK, sis. What do you want to talk to me about?'

'I'll tell you when I see you.'

* * *

Two hours later a courier came to the house with a big envelope addressed PERSONAL and PRIVATE, for Liza. She ripped it open, and out fell what she'd been waiting for, the list of outside names on the Hamcroft agency.

'It's arrived,' she called to her father, who was pottering in the garden.

Together they pored over it, scanning the names and particularly the addresses, in the hope of recognising someone who could be linked to Henry Granville.

'I know a lot of these people,' Liza remarked after a few minutes. 'I'm sure many of them were introduced to Lloyd's by Toby. God, I hope they haven't all lost their money.'

'But they're not the sort of people who would seek revenge in this way, are they?' Sir George asked.

'I wouldn't have thought so, but you can never tell.'

Suddenly her father went rigid, as he stared at one of the pages. He gave a sharp intake of breath.

'What is it, Daddy?'

'Bingo . . . in one, I think.' His voice was dangerously quiet.

'Who? What? Tell me?'

'First of all the address is Newbury.'

'And . . . ?'

'Colonel Raymond Mackenzie. Mallows Hall, Newbury, Berkshire,' he read aloud.

'Well . . . ?'

'I know him. He was in my regiment. I remember he joined Lloyd's when he came out of the army, in 1973.

I've lost touch, but there's nothing to stop me giving him a ring, is there? For old times' sake. I doubt if he knows you're married to Toby, so he wouldn't connect me with Toby's disappearance.'

'My God! Is there anyone else in the Newbury area, I wonder?' Liza scanned the lists again. 'Yes! Look! There's someone else listed here, a Brian Todd, living at Longacre Farm, Bonwell, near Newbury, Berkshire. I wonder if he's involved, too?'

Sir George's face was flushed with excitement.

'I have a feeling, Liza, that this could lead us to Toby. I'm going to call this chap, Mackenzie, right away.'

Across London, it was Question Time in the House of Commons, and Anthony sensed something was brewing. Tuesday and Thursday afternoons were always lively, with the Prime Minister jumping to his feet to answer the questions that flew in his direction like bullets from a gun. He was always prepared, though. Nothing was left to chance. His Parliamentary Private Secretary always presented him with the facts and figures he was going to require in answer to the list of questions presented to the Speaker earlier.

'What's going on?' Anthony leaned forward to ask a member of the Cabinet, as he took his seat on the front bench.

'The other side seems to have got hold of some rumour about Lloyd's,' the Minister of the Environment told him.

They both looked across the House at the Opposition,

some of whom were looking very pleased with themselves.

'Does the PM know?' Anthony asked, frowning.

'I think he knows something's up, but no one's sure what it is.'

Anthony knew, though. Emma had heard and had told him late last night, when he got back from his meeting. It was the sort of titbit that certain members of the Labour Party would love to throw at the Conservatives; a motion, no doubt, that had been conceived by some mischief-making newspaper editor, in the hope of setting the cat among the pigeons.

'I must get a message to the PM,' Anthony said with some urgency.

Two hours later, the Leader of the Opposition rose to his feet to face the Prime Minister. His 'question', although long, was to the point.

'Only this government,' he began, 'would allow an institution like Lloyd's of London to regulate itself. No less than three governors of the Bank of England have in past years sought to enforce regulations on that institution, only succeeding in 1983, when at last a council was formed. However—' here the Opposition Leader paused for dramatic effect – 'what else can one expect from an establishment that is governed by dynastic despots, and which, one might say, resembles an English aristocratic mafia rather than a respectable place of insurance?'

There were growls of anger and dissent from the government benches, and Anthony Turnbull mentally braced himself for the moment when the Leader of the Opposition closed in for the kill. He didn't have long to wait.

'It's a case of jobs for the boys. . . . yet again! There is corruption at every level . . . Funny, isn't it, that when the working classes lose money, it's down to their own recklessness; it's not up to the government to bail them out.'

Up to now, the Leader's manner had been light and bantering, if sarcastic. Everyone, on both sides of the House, was enjoying the usual comparisons between the Left and the Right. Then suddenly, Anthony knew they were about to be knifed in the back.

'But what happens,' roared the Leader of the Opposition, 'when one of those gentlemen on the opposite side of the House gets his fingers burnt and loses money, as fifty-one Members have so far done at Lloyd's? Do they pay up like the gentlemen they purport to be? Do they sell their houses? Hock their wives' jewellery? Get rid of their cars and their servants and their private doctors? No! No, they get the poor man in the street, trying to earn an honest living, to pay their losses! That's what they do!' His voice was drowned by cheering on his side of the House, and angry shouts from the government.

'The taxpayer is going to be asked to meet their losses! That's what is going to happen! Tell us, Prime Minister; are you going to allow these honourable gentlemen, who represent the Conservative Party, to sponge off the average working man so that they can continue to live in luxury? And not only to live in luxury, but to remain Members of this Parliament? Because we all know that, if they had to meet their losses, many would be rendered bankrupt! Then what would happen? *You'd be faced with dozens of by-elections! And the result would be that the Conservative Party would lose fifty-one seats, and we'd gain them!*'

'There was pandemonium,' Anthony said to Emma when he got back to their London flat that night. 'Thank God I'd got a message through to the PM before Question Time began, but I'm worried about this series you're writing on Lloyd's.'

Emma, who was whipping up an omelette for their late supper, stopped to look at him.

'What do you mean?'

'I wish you'd turned it down, Em.'

She looked stunned. 'But it's the biggest break I've had in my career,' she protested.

'Maybe, but you're no longer a full-time journalist now. It's only something you do on the side. You could easily refuse to do it, you know.'

'But I don't want to refuse it. I'm *dying* to do it, Ant. It's my big chance. You know I've always wanted to be a leading investigative journalist, and this gives me the perfect opportunity to show what I can do!'

Anthony looked at her stiffly, and there was an expression on his face she'd never seen before. 'But it might affect my career,' he said.

'*Your* career?' Her eyes were wide, confused and hurt-looking. 'So what happened to *my* career?'

'You got married and had children.'

'You got married and had children, too,' she retorted. 'Have you let that affect your career?'

'Don't be silly, Em. You know perfectly well what I mean. The wife of a Member of Parliament has to be supportive. Anyway, there are the children,' he added lamely.

Emma looked at him angrily. 'So you expect me to give up my career, just because I'm married to you?'

'I don't mind you doing odd freelance bits, here and there.'

'Oh, you don't? That's big of you, I must say! I'm allowed to do prissy little articles, as befits an MP's wife, but given the chance of a lifetime to show what I can really do, you want me to refuse? Say "in my position" I'm unable to accept the offer? Is that it?' She was simmering now, banging down the omelette pan on the hob unit with fury.

'Steady on, Em. There's no need to get in such a state. You have to realise that, as my wife, it's not a good idea for you to write about anything controversial. Especially if it's something I'm involved in.'

'If you're so perfect, why are you involved in something controversial in the first place?' she demanded. 'Hundreds of people are losing money, many in the most scandalous way as a result of corruption on a grand scale, but because you, and the government, are in the firing line, I'm supposed to keep quiet, and let this chance of turning out a first-rate feature pass me by?'

Her eyes blazed with tears of anger. Her disappointment in Anthony was huge. She'd expected him to be proud of her achievement; when the children were older she had planned to join a newspaper as a regular feature writer. Was this argument going to happen every time she wrote anything that might embarrass him as a Member of Parliament?

'The Prime Minister doesn't need to be stabbed in the back by his own party or their families,' Anthony pointed out coldly. 'This Lloyd's business was a great embarrassment to him today. If, as the Opposition said, people like myself go bankrupt, it will be devastating for the Conservative Party. We want to keep the whole Lloyd's business as low-key as we can. We have enough problems without that as well.'

Emma looked at him long and hard, and suddenly she no longer liked what she saw. 'So you'll let the government, which means the taxpayer, which means the ordinary man in the street, pay your losses for you, so you can keep your cushy job as an MP?' she asked.

Anthony flushed angrily. 'You're deliberately misunderstanding me!' he retorted.

'I don't think I am, Anthony. I think I've got the picture loud and clear. All that remains to be seen is how you deal with your own conscience. Meanwhile, if you'll excuse me, I'm going to go over my research notes, in readiness for an editorial meeting tomorrow. Your omelette's there.'

She pointed at the hob, turned, and without a backward glance, walked out of the kitchen, her head held high. Not for a moment was she going to let Anthony see how hurt and upset she was.

Lady Rosemary lay flat on her back, gazing up at the heavy brocade hangings on the four-poster bed. Beside her, Sir Humphrey, propped on one elbow, read with slow interest an article about hunting in *Horse and Hound*. Tears trickled silently from her eyes on to the pillow, but it wasn't until a small sob escaped her parted lips that her husband realised anything was wrong. In consternation he rolled over towards her and looked anxiously into her face.

'What's up, old gel?' he asked in alarm. It wasn't like her to cry. In fact, he couldn't remember when it had last happened.

Lady Rosemary made an effort to control her emotions. Her mouth struggled to form a watery smile. 'It's . . . it's just that the die has been cast, after all these years. Now we've finally put this place up for auction, I feel . . .' She paused. She didn't have words to describe the terrible emptiness and misery she felt. It was like losing someone you love; it was like being cut in half, uprooted, combined with a feeling of failure that after three hundred years, it was she who was having to relinquish the home of her forebears. Cavenham Court had been entrusted to each generation in turn to look after and preserve, ready to be handed on to the next generation, but now it would never be inherited by her son or a grandson. The hammer, as it struck the auctioneer's podium, would be like a blow to her heart, and each time it struck again for the contents, which would add up to hundreds of lots, her heart would be smashed into smaller and smaller pieces.

'I know it's a great shame,' Sir Humphrey said sympathetically. He patted her shoulder. He was not very good with words.

'I didn't think I'd mind so terribly,' she said, twisting the lace edge of the sheet with her hands. 'I'd made up my mind that I was going to be brave but ... Oh! Humphrey! It's going to be awful, isn't it? Not living here any more.'

'The dogs are going to miss it, too.' His tone was sad.

She reached for his hand and held it tightly. 'We'll just have to stick together, won't we. And find a flat near a park, so you can take the dogs there.'

They lay in silence for a few minutes, each trying to imagine what it was going to be like without Cavenham Court to come to each weekend, and at Christmas. Lady Rosemary's throat contracted painfully again when she remembered past Christmases.

'It's my fault, isn't it?' Sir Humphrey said at last. 'All I can say is that I'm dreadfully sorry. I wish I'd been born clever, for your sake, if not my own. Then none of this would have happened.'

She held his hand tightly. 'At least we've got each other,' she said, rather to her own surprise. The money worries seemed to have brought them closer and when it came down to it, she told herself, people were more important than possessions.

* * *

'Mackenzie? My old fellow! Mortimer here; George Mortimer.'

'I'll be damned!' There was rich laughter on the line.

The two senior officers, who had not seen each other for twenty-five years, talked as if it had only been a few months.

'How's life?' Sir George asked.

The laughter died and Colonel Raymond Mackenzie spoke sombrely. 'We've hit a spot of trouble. Things are not too good.'

'Nothing serious I hope, old chap?'

'I'm having to sell the house. We've lost a packet at Lloyd's. Nearly wiped us out.'

'My God, that's a bad show.' Sir George pretended to sound surprised. 'I am sorry to hear that. What are you going to do about it?'

There was a pause before Mackenzie continued. 'We might go and live in Canada. I have a brother in Toronto who owns a timber business. Maybe he can give me a job if all else fails.'

'My dear fellow! You're in good company though, aren't you? From what I've been reading in the newspapers, hundreds of people have lost their money,' Sir George remarked.

'Oh, I'm not alone; I know that. I don't mind so much for myself, but my wife Kitty has been hit very hard by it all. Hates the idea of leaving Mallows Hall, too. It's a beautiful place.'

As if I didn't know, Sir George reflected silently. *I love Balnabreck, too.*

'What a shame,' he said aloud. Then, very gently, he began, 'I read in the papers about that chap who committed suicide. Did you see it? Grenville or Granville or something? Lived near you; that's why I remember it. Terrible tragedy.'

'Ummm.' Mackenzie's response was noncommittal.

'Ever come across him?' Sir George asked casually.

'No.' The response was too quick and too curt.

'Oh well. Keep your pecker up, old chap. The reason I was ringing is, I've got to go to Newbury on Friday, to pick up something from an antique shop, and I wondered if we could meet for a snifter? I hardly ever come down from Scotland these days, but when I do, it's nice to catch up with old chums.'

Mackenzie agreed, and they arranged to meet at a pub in a village on the outskirts of the town. It would mean hiring a self-drive car for the weekend, because he couldn't travel now with either Liza or Freddy, in case Mackenzie put two and two together, but no matter. He suddenly felt the *frisson* of anticipation he'd felt when he was in Intelligence and about to crack a case. It would be nice seeing old Mackenzie again; it would be even nicer if it led to discovering where Toby was.

It was only a small item on the third page of the *Globe*, but when Liza saw it she knew time was running out for Toby.

WIDOW OF LLOYD'S SUICIDE MAN VANISHES, ran the headline.

In smaller print it continued: 'Mrs Janet Granville has vanished from a boarding house in Barons Court, after leaving in a distressed state with two men. Her landlady Marion Peterson reported her missing when she failed to return that evening. Janet, who is fifty-two, was recently widowed when her husband Henry, fifty-nine, committed suicide. It is thought he became depressed after the couple lost all their money in the Lloyd's crash.'

That was all, but it was enough. Now it was only a matter of time before the police and the press linked the two disappearances together.

In a fever of anxiety, she put through a call to the chairman of Lloyd's. To her relief he was in his office.

'There's nothing more I can tell you,' Malcolm Blackwell said immediately, pre-empting the question he knew she would ask. 'There have been no further developments.'

'Have you seen page three of the *Globe*?' Liza asked.

'Yes,' he replied tersely. 'There's nothing we can do.'

'I'm going to the country for the weekend; have you got our number there?'

'Let me take it, anyway.'

Liza gave him the phone and the fax numbers. 'Are you staying in town?'

'Yes,' he said again. 'I'll be in touch if I have any news.'

'Thanks.' Liza hung up, feeling more frustrated than ever. Malcolm Blackwell seemed so negative. He seemed to be sitting and waiting for something to happen, with as much nonchalance as if he were waiting to hear the result of the test match. Why couldn't someone *do* something? she raged inwardly.

She rang Emma. Her friend sounded charged with energy.

'I'm working like mad on the feature,' she said, 'and I have a favour to ask.'

'What is it, Em?'

'Can I come over to Chalklands on Saturday afternoon, to interview your father-in-law about Lloyd's as it was in his day, and can I bring the children with me? They can play in the garden with your lot, can't they? Would that be all right?'

'Of course.' Liza sounded surprised. 'Do you really want to do it over the weekend, though? Wouldn't you rather come here? As you're in London, in any case, surely it would be easier?'

'No. Anthony and I have had a bust-up; we're not speaking. I thought I'd like to get out of the house on Saturday, as the weekend's going to be hell if we're both at home together.'

'Oh, Em! I'm sorry. You don't sound upset, though. What's happened? It's unlike you and Anthony to fight.'

'It's all too boring, Liza. He's being an arsehole! Wants me to turn down this feature, because he's afraid it might be embarrassing to him as an MP. He seems to think I should drop the whole thing because it might have an adverse effect on his career. What about *my* career?'

'Oh, Em . . . He has got a point, though, hasn't he?'

'Don't tell me you're taking his side? Why should a man's career be more important than a woman's?' she demanded. 'It's the most outrageous thing I've ever heard.'

'Well, anyway . . .' Liza didn't want to argue; she had more important things on her mind. 'Come over Saturday afternoon. The children will be thrilled when I tell them you're bringing yours over. Oh! and by the way . . . Have a look at page three of the *Globe*. It's not going to help.'

After she'd hung up, Liza picked up the newspaper and read the item again. Once more she felt a deep temptation to phone the police and tell them the truth about Toby's disappearance, and Janet Granville's, too. Surely they could be trusted to handle the situation in the best possible way? Surely that was better than leaving things to Malcolm Blackwell, who seemed to be letting the kidnappers call the shots?

Chapter Twelve

Liza led the way to Chalklands in her Mercedes, with Freddy following in his car. With him was his mother, Tilly and Thomas, and Ingrid, who had offered to work over the weekend. Liza took her in-laws and Sarah. They had decided to leave London in the early afternoon to avoid the mass exodus from the city on Friday evening. Sir George had already left in a rented car, to meet Colonel Mackenzie at the White Swan near Newbury.

'It seems like an age since we were at Chalklands,' Liza observed as she headed out of London on the M4. If the traffic was light, they'd get to the village of Kingsclere, on the Hampshire–Berkshire border, in an hour and a half.

'It's three weeks, in fact, because the children and I stayed with Emma when Toby was away . . . I mean, while I *thought* he was away.'

At times she experienced a total sense of unreality, as if nothing around her had any substance, and at any moment she'd wake up to find she'd been having a nightmare. Then harsh truths would assail her and, like a fresh blow to her senses, she'd realise that she might never see Toby again.

'I'm sure he'll be back before long,' Nina said comfortingly from the back seat, where she was showing a picture-book to Sarah. 'You never know, George may get some useful information out of this old army pal he's meeting.'

Martin, sitting in the front with Lottie on his knee, her nose snuggled under his elbow, said nothing. He'd been quiet all day.

'Are you all right?' Liza asked, glancing at his profile. 'Shall we put Lottie in the back? She weighs a ton.'

Martin stroked the deep amber-coloured silk ears and shook his head. 'No, I like her here. She keeps my legs warm.'

They arrived at Chalklands, a rambling, grey-stone, two-storeyed house, shortly before four o'clock. Liza clambered out of the car and looked appreciatively at the old tiled roof, the white-shuttered french windows leading on to the terrace, the climbing roses and clematis and jasmine that covered the walls in a clambering, tumbling mass, and she was glad they had come here for the weekend.

Freddy drew up behind and the children jumped out, to be greeted with hysterical joy by Lottie, as if she hadn't seen them for weeks. Then there was Bert and Margaret, hurrying from the back door, Bert taking their cases up to their rooms, Margaret telling them tea was ready.

'How is everything?' Liza asked, surveying the smooth camomile lawns and trimmed box hedges, the profusion of flowers in the herbaceous borders, and the white cane table and chairs set out invitingly under the old Victoria plum tree.

Liza remembered the first time she'd seen this garden, and how enchanted she had been by it. But was that enchantment real? she asked herself as she walked across the York-stone terrace to the lawn. Or was it because I was younger then, and untouched by sorrow, and the world seemed such a magical place to my innocent eyes?

'George should be here soon,' Helen observed, sitting on one of the garden seats and slipping off her sandals, so she could feel the cool lawn beneath her bare feet.

She was joined by Nina, and then, walking slowly, Martin. Liza and Freddy walked with him, while Lottie and the children rushed over to the swings and slides and sandpit at the far end of the garden.

Freddy dropped into a chair. 'Does Dad know Melissa's left me?' he asked Liza tentatively.

'We haven't told him,' she said. 'That's up to you, Freddy. Frankly, I think she'll come running back, anyway.'

'I'm not so sure. What have I got to offer her now?'

Helen looked at him severely. 'What you had to offer her at the beginning, and what you'll have to offer her at the end: yourself.'

'And she's very lucky to have you,' Liza added firmly.

Freddy smiled ruefully. 'You all think so because you're family. I doubt if Melissa shares your feelings now.'

'In that case she doesn't deserve you,' said his mother.

'How pretty this all is, dear,' Nina said, looking around her appreciatively. 'It's years since Martin and I visited you here.' She glanced beyond the gardens to the fields and hills beyond, green and lush in the soft English sunshine, with only a rippling breeze to cool the air.

'It almost makes one want to live in England again, doesn't it?' she remarked wistfully.

'No, it doesn't,' Martin replied with feeling. 'England's damp and cold and grey.'

'But the sun and the heat are so *unrelenting* in Spain,' Nina complained. 'It's a cruel, harsh sun. The nicest time is in the evening, when the light mellows, and then you get those gloriously balmy nights.'

'Ah! Here's tea,' Liza exclaimed, glad of a distraction. Nina and Martin had been disagreeing about the difference in the two countries all week, and it was getting tedious.

Margaret set the tray on the table, smiling as Tilly and Thomas crowded round to see what there was to eat.

They heard a car coming up the drive, and saw it was Sir George. Liza waved and hurried over to greet him.

'How did it go, Daddy?' she asked, looking up anxiously into his face.

He shrugged. 'It was a bit disappointing. Mackenzie was full of all the trouble he's had with Lloyd's: his losses, having to sell his house, trying to find himself a job – but not much else.'

'Do you think he's got anything to do with Toby's kidnap?'

'Yes. Without a doubt.'

Liza's eyes widened. 'You really think so?'

'I'm sure of it. When I started questioning him about the ins and outs of his losses, which syndicates he was on and all that, he became cagey and ill at ease. Then I mentioned Toby.'

'What?' Liza looked aghast.

'Oh, very much in passing,' her father replied. 'I remarked about the story in the newspapers of a Lloyd's broker vanishing. I didn't mention Toby by name, just that I'd read something about this broker who'd disappeared. Mackenzie pretended not to have heard anything about it. Seeing it was front-page news for several days, and on television, I fail to see how he could have missed it. He was lying all right. I know all the signs from interrogating people in the army. Just how much he knows, though, I can't be sure.'

'What do we do now?'

'I dropped in to see the man who lives at Bonwell. Remember him on the list? At Longacre Farm? It's about three miles north of Newbury. His name is Brian Todd. He's a farmer.'

'What did you say to him? You don't know him, do you?'

Sir George chuckled. 'No. I snooped around for a bit, and then I knocked on the door and said I was lost. I'd taken the map with me, and I said I was looking for Mallows Hall, Newbury, and could he direct me.'

'Colonel Mackenzie's address?'

'Exactly. This chap, Brian Todd, gave me a very funny look and said he'd never heard of it, but I don't believe him. I bet anything he and Raymond Mackenzie are involved in Toby's abduction. And we all know Henry Granville was part of the operation. What we now have to do is try and prove it.'

Liza felt a mixture of elation and despondency. It was one thing guessing who Toby's abductors might be, but another finding out where they were hiding him.

Sir George told the others what had happened as he had his tea under the plum tree. Freddy, who'd been told the truth about Toby's disappearance by Liza, listened intently.

'Dad, why don't we get someone to bug both your army friend and this Brian Todd? If they're really involved, we're bound to find out what's going on. Can't you get some of your MI5 chums in on this?'

'I still think we should call the police,' Martin said heatedly. 'They're obviously a bunch of cranks and, apart from holding Toby illegally, they're about to destroy the reputation of Lloyd's at this rate.'

Liza stiffened. She was getting heartily sick of Martin's protective obsession with Lloyd's.

'We may be able to solve this without any help from the police,' Sir George said. There was something mysterious in the way he spoke.

'How?' Helen asked, intrigued.

There was a mischievous twinkle in her husband's eye. 'After we'd had drinks at the White Swan, I said to Mackenzie that I'd like to see his house before it was sold. I said my son was thinking of moving out of London, and was quite interested in living in Berkshire.'

Freddy paused in helping himself to a piece of Black Forest cake, one of Margaret's specialities. 'He must have thought I was rolling in money.'

'He made a joke about *our* family obviously not being involved in Lloyd's, if my son was in a position to consider a house in the three-quarters-of-a-million-pound bracket, and I made no comment.'

'I wish,' Freddy said fervently, his mouth rimmed with chocolate.

'So,' his father continued, 'we drove to Mallows Hall. Pretty impressive it is, too. Seventeenth-century, and in beautiful condition. I envy the person who can afford to buy it.'

'Do get to the point, George,' Helen said in exasperation. 'What has your going to see Mallows Hall got to do with our not needing the help of the police?'

'I bugged the house.'

The others stared at him with a mixture of shock and amazement.

'You . . . ?' Liza's eyes blazed with excitement. 'Oh, my God! That's wonderful!'

'How did you do that without him noticing?' Martin asked.

'It's the easiest thing in the world these days. The mikes are so tiny you'd never notice them. Whilst he was putting on the kettle for a cup of tea, I fixed one by the phone on his desk, one in the hall on my way to the loo, and one in the kitchen, when I was kind enough to insist on washing up my cup and saucer before I left.' Sir George chuckled softly. 'I was glad to find I hadn't lost my touch!'

Freddy looked doubtful. 'But how are we going to pick it up? You need receivers and all that sort of thing, don't you?'

Sir George rose from his seat and gazed across the lawn to the house. It stood serene and gracious against a clear blue sky, surrounded by the beautifully tended garden.

'Can I set up everything in one of the bedrooms, Liza?' he asked. 'I brought all the equipment I might need and, as we're not far from Newbury, we should get excellent reception here.'

Nina gasped, while Helen looked quietly proud of her husband.

'You'll be able to listen in to what's going on at your friend's house?' Nina asked, her voice shocked.

Sir George smiled. 'I'm going to enjoy myself. It's a long time since I did any of this, but at least I still have my contacts, so I was able to borrow all the latest equipment necessary for this type of operation before I left London today.'

Liza looked at him with shining eyes. It was the first time for days that she'd felt they were really getting somewhere.

'Thank you, Daddy,' she said gratefully. 'I think you're brilliant.'

'It's pure luck that I happened to know Mackenzie. I wish I'd been able to plant a device at Longacre Farm, but I didn't have the chance.'

'Can I help you listen in, Dad?' Freddy asked with a boyish smile.

'Of course. If we're going to keep a watch around the clock, we'll all need to take it in turns to listen in. I think I'll go and get everything set up now,' he added.

'I'll help,' Freddy offered.

'Why don't you use the little blue bedroom at the end of the corridor?' Liza suggested. 'It's the far end of the house from the children, so you shouldn't be disturbed, and no one's sleeping in there this weekend.'

Father and son went off to unload the equipment from the boot, leaving the others to speculate on the possibility of hearing something of significance.

'I think I'll go into the house, too,' Martin remarked after a while, rising slowly.

'Are you all right, dear?' Nina asked, looking at him in concern. His face had a pinched look and it was obvious he was tired.

'I'm fine, but it's getting chilly out here,' he replied.

Liza and her mother exchanged looks. The temperature was in the eighties, and Liza was about to suggest to Ingrid that she put the children into bathing suits so that they could have a swim in the deliciously cool-looking pool, set to one side of the terrace.

'He does so feel the cold,' Nina remarked in a worried voice, as Martin walked slowly towards the house.

The phone rang just as they were going to have dinner. Sir George and Freddy had been sitting by the receivers all evening, and had decided to take it in turns to eat in the dining room with the family.

Margaret, answering it in the kitchen, told Liza it was for her brother.

'I'll get him,' Liza said quickly. She'd told Margaret that her father and brother had business to discuss, and were not to be disturbed, and so she ran upstairs and tapped on the door of the blue bedroom, which they'd also taken the precaution of locking. Freddy came to the door.

'What's up, sis?'

'There's a call for you. Why don't you take it in my room?' Liza indicated a door halfway down the corridor, that led into a spacious bedroom where a king-size bed was festooned in white muslin. A white carpet, several beautiful pieces of furniture, chintz curtains and a *chaise-longue* created an elegant, luxurious room.

'OK. Thanks. Is it Melissa?' he asked hopefully.

'Margaret didn't say.'

While Freddy shot into her bedroom, Liza went over to her father, who was wearing earphones and was surrounded by some complicated-looking electronic equipment.

'Any luck?' she whispered.

Sir George took off the earphones and grinned.

'Why are you whispering? Mackenzie can't hear *us*.'

Liza smiled back. 'I forgot! Are you picking up anything?'

'Everything,' he replied succinctly. 'He's alone in the house, but he's been talking to the cat, who incidentally purrs like a machine-gun; he's clanked around the kitchen, and uttered a few four-letter oaths when I gather he burnt himself on the oven, and he's been to the loo twice.'

Liza eyed the equipment with astonishment. 'You can hear all *that*?'

Her father nodded. 'And he's received no phone calls so far. That's what I'm really waiting for.'

'Oh, my God, supposing he's careful what he says on the phone?' Her momentary elation swiftly abated.

'There's a chance that will happen, and we mustn't be disappointed if it does. I still think we'll pick up something useful, though.'

'Maybe he'll have visitors? Someone else who is involved?' she suggested.

At that moment the bedroom door flew open, and Freddy was standing there, looking pale and distraught.

'It's Melissa!' he said breathlessly.

'What's happened?' Liza rushed over to him. 'Is she all right?'

'She's gone into labour! The baby's not due for eight weeks . . . ! Oh my God!' His voice broke on a sob. 'I've got to go to her.'

'Where is she?'

'Queen Charlotte's Hospital. Her mother's with her. I'll drive up to London now.'

'Do you want me to come with you?' Liza asked anxiously.

'Thanks, sis, but it's all right.' Freddy turned and ran along the corridor and they could hear him leaping down the stairs.

At midnight, Sir George turned off the radio receivers and went to bed.

'Mackenzie has turned in for the night, so there's no point in listening for anything to happen for the next few hours,' he explained to Liza.

She looked at him with tender concern. 'You must be exhausted, Dad.'

'I'm OK.' He looked tired though, and his smile was weary. 'Your mum's gone to bed, has she?'

'Yes. She and Nina and Martin went about an hour ago. The children, of course, have been out for the count for hours, thank God.'

Sir George leaned forward to kiss her cheek. 'You must get some sleep, too, my darling girl. Let's hope Freddy doesn't wake us all up in the middle of the night to inform us that Melissa's given birth. I don't think I could stand it,' he added with mocking amusement. 'Freddy a father, eh? Let's hope they sort out their problems.'

Liza flung her arms around her father as she'd done when she was a little girl. 'Oh, I love you, Daddy. And thank you for all you're doing to help get Toby back. You know how grateful I am, don't you?' She gazed earnestly into his face. 'And when all this is over, we'll stick by each other, even if Balnabreck has to be sold. Maybe Toby will buy it for you? I know he'll make sure you and Mum don't suffer because of Lloyd's.'

'Sweet girl,' Sir George replied huskily, patting her back. 'All your mother and I want is to see Toby home with you again. After that, the future can look after itself.'

It was a cold grey dawn when the phone beside Liza's bed rang, piercing the fragile sleep she had finally succumbed to. She reached out and grabbed the receiver.

'Hello?' She was sure it would be Freddy – jubilant, a father, and reconciled with Melissa. 'Is that you, Freddy?' she asked eagerly.

A woman spoke. At the sound of her voice, vaguely familiar at first, and then clearly recognisable, Liza sat upright, her body straining to hear, to take in, to remember every word the woman uttered. What she had to say was vital.

It was Janet Granville.

The cat's-eyes down the centre of the road blinked

hypnotically as Freddy put his foot down hard on the accelerator, and the miles slipped past in the enclosing darkness. From time to time he looked at the digital clock on the dashboard, and wondered how long it took for a baby to arrive. He was nearing the outskirts of London now; another twenty minutes and he'd be at the hospital. He blinked nervously, cursing himself for not being at Melissa's side at a moment like this. He should never have gone away, never left London, he reflected. From the beginning he'd promised Melissa he'd stay with her when the baby was born, and now he felt he'd let her down. Consumed by guilt, and with his heart beating fast, he swung the car into the drive of Queen Charlotte's, and parked it in the first available space he came to. Melissa's mother had told him the name of the ward she was in. Frenziedly he ran up and down between the tall, institutional red-brick blocks, looking for signs. At last he saw it: MILFORD. With a bound he pushed his way in through the double swing-doors. At a desk in the lobby a black, uniformed receptionist looked up at him enquiringly.

'Mrs Mortimer. . .!' he gasped breathlessly. 'Mrs Melissa Mortimer. She's having a baby. Right now.'

'They're all having babies in here,' she commented drily in an attractive Southern drawl. She tapped the computer on the desk in front of her lethargically. Freddy, watching her, felt like screaming with impatience. At last she looked up at him.

'Third floor. D3.'

'Thanks.' He ran towards the stairs, mounting them

two at a time. 'D3 ... D3,' he kept repeating under his breath as he arrived on the third floor.

He nearly collided with a senior nurse as he rounded the corner of a corridor. Just in time he stopped.

'I'm sorry ... I'm looking for my wife ...'

'Are you Mr Mortimer?' she asked, suddenly looking at him with curiously compassionate eyes. His heart skipped a beat.

'Yes. My wife's having a baby. Can I go to her?'

'Would you like to come this way, Mr Mortimer.' She turned, all crisp white starchiness and efficiency. But something in her manner made him acutely uneasy.

'My wife's all right, isn't she?'

The nurse glanced back briefly over her shoulder at him. 'Your wife's fine.' Something in her tone forbade him to ask any more questions. A moment later she had shown him into a small square room with a bench-seat along one wall, two wooden chairs and a small wooden table in the centre.

Freddy looked round, bewildered. 'Where ...?' he began.

'Why don't you sit down, Mr Mortimer. The doctor will be along in a minute. Can I get you a cup of tea?'

Freddy's confusion increased. 'I want to see my wife. I promised her I'd be there when the baby was born, but I had to go to the country and I've just driven up ...' He realised he was babbling hopelessly.

'You can see your wife presently.' Her smile was kind. 'Do you take milk and sugar?'

He could see she was not going to tell him anything. 'Just milk, please.'

He sank on to the fake-leather-covered bench and closed his eyes for a moment, trying to regain some measure of control. For some reason he felt afraid, and he wished now that Liza was with him.

A figure passing the open door caught his eye. It was Melissa's mother, but she passed along the corridor and did not see him. He jumped to his feet and was just about to follow her, to call her name, when a white-coated doctor stood before him.

'Mr Mortimer?' he asked.

Freddy started to tremble inside. 'Has my wife had the baby yet?'

The doctor nodded, but he wasn't smiling. 'Your wife is fine,' he said, stressing the word *fine*. 'She gave birth to a son an hour ago, but I'm very sorry to have to tell you that the baby died within a few minutes. We did everything we could, but I'm afraid he was very premature, and he didn't make it. I'm so sorry, Mr Mortimer.'

Freddy stared at him blankly, feeling his life crumbling, falling apart, demolished. The doctor looked at him with the same expression of compassion as the nurse.

'It's a great shock for you, I know,' he continued gently, 'but there is no reason why your wife shouldn't have as many children as you both want. We'll do tests, of course, but her physical condition seems excellent. Would you like to see her now?'

Dumbly, Freddy nodded. What was he going to say to

Melissa? They'd both been looking forward to the baby so much; they'd bought clothes and a bassinet, and turned the spare room into a nursery. He felt a sob rise from his chest, nearly choking him. What *was* he going to say?

Melissa was propped up against the pillows, her dark hair spread over her shoulders. In her white face her eyes looked like two smudges of charcoal, her mouth a swollen slit of pain.

Freddy went to the side of the bed and looked down at her. 'I'm sorry, sweetheart,' he said huskily, reaching for her hand. 'Are you all right?'

She nodded silently, not looking at him.

He leaned forward to kiss her. 'There'll be other babies.'

'Not for us.' Melissa turned her face away and started crying bitterly.

'But the doctor said . . .'

'I've left you. Don't you understand? It's over . . .' Sobs choked her and she pressed her hand to her mouth.

'But *why*? Surely not because . . .'

'It's no use, Freddy. We're finished.'

Blinded by his own tears, Freddy stumbled from the room, charging along the corridor like a wounded animal in flight. As he turned to go back down the stairs, he bumped into Melissa's mother.

For a moment they stood looking at each other, then he saw the steely determination on her face.

'Don't come back, Freddy,' she said. 'You must realise, Melissa doesn't want to see you again.'

Chapter Thirteen

'Janet Granville?' Liza repeated the name, sitting up in bed, tinglingly alert. 'My God! Where are you?'

'I'm in a call-box.' The voice was hoarse and whispery. 'Your husband's being held in a disused petrol station in Cornwall. Near Fowey, on the road from Polgarth ... But don't tell the police. Don't tell anyone.'

'But ...' There were a million things Liza wanted to ask, but she felt stupefied, her mind spinning. It was like receiving a message from someone who had died. In shock she gripped the receiver tightly, lost for words.

'I must go. I'm running out of money.' Janet Granville sounded agitated. A moment later there was a series of sharp peeps, and Liza knew they'd been cut off.

Grabbing her dressing-gown, she rushed along the corridor and tapped on her parents' door.

'Mum? Dad? Can I come in?'

Sir George and Helen sat up sleepily, then looked anxiously at Liza.

'What is it, darling?' Helen demanded in a scared voice.

'I've just heard from Janet Granville!' she blurted out. 'She's told me where Toby is.'

'Dear God!' Sir George swung his legs over the side of the bed and sat upright, rubbing his eyes with his hands.

'Toby's being held in a disused petrol station near Fowey.'

'In Cornwall?' Helen exclaimed.

'What did Janet Granville actually say?' Sir George asked urgently. 'Where is she?'

'I don't know, Daddy. She was calling from a phone-box. We only had a few seconds because she ran out of money. That's all she told me.'

He reached for dressing-gown and slippers. 'Do you think she'll ring again?'

'I don't know. She sounded frightened.' Liza paused as if she'd just thought of something. 'I wonder how she got this number?'

'You're not ex-directory, are you?'

'No, that's true.'

'Exactly. This house was mentioned in all the news-papers when Toby vanished. She'd get your number from directory enquiries in seconds.'

'Oh, I wish she'd made a reverse-charge call. Then I could have asked her more about Toby,' Liza fretted.

Sir George walked purposefully to the bedroom door.

'Where are you going, dear?' his wife asked.

'I want to start monitoring MacKenzie's place again.

Toby's abductors are going to get very edgy now that Janet's escaped. They'll be more afraid than ever that she'll talk.'

'Now that we know where Toby is, we can get moving,' Liza pointed out, following him down the corridor.

'Let's hope it's not a trap,' he said grimly.

Liza looked at him, startled. 'What do you mean?'

'They may have put her up to this. Got her to phone you to tell you where Toby is.'

'Why would they do that?'

'Maybe they'd like you and me out of the way, too, for a while. Allow them time to strike a deal with Lloyd's, without our interference. Have you thought of that?'

'You think they realise we know what's going on?' Liza asked.

'Malcolm Blackwell is bound to have told you, isn't he? I can't imagine they think he wouldn't. Then we call on Janet Granville, and the next thing is that she's been taken, too. I think they're running scared, and it's going to get worse. They're obviously very determined.'

'What are we going to do?' Hope of rescuing Toby was diminishing the more she thought about it. For one bright, wonderful moment she'd thought they would only have to drive down to Cornwall and, having located the disused petrol station, mount a rescue operation. What a naïve, childish notion!

Sir George unlocked the spare-room door and she followed him in.

'Let's see if there's any joy from MacKenzie, before we make plans.' He seated himself at the table where he'd set up the equipment, and put on the headphones. 'If Janet Granville really has escaped in the night, you can bet the telephone lines are going to be hot.'

While he switched on the power and adjusted the control buttons, Liza went to open the curtains. A rosy, misty dawn was breaking in the east, melting the darkness away, revealing the glistening dew on the camomile lawn. Another day was beginning, and it would be another day without Toby. Would he be seeing this sun rising too, somewhere far to the west in Cornwall? Or was he locked in some dark place where the sun never shone? She ached with a longing that felt like a pain in her chest as she wondered how she was going to get through another day without him. And maybe another week? Or even several months? It was then that she knew what she must do. There was no other way. If Janet Granville had been forced to set a trap, no matter; she would not heed it.

'I'm just going to get dressed,' she said quietly as she left the room. Her father hardly noticed her departure, so engrossed was he in what he was doing.

Early that morning, Freddy went back to visit Melissa, and as he was leaving the hospital he saw with dread the stout figure of her mother approaching, her arms full of flowers.

'You've been to see her, haven't you?' Her manner was aggressive.

'Yes,' he answered uncertainly, 'but she was asleep.'

'You've ruined her life. You realise that, don't you?'

He looked aghast. 'I haven't done anything!'

Mrs Blagdon eyed him beadily. 'That might be the truest thing you ever said,' she retorted. 'You've put Melissa through hell. Sheer hell. How would you like to be told you had to leave your home? Do without a nanny or servants? Have no money to live on? It's a perfect disgrace the way you've behaved towards my daughter. That brought on the baby prematurely, you know. The shock. It's a miracle it didn't kill her!'

'Really, Mrs Blagdon, I do think you're overreacting. We're not the only people to lose money at Lloyd's. Ask anyone, people are having to get rid of their houses, take their children away from school, sell everything! Melissa knows that.'

'I don't suppose your sister and her husband have lost *anything*!' A blob of spit flew from her mouth and landed on the lapel of his jacket. He didn't know whether to wipe it away or not.

'You've only got to read the newspapers to see that Toby Hamcroft has absconded with millions of pounds. They're going to be all right, aren't they? Unlike Melissa, towards whom you seem to have no sense of responsibility at all.'

Turning sharply away, she marched down the corridor in the direction of her daughter's room. Freddy looked after her, appalled. No one had ever talked to him like that. He felt sure that it was she who was behind Melissa's misery and fury at losing their money. Returning to the car, he sat in it for several minutes, lost in thought. It was hard to believe, he reflected, that his whole life had changed within the space of two weeks. He'd lost his wife, his baby, and a financially secure future.

It was a hard and painful realisation, and the most painful part of all, he found to his surprise, was the loss of the baby. He hadn't realised how much he wanted a child. A son. Robert, they had been going to call him. Now Robert was gone, the child he'd hoped would climb the Scottish hills with him, and fish and shoot, as he himself had done at his father's side. His son had been and gone, a tiny spark of life that had been so quickly extinguished. And the worst part of all was that he hadn't even been there to greet him before saying goodbye.

It was madness, total madness, but the moment Liza turned out of the drive of Chalklands, she felt such a powerful surge of elation that she pressed her foot down hard on the accelerator, heading through Kingsclere for the motorway.

Now that she was on the road, she had no doubts that she was doing the right thing. After two weeks of waiting, of doing nothing, of impotence and frustrations, it was a relief to be on her own. She felt a pang of guilt at not having told her father what she was doing, but she'd told her mother, though she had sworn her to secrecy until she was well away.

'I don't like it,' Helen had warned her, looking alarmed. 'You don't know what the hell you're getting into.'

'I know, Mum, but I can't sit around for another minute, waiting for something to happen. I could wait *months*! If Lloyd's refuses to pay the ransom money, Toby could be kept a prisoner for God only knows how long! Something has to be done quickly. I'm sure Janet Granville is on the level.'

'But you don't even know where this petrol station is. It will probably be heavily guarded, too. What are you going to do when you get there? These people may be armed. Oh, Liza, for God's sake, think again.' Helen looked increasingly appalled.

Liza, who had slipped into jeans, a dark shirt and trainers, hitched her shoulder-bag over her arm. She did not tell her mother that a few minutes ago she had put Toby's rifle and some ammunition in the boot of her car.

Sir George had taught both her and Freddy how to use a gun when they'd been in their teens in Scotland and, although she rarely went shooting these days, she knew she was still quite capable of handling a gun if she had to.

'Don't worry,' she assured her mother, her face flushed, adrenaline making her feel charged with energy. 'I shall do a very careful recce, making sure no one sees me. I'm not crazy enough to imagine I'm a female James Bond but, once I've seen where he is, and have got the general lie of the land, then we might be able to go back and mount a proper rescue operation, with the help of the police.'

'Why not take Daddy with you?' Helen appealed, anguished. 'He'll kill me when he finds out what you're doing.'

'Mum, please, for me, don't let Daddy come after me. I can't explain, but I really want to do this on my own. I must go.' Liza kissed her mother briefly. 'I've got my mobile phone. I'll stay in touch.'

'Oh, God, Liza . . . !'

But Liza was gone, slipping out the back way, to where the cars were parked in a courtyard beside the old stables. Her one thought was to get away, although she knew she was being reckless. *I won't put myself in danger*, she told herself, remembering her responsibility to the children, *But, oh God! I so want to find Toby*.

The thought that in a few hours she might be in close proximity to him, even if he didn't know it, made her feel dizzy with excitement.

The roads were clear at that time in the morning, and by ten o'clock, Liza had reached Honiton. Suddenly realising how hungry she was, she stopped off at a roadside café, ordering eggs, bacon and coffee. Then she filled up the car with petrol at a nearby garage, bought a copy of the *Daily Mail* and the *Globe*, and continued on her way. At this rate she reckoned she'd be in Polgarth by lunchtime. Her elation increased with every mile, and now she felt heady, powerful. *Who knows?* she thought. *I might even be able to rescue Toby, if he's locked in the petrol station on his own, if his captors don't guard him day and night ... if ... if ...*

Liza hardly noticed the countryside as she sped along, so filled was her mind with the fantasy of finding Toby and releasing him.

She was startled by the ringing of her mobile phone, then she remembered she'd switched it on again once she was a safe distance from Chalklands.

'Hello?' she said cautiously, speaking to the microphone above the windscreen.

'Liza!' It was her father and he sounded furious.

She tried to sound cheerful and in control. 'Hi, Dad! I'm nearly there, I was going to call you when ...'

'For Christ's sake, girl, stop! Stop at once.'

She'd known he'd be annoyed with her. She had to try and calm him down. 'Daddy, don't get in such a state. I'm only going to get the lie of the land and see what sort of place this petrol station is,' she replied. 'I'm not going to let myself be spotted. I just want to know what we're up against.'

'You had no right to go off like that, without telling me. I thought you were out with the children. I don't know what your mother was thinking of, letting you—'

'I'm not a child,' Liza cut in. 'I'm perfectly all right, and I'll call you.'

'*No!*' Sir George was bellowing now. 'Liza, I forbid it.'

'I'm sorry, Dad. This is something I have to do. I'll call you later. Give my love to Mum, and don't worry.'

Defiantly she switched off the phone. She'd seen a

signpost pointing to the right marked Polgarth. A tremor of nervous anticipation made her heart stumble, before it raced faster. Her plan was to drive through Polgarth, and then take the road to Fowey. Janet Granville had said the old petrol station was between the two.

'Where are you going?' Anthony demanded when, after breakfast, he found Emma in the drive of their house in Surrey, helping the children into the car.

'I'm driving over to see Liza, and to interview Martin,' she replied coolly, loading up the boot with large baskets containing swimsuits and towels, and a picnic lunch for them to have on the way.

Anthony scowled. 'You're still determined to go ahead with this feature?'

She stood stock-still, looking at him, a breeze blowing the ebony tendrils of her hair around her face. 'This is my life, too, you know, Ant,' she said steadily. 'I won't do anything to tarnish your career, but I'm going to have to be honest about Lloyd's. It's not as if you're the only MP who's an Outside Name. I don't know why you're being so paranoid.'

'As an MP I prefer not to get involved in anything controversial. You're being pig-headed, Em. I don't need you to do a Women's Lib all over me.'

'Now you're being pompous,' she shot back. 'I've arranged to go to Chalklands today and I'm going. The children are looking forward to playing with Thomas and Tilly and Sarah, anyway.'

'But you know I've got meetings with several constituents this afternoon, and a huge backlog of paperwork to catch up on,' he protested childishly.

'Great! You do your thing and I'll do mine. Mrs Hudson will be here in an hour to do your luncheon, and I'll be back this evening, so what's your problem?'

'You know perfectly well! Go to the Hamcrofts' if you want to, but I'm asking you to drop this idea of a feature on Lloyd's.'

Emma shook her head, almost sadly. 'No, Anthony. I can't do that.'

'*Won't*, you mean!'

'No. *Can't*. I've agreed to write this series of articles for the *Globe* and, if nothing else, I'm a professional. If I accept a commission, I do it. They'll never ask me to write for them again if I back out now just because my husband is scared it will look as if he's involved in what might be a controversial issue.'

'Do as you like then.' Anthony turned and stormed back into the house, slamming the front door shut.

'What's the matter with Dad?' Robin asked.

'He's just being a big baby!' Emma said lightly, getting into the car and turning on the ignition.

Rosie giggled with mirth, waving her rag doll in farewell. 'Daddy's not a big baby!' she chortled. 'He's a big Daddy!'

As Emma drove cross-country to Kingsclere, she kept the children entertained with audio-cassette stories, while she worked out in her head the type of questions she wanted to ask Martin. No doubt he'd like to expand on the good old days when a handshake was a gentleman's agreement, but she really wanted to get his opinion on how Lloyd's had changed in the past twenty years.

When she arrived at Chalklands, the place seemed to be deserted, and then she saw Helen Mortimer carrying a tray of plastic beakers filled with orange juice on to the terrace. Helen looked up, surprised, when she saw Emma.

'Hello there,' Helen called out, and Emma thought she looked strained and not entirely welcoming.

'Hello,' Emma called back, letting the children out of the car. They swarmed across the lawn, shouting excitedly.

A moment later, Thomas came hurtling out of the house, waving a tennis racket, followed by Tilly.

'Have you brought your swimming things?' he demanded, before saying hello.

''Course!' Robin replied scornfully. 'And my new cricket bat.'

'Wh-e-e-e!' The two boys dashed off, followed by Tilly and Barnaby. Watching them, Emma laughed. 'Go on, Rosie. Go and find Sarah.' Obediently, Rosie trotted off, dragging her rag doll behind her.

'I wish I had that energy,' she commented.

Helen smiled. 'Is Liza expecting you?'

Emma's face fell. 'Don't tell me she's forgotten! Oh, how awful. Is it frightfully inconvenient?'

'Not at all, but Liza isn't here, you know.' She sounded harassed.

'Where is she? She said it would be all right if I came over with the children today; I'm supposed to be interviewing Martin about Lloyd's.'

'Are you?' Helen raised surprised eyebrows. 'Listen. Let me give these drinks to the children, and then we'll have some coffee and I'll tell you what's happening. We're in the middle of a crisis and George is doing his nut.'

Later, on the terrace, Helen told Emma everything.

'Where are Martin and Nina?' Emma asked, looking around.

'Still upstairs in their room. They had a snack on a tray instead of lunch. I'm a bit worried about Martin. He's suddenly got awfully old,' Helen replied.

'Do they know Liza's rushed off to Cornwall?'

'No. I've managed to keep it from them.'

'I wish I'd known she was going; I'd have gone with her,' Emma said, almost enviously. 'I can't believe it.' She shook her head. 'It's so *unlike* Liza to go dashing off like Wonder Woman. It's very brave of her, too. What a story it would make, if only I could write it,' she added soberly.

'Once a journalist, always a journalist, eh, Emma?' Helen remarked, smiling at her.

Emma looked thoughtful. 'Anthony would agree with you on that.' Then she glanced at her watch. 'She'll be there now, won't she? What time did Sir George speak to her on the phone?'

'About half-past twelve I think. Then she switched it off. Yes.' Her eyes were troubled. 'She'll be there. Oh, my God, I hope she's all right. I really feel frightened for her.'

'So do I, actually,' Emma echoed hollowly.

Liza's skin was prickling as if feathers were brushing her bare arms. She felt breathless, as if she'd been running and then had suddenly stopped and entered a very cold atmosphere.

The petrol station looked derelict, and the broken 'Esso' sign, swinging creakily, was encrusted with dirt. Abandoned, the three old petrol pumps stood like scrapyard sentries, guarding a forecourt overgrown with weeds forcing themselves through the cracked concrete surface. In a corner, a clutch of garbage-filled black plastic bags huddled together, waiting to be collected by the refuse van that never came. Beside them, propped against the wall, was a folding board that had once said OPEN.

Driving past as slowly as she dared in case she was being watched, Liza took in the scene. She was trying to think clearly, but the only thought flashing through her mind was *Toby's in there. Not more than a couple of hundred feet away*. And there was no sign of anyone. The place looked deserted. That could mean ... she might be able actually to get into the building unopposed. It could also mean Toby might be bound and gagged and locked inside without food or water.

Forcing herself to keep going, although she ached to stop the car and get out, she drove on down the road. There didn't seem to be any houses or other buildings about, and her excitement grew. If she could find a quiet lane leading off the road, she might be able to park her car out of sight. Then she could make her way back to the petrol station on foot.

The road dipped, and hedges, overgrown and wildly festooned with blackberry branches, rose high and blocked out the view for a moment. Then the road turned right, the high banks fell away and Liza could see on the horizon the blue rim of the sea in the distance. Fowey lay ahead. At that moment, as the road entered a heavily wooded area, and a canopy of overhanging branches obliterated the sky, she saw a wide path to the left. It led into a forest, winding its way out of sight among the trees. It was a perfect place to park. Turning off the main road, she eased the Mercedes down the path. As it narrowed, the undergrowth thickened, brushing the sides of the car, leaves flipping the windscreen, branches scraping the paintwork, closing around her to form a perfect screen from prying eyes. The only thing that worried Liza was: will I ever be able to get out of here again? The tyres were sinking into the soft mulchy ground, which was slippery with pine needles. She edged slowly forward, and when she came to a wide clearing, a hundred yards into the forest, she decided to turn the car around, so that she was facing the way she'd come, just in case she needed to make a quick getaway. Then she turned the engine off, and for a moment sat with her head resting against the grey leather upholstery. Her neck and shoulders ached from tension, her clothes stuck uncomfortably to her with sweat. Feeling both exhausted and apprehensive she climbed out of the car, anxious to get on. A quick glance around assured her no one was about. Lifting the large black leather bag out of the boot, she hung it on her shoulder, a universal receptacle for shopping or picnicking, and at this moment the perfect container for the tools she'd packed earlier, which included wire cutters, a sharp knife, a hammer, the first-aid kit from the kitchen at Chalklands, and, of course, Toby's gun, wrapped in a car rug, and the ammunition. Then she locked the car, and looked round once more to make sure there was no one about. It was all right. The forest was still and silent. It was time to go.

The children were playing, splashing about in the pool, supervised by the indefatigable Ingrid, who rather relished being at the centre of a drama, even though she didn't know the whole truth: as far as she was concerned, Toby had merely vanished without trace. Emma sat under the plum tree, talking to Martin.

'I probably had the best years,' he admitted. 'During the fifties, sixties and seventies, Lloyd's was a wonderful place to be. One had so many friends, and the atmosphere was so convivial. One worked hard, of course,' he added, smiling.

'Did everyone work hard, or just you?' Emma asked.

'I worked hard, because I wanted to build up the syndicate until it was one of the most powerful in The

Room. There were others who didn't, of course. I used to know a broker who managed to play five games of chess a day.'

Emma looked at him in astonishment. 'Wasn't he sacked?'

Martin shook his head, rubbing the palms of his hands together all the time, as if to bring back the circulation. 'You've got to remember that a broker has to join a queue at each underwriting box to place a line on a policy. It's extremely bad form to join more than one queue at a time.'

'You mean you have to stake your place in a queue, and you can't go to another box until you've completed your business with the first one?'

'That's right.'

'Has anyone ever tried to do a time-and-motion study? Brokers must waste hours hanging around,' Emma exclaimed.

'But you're talking to people all the time: "networking", I believe you call it these days. Lunch could be lengthy, too. A lot of business was actually done over a good lunch.'

Nina joined them, her skin like chocolate-coloured crêpe fabric in a white sundress. *Remind me not to stay in the sun too much*, Emma told herself.

'How's it going?' Nina asked, smiling.

'I think we're about finished,' Emma replied. 'We've talked for nearly two hours.' She turned to Martin. 'I hope you're not too worn out.'

'I've enjoyed it,' he said graciously. 'Is there any news

from Liza?' he asked his wife. They'd been told by Helen what Liza was trying to do.

'No, nothing.' She looked at her wristwatch. So did Martin and Emma.

'I wish she'd ring,' Emma fretted. 'I'm worried about her.'

'It's a mad but wonderful thing she's trying to do,' Nina observed, 'although I wish she hadn't gone alone. Helen and George are frantic, and it hasn't helped that Freddy's wife had a baby in the early hours of this morning; a premature boy who didn't survive.'

'My God, I'd no idea!' Emma looked appalled. 'I thought Helen looked fraught when I arrived, but I thought it was just about Liza. Poor Freddy and Melissa! They must be dreadfully upset. Has George picked up anything on the radio?'

'Not that I know of. Poor man, he's feeling very down at the minute. It's a terrible time for us all, isn't it?' Nina reflected. 'I feel as if I've aged ten years in the past ten days. If we could only get Toby home . . .' Her voice broke, and she blinked rapidly. Tears glistened, merging with her iridescent blue eyeshadow. Emma reached out and took her hand.

'Toby is a great survivor, and so is Liza. I know they'll be all right,' she said, sounding more reassuring than she felt.

'But supposing Toby's captors spot Liza?' Martin pointed out. 'If they were capable of abducting Mrs Granville, what do you suppose they'd do to Liza?'

Chapter Fourteen

The five-barred gate was padlocked. Liza dumped her shoulder-bag on the side, then climbed over. It led into a large field of unripe corn, which shivered silvery and fragile in the breeze. So far she'd seen no one since leaving the shelter of the forest but, as a precaution, she kept close to the hedgerows that divided the fields. Hoping she was going parallel to the road she'd just driven along, she wondered how soon it would be before she got back to the petrol station. Distances could be deceptive, a car ate up the miles that made weary work of walking. There was no way of being sure she was going in the right direction, either; no telegraph poles or landmarks. Not even the sound of traffic.

In the still heat of the afternoon, she hurried on, the bag heavy and the straps digging into her shoulder; the ground was soft under her feet, making the going harder. And yet, a constant quiver of excitement kept her going: Toby was at the end of her journey, whether she got to see him or not. At least she would be near him.

For that she was prepared to do anything. On the far side of the field, she had to jump across a ditch, and then climb through wire fencing to get into the next field. A hawthorn bough caught on the back of her T-shirt, scratching her painfully. Swearing, she rested for a moment. Her legs were aching, and the sweat was trickling down between her breasts. A cloud of midges danced with maddening persistence around her head, increasing their activity as she tried to wave them away.

This field was lying fallow, meant perhaps for grazing. Still looking around to make sure there was no one about, Liza got to her feet. Once again she walked around the outskirts, in the shelter of beech and oak, briar and horse chestnut. It was at that moment she realised the sun was shining directly into her face, stinging her fair skin with its intensity, dazzling her eyes even though she wore dark glasses. It should have been on her right. She was going too far in a southerly direction. This way she'd pass behind the petrol station and might miss it completely.

Ahead of her lay a wooded area. It looked light beneath the trees, so it couldn't be very large. Once she was able to leave the shelter of the hedge and enter the wood, she'd be able to walk in any direction she liked. She had to go more east, she reckoned, to get back to being near the main road.

The wood was similar to the one in which she'd left the car. The cool shade was refreshing, after the merciless glare of the sun. She walked quite briskly now, feeling safe in the shelter of the trees. Then she heard it. The sound of a car approaching, changing gear and then roaring past. Her stomach tightened. The road must be only thirty or forty yards to her left, and on a lower level. She remembered the high bushy banks that had obliterated the fields from the roadway. She must be nearing the petrol station. Who had been driving past? One of Toby's captors? Had they spotted her entering the area?

Liza decided to keep going, even if she had been seen. There was no turning back now. Not when she was so near to Toby. Not while there was a chance of being able to rescue him. For a moment she wondered if it wouldn't have been better if she'd gone to the local police station and got them to mount a rescue operation. But supposing Toby's abductors had got wind of that? They'd threatened to kill Toby if the police were brought in; it was a risk she knew she could never take. As she walked quietly and steadily on, keeping out of sight of the road on her left, she heard a rustling sound, as if someone was following her, their feet stirring the mouldy leaves. Then there was a scuffle followed by silence. Freezing instinctively, she stood still, holding her breath, while the blood thundered in her ears. Something flashed past the corner of her eye and she turned sharply. As the rustling started again, she realised it was a rabbit, its paws pattering as it shot off among the trees. For a moment she leaned against the nearest tree, almost collapsing with relief. What if it had been one of Toby's captors?

Continuing along the path, more slowly now, she

knew she must have almost reached the petrol station. Still she had no fixed plan. She didn't know whether the entrance to the building faced the road or was at the back. The place had seemed quite deserted when she'd driven past, but were there guards inside? Holding Toby captive and maybe armed? For a moment the foolhardiness of what she was doing hit her forcibly. Her father was right. She was crazy to attempt to get close enough to find out what was happening. And yet . . . The thought of being able to help Toby made her resolve to go on. There could be no turning back now. If he was alone she'd somehow get into the petrol station and release him, no matter what. Without guards, there would be nothing to stop her. But she must be prepared for the worst. It was unlikely he'd been left alone.

With hands that shook and were damp with sweat, she checked the contents of her bag again, and then, crouching on her haunches, unwrapped the rifle and loaded it. Making sure the safety-catch was on, she held it down by her side, unbroken. Her father would die if he saw her walking with her gun like that, she reflected, but if someone suddenly appeared she had to be ready.

Another three hundred yards, winding her way carefully through the last of the trees, and she came out on the far side and found herself on the edge of a field of rape. Its brilliant yellow blooms were waist-high. It made perfect cover, and she edged forward now, crouched low.

Then she saw it. On a lower level to the left, on the far side of a wooden fence, was the corner of a building. Liza dropped down on to her knees and, with the gun in her right hand, crawled slowly forward.

The petrol station lay forty feet ahead of her, built into a cutting by the roadside, twelve feet lower than the grassy bank on which she lay.

Liza edged forward and peered through the fence. The row of disused pumps, the creaking sign and the stack of plastic bags looked less sinister from this higher angle. The place seemed so deserted-looking now, she wondered, in a moment of panic, if this was the petrol station Janet Granville had referred to. But of course it was, she assured herself. On the five-mile stretch of road between Polgarth and Fowey there were unlikely to be *two* disused petrol stations.

The building itself was oblong-shaped, a cheap concrete construction with a flat roof and no windows. And it was impossible to tell whether there was anyone inside or not.

She lay there for several minutes, listening. There was not a sound. The silence was eerie, a listening, watching silence. From her vantage point she realised two things. The entrance to the building must be at the front, and there was no way down to the level of the road. She was going to have to jump.

After a moment's thought she decided she'd better drop down by the side of the building rather than behind it. If she landed badly, there were eight to ten feet at the side, in which she could sprawl. At the rear there was only three feet between the sheer drop of the cutting and the concrete back wall.

One more look around to make sure no one was watching her, another moment to listen for approaching cars; the coast was clear. Liza puffed out her cheeks as she exhaled, deciding to go for it. Breaking the gun, she hastily wrapped it in the rug again, jammed it into the bag and after climbing through the fence, crawled further forward. Leaning over, she dropped the bag at arm's length down behind the building. It landed with a thud. Liza drew back, in case the noise had been heard by whoever was guarding Toby. She lay there for several minutes, head flat on the grass, listening tensely. Clover and meadow-rue, cow-parsley and hog-weed provided a screen which hid her from the road. Now that she was so close to Toby, a moment away from him in fact, the longing to see him again was acute. It made her throw caution to the winds. She *had* to get to him, now, this minute.

Getting on to her hands and knees, Liza moved round to the side of the cutting, still keeping low, but too anxious to complete her mission to wait and watch and listen before taking action. She sat upright, slid her legs over the side, feet dangling, and pushed herself forward with her hands.

The ground was hard as she hit it, her knees buckling so that she rolled on to her side. Her elbow hurt, but she didn't care. Before she rose and darted behind the building to pick up her bag, she was able to get a quick look at the front. There was a double wooden door, wide enough to get a car through. It looked forbiddingly shut.

Round at the back of the building, Liza was unwrapping the gun when she heard a car coming. Hidden from the road, she nevertheless dropped on to her haunches again and, crouching, strained to hear the engine coming closer. Supposing it was Toby's kidnappers, bringing reinforcements to guard him? And how many might there be? Now that Janet Granville had escaped, they were going to make sure Toby couldn't do the same. What if...? The thought that if only she'd come a few minutes earlier, she might have been able to rescue him made her feel sick with misery.

She held her breath. The car swished past, driving inland towards Polgarth. Trembling violently from anxiety and fear, she decided it was now or never. Dropping the bag, she cocked the gun and, keeping close to the grimy concrete wall, made her way around the side of the building to the front.

Sir George sat rigidly at the table, the earphones clamped on his head as he listened to the conversation he'd been waiting for twenty-four hours to hear. Colonel Mackenzie had taken a call from Brian Todd a few moments before, and Sir George was recording their conversation, hoping they would give themselves away by saying something incriminating. So much, he scoffed mentally, for Brian Todd saying he'd never heard of Mallows Hall, where Mackenzie lived.

'There's been no response, then?' he heard Todd ask.

'None.' Mackenzie sounded cryptic.

'Anything from D. W.?'

Sir George scribbled down the initials: D. W. must be the initials or the code name for another of the kidnappers.

'I've arranged to contact him at 1900 hours. I'm worried about him. I think he's gone over the top.'

Sir George glanced at his watch. It was now four o'clock; three hours to go before Mackenzie made the call.

'What are we going to do about M. B.? I have a feeling he's not going to budge.'

'He will. In time.'

'You think so?'

'Yes.'

'I didn't think it would be like this.' It was Brian Todd speaking. Sir George concluded that 'M. B.' must be Malcolm Blackwell.

'That's what I mean,' Mackenzie replied. 'I think he's flipped.'

'I don't think I'd have gone along with the plan, if I'd known we were in the hands of a nutcase,' Todd agreed.

'We can't go back now.'

'What about Janet?'

'He'll put her back in her cage again, no doubt. I fear her singing days are over.' Mackenzie, Sir George thought, might have been referring to a pet canary. He shuddered at the cold-blooded way they were talking about the widow of one of their group, and the realisation that Liza might have put herself at the mercy of these ruthless people appalled him afresh. And who was the nutcase they were referring to?

Mackenzie and Todd continued to talk in a careful, stilted fashion, referring to people by initials only. Six sets of initials in all, Sir George noted, writing them down. When this conversation was over, he'd go through the list of Outside Names Declan had provided, to see if he could trace who they were.

Mackenzie was speaking again. Sir George strained to listen. A moment later, he had thrown up his hands and let out a yell of despair.

'Helen!' He called to his wife. 'Helen, for God's sake, come here quickly.'

Holding the gun across her front with her left hand, Liza placed her right hand on one of the double doors and pushed it. It was locked. She wasn't surprised. It would hardly have been left open. Pressing her ear to it, all the while listening out for passing cars, she began to think Toby *must* have been left here on his own. If they'd bound and gagged him, and then left him in this building which was on such a lonely road, he was unlikely to be found. Unless of course . . . ? Oh, dear God, could they have already killed him . . . ?

In sudden panic she kicked the door, the flat of her foot slamming hard against the rotting timbers. Nothing happened. She kicked again, more savagely this time, terror at what she might find causing her to shout, wildly, '*Toby*! Toby, are you there?'

In the deathly silence that followed her cry, the door

suddenly gave, and she almost fell into the darkness of the disused building.

Gripping the gun, she looked around, her eyes searching the gloomy depths of a space twenty-five feet by eighteen. Petrol cans, oily rags, worn tyres, the chassis of an old car and rusting tools cluttered the place. Opening both doors to let in more light, she realised there was no one here. The building was as deserted as the yard outside.

'Toby . . .' His name was a lament as she sank to her knees, the tears pouring down her cheeks. She'd been so sure, so certain; Janet Granville had *told* her he'd be here. Was it a trick, as her father had feared? It seemed unlikely. If this had been a trick to capture her too, she would surely have been jumped on by now. As it was, she was sure this was an isolated place with little passing traffic, and not a soul – kidnapper or otherwise – in sight. Disappointment, after her hopes had been so high, was profound and deep. She was back to square one, with no idea where they'd taken Toby, and probably little hope of finding him.

Blinded by tears, she rose, looking slowly and sadly at the mess lying everywhere. She walked round the space, idly tapping old cigarette and sweet packets with the toe of her trainers. They looked as if they'd lain there for years. Then, with a great lurch, her heart skipped a beat. On the far side of the remains of the car, some matting had been piled up on the floor. It was filthy and torn, but she felt she could detect a hollow impression down the centre. Had this been Toby's bed while they locked him in here? She looked more closely, bending over the pieces of grey carpeting. Her foot slipped on the concrete floor and, thinking it must be engine oil, she glanced down at her shoe.

The icy *frisson* started at the back of her neck and seemed to spread down her spine like trailing fingers. It wasn't oil. It was blood; recently spilt blood, for her white rubber sole was smeared dark red and, when she stepped backward in horrified revulsion, her shoe left the imprint of her rubber sole on the concrete. A crimson imprint.

'Dear God...' An overwhelming sense of nausea swept through her, leaving her wet with perspiration and so weak she could hardly stand. She had to get out of here. The place smelt of oil, and rubber, and petrol, and now she imagined it smelled of sweat and blood as well. What in God's name had they done to Toby? With her hand clasped over her mouth to quell the rising nausea, she was just about to leave when she noticed something tucked down the far side of the carpeting. There was something familiar about it. When she picked it up she realised it was a flat pack of matches. But these were not just any matches you'd buy at a tobacconist: the glossy white folded card was grubby and crumpled-looking, but the name on the front was clear. Le Caprice. And on the reverse side: Arlington Street, SW1. It was their favourite restaurant. Then she remembered. Toby had taken her there for dinner a couple of nights before his trip to the States. She even remembered him pocketing the matches, while she laughingly asked him why he wanted them, as neither of them smoked? Toby had smiled and said matches were always useful.

'Oh, Toby!' The tears gathered in her eyes. 'What have they done?'

'What on earth is it, George?' Helen asked breathlessly. She'd hurried along the corridor to the spare room as soon as she'd heard him.

Sir George sat slumped, still wearing the earphones.

'I think they've moved Toby,' he said in distress. 'I was afraid it might be a trap, and now Liza's walked straight into it.'

'Oh, my God!' Helen gasped in dismay. 'What did you hear?'

'Mackenzie's been talking to Brian Todd. He was talking in riddles, of course. Anyway, Todd got another call on his mobile phone, and then he told Mackenzie that "the pawn" had been moved.'

'"The pawn" being Toby?'

'I believe so. Todd's actual words were: "The leader just said he's moved the pawn two spaces forward. Next move to castle."'

'As in chess?'

Sir George nodded, drawing the squares of a chessboard on his pad as he did so. He drew a small pawn, and two squares away a battlemented turret. He stared down at it, frowning, as if he were studying a map. Then he threw down his pencil.

'God, I don't like it!' he exclaimed.

'What can we do?'

'Nothing, until we hear from Liza. *If* we hear from Liza,' he replied grimly. 'Christ, she should never have gone. It was mad and absolutely irresponsible!'

Helen gave the ghost of a wry smile. 'Her father's child, through and through.'

'I was in the army. Trained for the job. If Liza comes up against trouble she'll be like a lamb to the slaughter. She won't stand a chance in hell!'

Helen remained silent. She'd always known that under the feminine charms of her daughter lay a strong and valiant spirit, capable of looking after herself if she had to. Just as she'd always realised Freddy was the weaker of the two. He always had been, even as a small child. It was something she never discussed with George, but she knew he was aware of Freddy's lack of backbone. The disaster of Lloyd's could well reduce her son to a nervous wreck; Liza, however, would always be able to cope.

'Do you think they'll be waiting for Liza at the petrol station?' Helen asked in a small voice.

'God knows. She should never have gone,' he repeated. He turned back to the receiver. 'I'm going to keep listening. Mackenzie may talk to other people. They might even mention Liza.'

Helen knew he was angry with her for letting Liza rush off to Cornwall, although he didn't say so. *As if I could have stopped her*, Helen reflected. *As far as Toby is concerned, Liza would give her life for him.*

There echoed the terrible thought in her mind, that perhaps her daughter might have to.

* * *

Liza lost track of time as she sat crouched on the ground, fingering the empty pack of matches, turning it over and over, as Toby must have done. She'd remembered he'd worn the same suit when he left for America as he'd done on the night they'd dined at *Le Caprice*. They must have fallen out of his pocket. At least it proved he'd been here, she thought, looking around, trying to imagine what he'd gone through. He must have been tied up, bound and gagged, otherwise he'd have escaped. There were no windows, but the lock on the door was flimsy. A child could have escaped – as long as he wasn't tied up. Or guarded night and day. But what did Toby eat and drink? There were no signs of crumbs or discarded food packaging, no empty tins or bottles of drink. And whose blood was it spilled on the floor?

As a sense of desolation swept over her, she rose slowly. A car swished past at that moment, and she saw it briefly, black and sleek through the open doors; but she didn't care. Her misery was so great that it didn't seem to matter to her what happened now. She knew instinctively, anyway, that the kidnappers wouldn't come back. What would be the point?

Picking up the rifle, she walked on to the front courtyard, shutting the double doors behind her. Then she went round to the back of the building, collected her bag and set off along the road to pick up her car.

'I'm on my way home, Mum,' she told her mother on the mobile phone, as she drove along the A3269 to

Lostwithiel. It was now half-past four. The children would be in bed and asleep by the time she got back. Briefly she explained what had happened.

'I'm sorry,' said Helen, immediately. 'You must be disappointed. Your father was listening in to Colonel Mackenzie and it sounds as if they've moved Toby to a castle.'

'A castle?' In spite of being downcast, Liza felt a fresh thrill of hope. At least it meant Toby was still alive.

'I wonder which castle?' she said.

'Daddy's still listening in; maybe he'll find out some more before you get back. I'm just thankful you're all right. We got a fright when we heard Toby had been moved. We really did think you'd walked into a trap. Emma's here, you know, with her children. She's been interviewing Martin.'

Liza gave a little shriek. 'Oh, my God! I'd completely forgotten. Give her my love, Mum, and say I'm really sorry. I suppose she wouldn't like to stay the night? We could put up beds for the children in Thomas and Tilly's room. I'd love to see her.'

'All right, darling. I'll ask her. You'll be home in a couple of hours?'

Liza glanced at her wristwatch, suddenly thankful Chalklands was going to be filled with people for the rest of the weekend. She needed the companionship of friends and family more than ever, now she knew there was no chance of Toby being home tonight.

'Yes. Tell Margaret to prepare an enormous dinner for everyone, will you?'

Liza settled back in her seat, concentrating on the road ahead. Then she turned on the car radio. Music would help pass the time. As she tuned the set, she found herself listening to a news bulletin.

'... And the Prime Minister has expressed delight that Britain has won its fight against a European rule slashing the number of hours teenagers can work,' the announcer reported. Liza was about to switch channels when his next words made her sit up, rigid.

'... The findings of the Council of Lloyd's, investigating the financial dealings in the insurance company, Martin E. L. Hamcroft's, will be announced on Monday. It is thought hundreds of members and especially Outside Names have suffered massive losses, which have led to this inquiry being held. Two weeks ago, the son of the founder, Toby Hamcroft, vanished whilst supposedly on a business trip to America...'

'... Mortgage rates are set to—'

Liza didn't wait to hear any more. She switched off the set, maddened that the media were still linking the story of the losses to Toby's disappearance, and put her foot down hard on the accelerator. The Mercedes roared forward. If it was the last thing she ever did, she was going to clear Toby's name, whether he was dead or alive.

Chapter Fifteen

'Have you heard about this "Hardship Committee" Lloyd's are setting up?' Freddy asked his father. It was the next afternoon, and he'd driven down to Chalklands for the day, to join the rest of his family. Scarcely able to think about the death of his baby, he was grasping at any distractions. Melissa was still refusing to talk to him, telling the nurses in the hospital that she wanted no visitors at all, with the exception of her mother.

Sir George put down his copy of the *Sunday Times*, and looked at Freddy as he lounged in the garden chair. 'Do you think they'll be able to help you?'

'From what I've heard,' Freddy replied, 'it's more an organisation to bolster the hardship Lloyd's believes *it's* suffering from! It's not setting out to help people like me. I talked to someone last week, who'd been sent a form to fill in that was incredible! Pages and pages of questions. Believe me, Lloyd's is not rushing to give handouts to people on the brink of bankruptcy.'

Sir George raised bushy eyebrows over beady eyes. 'I didn't know that. Are you sure?'

'I read of a widow who had lost the nest-egg her husband had left her, and who lives in a small three-bedroom house. It's been her home for forty years, for God's sake! When she applied, the Hardship Committee wrote back and said she didn't need three bedrooms, one was enough; and she must sell her house, buy herself somewhere much smaller, and give them the balance from the sale! The rest, they graciously said, they'd expect when she died.' Freddy's voice was rough with bitterness.

'I hope she refused to have anything to do with them,' Sir George said indignantly.

'You can't, Dad. That's the point. If you once apply to the Hardship Committee, you're stuck with it. They won't let you change your mind! In reality, it's been set up to help Lloyd's screw people for everything they've got – only slowly, instead of very quickly.'

'Good grief.'

'Oh, you've no idea, Dad.' Freddy was warming to the subject, glad to be able to unburden himself of all his worries to someone and to think of something other than Melissa and the baby. 'I heard of a man who lost everything. I mean, everything, right down to those proverbial cufflinks. Assessors were due to look over his house, and *all* the contents had to be valued, so they could be sold to pay what he owed Lloyd's. Well, he was damned if he was going to let them have the contents of his wine cellar. He'd been laying down the most superb wines for twenty years, and some of the bottles were worth several hundred pounds.'

'God!'

'So he made a deal with their next-door neighbour, to store the wine in his cellar for the time being. They all lent a hand, moving hundreds of bottles in the middle of the night, so when the valuers came the next day, there was nothing in the cellar but a few old boxes.'

'Fantastic!' Sir George beamed with delight. 'And they weren't caught?'

'Not exactly, but it rained the following night. A real storm that was so bad their neighbour's cellar got flooded,' Freddy explained.

'And . . . ?'

'When they went to look the next day, they found all the labels had come unstuck and were floating about everywhere. Now they have hundreds of bottles of wine, and no idea what anything is.'

'No!'

'At least – unlike most – that story is more comic than tragic.' Freddy glanced at his watch. 'I must go and relieve Liza. She's been listening in for the past hour, in case Mackenzie has had any more calls.'

'Thanks. I'll take over after you. I'm staying down here with your mother for a few days. I could do with a bit more country air, and I might hear something useful . . .'

'You're right, Dad. I'm going back to town tonight

with Liza. I don't think she should be on her own, but she's decided to leave the children here with Ingrid and Margaret.'

'Martin and Nina are going back to London, aren't they?'

Freddy made a grimace, and dropped his voice. 'I don't think they're much help to Liza. Martin's very crotchety and they're both a bit old for this sort of stress and pressure.'

Sir George looked surprised. 'They're only a couple of years older than your mother and me.'

'I know. They just seem so old compared to you.' Freddy grinned. 'Thank God for you and Mum. I don't know what Liza and I would do without you.'

Up on the first floor, Liza sat hunched over the receiver. When Freddy entered the room, she turned to him with a wan smile.

'I think Mackenzie must have gone out to Sunday lunch,' she said, taking off the headphones and rising. She stretched, feeling so tired she longed to go back to bed. The trauma of the previous afternoon had really hit her now, making her wonder just how much longer she was going to be able to carry on.

'Are you all right, sis?' Freddy asked anxiously as she gripped the back of the chair for support. 'You look like death.'

'I'm just tired and worried.' Her eyes were blank, dead-looking, and there were heavy mauve shadows beneath them. 'I'll be glad to get back to town, actually. I feel so out of touch here, in spite of this radio.'

'I know what you mean. Are you going to contact Malcolm Blackwell when you get back?'

'I'll wait until they've announced the findings of the council. Whatever they've discovered should clear Toby's name, and then I want an all-out bid made to get him released. Malcolm Blackwell has obviously decided to adopt the policy of let's wait and see what happens, and that isn't good enough. Oh, if only Toby had been at that petrol station yesterday. I can't believe I probably only missed him by *hours*.'

'That must have been awful for you,' Freddy sympathised.

'The worst. It was hideous. I felt so cheated and I'm so worried in case he's badly hurt.'

'And you're certain he'd been there? I mean, the match packet could be a coincidence. Le Caprice is a famous restaurant. And it wasn't necessarily his.'

Liza thought for a moment. 'Toby and I are so close, Freddy; I just sort of *felt* his presence. I also think that when Janet Granville escaped, they feared she'd tell us where Toby was being held, and that's why they moved him somewhere else. I wonder where she is now? I do hope she's all right, and that they haven't caught up with her again. When you think of it, it was really wonderful of her to contact us like that.'

'Brave, too. God, Liza, what a mess! I wonder how it's all going to end?' he said fretfully. Flopping into the chair he reached for the headphones. 'Let's hope this produces something this afternoon, other than Mackenzie going for a pee, or his blasted cat mewing all the time.'

'I'll see you later.' Liza slipped from the room in search of Margaret. In spite of everything, she still had a large house in the country to run, and a house in London, too. There were instructions to give, food to be ordered, plans for the following week to be carried out, and then there were the children. Glad that she'd decided to let them stay at Chalklands for a few more days, there were still a lot of arrangements to be made to make sure both houses ran smoothly. Sometimes Liza wondered if hers and Toby's lives weren't made more complicated by having two establishments to keep up; it had only recently occurred to her, when she heard people talking about their losses, that the running costs were enormous. In a week she thought nothing of spending a hundred pounds on flowers alone for the house in Holland Park Walk.

At moments like this she wondered how she would really feel if she and Toby lost everything. There were some things she would be sad to lose, of course, but as long as she had Toby, and her children and the people who had been lifelong friends like Emma, she felt she could adjust quite quickly to a much lower standard of living. Her mother had always said 'possessions can be a burden', and there were times when she knew that was true. The less you have the less you have to worry about. Life could be simplified. If Toby didn't have to work so hard to maintain all he'd striven for, they could have much more time together.

Once Liza had seen to all the usual Sunday chores at

Chalklands, she joined her parents and Martin and Nina on the terrace. Emma had left earlier, taking her children with her back to Surrey, but promising to call her the next morning.

'I've been speaking to Charles Bryer,' Martin announced.

They all looked at him expectantly.

Liza was the first to speak. 'What did he say about the Council's findings?' she asked.

'He doesn't know what their findings are, as yet,' Martin replied, his chin held high. 'He's got a meeting with Malcolm Blackwell first thing, before an announcement is made.'

'That sounds serious,' Sir George observed.

'Not at all. It's common courtesy,' Martin snapped. 'I think I'll go up to Lloyd's tomorrow. Maybe have lunch in the City. I want to find out what's going on, first hand.'

'Is that wise?' Liza asked gently.

'What do you mean by "wise"?'

'Well . . . er . . .' she floundered. 'Won't you find it very upsetting if the findings are unfavourable? After all, you started the company, and it will be heartbreaking if something's gone wrong. Wouldn't it be better if you stayed at home, and you could keep in touch on the phone?'

'Certainly not,' Martin replied arrogantly. 'I hardly think they're likely to report anything more distressing than the losses that are being suffered by everyone in Lloyd's. I'm surprised at your lack of faith, Liza.'

'It's not lack of faith, but doubt about the management of the syndicate,' Liza replied hotly. 'Something's been going on, and I want to know what it is, so we can clear Toby of suspicion.'

'You've always had great faith in Charles Bryer's ability, haven't you, Martin?' his wife remarked. 'That's why you appointed him chairman of the company when you retired. Toby was too young and inexperienced to take over then, wasn't he?'

'Total faith,' Martin echoed. 'He's looked after our interests, hasn't he?'

'But maybe at the cost of others,' Sir George murmured under his breath.

Martin bristled. 'What was that?'

'I said, "Maybe at the cost of others",' Sir George repeated more loudly. 'In fact, when you think of it, Toby's probably only been kidnapped *because* there are a lot of people who have lost substantial amounts.'

Liza sighed. They were heading for another argument. 'I'll get Margaret to bring us tea out here,' she said, rising, to cause a distraction. As she left the terrace, she heard her father-in-law say, 'What people don't seem to realise is that Lloyd's is a gamble. It's no good complaining when you lose . . .'

She'd heard it all before, a hundred times. But there was losing and losing. There was also something called Being Taken for a Ride.

As she crossed the hall, with its polished floors and oak furniture, and great arrangements of flowers in copper bowls, scenting the air with a fragrance of white peonies and lilies, she had to admit, fleetingly, that she would miss all this if they had to give everything up. It would be no good pretending otherwise. On the other hand, how badly she would feel if they'd lost nothing, while Emma and Anthony, and the rest of their friends, were wiped out.

As she stood in the kitchen a moment later, talking to Margaret, the phone rang. Breaking off in mid-sentence, she flew to where it hung on the wall by the window. Maybe it was news of Toby. Maybe—

'Hello?'

'I'd like to speak to Sir George Mortimer.' The man spoke with a West Country accent.

'Who is that?'

'This is the Shepton Mallet constabulary. Police Constable Grey speaking.'

Liza's mind whirled in dizzy circles. 'What is it about?' she asked. 'Sir George is my father.'

'We've been particularly asked to speak to the gentleman.' The policeman sounded determined. 'Is he at that number, please?'

'Yes. Yes.' She must be helpful. He might have information about Toby. 'Wait a minute. I'll get him.'

Liza ran out of the kitchen and across the hall to the terrace.

'Daddy! Phone! It's the police from Shepton Mallet. They want to speak to you.'

Charles Bryer's hand shook as he lit another cigar. Across his study, blue with acrid smoke, Declan sat, staring at him anxiously. In all the years he'd known Charles, he'd never seen him in such a state.

'You're not seriously worried about your meeting with Malcolm Blackwell tomorrow morning, are you?' he asked.

'Aren't I?' Charles riposted sharply. 'Give me some more of that coffee, will you?'

Declan and Maxine had been invited to Sunday lunch by Charles and Jane Bryer at their penthouse flat in Arlington Street. It had been a strained affair, until Jane and Maxine had decided to drink their coffee outside on the roof garden, which commanded a superb view of Green Park. Charles had declined, saying he wanted to talk to Declan, and he didn't like being out in the sun anyway. Once settled in his cluttered study, which he wouldn't allow anyone to enter, even to clean, he became nervously fretful.

Declan refilled their cups, wishing he could sit outside with the others on such a beautiful afternoon.

'But there's nothing to be worried about, Charles,' he pointed out. 'There's been nothing going on in the syndicate that isn't recognised as normal trading procedure in Lloyd's. Several syndicates have baby syndicates, too, so there's no problem there. Using insider knowledge has been practised for three hundred years, so they can't object to that!'

Charles nodded, but he didn't seem to be listening. It was as if he were in a world of his own, tortured by worries of which Declan had no knowledge.

'Look,' said Declan, trying to get through to him. 'If

anyone should be in hot water, it should be me, but I'm not worried. Who's to know that, when I made someone an Outside Name, I'd choose to put him on a syndicate with the greatest potential profits, if he was lucky, the greatest loss if he wasn't. I got good commission, and if disaster struck, then it was tough! The member lost his shirt! But that's the name of the game, and it was you who taught me that.'

There was silence in the room. Charles puffed away distractedly, gazing into space. Declan might as well not have been in the room.

'At the most,' Declan continued, 'Malcolm Blackwell will say you've been a naughty boy, and will rap you on the knuckles, and tell you that you shouldn't have let it become obvious you were favouring those who work in Lloyd's to the detriment of those that weren't. But what can he do about it? I say fuck the ten commandments; it's the eleventh that matters: *thou shalt not get caught*!'

Charles's voice was thick with worry. 'I know Hamcroft's isn't the only company—'

'What? *Of course* it isn't!' He paused, then added, 'Everything was fine, actually, until Toby goddamn went missing. That's what has drawn attention to us. I wish they'd find his body or something, so that we could all get back to normal. I could kill him for running off like this. What the hell was he playing at?' Declan added, incensed.

'I wish Martin Hamcroft would get off my back. He's far too nosy for my liking, and with his precious son missing, he's driving me mad.'

'You don't have to tell him anything, though. He's on the baby syndicate, isn't he? His money's safe?'

'Yes. I owed him that much. He was very good to me in the days when I first joined the firm.'

'And Toby? What about his money?'

Charles shrugged. 'He could have lost the lot, for all I care. He refused to join us on the baby syndicate, saying he preferred to take his chances with everyone else. Stupid bugger.'

'Perhaps he's topped himself *because* he's lost everything?' Declan speculated.

Charles lapsed into silence again. The smoke from his cigar was starting to make Declan's eyes sting. He rose and put his coffee-cup on the tray.

'I think it's time Maxine and I were getting home,' he observed. 'We're supposed to be going out to dinner tonight.'

Charles roused himself. 'Sit down again, Declan. There's something I want to tell you.'

If Declan felt a shudder of apprehension, he gave no sign. 'Oh, yes? What is it?' He seated himself opposite his boss again.

'As you know, Jane and I have no children, Declan.'

Declan looked startled at this sudden change in the topic of conversation. He nodded, smiling uncertainly. Charles continued.

'Jane had a problem, you see. A great shame . . .' He lapsed into silence once more.

'Yes?' Declan tried to sound encouraging, though he couldn't quite see where this conversation was leading.

'That's why I've always kept an eye on you. Taken you under my wing, in the early days, so to speak.'

Declan nodded. It was true. Charles Bryer had encouraged him from the start, sometimes to the chagrin of more senior people in the firm. From the beginning he'd guided Declan, teaching him everything he knew.

'I'm very grateful, Charles. You know that,' he told the older man.

'I shall be retiring in a couple of years, and I very much hope the board will see fit to make you chairman of Hamcroft's in my place.'

Declan's eyes popped, and he flushed deep red. This was something even he hadn't hoped for, in spite of his ambitions. Deputy chairman was as far as he'd ever aspired to, and only then when Toby became chairman.

'But Toby...!' he protested. 'What about him? I thought it had always been understood that Martin Hamcroft made you chairman when he retired, the understanding being his son would succeed you eventually.'

'But what if Toby never comes back?'

The two men looked at each other, but neither spoke.

'In any case,' Charles continued, 'what I really wanted to say was that I've made you my heir. Jane will be looked after for life, but everything will come to you eventually.'

Declan felt his jaw drop open in total astonishment. His imagination soared, racing ahead to the future.

Heir to Charles Bryer, who was reputed to be worth in excess of £20 million, was something else.

'But ... but why me?' he floundered, all his usual *savoir faire* deserting him.

The chairman's eyes seemed to water, and he cleared his throat gruffly, before answering. 'Let's just say ... you're the son ... I would have liked,' Charles mumbled. He turned away to stub out his cigar.

'I don't know what to say,' Declan replied in genuine bewilderment. 'It's quite a shock ... but thank you. Thank you very much. I don't know what I've done to deserve this, but ...' His voice drifted off in unaccustomed embarrassment.

Charles looked at him then with an expression that Declan didn't understand. It seemed to appraise him, to search for something in his face, and then to be satisfied with what he found.

'George Mortimer speaking? Who is that?'

Liza stood beside her father as he took the call.

'This is Police Constable Grey from the Shepton Mallet constabulary speaking.'

'Yes?' Sir George's manner was brisk. 'What can I do for you?'

'We have a lady here, sir. She says she's a friend of yours.'

'A friend ... ?' He drew his brows sharply together.

'Yes. She turned up at the station earlier today, in a state of exhaustion. She says she's got nowhere to go, and no money either. She says, though, that if we can fix transport to get her over to where you live at Kingsmere, you'll be able to help her. Is that true, sir?'

'What's the lady's name?'

'Janet, sir. That's all she'll tell us. Would you like to speak to her?'

The police car containing Janet Granville arrived two hours later. Liza had delayed her return to London so that she could be at Chalklands to greet her.

The figure that staggered out of the police car bore little resemblance to the elegant woman they'd visited at Barons Court. Her clothes were dirty and crumpled, her tights were in shreds. Bedraggled hair and a face devoid of make-up made her almost unrecognisable.

Sir George was first down the front steps of the house to welcome her, hands outstretched. 'My dear Janet; what you must have been through,' he said as he guided her into the house. Liza rushed forward and impulsively kissed the older woman on both cheeks.

'Thank you for phoning me about Toby. I do hope you didn't put yourself at risk to do it,' she said anxiously.

Janet's face lit up at the warmth of Liza's greeting. 'Did you find him?' Her voice was low, and she glanced anxiously over her shoulder to make sure the police couldn't hear her.

Liza shook her head. 'He'd gone when I got there. We don't know where he is now.'

'Oh, my God!' Janet looked distressed.

Sir George had a few words with the police before

waving them off and joining the women. 'I gather you didn't tell them what this is all about?' he said.

'Of course not! That's why I said I'd been ill and had suffered from loss of memory. I had no money on me and I didn't know what else to do. But I knew I'd be safe if I could get here.' She turned to Liza and Sir George. 'I hope you don't mind my asking to be brought here? You're the only people I know who I could turn to for help.'

'Of course not,' Sir George replied.

Liza echoed his sentiments. 'You must stay with us until you are fully recovered,' she said. 'Come and meet the rest of the family.'

They took Janet on to the terrace, gave her tea, but did not press her for details. It was only when she seemed rested and more relaxed that Liza suggested taking her upstairs, where she could bathe and get settled into one of the luxurious spare rooms.

'We're about the same size, aren't we?' Liza observed. 'You can borrow some of my clothes.'

'You're so kind.' Janet shook her head, near to tears. 'It's been so awful. You've no idea.'

'I don't want to upset you now, because you must be exhausted, but can you tell us who they are? The people who kidnapped you? Did you know any of them?' Liza asked.

'That's the dreadful thing: I don't. I only saw the ones who came to . . . to take me away with them, but I've no idea who they were. They didn't call each other anything, and I didn't dare ask them, of course, because I was so frightened. I had the feeling they were hired by someone they called "the leader". I don't think they knew *why* they had to abduct me, or what it was about.'

'You've no idea where they could have taken Toby to now? Did they mention a castle?'

'No. I only know they'd taken him to the petrol station near Fowey because I overheard one of them saying so. I was locked in a room next to them in a remote cottage they took me to, and I was able to hear snatches of conversation.' As she spoke, Janet sank on to the spare-room bed, her voice reduced to a whisper. It was obvious she was on the point of collapse, and Liza hardly dared think what she must have suffered.

'Janet,' she said softly, 'have a bath, get into bed, and I'll get Margaret to bring you up some supper on a tray. You must sleep and get over your ordeal. I've got to get back to London tonight, but my parents are staying down here. Why don't you tell my father everything in the morning? You'll be safe staying with us. No one will know you're here and then, when you're ready, we'll get you on that plane for New Zealand, if it's the last thing we do!'

Janet dissolved into tears of gratitude and exhaustion once again. Then she whispered, 'Thank you. I don't know what I'd do without you all. Henry used to arrange everything . . .' Her voice trailed off pitifully.

Liza laid a hand on her shoulder. 'Now get some rest. I'll send my mother up to see you presently, and I'll talk to you on the phone tomorrow. All right?'

Janet nodded silently, her hand covering her mouth.

Dear God, Liza thought, as she went to fetch the older woman some nightclothes. If they have reduced this harmless woman to a nervous wreck, what are they doing to Toby?

Chapter Sixteen

It was nearly midnight when Liza drew up outside the house in Holland Park Walk. Nina and Martin had dozed for most of the journey, and now they woke, confused and crotchety. Freddy, following in his own car, unloaded the luggage and carried it into the hall.

'Why don't you go straight up to your room?' Liza suggested to her in-laws. 'Would you like a drink?'

'Tea would be nice,' said Nina, and Martin grunted in agreement.

'I'll take up all our cases,' Freddy offered. At Liza's request he was going to stay for the next few days.

'There's not much point in going home anyway,' he remarked sadly. 'Melissa's still in hospital and, even if she weren't, I doubt she'd want me back at the house. I don't think she even wants to see me again.'

'We've got to try and get you two sorted out as soon as things are back to normal,' Liza said. 'Someone is going to have to knock some sense into her, and from what you've told me, get her away from the clutches of that dreadful mother of hers.'

Down in the kitchen, left sparkling and spotless by Liza's daily cleaner, Odete, she put on the kettle and was getting out the cups when Freddy sauntered in, holding a stack of mail.

'Are they all right?' Liza asked, referring to Nina and Martin. In the last few days she'd felt they were becoming more of a liability than a help. Far from being supportive, Martin grumbled about feeling cold, and picked endless little quarrels with anyone who said a word against Lloyd's, while Nina wept a lot, adding to Liza's fears that none of them would ever see Toby again.

'They're getting ready for bed, poor old things,' Freddy replied.

'I feel sorry for them, too.' Liza set cups and saucers on a tray as she spoke. 'They're too old for this sort of nightmare.' She felt guilty for judging them harshly: they were suffering as much as she was.

Freddy, sorting out the mail on the kitchen table, came to a letter addressed to Frederick Mortimer, Esq. It was typewritten and the envelope was white and expensive-looking.

'Who can be writing to me at this address?' he asked, startled.

Liza looked up sharply. 'Open it, Freddy. Perhaps it's got something to do with Toby?'

'That's not very likely, is it?' He slit the envelope with a knife and, as he unfolded the sheet of writing paper, gazed at it in disbelief, his mouth open.

'Who is it from?'

'A firm of solicitors! I've never heard of them . . . What an extraordinary thing. They say—'

Liza had picked up the envelope. There was no stamp on it. The letter had been delivered by hand. She looked anxiously into Freddy's face.

'What does it say?'

'Melissa has had the locks changed at the house to prevent me from getting in, and they say they will arrange for my personal belongings and clothes to be delivered here early this week! Jesus, Liza! She's starting divorce proceedings right away, and barring me from going home! She's kicked me out!' He sat down rather suddenly on one of the kitchen chairs, looking extremely flaky.

'Oh, God . . .' Liza shook her head, shocked.

'Can you believe it?' He looked at his sister in a dazed fashion.

'I wonder if she thinks she can keep the house – prevent it having to be sold to meet Lloyd's losses – by kicking you out and living there by herself?'

'I don't know.'

'Get yourself a good solicitor, Freddy. I'll give you the name of the one Toby always uses: he's the best.'

'Christ, she's moved fast, hasn't she? I only left the house on Friday lunchtime, to go down to Chalklands with you. I suppose she got her mother to arrange everything.' He sounded sad and despairing.

'She's a bitch, and you're better off without her, if this is the way she's going to behave,' Liza retorted angrily.

'I could kill the silly little fool for letting you down like this.'

Freddy couldn't help smiling at his sister's vehement loyalty. 'Toby's a lucky man to have someone like you,' he said softly. 'You'd never treat him like Melissa's treated me, would you?'

'I certainly would not. What gets me is that none of this is your *fault*! If you'd cheated on her with someone else, or squandered the money at the races, or got drunk every night, then maybe she'd have a point; though I'd still think she'd behaved badly,' she added illogically.

'I don't know what to do. Nothing, I suppose. There's not much I can do if she won't have anything to do with me.' He was sitting hunched at the kitchen table; abruptly he covered his face, suddenly pink and puckered, with his hands. In a moment Liza had her arms around him, consoling him as she'd done when they'd been small.

'Maybe she's suffering from the natural grief of losing the baby. It's enough to make anyone go off-keel, so maybe this is not the end, Freddy. Maybe you can work something out when she's better?'

'But she had it in for me from the moment she heard about Lloyd's. From then on she was so angry; angry and disappointed because she thought she was set for life and that everything was going to be perfect. As soon as she realised we were going to be poor – broke in fact – she changed. I don't think it's got anything to do with the baby.'

'Oh, Freddy, I'm sorry.' Liza rested her head against his. 'Do you still love her?' she asked gently.

It seemed several minutes before he nodded, slowly. 'Yes,' he mumbled, almost inaudibly. It was as Liza feared. If he still loved Melissa, it was going to be much more difficult for him to let go, if it came to that.

'You must stay here as long as you like,' she said immediately. 'It will mean sharing a room with Thomas until all the parents go, but you won't mind that, will you? We can spend weekends at Chalklands where there's more room...'

Freddy dropped his hands from his face and, with eyes glistening, looked up at Liza with genuine amazement. 'As if you hadn't got enough on your plate without worrying about me! You must be frantic about Toby and what's happening to him, and worried that you may have lost all your money, too, and yet here you are, caring about me. You really are the most remarkable woman.'

Liza gave him a little crooked grin. 'If we don't all stick together, we *are* finished, Freddy. Come on, let's get this tea upstairs to Nina and Martin.'

'I'll take it up.'

'Thanks. I suppose I'd better check the answering machine in case there have been any messages left over the weekend.'

'OK.' He kissed her briefly and gratefully on the cheek.

As Freddy turned to leave the kitchen, Liza flipped

through the rest of the mail. When she came to a brown padded envelope she paused; the handwriting was unknown to her and the postmark smudged. Inside, she could feel something slightly oblong and hard. Who could be sending her a book? Ripping off the arrowed strip down one side, she drew out a black plastic object. It was a video cassette, unmarked, without a label and with no accompanying note.

Liza ran up the stairs to the ground floor in a fever of impatience. Dashing into the sitting room, she switched on the combined video and television set, and jammed the tape into the machine.

Then she heard it. In a heart-stopping moment that nearly made her faint, she heard the voice that was more familiar, more thrilling, than any other voice in the world. The warm, rich, beautifully modulated and deep-timbred voice that had filled her days and nights and every moment of her life for so long now. A second later, the picture filled the screen. It was Toby. She stared at the unshaven features, the swollen eyes that looked as if he hadn't slept for days, and the strip of Elastoplast on his temple. He looked unwashed, unkempt and drawn, and there was something about the way he was speaking that struck a false note. Had he been forced to read a prepared script? Was he trying to convey something that he was not allowed to say outright? Liza's mind was in such turmoil, her wits so scattered and confused, that she realised she was not actually listening to what he was saying. Toby, her beloved Toby, was talking to her and she must pull herself together; listen to what he had to say, take in every word, every nuance of expression, and make of it what she could. With shaking hands she pressed the rewind button. Then she pressed play.

'Liza, my darling, I hope you are listening to this,' he began. 'It will be the only chance I'll have of talking to you. I can't speak for long, but you've got to persuade Malcolm Blackwell to come up with the goods. He knows the terms. They're running out of patience this end and he must get on with it as soon as possible. Liza, my days are numbered if Malcolm ignores these demands. I mean it. These people are serious. They will kill me if they don't get what they want, and they will kill me if my position is made public or the police are brought in. I hope you and the children are all right, darling, and I hope we can be together again soon, but it will only happen if Malcolm obeys the instruction. Goodbye, Liza. I love you.'

The soundtrack and picture stopped at that moment, and Liza was left with the tears pouring down her cheeks, looking at a black and white flickering screen. Her sobs were the only sound that broke the stillness of the room that minutes before had been filled with Toby's voice.

'Toby . . .' her anguish was deep, profound. Toby, so near and yet so far. His voice still rang in her ears. The longing to be with him again, to hold him in her arms and tell him how much she loved him nearly overwhelmed her. Tears blocked her throat and blinded her eyes. The pain inside was real and took her breath away.

'Liza! My God, what is it?' It was Freddy, staring at her from the doorway.

Liza switched on the video again.

'Watch this,' she whispered.

Freddy looked shaken when the recording came to an end. 'But at least it means he's still all right,' he said comfortingly.

'I know.'

'Do you think they really will kill him if they don't get the money?'

'He's been made to say that, I'm sure,' Liza replied, wiping her eyes, trying to think coherently. 'I must get a copy to Malcolm Blackwell first thing in the morning.'

'I expect it was a bluff,' said Freddy. 'They're not going to want a murder on their hands, are they?'

'We don't know that.'

'What? The likes of Dad's army friend, Mackenzie? And the chap who farms? Don't you think it's unlikely? I think there's someone else calling the shots. Someone who is utterly ruthless, and desperate, too.'

Liza still looked deeply upset. 'Oh God, this whole thing is a nightmare, isn't it? How much longer is it going to go on for?'

Freddy sighed deeply. 'I wish we could tell the police. If you'd been able to tell them that he was being held in that petrol station, I bet they'd have got there hours ahead of you and rescued him in minutes.'

'Don't, Freddy,' she begged. 'It doesn't bear thinking about.'

'Are you going to be able to sleep tonight?'

'I shouldn't think so.'

'What time tomorrow are we going to know the council's findings on the Hamcroft syndicate?'

'Midday, maybe. Or the one o'clock TV news. Not that it's going to make a difference to Toby. It's Malcolm Blackwell we've got to get hold of.' Liza sounded distraught. Freddy hardly dared ask the next question, but he had to.

'You think Lloyd's will pay up now?'

The question lingered in the air, hovering between them, unanswered and unanswerable.

At eight o'clock the next morning, Charles Bryer left the elegant marble lobby of Arlington House, carrying a briefcase. He'd kissed Jane goodbye, and left her, as he always did, to her own devices. No doubt she'd go shopping, have her hair done, meet a friend for lunch, and perhaps do a little more shopping before returning to their penthouse to get ready for another round of business parties. The best thing that could be said about Jane, Charles told his cronies, was that she never gave him any cause to worry. She kept within the spending limits he'd set for her, and she mixed with nice plain women like herself, who would never draw any of them into a network of scandal. She didn't drink, and she didn't gossip. And she always did as she was told. They'd been married thirty-nine years, and she'd never caused him anxiety in any way.

The car was waiting for him as usual, a dark green

Daimler with a chauffeur he'd had for nearly fifteen years. If he felt apprehensive about his coming meeting with the chairman of Lloyd's, he gave no sign. His jitters of the previous day when he'd had Declan and Maxine to lunch had vanished. Deadly calm, as only a man who knows what fate has in store for him can be, he read *The Times* as they drove through the heavy traffic to Lime Street.

Here, in the shadow of tubular steel and glass and an awakening empire, he alighted and, entering the building, went straight up to the chairman's office. It was eight forty-five. He'd been punctual all his life. He was shown straight into Malcolm Blackwell's office, where his destiny awaited him.

Liza didn't sleep at all. She remained in the sitting room for some time after Freddy had shambled off to bed, playing the video of Toby, and copying it on to blank tapes to give to both Malcolm Blackwell and Declan. It was so wonderful just to hear his voice again, and to close her eyes and imagine him in the room. At last, exhausted, she went upstairs and had a bath and got into bed, but she couldn't sleep. It was four o'clock in the morning and she still had no idea what she should do, beyond putting Malcolm Blackwell in the picture. But what good was that going to do? It was unlikely he'd concede to the kidnappers' demands, even if they did threaten to kill Toby. So then what? Did she dare go to the police? Toby had said not, but then he'd have been told to say that.

It seemed, she reflected, as the clear blue dawn of another day washed over the rooftops of London, that the only chance of finding Toby and rescuing him lay in the slender hope that either her father would pick up some useful information on his receiver, or Janet Granville, once she had recovered from her ordeal, would remember what might be a vital link to finding Toby.

At six a.m. she clambered out of bed, missing for once the early-morning chattering of the children, like birds eager to leave the nest to join the dawn chorus. Downstairs it was quiet and still, and she opened the french windows that overlooked the garden, smelling the jasmine and honeysuckle as their fragrance came floating in to her, bringing with it memories of weekends at Chalklands when she and Toby had lazed on the terrace, enjoying the rich trappings of his success. Now, she would trade in everything they possessed just to have him back.

Freddy was the first to come downstairs, by which time Liza had dressed, given Odete a shopping list and instructions for the day, and gone through her mail.

'Did you sleep?' she asked.

Freddy nodded, rather sheepishly. 'I did, actually. Well, for a couple of hours, anyway. Are the others down?'

'No, I've sent Odete up with a tray. Martin is going to be on tenterhooks until the Council's findings are announced,' she observed.

'Aren't we all? Surely this is what is needed to clear Toby's name of nasty rumours though, isn't it?'

'Yes, if it's conclusive, but I'm afraid it will be one of those reports where irregularities have been found, but no one says who has committed them, and so everyone's under suspicion while further investigations are carried out.'

'Cheer up, sis. They might point the finger at who really has been on the fiddle in the syndicate.'

Liza smiled. 'You're much more cheerful this morning, Freddy.'

'Well, I got to thinking before I fell asleep, that really Melissa is completely dominated by that dreadful mother of hers. I've got to try and make her see sense, Liza. I have to make her realise that now we're married, I do come before her mother.'

'*Quite*,' said Liza with feeling.

Just before one o'clock, Liza turned on the television to listen to the news. Martin and Nina sat on the drawing-room sofa, watching the screen nervously; Freddy had promised to phone from his office shortly after one to find out what had happened.

It was the first news item.

'The council of Lloyd's, as a result of their investigation into the management of the Martin E. L. Hamcroft syndicate, have brought in the Director of Public Prosecutions and the City of London Fraud Squad to assist them in their findings. Five thousand investors in the syndicate have lost excessive amounts, notwithstanding the recent heavy losses suffered by Lloyd's in general. It is thought something in the region of forty million pounds could be missing. The chairman of the insurance company, Charles Bryer, has been fined one million pounds and has been suspended from Lloyd's until further investigations have been carried out.'

It was short and to the point, and Liza sat gazing at the screen, even when the announcement had ended, in a state of shock.

'Forty million pounds!' she echoed, stunned. 'What on earth could have happened?' She turned to Martin, who sat slumped, his face a sickly shade of grey.

'What's gone wrong?' she asked.

'I don't know. I don't believe this.' His voice sounded like a gurgle deep in his throat. 'There must have been a terrible mistake.'

'Charles has always been the essence of honesty, hasn't he?' Nina remarked. 'He can't possibly have gone off with all that money? How could he get hold of it in the first place?'

Martin looked up in anguish. 'This is appalling. This is the end of the company; everything I built up over the years. I don't understand how Charles could have let this happen.'

'It doesn't help Toby, either,' Liza pointed out tartly. 'I'm sorry, Martin, but my feelings are *screw the syndicate*! There was nothing in that statement to lift the shadow of suspicion that's hanging over Toby.' The thought that people might still think he was involved filled her with indignant rage.

'I've got to go and see Malcolm Blackwell, and get him to issue a statement clearing Toby's name, without revealing that he's been kidnapped. I've also got to give him a copy of Toby's message.' As she spoke she was gathering up her things, her energy restored by the strong motivation to get something positive done.

Martin had risen also. 'I must see Charles,' he said in agitation. 'I must talk to him. I don't believe he's done anything illegal; if he's guilty of anything I'd say it was only management failure.'

'Will you be long?' Nina asked, anxiously. 'Are you going up to Lloyd's? Or will you go round to his home?'

'Why, the office, of course. He may have been suspended, but he won't have left yet! God, this is a tragedy.' Muttering, he walked slowly out of the drawing room.

'Let's go together,' said Liza decisively. 'If I have to hang around any more, I'll go crazy.'

Emma sat stunned, looking at the letter she'd received that morning, as if she couldn't believe her eyes. It was typed on thick cream writing paper, and in the top right-hand corner Lloyd's of London, Lime Street, EC3 was printed in embossed red. It was no surprise to her that the letter was unsigned.

She phoned the editor of the *Globe* immediately. This was a news item in itself. When she was put through to Richard MacDonald she came straight to the point.

'I've received a death threat this morning, Richard, on Lloyd's writing paper. I've been warned about my investigative journalism into what is happening and the letter says, in no uncertain way, that if I continue to pursue the subject, and write about my findings, it will be the last thing I do on this earth.'

There was a long silence. Then Richard spoke in shocked tones. 'My God! This is unbelievable. Have you any idea who it's from?'

'None. It's anonymous, but posted in EC3, so I'd say it was someone working in Lloyd's who doesn't want what is going on exposed in the press.'

'You can say that again! Christ! I can't get over it. Listen, Emma, this is serious. I don't know that I can allow you to continue to put yourself in danger. You are, after all, a freelance journalist, and it seems to me we ought to protect you—'

Emma interrupted him. 'Please don't take me off the story and give it to one of your staff writers,' she begged. 'I've no intention of letting this scare me. It only deepens my resolve to expose whatever is going on. I think this shows they're running scared.'

'Don't you think you should discuss this with your husband, first?' Richard asked. 'I wouldn't want—'

Again, Emma cut in. 'There's no need for that. I shall continue to do everything I can to get the whole picture;

if they've got something to hide, then it must be exposed. I just wanted you to know that this is a much bigger story than I at first envisioned.'

'You'll keep me fully posted, won't you? And you'll take care, Emma? I can't say I'm very happy about this.'

'Don't worry, Richard. I can look after myself.' And I won't be telling Anthony about this either, she said to herself.

At one o'clock she watched the television news. Things were developing in a way her journalistic instincts found fascinating. And who could have sent her this letter? Charles Bryer? Declan Connolly? Malcolm Blackwell himself? Whoever it was certainly didn't want her revealing their secrets.

Declan felt too sick to eat. He'd arranged to have lunch at the Savoy with a self-made businessman from Hull who, apart from having got rich by getting into the software computer business before everyone else realised its potential, had now been bitten by the social climbing bug. Lloyd's of London was considered in his part of the world as providing a respectable background of upper-class affluence from which to climb a ladder that might lead to being an accepted member of the Establishment. His name was Frank Walters, and *bonhomie* oozed from every pore of his red and rotund face.

'So what are you having?' he demanded, scrutinising the menu.

'Asparagus, and the poached salmon,' Declan replied faintly, sipping his glass of iced water, regretting now that he hadn't cancelled this appointment. Earlier, he'd been in Lloyd's when the word had spread like a tornado around The Room that Charles had been fined £1 million and, worse, suspended under suspicion of having embezzled £40 million. Was it because of the baby syndicate, which he'd insisted on continuing, even after the committee had rendered them illegal? Or was it connected to insider knowledge? A forbidden and punishable offence in the stock market, but practised in Lloyd's as a matter of course by those who lacked integrity.

'I'm sorry I haven't been able to get down to London before now to discuss your little proposition,' Frank Walters was saying, tucking his pale pink damask napkin into his shirt collar. 'But I've been ever so busy, and I haven't been able to get away.'

'That's nice,' Declan replied absently. 'Being busy, I mean. Good for business.'

'Oh, I'm making a packet all right. Will you have red wine?' Frank Walters's beefy forefinger ran down the list of wines as if he were checking the football pools.

'I think ... just water, please.' Declan tried hard to stop his hands shaking, holding them down on his lap, pushed between his thighs.

'Just water? You must have a drop of wine.'

'Oh, well, thanks. A little white wine then.'

Frank Walters looked even more surprised. 'White,

eh? That won't put any blood into your system!' He guffawed loudly. 'Blood into your system! D'you know when I was poorly last winter, with a bit of a chest infection, they gave me a blood test.'

'Oh, yes?'

'And d'you know what they found?' he boomed.

Declan shook his head, wishing he were a million miles away.

'Blood in my alcohol stream! How about that, eh? Blood in my alcohol stream! Ha, ha!' He chortled some more, and finally chose a bottle of Chablis.

'So, how about this Lloyd's lark? Saw a headline in a newspaper on my way here about someone being suspended and fined a million pounds! Anything to do with your outfit?'

Declan swallowed. 'In any walk of life, there's always the odd bad apple,' he said, talking in clichés as he always did. 'Of course, the newspapers are going to blow it out of all proportion, but it's nothing for you to worry about. As the members' agent, I look after all the Outside Names, and you can be sure I'll pick and choose each syndicate I put you on. Spreading the losses, it's called,' he added, desperately trying to bring a note of joviality into what he was saying. 'Amongst the Names I handle,' he continued, 'it's known as "spreading the profits".' His smile was sickly, but it was good enough for Frank Walters.

'That's the word I like to hear!' he said. 'Profits! So which syndicates will you put me on? Marine or non-marine?'

'Both,' Declan replied, unhesitatingly. He could think of quite a few syndicates where the risks were high, and where losses had already been reported. Frank Walters didn't know it, but his money, before he'd even had to produce a penny, was already lost. Frank Walters and the fortune he'd made might only be a drop in the ocean when total losses, at the end of the day, could reach £20 billion, but every little helped.

Frank raised his glass now, looking like a man who thinks he's arrived. 'Here's to Lloyd's,' he beamed. 'And to making a packet.'

'Here's to Lloyd's,' Declan echoed hollowly, thinking the packet might not contain quite what Frank Walters hoped for, when it eventually did arrive. But he felt no guilt. The last few years had been all about getting people to join, because there was commission to be made that way, especially if he headed them in the direction of the high-risk syndicates. Their money was also desperately needed now, or the jolly old Lutine bell would start tolling, and it wouldn't only be for ceremonial occasions.

Back at Lloyd's by three o'clock, he bumped into Liza in the main entrance, just as she was leaving. She looked so thin and harassed he didn't recognise her at first.

'Liza!' he exclaimed, 'what on earth are you doing here? Have you been seeing Charles?'

For a second her blue eyes looked blankly into his, as if she neither knew him, nor what he was talking about. Then she recovered herself. Declan mustn't know she'd been talking to Malcolm Blackwell, having waited for over four hours, while he was closeted in meetings, before she got to see him.

'No, I haven't been to see Charles, but my father-in-law has. I just accompanied him,' she said quickly. 'How's everything going with you?'

'It's a disaster about Charles. I don't know what's going to happen now. I'm on my way to see him myself, after I've done a bit of business in The Room.' Declan looked at her more closely. There was something about her manner he didn't understand, an evasiveness that was totally unlike her. 'If you and Martin have been to see Charles, what are you doing coming out of Lloyd's? Hamcroft's is in Fenchurch Street.'

'I know *that*!' Her laugh was brittle and false. 'I just wanted to say Hi to an old friend of ours – an underwriter,' she added unnecessarily. Declan was looking at her; she knew he didn't believe a word she was saying.

'I've got to go now, Declan.' She started down the steps to the street. 'I'm late as it is.'

'Any news of Toby?' he asked urgently, following her.

'Not a thing,' she lied smoothly. At that moment an empty taxi came cruising along. She hailed it and, giving the driver her address, jumped in. Declan was left staring after her.

'I'll ring you . . .' he called out, but the taxi had pulled away from the kerb. The last he saw of Liza was her profile. She was crying.

Jane Bryer returned to Arlington House shortly after

five. Time, she reflected, for a nice bath and another cup of tea. Then she'd get dressed for the banquet at the Fishmongers' Hall – yet another evening spent with Charles's business friends. Maybe she'd wear the new navy-blue silk evening dress? Or the black lace? Charles thought the black lace was dull, but it was comfortable. It also set off her pearls rather nicely. Jane laid the black lace on her bed, and got out her black satin shoes and purse.

Knowing she had nearly two hours before Charles returned in a whirlwind of phone calls and barked commands, mislaid gold cufflinks, curses that the evening shirt wasn't crisp enough, and shouts about *why the hell hadn't a fax arrived from Mexico?*, she decided to make the most of the peaceful atmosphere. Lying on the living-room sofa, she drank her tea and contemplated the delightful day she'd spent in the company of her sister, Priscilla.

They'd lunched at Claridge's, in the Coserie, where she usually ran into several old friends, and then they'd strolled along Bond Street until they came to the grandest shop in the area, Asprey's. Here, amidst the lavish displays of silver and jewellery, antique furniture and items designed to give as wedding presents, they bought several trinkets to put aside as presents, ready to give when Christmas came round again. Then, soothed by the supreme elegance and old-world courtesy of the assistants who served them, they walked on to the Ritz, where Jane was always able to secure a table for afternoon tea, because they all knew her so well.

Surrounded by the gilt embellishments of the tea lounge, the crystal chandeliers and the red carpeting, stretching for hundreds of yards like a crimson lake, Jane lapped up the opulent splendour, like a plain brown sparrow who finds itself in a magnificent garden, but believes it only deserves to hop along the gutter. She loved splendid settings. It was as if, by some secret system of osmosis, she hoped to absorb some of the glorious grandeur, and make it a part of herself. Yes, it had been a very nice day, she thought, wanting to keep the mood of placid contentment that had cocooned her in its gently enveloping wings ever since Charles had left for Lloyd's that morning.

Then she switched on the television to watch the six o'clock news. Five minutes later, the full impact of what she'd just heard made her senses reel. In those few moments her life had been shattered. She could hardly take it in. Why hadn't Charles said anything? Why had he let her find out in this dreadful way? And what did it actually *mean*? 'Suspended'? He couldn't carry on underwriting? He couldn't, God help her, even go to work? Providing £1 million wasn't a problem, but the disgrace would be. Oh, my God, she thought, think of the disgrace! How would her hairdresser react? What about all the nice people in shops she knew? The staff at the Ritz? The head waiters at Claridge's and the Connaught?

Jane sat on the edge of the sofa, staring with unseeing eyes at the screen, wondering desperately how she should act at the banquet they were going to tonight?

And on all the other nights that lay ahead, stretched out like the signposts of their future?

. . . But had they a future? She never knew what made her do it; never guessed what presentiment made her go into Charles's cluttered, dusty study, but that is what she did. She went over to his safe in the corner, where he kept important papers and her jewellery and, without hesitation, she opened it using the combination she'd committed to memory years ago. She knew just where to look, too. Her hands went straight to the second shelf. It was as she'd thought. Charles's passport was missing.

Chapter Seventeen

Liza flung herself on to the pale pink drawing-room sofa, her eyes swollen and her mouth dropping at the corners. She looked across at Martin, who had returned from the City some time earlier. There was a raw edge to her voice.

'I saw Malcolm Blackwell. He's had another anonymous letter. They're still demanding fifty million, to be paid into the different Swiss accounts, but this time they've given him a deadline. Oh, dear God, what are we going to do? He says he won't pay out a penny.'

Martin was in a foul temper, having failed to get to see Charles Bryer. Supposedly he'd been 'in meetings' all day. He regarded Liza wearily. 'What sort of deadline?' he asked, putting down his newspaper.

'One week. Seven days from yesterday.' Her hands shook as she reached for her handkerchief, trying to control the terror that was threatening to engulf her and push her down into a slippery dark hole. Only six more days to achieve the impossible, her mind screamed, because she knew Malcolm was speaking the truth when he said he had no intention of meeting the demands. Only six days in which to discover who the other kidnappers were, and perhaps thereby to discover where Toby had been moved to.

Martin cleared his throat before speaking. 'Malcolm is quite right, of course. On no account should the ransom be paid.' Creakily he arose, and shambled over to the drinks tray to refill his glass.

Liza looked at his back view with ill-suppressed anger and frustration. 'How can you *say* that? I don't understand you. This is your son, your *only* son, we're talking about.'

Martin returned to his seat on the opposite side of the fireplace, placed his glass carefully on the side table and looked at her steadily. 'No one individual is greater than Lloyd's. In the army a soldier's life is secondary to the importance of his regiment as a whole, and his country. It's the same with Lloyd's.'

'I don't believe I'm hearing this,' Liza said appalled. 'Of course soldiers sometimes have to die to save others; but to sacrifice a human being for an *insurance* institution? That's the biggest load of crap I've ever heard.' She had risen, reed-slim and taut with nerves in a white summer dress. Her gold bangles clicked softly as she gestured expressively with her hands, pushing her long blonde hair out of the way.

Martin's wizened face was a study of cold disapproval. 'There's no need to be abusive, Liza,' he said coldly.

'I'm sorry, but I really can't go along with this idea

that Toby is of less importance than a bunch of businessmen, half of whom strike me as crooked, anyway,' she replied wildly. 'I know Malcolm can't transfer fifty million pounds to Switzerland, just like that, but he could send something; then it might open the door to negotiating. As it stands, he's sitting like a fat cat in his splendid office, and he's bloody well doing *nothing*!' Fired by passionate anger, she started walking around the room, back and forth. 'He just looks at these ransom notes, says "Dear, dear, there's nothing we can do," and then he goes out to a dinner party!'

Martin remained silent, sipping his drink, making her feel she was like a child having a tantrum, but she didn't care.

'You don't give a damn for Toby,' she went on. 'All you care about is Lloyd's.'

The dark wrinkled face and the wizened neck stretching out of the collar reminded her once again of a tortoise. 'Of course I care about Toby. Why do you think Nina and I flew over here the moment we heard he'd gone missing?'

'I'll tell you why,' Liza shot back. 'It was because at that time we all presumed Toby had had an accident, or maybe a nervous breakdown; even loss of memory. Nothing, though, that would bring disgrace on Lloyd's. *That's* why you came. Now that we know Toby's been kidnapped, probably because of what's been happening on the Hamcroft syndicate, it's a different story, isn't it?'

Martin sipped his whisky fastidiously. 'Just because I don't rush around the countryside playing at being a spy like your father, who seems to think he's still in military Intelligence, doesn't mean I don't care. You've also overlooked one very important factor.'

Liza ran her hand distractedly through her hair. 'What's that?' she asked with forced patience.

'Toby wouldn't *want* Malcolm Blackwell to pay out the ransom money. Think about it, Liza. If it had been someone else who had been kidnapped and Toby had received the ransom note, he'd be the first to say one mustn't give in.'

Miserably, Liza looked at him, recognising the truth of his words. Toby would have taken exactly the same line as Malcolm Blackwell. She covered her face with her hands. Something inside her felt as if it were crumbling, breaking, so that in a moment she would disintegrate so entirely that she'd never be able to gather herself together again. They sat in silence for a few minutes, then Martin spoke.

'That's why I believe he was forced to make that video. Toby would never have talked like that, begging for the ransom money to be paid, of his own volition.' Martin seemed to be thinking aloud. 'It's the new element – the get-rich-quick lot – that has destroyed the code of behaviour by which we all worked.'

'But they were invited to join! Coaxed into joining, even.'

'Oh yes. Again, by a new and rather unsavoury element in The Room, who were after commission for themselves, and so piled in these new members regardless.'

'Toby introduced a lot of new members out of a genuine belief that it was the best investment, if you could afford it,' Liza protested.

'My son is a man of integrity,' Martin said with dignity. 'It's not his fault that the likes of Declan Connolly muscled in on these new members, and, as their agent, was able gradually to get them on to whatever syndicate he wanted. *That's* what's gone wrong. I believe Toby intended that they should be looked after, fairly and in a straightforward manner. Declan thought otherwise. To him they were gambling fodder; I don't think he cared what happened to them or their money. Declan is exactly the wrong type to be in Lloyd's. He's more suited to the second-hand car trade.'

'The Davenports...' Liza said thoughtfully. 'That explains a lot. Declan probably changed the syndicate they were on.' Then she looked directly at her father-in-law. 'Why on earth does Declan have such a responsible job?'

Martin pursed non-existent lips. 'Charles Bryer appointed him.'

'Why? Charles must have known what was going on.'

'He's always been a favourite with Charles. In fact it was Charles who first employed him, years ago,' Martin replied drily.

'Do you think Declan realises what Charles has been up to?'

'Who knows? The committee obviously haven't been able to prove anything against Declan, otherwise he'd have been suspended, too. Personally, I wouldn't touch Declan Connolly with a bargepole. Or that frightful greedy little French wife he's got, either!'

They sat on in silence, each buried deep in a world of their own thoughts; both of them exhausted by the events surrounding them.

'So what do we do now?' Liza asked at last.

'There's not a great deal we can do.' He drained his glass and put it back on the table. 'Emma is coming to supper tonight, isn't she?'

'Yes.'

He struggled to his feet, and she was struck afresh by his frailty.

'Are you all right?' she asked, suddenly contrite.

'I think I'll go up and have a little rest before dinner,' he muttered, leaving the room.

Emma arrived an hour later, her black hair held back by a velvet bow, and one of the suits she wore to constituency functions giving her a businesslike air.

'We're handling a really hot potato now,' she said as soon as she'd hugged Liza. 'Guess what I got today? A death treat, to try and stop me writing these articles.'

Liza gasped. 'You're not serious! Christ, Em! This whole situation is getting really scary, what with Charles Bryer being suspended and the Fraud Squad called in, and Malcolm Blackwell refusing to have any dealings with the kidnappers.' Then she told Emma about the video.

'Oh, Liza!' She clutched her friend's hand. 'I wish to

God there was something I could do; has there been no word of where they've taken Toby?'

'Janet Granville hasn't been able to tell us any more than we already knew, unfortunately.'

'What … nothing? God, I bet I could get something out of her if I were to interview her.'

'There honestly doesn't seem to be much to tell. When she was taken from the house in Barons Court, she was bundled into a waiting van and blindfolded, and driven for several hours – we think down to the West Country. She was locked in a room in a remote cottage which is where she heard them talking about Toby being in the petrol station. Miraculously, she managed to escape through a window in the middle of the night. God knows how many miles she walked before she arrived in Shepton Mallet,' said Liza.

Emma's dark eyes widened. 'And she never discovered who the kidnappers are?'

Liza shook her head. 'She's no idea. They gave nothing away about themselves.'

'Oh, shit!'

'There's been nothing more from Mackenzie's house, either. Daddy thinks he's discovered the bugs. I've reached desperation point, Em. If something doesn't happen within the next week, it may be too late to save Toby.' Liza outlined what Malcolm Blackwell had said to her earlier.

'Have you thought of calling their bluff and going to the police?'

'I think of it all the time,' Liza replied with feeling.

'So what about it?' Emma sounded almost eager.

'God, I don't know. What if they aren't bluffing? What if they're serious about killing Toby if we tell anyone?'

The two women looked at each other. Liza was as anxious to bring in the police as Emma, but supposing it all went wrong? How would she live with herself, or face her children again, if the kidnappers carried out their threat?

'I don't know what to do, Declan,' Jane Bryer said, clutching the phone. 'Charles's passport is missing, and so is some cash we keep in the safe for emergencies. Did he tell you he was going away?'

'No.' For the second time that day, Declan was thrown into a state of severe shock. The fact that Charles had been fined and suspended that morning, and the Director of Public Prosecutions and the Fraud Squad had been called in was bad enough, but to hear that he'd fled the country was a terrible blow. Charles was his mentor, his boss, and a friend who had guided his career and taken care of him since he'd first joined Lloyd's as a raw recruit. It was Charles Bryer who had encouraged him to try and become as polished and successful as Toby Hamcroft. He'd also taught him how to benefit from Toby's social contacts, and take advantage of them for himself. Now Charles, according to his wife, had left the country without even saying goodbye.

'Are you sure he hasn't left you a note, Jane?' he asked, suddenly rattled. He'd always thought she was a dull, colourless woman, but now he knew she was also stupid. How come she had no idea that her husband was planning to skip the country if things got too hot?

'There's no note, Declan. I expect he'll get in touch in due course, but I wondered if you knew where he'd gone?' she said mildly, as if apologising for disturbing him.

'I've no idea,' he said shortly. 'Let me know when he contacts you, will you?'

'Yes. Of course. I suppose I'll have to go to this dinner tonight on my own.'

'Are you serious?' Declan was incredulous. 'You can't possibly go! Charles being suspended today is the talk of the City! You'll be hounded by people if you show your nose outside the door; especially when it gets out he's fled abroad.'

'Oh, dear. What shall I do?'

'Sit tight, if I were you. Look, I must go now, but I'll ring you tomorrow. OK?'

'Yes. All right.' She sounded uncertain.

Declan immediately phoned Liza. He didn't waste time on the niceties of polite small talk.

'Did you know that Charles was going to do a bunk?' he demanded.

'What do you mean?'

'Come on, Liza. You and Martin went to see Charles today, didn't you?'

'Martin did,' Liza replied, 'but I don't think he actually saw him; Charles was in meetings all day.'

'So you didn't know he was bailing out?'

'Bailing out?' Liza, dazed from lack of sleep and

stress, was having a problem keeping up with this conversation.

'He's skipped the country,' Declan said succinctly.

'No!' Liza felt a stab of genuine surprise. She'd never thought of the gutsy Charles as someone who would run away.

'Jane has just phoned me. He never even said goodbye to her. He took his passport and some cash this morning, so it looks as if he never intended returning home after his meeting with the chairman.'

Liza felt pain for his wife. Though she didn't know her very well, she could sympathise with her situation.

'How awful,' she exclaimed. 'Do you know where he's gone?'

'No idea.'

'It is because of the baby syndicates? They're not legal any more, are they? Didn't Margaret Thatcher put a stop to them?'

Declan groaned. 'I have a feeling it's more serious than the baby syndicate business. So many people are involved in that, that unless Lloyd's wanted to use Charles as a scapegoat, I very much doubt that's why he's been suspended.'

'Then what about this £40 million that's missing?'

'That's probably why he's gone. This is serious, Liza. We could all be for the high jump. I suppose there's no news of Toby?'

'None,' she said, tight-lipped.

'He's not doing himself a favour by staying away as long as this.' Declan sounded bitter. 'Everyone is going to think he's definitely involved with Charles and the missing millions, now. I suppose he's not, is he?'

'How can you *think* a thing like that?' Anger made her voice sharp.

'Come on, think about it. Toby goes missing, then forty million pounds go missing, and finally Charles does a bunk! What else are people going to think?'

'Yes, but . . .' she stopped herself just in time. 'Oh God, I don't know,' she said lamely. 'I wish Toby would come home, too.'

'What the hell are the police doing?'

'I expect they're doing all they can.' Liza spoke carefully.

'And you've heard nothing at all?' Declan probed. He reminded Liza of Lottie worrying a bone. It made her wonder if he didn't know something, and was testing the ground to see if she knew, too.

'Nothing,' she replied firmly. She said goodbye and, when she'd hung up, she turned to Emma who had been listening to the conversation.

'Declan sounds as if he's in a panic,' Liza observed. 'Charles has fled the country without even telling his wife, and Declan thinks it's to do with the missing millions.'

'Wow!' Emma looked riveted. 'Have you got her phone number? I must talk to her right away. What a twist this is! Oh, I hope the other newspapers don't know about it yet. If I'm lucky I could get an exclusive.'

'Oh, Em, you can't possibly phone the poor woman now,' said Liza, shocked.

'Why not, for God's sake? Everyone else is going to be phoning her as soon as the story breaks; she might as well talk to me first.'

'But that's awful, Em. Remember how I felt when the press arrived that morning after we knew Toby was missing? It was horrible. And if I had a problem dealing with them at first, think what it will be like for Jane Bryer. She's shy, nervous, and has never moved out of Charles's shadow. She'll have no idea how to cope.'

Emma had reached for her capacious bag, and was taking out her portable phone.

'OK, Liza. I won't involve you in this but it's something I have to do.' She dialled 192. After a moment Liza heard her say: 'Can you give me the number of Bryer, please? Charles Bryer. Arlington House.' Then she looked at Liza with a wry smile. 'I'm not even asking you for the phone number, so you won't feel involved.'

A few minutes later, Emma was talking to Jane Bryer. 'I hear your husband has left the country, Mrs Bryer. Isn't that rather unexpected? How do you feel about...'

Liza rose abruptly, and walked through the french windows into the garden. It made her feel sick to hear Emma putting Charles's wife through this gratuitous interrogation. How did Emma *think* she felt? Liza moved to the rose bushes, breaking off the dead heads with impatient hands. The sound of music came floating on the air from a neighbour's open window. It was Ravel's *Concerto for Piano and Orchestra in G*. She lifted her head to listen to the familiar strains, for this was one of Toby's favourite pieces of music. The notes, exquisitely sweet, found an echo in her heart, and a voice within seemed to say it was a good omen that she should hear this particular piece of music. It brought with it a renewed determination to save Toby; to get him home again, to have him back amongst his family.

When she returned to the drawing room, mentally refreshed by her few minutes alone, she found Emma still on the phone, clearly dictating her story to someone on the other end.

'...It is thought,' Emma was saying, 'that Charles Bryer may by now be in Switzerland. He leaves behind a wife, and a tangled web of financial corruption, making Lloyd's the centre of the worst scandal to have rocked the City in its three-hundred-year history. End of story. OK?

'It's all right, Liza,' she said gently, when she'd switched off the phone. 'I didn't grill the poor woman. Someone has to write these pieces, and it's better I should do it than some uncaring hack.'

'What did she say?'

'She sounded remarkably calm. She thinks Charles has probably gone to Zermatt, where they have a flat. That was all she could tell me, because it's obvious he never discusses his financial dealings with her,' said Emma.

'Can the Swiss government extradite him?'

'I'm not sure, but I'll find out.'

Liza frowned. 'I suppose he couldn't possibly have anything to do with Toby's kidnap, could he? Remember, the ransom notes wanted the money paid into Swiss banks.'

Emma shook her head. 'I think that's too obvious and simple an explanation.'

'But if *all* the numbered accounts mentioned actually belonged to Charles, he might hope to get fifty million, on top of the forty million he's already pinched,' Liza said, thoughtfully.

'Whilst hiring people to do his dirty work, like kidnapping Toby?' Emma thought about it. 'It doesn't sound right. I don't think that's the explanation.'

They fell silent, Emma wishing she'd got some better quotes from Jane Bryer, and Liza realising it was time to dish up the dinner Odete had cooked for them earlier.

At that moment Nina came scurrying into the room, her face a terrible shade of grey. Her eyes screamed silently. 'It's Martin . . .' she gasped. 'Come quickly.'

Martin was lying on the floor beside the bed, his skin cold and clammy, his face bleached white. Kneeling beside him, Liza felt for a pulse, a sign of breath, the flicker of an eyelid.

'I'll ring for an ambulance,' Emma said immediately.

Carefully, gently, Liza managed to roll him on to his side. Remembering all she'd learnt at a St John's Ambulance course she'd taken, she made sure he had not swallowed his tongue, that his collar was loosened, and his air passage clear.

'What happened, Nina?' she asked. Her distraught mother-in-law sat on the bed, gazing down at Martin in disbelief. Martin, who had never had a day's illness in his life ... who was always so fit...

'He complained of a pain in his chest and his jaw. Then he collapsed. He is going to be all right, isn't he?' She was shaking all over and tears were coursing down her cheeks.

Liza didn't answer. She'd found a pulse-beat, but it was faint and thready.

'The ambulance is on its way,' Emma announced. 'I'll go and wait by the front door to let them in.'

'Please, God, let him live,' Nina sobbed. 'Please let him be all right.'

Liza continued to kneel by Martin, her own heart hammering with fear. If Martin were to die, it would compound the nightmare of Toby being held hostage. She also felt deep regret that she'd lost her temper with him earlier. Holding his blue-veined hand in hers, she watched him closely, saw him breathe shallow intakes of air through blue-tinged lips, observed the sickly pallor beneath the suntan.

They waited for the ambulance, every minute seeming like an hour, time that dragged heavily and would not be hurried; and all the time Nina wept copiously.

Liza looked back to Martin again, and in that moment a strange change had come over him. His eyes had half opened, but they were unseeing, gazing beyond her at some secret horizon, and his lips had turned so white they might have been painted.

'Martin...!' Liza felt for his pulse again, saying his name with urgency, praying it wasn't true, couldn't be true . . . Nina rose from the bed and crouched over him, too.

'Martin?' Her tear-stifled voice seemed filled with surprise that there was no answer. He had no pulse, no rise and fall of breath, no movement of the eyes. A terrible stillness held the moment for ever in its silence, and they knew he had died, drifting away as quietly as a feather in the breeze.

Nina was on her knees, gathering Martin into her arms. 'Martin! . . . Martin, don't leave me! Please don't leave me.'

Too stunned to cry herself, Liza put her arm around her mother-in-law, wondering how Nina would manage without the husband she had adored for nearly fifty years.

Chapter Eighteen

Sir George came back from Chalklands the next morning and, together with Freddy, saw to all the arrangements for Martin's funeral, as Nina was too shocked and devastated to cope. Helen Mortimer returned also, bringing with her Thomas, Tilly and Sarah. It had been decided they should return to school for the last couple of weeks of the summer term, because the media had lost interest in Toby, whose disappearance seemed of little consequence compared to the new scandal that was rocking Lloyd's and the City of London.

FORTY MILLION POUNDS MISSING! screamed the headlines. SUSPENDED LLOYD'S MAN FLEES THE COUNTRY!

Only in very small type, at the bottom of the last column, were a few lines mentioning that 'another Lloyd's member, Toby Hamcroft, went missing two weeks ago and has not been seen since'.

Emma, dropping in for coffee the following day, gave a wry smile as she glanced at the stack of newspapers on a side table in the drawing room.

'Isn't it *typical*!' she exclaimed. 'Here they are, these gutter-press tabloids, making a big drama out of Charles Bryer going to Switzerland, and completely missing the *real* story, which is Toby being kidnapped!'

'It is ironical, isn't it!' Liza agreed. If Emma had not been such a good friend she'd have been nervous that she might get carried away by the demands of her profession and scoop the story of the year. It must be very tempting, Liza reflected. Being the first one with a major story was every journalist's dream.

'How is Nina?' Emma asked.

'She's stayed in bed since it happened. I hope she'll be able to manage the funeral tomorrow. Martin's death has really hit her hard,' Liza replied. Her voice shook. 'Honestly, Em, I don't think I could bear anything else to happen. I don't know how I'd have managed without Mum and Dad since this whole nightmare started.'

Emma, seeing how much weight Liza had lost, and how chronically tired she seemed, wondered as well how much longer she could carry on. She gave her friend a sympathetic hug.

'When Toby is back,' she said with emphasis, 'you must both get away for a holiday. On your own. Just the two of you. Kick everyone off *Morning Glory* and set off around the world or something!' she added dramatically.

Liza smiled, though tears were never far away, especially now she had the grief of Martin's death to cope with, too. 'Dream on, Em! We probably won't be able to keep the boat! I don't know if we'll have any money. Have you heard if Anthony has suffered any losses?'

'Not so far. I'm praying, Liza. Mind you, as I said, Anthony and I are not talking at the moment. He's angry at my doing an exposé on Lloyd's, and he's scared it may affect his position. God, I don't know what to do. My career means a lot to me. I think he's being unreasonable.'

'Members of Parliament do have to be more careful than the average person about getting involved in anything unsavoury, don't they?' Liza pointed out.

'I suppose so. Nothing's going to stop me doing this particular story though. Not even death threats.'

Liza looked concerned. 'You haven't heard any more? Who on earth, in Lloyd's, could have sent you that letter?'

'God knows!' Then Emma smiled affectionately. 'We do go back a long way, don't we? When this absolutely stinking time is over, we've got to give a party, Liza, even if we're all broke. We've got to give a party if only to celebrate the fact we're still *here*, and that we've survived all this.'

'I agree. Oh, wouldn't it be wonderful?' Liza closed her eyes, trying to imagine Toby home, safe and unharmed, and all of them together again. Then she frowned and opened her eyes again. 'Toby's going to be terribly upset about his father.'

'They were quite close, weren't they?'

'Yes and no.' Liza put her head on one side. 'I don't

think they shared quite the same values. Money means a lot to Toby, because, as he always said, it enabled him to give the children and me the sort of lifestyle he wanted for us. I'm sure he wouldn't have gone along with Martin's blind loyalty to Lloyd's, though. People have always been more important to Toby than money or possessions.'

'Talking to Martin the other day,' Emma said thoughtfully, 'I got the feeling that his first, only and great love was Lloyd's itself. Not even the money it produced for him. It was his spiritual home; its history became his history; all it stood for – before this financial calamity – was everything Martin himself stood for.'

'Yet he appointed a rogue like Charles Bryer to be chairman until Toby was old enough and sufficiently experienced to take over,' Liza pointed out. 'It's a long time since he actually worked there.'

'And you've no idea why he left and went to Spain?'

'I think it was for health reasons. The English climate didn't suit him.'

'He did complain of the cold, although the weather's been lovely.'

'I should have noticed he was unwell,' Liza spoke as if she felt guilty. 'They should never have come over here; there hasn't been much they could do, anyway, except sit and fret.'

Emma lowered her voice. 'Is Nina going back?'

'No. She wants to sell the villa and move back to England, permanently,' Liza replied.

'I think she's wise. She'd be awfully lonely otherwise,

wouldn't she? At least she's got all of you around her, if she stays here, and Martin will have made sure she's financially looked after, won't he?'

'I imagine so, though money isn't much of a consolation if you've lost the person you love.'

'I agree, but as they say: it helps to be miserable in comfort. What's happened to Janet Granville, by the way? Is she still in hiding at Chalklands?'

'No. That's one story with a happy ending. Daddy put her on a plane for New Zealand two days ago to be with her sister, and we gave her enough money to get started again. I do hope she's going to be all right.'

Emma's face softened as she looked at Liza, and she spoke with affection. 'Do you know what you deserve, Liza? A chamois to polish your halo! You're an angel. God, Janet Granville must be so grateful. That woman's life was over, washed up, until you and your father befriended her.'

'She was nearly washed up *because* we befriended her,' Liza retorted. 'She'd never have been abducted if she hadn't been trying to help us find Toby.'

Emma smiled fondly at Liza. 'Toby will be so proud of you when he hears how marvellously you've carried on during this whole ordeal,' she said sturdily.

For a second a mischievous gleam flashed in Liza's blue eyes, and she grinned. 'You think so, Em? You really think so?' For a moment she allowed herself the luxury of imagining Toby's approval when he heard how she'd held things together in his absence.

'I know so! You know it too, but you're so flaming

modest and self-deprecating, you'd never admit it,' Emma scoffed teasingly.

Liza chuckled, feeling better. All this positive talk about what they'd do when Toby returned was what she needed to keep her own morale up. And if he didn't...? She wasn't even going to think about it at present.

Three hundred people attended Martin Hamcroft's funeral at Holy Trinity, Knightsbridge, followed by the cremation at Golders Green. Sir George had organised everything with military precision, from putting the announcement in *The Times* and *Telegraph*, to booking the church, with a full choir, and, after long and tearful consultations with Nina as she chose the hymns and readings, the printing of the service sheet. Freddy and six of his friends were to usher the guests into pews, the church was to be decorated with Martin's favourite white iceberg roses, limousines had been hired to transport all the family, and the coffin itself he'd chosen for its beautiful oak.

Nina, unable to speak, or think, or plan or concentrate on anything for more than a few seconds, was 'kitted out', as Sir George insisted on calling it, in a black dress and hat bought by Helen at Harrods.

'I don't know how she's going to get through the funeral,' Helen confided to the rest of the family. 'She's out of her mind with grief. It's going to be the most terrible ordeal for her.'

'Get her a pill or something from the doctor,' Sir

George suggested, 'and we'll give her a stiff brandy before we leave for the church.'

The funeral was to take place at ten-thirty and, by the time they arrived at Holy Trinity, the church was filled with mourners, mostly elderly and middle-aged couples who had been the Hamcrofts' friends during Martin's long years in the City. Liza, slipping into the front right-hand pew with Nina, recognised many of their own friends as well. They all seemed to be staring at her, and her cheeks flamed at the thought that they might believe Toby had vanished along with Charles Bryer, taking the missing £40 million with them.

There were Sir Humphrey and Lady Rosemary Davenport whom she'd heard had lost a fortune, and who were being forced to sell Cavenham Court and all its contents. They looked surprisingly composed in the circumstances. In contrast, Declan and Maxine Connolly looked hard-jawed and worried, Maxine swathed in black chiffon, Declan trying to tone down his loud blue pinstriped suit with a black tie. Liza briefly scanned the other faces, wondering who had lost money and who had escaped the financial reaper; wondering even, in a heart-stopping moment as the thought occurred to her, whether any of the people here might be Toby's kidnapper? The thought made her jittery, and she had to clasp her hands tightly in her lap to stop them shaking.

The coffin was now in place before the altar. Nina, having taken her prescribed pills, and had a brandy, seemed controlled if a little excitable. The choir began to sing 'Jerusalem', and Liza braced herself for the coming ordeal. She'd never been good at handling funerals, even if it was someone she hardly knew, but today her thoughts and prayers were so filled by Toby that she found it hard to concentrate on Martin. Toby, her love, the one person in the whole world she revered above all others, should have been here today, mourning the loss of his father, and his absence was like a large hole in the atmosphere that nothing else could fill.

'Let us pray...' said the minister, and Liza found all her prayers were for Toby. God would take care of Martin now; it was Toby who needed help.

The service was dignified, the chosen music beautiful. Nina seemed to bear up with remarkable stoicism, and afterwards she stood with Liza in the doorway of the church, greeting friends and thanking them for coming. If she seemed dazed, no one was surprised. If what she whispered confidentially to some of her friends sounded far-fetched and slightly deranged, no one felt anything but sympathy for the widow whose husband had been so suddenly and tragically taken from her.

Two hours later, back at Holland Park Walk, her words were to have a devastating effect.

It had been Sir George's suggestion that Liza hold a reception after the funeral. She had readily agreed. Caterers had been ordered to serve drinks in the drawing room, and a light buffet lunch in the dining room to those who went straight from the church to Holland Park Walk. Freddy had been roped in to act as host, while the rest of the family went to the cremation service; and when they returned, Liza found over a hundred people milling around, crowding into all the ground-floor rooms and even spilling into the garden.

'There are so *many*...!' she exclaimed in dismay. 'Have you ordered enough of everything, Dad?'

'Of course, Liza.' He spoke with confidence. 'I knew half the City would turn up for Martin's funeral; all his old chums, you know. I think it's going rather well, don't you?'

'Once a general always a general,' she whispered, smiling. 'You're wonderful, Dad. Thank you very much for organising everything.'

'Where's Nina gone? Is she all right?'

'She's fine. She's sitting in the dining room, surrounded by all her old friends. She's bearing up very well, considering.'

Freddy came up to her at that moment. 'Everything OK, sis?'

'Thank you for holding the fort,' Sir George interjected. 'Damn useful, m'boy. Couldn't have got it started without you.'

'That's OK. I never object to getting to the champagne before everyone else,' he responded with a grin.

'I suppose I ought to circulate,' Liza said reluctantly. Her head ached and she wished all these people, the majority of whom she'd never seen in her life before, would go home. As she squeezed past a group in the hall, to go into the drawing room, she bumped into the Davenports.

'My dear Liza,' Lady Rosemary greeted her with a kiss on both cheeks. 'I am most awfully sorry about everything. You're having a wretched time, aren't you?'

'We've been thinking a lot about you, m'dear,' Sir Humphrey interjected.

I'm sure you have, thought Liza. *But for us, you'd still be rich.* Aloud she said: 'It's really good of you to come today.'

'Not at all, and we're terribly worried to hear about Toby, too! You must be quite frantic,' Lady Rosemary sympathised.

'One doesn't expect this sort of thing in England, does one? Quite barbaric!' Sir Humphrey continued.

Liza looked from one to the other and smiled uncertainly, not quite sure what they meant. 'It is worrying . . .' she replied, and at that moment an elderly lady tugged her arm, drawing her away.

'This is frightful news about Toby,' she rasped. 'I was terribly shocked when I heard.'

Someone patted Liza on the back, and she turned to see a tall white-haired old man looking down at her with concern. 'It's a dreadful business. My God, it's not what you expect, is it?' he commented with a knowing look.

Bewildered and suddenly apprehensive, Liza hurried into the drawing room, wondering what was going on. Why all this sudden talk about Toby? Everyone would know he was missing, but she'd been trying to play it down; and yet, she could detect a definite buzz in the atmosphere, with guests giving her darting, sympathetic looks.

Liza rushed up to Helen, who was talking to a group of guests. 'Will you excuse me if I have a quick word with my mother?' Charmingly, Liza edged Helen away.

'What's going on, Mum?' she asked urgently. 'People are talking about Toby as if they knew what had really happened.'

Helen looked aghast. 'Surely not!'

At that moment, one of the butlers provided by the catering firm came up to Liza.

'Madam, there's a phone call for you. Will you take it, or shall I say you're not at home?'

'I'll take it,' Liza said immediately. She hurried to the small sitting room and picked up the receiver.

'This is Liza Hamcroft; can I help you?'

'Good afternoon, Mrs Hamcroft. Shane Warwick here, from the *Globe*. We've just heard your husband has been kidnapped and held hostage. Can you confirm this is true?'

Liza froze, her mind free-falling into a spin. She didn't speak; couldn't speak. Clutching the phone, she stood as if paralysed.

'Are you there, Mrs Hamcroft? Your husband is Toby Hamcroft, isn't he? Can you tell us about his kidnap? When exactly—'

'I have nothing to say,' she said, slamming down the phone.

The phone rang again almost at once. In a fury born of fear, Liza snatched up the receiver and held it to her ear. 'Yes?' Her tone was forbiddingly clipped.

'Is that Mrs Liza Hamcroft?' The man's voice was uneducated and chummy. 'This is Jeff Harper from the *Evening News*. We've just received a report about your husband. Is it true he's been kidnapped and held for ransom, because he's a member of Lloyd's . . . ?'

Liza replaced the phone while he was still talking then shot out of the sitting room and looked around, frantically trying to find her father. At that moment she saw Emma coming out of the dining room, holding a plate of food.

'Emma!' She pounced on her friend and, grabbing her by the elbow, manoeuvred her into a corner of the hall.

Emma looked startled. 'What on earth's the matter?'

'I'll tell you what's the matter.' Liza was almost out of control with rage and fear. 'Someone has told the press about Toby! Don't you realise what this could mean? Remember what they threatened if it got out?' Blinded with anguish, she seemed to be seeing her friend through a red haze.

'What about Toby?' Anthony asked curiously, coming over to talk to them at that moment. 'Everyone knows he's vanished. The press have already written all about it.'

'Anthony doesn't know,' Emma cut in quickly. 'Tell me what's happened, Liza.' Her face suddenly turned white. She turned her back on Anthony, who looked annoyed at being ignored.

Liza told her about the phone calls. Even as she spoke, the butler came up to her.

'The ITV newsroom on the phone, madam.'

'Oh, God!' A sob escaped from Liza, and she covered her face with her hands.

'What's the matter, sis?' asked Freddy, as he passed her on his way to the drawing room.

'Someone's blown the story about Toby,' Emma whispered distractedly.

Freddy looked shocked. 'Jesus! What are we going to do?'

'Will someone tell me what's happened?' Anthony demanded in a loud voice.

'Later, Ant,' Emma said crisply. Then she gripped Liza by the shoulders. 'Liza, you don't think it was me, do you? I'd never do a thing like that.'

Liza nodded. 'I know, Em. I never thought it was you, but *who* is it?'

'What's going on?' Sir George strode up to them. 'What's all the commotion . . . ?' He caught sight of Liza's face. 'What's happening?'

'It's got out what happened to Toby. It seems every journalist in London is on to it.'

'*What?*' His face flamed red. 'How can they know? Are you sure they haven't just guessed, and are trying to trap you into confirming it? I hope you haven't said anything . . .'

'Of course I haven't,' Liza snapped. They were all on edge now.

'Let me go and sort this lot out!' Sir George said decisively, striding to the front door where a cluster of newspaper people had gathered. He looked them over as if they were a bunch of new recruits who didn't even know how to stand to attention.

'Look here. We've just come from a family funeral, we're all very tired and upset, and I'll ask you to leave us alone, please. We do not wish to be disturbed. Thank you.' Then he closed the front door quickly, before they could respond.

'Do not let *anyone* in,' he commanded the butler who was standing watching the proceedings, open-mouthed. 'And,' he continued, 'take the phone off the hook.'

Emma looked up at him in astonishment. 'Well, that's one way of handling it, I suppose,' she remarked, 'but I'm not sure it's the right way.'

'It's the *only* way until we have drawn up a plan of action,' Sir George said fiercely. Then he turned to Liza who was leaning against the door-lintel, her arms clasped round her ribs as if she were nursing a pain.

'Is Malcolm Blackwell here? We'd better get on to him right away and warn him.' He clasped the top of his head with the palm of his hand. 'This is a disaster. Who in God's name could have let the secret out?'

Sir Humphrey, strolling past to get his glass refilled, overheard Sir George.

'Are you talking about Toby being kidnapped?' he asked. 'We were told in the strictest confidence, but several people seem to know.'

'But *who* told you, Humphrey?' Liza asked.

'Why, your mother-in-law, of course,' he replied blandly. 'She told us as we were leaving the church.'

Liza recoiled, shutting her eyes as the realisation of

what had happened sank in. Doped on pills and alcohol to help her get through the funeral, Nina had obviously had no idea what she was saying.

'God help us,' she said faintly. 'What are we going to do now?'

Sudden hammering on the front door startled them all.

'Let the buggers wait while we decide what to do,' said Sir George firmly. 'No one is to open the door.'

'You're going to have to open it sooner or later in order to let the guests out,' Emma remarked in a sensible voice. 'Anyway, there's no point in denying Toby's been kidnapped, because it seems half London knows already.'

The hammering continued. It was so loud some of the guests stopped talking.

'Perhaps it's not the press this time,' Liza pointed out as she struggled to keep calm. Inwardly she felt incandescent with rage. How could Nina have been such a fool! She felt terrified too: what if the consequences of Nina's stupidity proved fatal?

Furious and scared, she felt in the mood for confrontation. She strode swiftly across the large square hall, a slim figure in a simple black dress, her black high-heeled shoes tapping on the marble floor.

She flung the front door wide open.

'What do you want?' she stormed furiously.

Then she realised she was staring into the face of a police officer, whose cold eyes only matched hers for hostility.

* * *

Several hours later, Detective Inspector Robin Buck sat facing Liza. He looked tight-lipped; he was clearly having a problem containing his temper.

'Hundreds of hours of police time have been wasted while we pursued the wrong lines of enquiry because you failed to tell us the truth,' he said severely. 'That is withholding information, Mrs Hamcroft, and a very serious offence. You should have informed us immediately you knew your husband had been kidnapped.'

'But I've told you over and over again that they've threatened to kill Toby if we told *anyone*,' she shot back, equally angry. 'Anyway, as I said, it was the chairman of Lloyd's who got the ransom note, not me.'

'I will be talking to him later on this evening. Meanwhile I gather you, General, have been conducting your own enquiries?' Buck's voice was icy, his manner barely civil as he turned to Liza's father.

'I most certainly have,' Sir George responded robustly. 'Let me tell you, I was in Intelligence for years, so I *do* know what I'm doing.'

'It's absolutely dreadful that this has got out,' Liza said. She was distraught with worry. 'Don't you realise these people mean business? Now it's going to be in all the newspapers, and on the TV news . . .'

'That is hardly our fault,' Buck informed her. 'We could have prevented that happening if we'd been informed of the true facts. We would have imposed a news blackout.'

'We still thought it was too risky,' Liza said. 'We

believe these people, whoever they are, mean business. I'm terribly frightened for Toby's safety now. Can you trace where he's been taken? We think it might be a castle.'

'We can let you have list of everyone who was at the funeral today,' Sir George added. 'I'm of the opinion the kidnappers are on the Hamcroft syndicate.'

Buck's expression remained cold. 'Have you told us everything now?'

Liza and her father looked at each other.

'I think so,' Liza replied. 'Is there any way we can fix a news blackout now, do you think?' she added desperately.

Buck rose. 'Seeing you had most of the media here this afternoon, I think it's highly unlikely,' he replied curtly. 'And please, Mrs Hamcroft, General, if you hear *anything* more about Toby Hamcroft, let us know immediately. We may already be too late. If we'd had this information sooner, things might have worked out very differently.'

Liza gave a sharp intake of breath. 'Too late?' she repeated in anguish.

Sir George put his arm round her shoulders. 'We had no choice,' he told Buck.

'There is always a choice, sir. We have ways and means of dealing with every crime, including kidnapping, and we are as able to work undercover as any branch of Intelligence. I have to say, General, that this case has been severely bungled from the start, including the handling of a potential witness, Mrs Janet

Granville, who you tell me isn't even in the country any longer! I can't impress on you strongly enough that it is better to leave this sort of thing to the professionals. I'd have thought you, of all people, should know that.'

Sir George snorted but said nothing. Liza now realised they'd made a possibly fatal mistake in trying to get Toby back by themselves.

Declan Connolly came round to see Liza early the next morning. One look at his face told her he'd seen the morning newspapers.

'Christ, Liza! Why the fuck didn't you tell me?' were his first words. He looked shattered, as if he hadn't slept for nights. 'Did Charles Bryer know?'

Liza shook her head. 'No one knew except Malcolm Blackwell.'

'And all this time, when we thought Toby had gone missing, he's really being held for ransom? It's unbelievable! Absolutely unbelievable! Why didn't you tell me?' he asked again. His squat fingers kept rubbing his face, as if trying to brush away something.

'They threatened to kill Toby if it got out. You've no idea how serious this is,' Liza replied, leaning back in her chair, closing her eyes for a moment. She hadn't slept at all and now she was feeling nauseous from exhaustion, the coffee she'd just had still bitter in her mouth.

'But at least this clears him from any suspicion of being involved in the missing forty million, doesn't it?'

'His honesty has never been in question,' she said coldly.

Declan looked taken aback by her manner. 'You and I know he didn't embezzle the money, but there are others who don't, and who would be delighted to see the high-and-mighty Toby Hamcroft fall from grace,' he pointed out.

'Really?' She opened her eyes for a moment and then closed them again. 'What small-minded people they must be,' she said.

Declan leaned forward, eager for her to know he wasn't one of them. 'This changes everything though, doesn't it?'

'What, for instance?' She wished he'd go away and leave her alone. Here he was, while Toby's life was in danger, wanting to gossip and speculate on the future. What future? she asked herself. She'd failed to find Toby and she felt terrible about it. She'd let him down and now it might be too late to do anything. If only she'd realised what Nina was saying to her friends. If only they'd all kept her confidentiality. But someone had spoken. A word here, a whisper there, and then the beast was out of the cage, rampaging everywhere, never to be captured and silenced again.

'Toby and I will be able to run the company together, now that Charles has gone,' she heard Declan saying.

'Will you?' she asked absently, too sick at heart to really listen.

'Well, when Toby's been released, he's going to want to get back to work, isn't he? Pretty damn quick, too.'

Liza looked at him. 'Why should he ever want to set foot in Lloyd's again?' she asked.

'Oh, God, Liza. I'd forgotten, in all this hullabaloo, that you hadn't heard about Toby's losses. He'll want to get going again, I'm sure, to try and rescue the situation.'

'Losses?'

'Yeah. I'm sorry you had to find out like this. Toby always refused to join the baby syndicate, you know. He's lost a packet, Liza, especially through the asbestosis claims in America. Toby has really copped it in a big way; and for the next three years, too. I'm all right, because Charles and I were on the baby syndicate.' He tried to keep the triumph out of his voice, but he looked pleased with himself as he glanced across to see how Liza was taking the news. He'd always tried to emulate Toby, and now, for a change, it was he who was ahead of the game.

'Bully for you, Declan,' she said quietly. 'Money happens to be the last thing on my mind right now.'

Chapter Nineteen

Liza awoke the next morning after a few hours' snatched and troubled sleep, expecting the top of the world to have blown off. Instead she found everything to be unnaturally quiet. The desperate jittery feeling of yesterday had worn off, and now a quiet sense of desperation made her feel strangely detached, as if all the terrible events of the past few weeks were happening to another person.

Outside on the pavement, an encampment of journalists and photographers waited patiently. That meant another day of lying low and of not leaving the house unless it was absolutely necessary.

As she made herself some coffee in the kitchen, still deserted at this time in the morning, Liza wondered if she'd hear from Malcolm Blackwell today. Her efforts to contact him yesterday had been frustrated by his secretary telling her that he was in meetings and couldn't be disturbed. No doubt the police had been to see him, and she wondered vaguely if Buck had been as angry with the chairman of Lloyd's for withholding information as he'd been with her. Somehow she doubted it.

A few minutes later Helen appeared, took one look at Liza and said gently, 'Darling, why don't you go back to bed? You look worn out.'

'I didn't sleep well. Maybe I'll have a rest this afternoon, but I can't stay in bed once I wake up. I start thinking . . . and that's fatal.'

Her mother nodded. 'I know what you mean. Everything seems worse from a horizontal position. Once you're on your feet, one's sense of perspective comes back.'

Liza poured Helen a cup of coffee, and they sat on each side of the kitchen table looking at each other, a younger and an older version of the same pattern, the shared genes.

'What are you going to do today, Liza?'

'I was going to let the children go back to school, but it's obviously hopeless. The press are waiting outside, and I bet they'll follow them to school. I'm beginning to feel we're all hostages in our own home.'

'Why don't Daddy and I drive them down to Chalklands again? After all, the summer holidays start very soon; there's no point in keeping them in London if they can't go to school, is there?'

'You're right. Would you and Daddy mind staying down there with them? They're beginning to feel insecure, and I feel they need to be with family. You'll have Ingrid and Margaret and Bert to help.'

Helen reached across and patted Liza's arm. 'We'd

love to, sweetheart. Shall we take Nina, too? She'd be happier in the country, wouldn't she?'

'Oh! Nina.' Liza looked as if she'd had a sudden pain, her brows drawing sharply together, her mouth tightening. 'How *could* she have told everyone about Toby? I still can't believe it.'

'It was the tranquillisers mixed with brandy that did it. I don't think she knew what she was doing. She was devastated when she realised what she'd said.'

'I know. God! What a mess.'

'Will you be all right here, on your own?' Helen asked, suddenly anxious.

'Freddy will keep me company in the evenings ... Anyway, how long is this hell going to last, for God's sake?' Liza looked up, her eyes shot with pain. 'It *can't* go on for much longer. We've passed the stalemate mark, when the kidnappers were demanding money and Malcolm Blackwell was refusing to give in. But now ... ? Surely ... ?' Her voice drifted uncertainly. She was no longer sure of anything.

Late that evening, after it was dark and the press had finally left, convinced the family had gone to bed and nothing of interest was likely to happen, Sir George and Helen set off for Chalklands with Nina, the children, and Ingrid, who had Lottie on her lap.

'You're unlikely to be bothered by the media at Chalklands if they don't know you're there,' Liza told them, 'and at this time of night it should only take just over an hour.'

Sir George had been reluctant to leave what he called 'the scene of action', but Liza had pacified him by saying the children badly needed the presence of a father-figure at this time. It was true, but she was also anxious about her father's health. Martin's death had shocked them all.

'Why aren't you coming too, Mummy?' Tilly whined anxiously as she climbed into the back of the car with Nina.

'Because I have a lot of things to do here, but I promise I'll be down at the weekend,' Liza assured her, giving her a final kiss.

'But that's not for *ages*.'

'The time will go very quickly, Tilly.'

'Are you going to wait for Daddy to come home?' Thomas asked, intuitively.

Liza looked into his blue eyes. They were so like her own, it was as if a part of her soul lay within him. 'Yes, I am,' she said with as much conviction as possible. 'But even if Daddy isn't home this week—' her voice faltered for a second before she controlled it – 'I'll still come down on Friday night.'

Liza waved them off, suddenly upset to see them all go. She'd longed for the peace of solitude earlier in the day; a moment to herself in which to gather her personal resources about her like a protective cloak, but now that they'd gone, a wave of sorrowful loneliness swept over her as she hurried back into the house. Freddy had gone out to dinner, saying he'd be back late. The house was eerily quiet. She'd never felt as low as she did at this moment.

* * *

When the police rang the front door bell early the next morning, Liza knew instinctively that something was wrong. They *could* have been bringing her good news about Toby, but something inside told her they weren't. Odete, opening the front door, seemed to recoil when she saw Detective Inspector Buck standing there. By his side was a policewoman Liza had not seen before.

Odete gestured for them to enter and, as Liza walked towards them, she braced herself for what was to come.

'I'm sorry to arrive like this, unannounced,' Buck began, and for a wild moment Liza nearly laughed hysterically: it sounded as if he'd gatecrashed a cocktail party or something, and was apologising for his *faux pas*.

'What is it?' Fear, like a cold hand, clutched her heart and squeezed hard. She looked up into his face and for the first time noticed that he had quite compassionate eyes. That frightened her even more. 'What's happened?' Her voice sounded harsh to her own ears.

'Shall we go into the lounge and sit down?' he suggested gently.

I can't bear it, Liza thought. Please God don't let him tell me . . .

She found herself being guided towards one of her drawing-room sofas. Buck stood in front of her, but the policewoman sat down beside her: she was a perky-looking young woman with a face like a cheeky little bird, and she looked ready for anything.

Buck gave it to her straight.

'They've found a body, washed up on the South coast, on a beach near Bexhill. We have reason to believe it may be your husband, but I'm afraid you're going to have to identify it before we can proceed.'

Liza continued to breathe; short, shallow breaths that did nothing to stop the feeling that the life was draining out of her body. 'I'll come right away,' she heard herself say. Then, practically: 'I'm afraid I haven't got a car at the moment, is there someone who can give me a lift?' She'd risen, as she spoke, and was distractedly checking the contents of her handbag.

Buck blinked. 'There's a car waiting to take you, Mrs Hamcroft. Whenever you're ready.'

Emma gathered together her notes, stunned by what she'd discovered. If all she'd been told was true, it was the most appalling example of blatant corruption she'd ever come across. It went a long way to explaining why Toby had been kidnapped; it also explained why Charles Bryer had fled the country.

Her source, which as a journalist she was honour-bound never to reveal, had provided her with enough information to sink Lloyd's along with its Lutine bell and everything else. The point was, though, would Anthony ever speak to her again if she did? Was any story worth risking one's marriage for? After a sleepless night she decided to tell him what she'd discovered before she wrote anything. They were spending two nights in London, and for once, they'd had a leisurely breakfast on their own, going through the mail and reading the newspapers. 'Ant, I want to ask you something,' she said softly. They were talking again, but hadn't yet recaptured their usual rapport.

'Ummm?' He seemed preoccupied, ticking something on a list.

'Please listen, Ant. This is very important.'

He looked up, frowning. 'What is it, Em?'

'I think I've rumbled what's going on in Lloyd's, and why Toby has been kidnapped.'

His expression hardened. A flicker of wariness skimmed across his eyes.

'And...?'

'I want to write about it, because it's very important. I truly believe the facts should be made public.'

'Go on.'

'You've read in the papers that forty million is missing from the Hamcroft syndicate, and that's why they're not able to meet all their claims?'

Anthony nodded, listening intently now.

'Apparently, for some time now, it has been a perfectly legal tax-haven scam for members' funds to be transferred abroad through an offshore reinsurance scheme. The capital growth is tremendous, of course, even after the interest is paid out to members,' Emma explained. 'These offshore companies are in places like Jersey and the Cayman Islands; even the Isle of Man.'

'These are funds from low-risk, high-profit reinsurance premiums, aren't they?' Anthony asked, listening carefully.

Emma looked surprised at how knowledgeable he was. 'Yes, that's right.'

'The Treasury knows all about it. It *is* a tax-dodging scam, but not illegal.'

'So I gather,' Emma continued. 'Now, on top of that, Charles has been running a baby syndicate, for himself and his friends, all on stop-loss policies, which ensured they couldn't lose money beyond a certain amount. Declan Connolly alone brought in eleven million in underwriting capacity, but most of the Names seemed to have been Toby's friends, whom he had originally made certain were on safe syndicates. Are you with me?'

'Yes, so far, but I don't see what you're leading up to,' Anthony commented. 'It all sounds like a bit of sharp practice, and very unfair, but no more, except that Declan must have been making a packet in commission.'

'It became a lot more when it was discovered the other day that Charles Bryer has diverted forty million pounds' worth of members' funds, held in offshore companies, into companies of his own in other countries.'

Anthony let out a low, long whistle. 'How glad I am that I listened to Toby,' he remarked after a moment.

'What do you mean?'

'I asked him about this baby syndicate business a few years ago, because a lot of people in the House feared it was for the benefit of those who worked in Lloyd's, to the detriment of those who didn't, and that sooner or later there'd be a scandal. Margaret Thatcher was dead against it.'

'And . . . ?' she asked, fascinated.

'Toby said on no account would he let me join a baby syndicate in my position as an MP, because he was sure there *would* be trouble in the future.'

'That was nice of him . . . but doesn't it mean we'll have lost our money?'

'If we've been unlucky, yes. But frankly, I'd rather that happened, because at least it would be an honest loss, rather than getting caught up in a City scandal. That would be the end of my career.'

'So you don't mind my revealing that Charles Bryer has gone off with all this money, and that's why he's fled the country?'

Anthony reached across the table and took her hand. 'Under these circumstances I don't mind at all, and thank you for telling me what you're doing. I'm sorry I've been such an arsehole, darling. I got scared because I feared a scandal at Lloyd's might backfire on us, but you're right. This type of wrongdoing must be stopped. Have you told Liza what you've discovered?'

'Not yet.'

He grinned at her and looked intrigued. 'Just how *did* you find all this out?'

'I don't think it would be fair to tell you his name, but there's a young chap who works in Hamcroft's, and he discovered what had happened when the committee investigated the company. Charles Bryer only missed the arrival of the Fraud Squad by an hour. He must have guessed what was likely to happen, and that's why he took his passport to work with him that morning.'

Liza was barely aware of the drive down to Bexhill. The police car was driven carefully and within the normal speed limits, and there was no dramatic flashing blue light or wailing siren, except in her mind. She mustn't *think*. As they drove through towns and villages, no one paid any attention to the car as they went about their business, and yet, she wondered, why not? Did she not give off a strange aura, livid and incandescent in its intensity? She mustn't *feel*. She looked down at her hands. Ordinary hands with well-kept, unpainted nails, her wide old-fashioned wedding ring still shining as if it were quite new. She clasped them together and kept her eyes on the road ahead. She mustn't *grieve*. Not yet.

The windscreen became blurred. It had started to rain.

Melissa's mother collected her from Queen Charlotte's Hospital that same morning. She'd tactfully packed away all the baby clothes and nursery equipment so that Melissa wouldn't be upset by the sight of them, made up the spare-room bed for herself, and filled the dainty little house with vases of fresh flowers and a fridge full of goodies. Now it was time to take her daughter home.

Emptied of her precious and longed-for burden, Melissa sat in silence, feelings of guilt filling her instead.

God's punishment, a voice kept saying in her head. She'd cared too much at the thought of losing the house. She'd been tortured with jealousy of Liza, who had everything, and now God was punishing her for her avarice. But was it greed? she asked herself. The house meant more to her than just a smart little home she could show off to her friends; she loved it because it was a haven, something that belonged to her, away from her mother. The realisation was quite a shock. And now they'd played right into Eileen Blagdon's hands by letting her pay their losses. The awful truth was that she'd managed to get away from home, to avoid living with her mother, only to end up with her mother coming too.

'We're nearly there,' Eileen announced as they turned off the King's Road.

Melissa nodded in silent despair. Mechanically she reached for her handbag.

'I hope I've got my front door keys.'

'You won't need them,' Eileen replied, smiling briefly.

'Why? Is there someone at home?' Could it be Freddy?

'No.'

'Then you've got my keys, have you?' Something wasn't right. Why was her mother hedging, as if she had an exciting secret she wanted Melissa to discover for herself?

'You'll soon find out, dear.' Again that tantalising little smile.

As her mother produced some bright new keys from her pocket, Melissa knew what had happened.

'What have you done?' she asked, appalled.

'Don't worry, dear. Everything's under control. You won't need to be married to Freddy much longer. I always knew you could do better than him. Meanwhile, I'm going to raise a mortgage so you can buy this house for yourself. It will make a very good launch pad for the future, won't it?' Her mother was beaming now, her own ambition finding root in her daughter's future.

'You must get back into circulation fairly quickly,' she continued. 'I know you'll soon find the right sort of husband. Successful, you know. A man who is going places. Titled, even. That's what you need.'

Melissa started to cry very quietly.

The mortuary smelled of death. The silence was the silence of the tomb: total, absolute, like an empty cave where no one had ever been before. The absence of souls was the worst part of all, a void where there had once been spirits, like a flame after it has been extinguished, or a ray of sunlight after it has been obliterated by a passing cloud.

They brought forward a trolley, the form lying on it covered by a sheet.

Liza dug her nails into the palms of her hands and hoped she wasn't going to faint. Buck and the police-woman closed in on either side of her, as if to support her. Slowly, the mortuary attendant drew back the sheet that covered the face. It was bleached of all colour; still, remote, no longer of this world.

Liza stepped nearer. A voice spoke gently beside her.

'Are you able to make an identification, Mrs Hamcroft? Is this your husband?'

'What do you think, Humphrey?' Lady Rosemary looked around at the pleasant living room of the flat they'd gone to view in Pimlico. It was large and light, with windows overlooking the central garden of Warwick Square, and it had three bedrooms, a large dining room and a very nice kitchen. 'The only snag is there's no garden, but I daresay we could use the middle garden.'

Sir Humphrey blinked, perplexed. 'How are we going to fit everything in?'

She slipped her arm through his, walking him into the rectangular hall. 'We'll choose some furniture from Cavenham Court, and some from the flat in Eaton Place, and we'll try not to be cluttered and I think we'll manage very well,' she said cheerfully. 'Remember, Richard and Laura will be at university most of the time. There will just be the two of us, and I think I'll do my curtain-making in the dining room.'

He nodded sadly. 'By then everything will be gone, won't it? Cavenham, Eaton Place, the lot.' His voice dropped to a whisper.

'But I tell you what we *will* have, Humphrey, and that's each other.' It amazed her how close they'd grown since their world had fallen apart. A few years ago she'd never have believed they could be so happy together. Perhaps, she reflected, her great wealth had been a barrier between them, destroying his confidence, highlighting his inability to have a brilliant career, isolating her from the real world.

Sir Humphrey smiled at her and looked grateful. 'Yes, we'll have each other, and we will have a little money, not much, but enough for the odd bottle of wine, eh?'

'Of course we will,' she assured him, smiling back, realising that it had been a long time since she'd noticed the clear pale blue of his eyes.

'I suppose,' he continued, 'the bit I get from Meldrews will come in handy.' The import-export company of which he'd been a director for twenty years had now grown into a very large organisation, and as he told his friends, his title still looked quite good on their headed paper. In fact, his lack of snobbery and genuine interest in the employees had endeared him to everyone, making him, over the years, feel wanted.

'Your director's salary will be a godsend,' his wife assured him firmly. 'So, shall we take this flat?'

'Yes, I think we should,' he replied with such unusual determination she looked at him in surprise. 'I know you'll make it lovely, my dear. I think we could be very happy here.'

Chapter Twenty

Liza sipped the glass of water Detective Inspector Buck had put into her unsteady hand. A series of conflicting emotions, like cross-currents in a narrow river, swept her this way and that, making her feel like a piece of driftwood, destined to hurtle along to an unknown destination.

'Are you feeling better now, Mrs Hamcroft?'

She'd nearly fainted when she'd seen that waxen face. Relief, she supposed. Overwhelming relief because it wasn't Toby.

'Yes. Thank you.' They were sitting in the police station adjoining the mortuary. Buck and the policewoman had helped her here, guided her stumbling feet until they could lower her on to a chair.

'What happens now?' she asked.

'We continue our normal lines of enquiry,' he replied, lapsing into typical noncommittal police-speak. 'When you're ready, I suggest we get back to London.'

'Of course.' The moment of near intimacy when he'd

stood close to her in the mortuary was over. She was once again the wife of a kidnapped man, who had previously hindered police enquiries by keeping the truth from them. The hint of hostility had crept back into his voice. He was not going to forgive her.

In silence they drove back to London.

When they arrived back at Holland Park Walk, Liza looked up at Buck as he held the car door open for her. There was something she had to know.

'Do you think they'll kill Toby?'

He seemed taken aback by the suddenness of her question.

'Not necessarily,' he replied, hedging once more. 'It's difficult, in a case like this, because we don't know what we're up against.' Buck turned away, his eyes distant, his mouth tightly shut. It was obvious he wasn't going to say any more.

As soon as Liza entered the house she stood in the hall, momentarily wondering what was missing. Then she remembered. There was no ecstatic greeting from Lottie, who usually launched herself at Liza with lunatic joy. There were no calls from different levels of the house, of 'Mummy?', 'Mummy?', 'Mummy, is that you?' The distant hum of the washing-machine was missing, too, as was the perfume of fresh flowers or the aroma of hot chocolate, as Tilly proudly baked a batch of brownies. The family were all down at Chalklands and, apart from Freddy in the evenings, she was alone in the house for the first time in years.

When the phone rang she jumped, nerves jangling.

'Hello?'

'Liza? This is Melissa. Is Freddy there by any chance?'

She sounded so unlike herself that Liza hardly recognised her voice.

'He's not here, Melissa, he's at work,' she replied coolly.

'I've tried, but they say he's not in his office.' She sounded as if she was crying, and Liza found herself relenting a bit towards her.

'Can I give him a message for you?' she asked more kindly.

'Could you? Could you tell him I'd . . . I'd like to talk to him?'

'Yes. All right.'

'I'm sorry about Toby. Is there any more news?'

'None, I'm afraid.'

'Oh, dear.' Melissa sniffed, and Liza brought the conversation gracefully to an end.

'I'll tell Freddy you phoned when he gets in this evening,' she said.

'Thank you. I'd be very grateful.' Melissa sounded positively meek.

For Declan the day had been sheer hell. Mr Stanley Houseman, a controller of Fraud Investigation at the office of the Director of Public Prosecution, along with his team, had been pulling the offices of Martin E. L. Hamcroft's apart since dawn.

Declan had been singled out, it seemed to him, for special interrogation.

'Look! I've told you all I can!' he exclaimed in desperation after hours of questioning. At times he'd thought they were merely trying to find out from him about the intricacies of the world of insurance, and Lloyd's in particular, but at other times he felt certain they were trying to catch him out, get him to admit to some illegal practice, trip him up so that he'd be forced to confess to some misdemeanour.

It was so unfair, he told himself, because he'd done nothing wrong; a bit of sharp practice here and there didn't count: looking after one's own interests went with the territory. No big deal. Everyone was at it.

They left at last, staggering under dozens of boxes of papers, files, tapes and computer printouts.

By order of the Director of Public Prosecution, Martin E. L. Hamcroft had ceased trading as from nine a.m.

The careers of all who worked in the company had, overnight, been disrupted, and in the case of some of the older men, destroyed. Many left in tears, wondering if they'd ever find work again.

Declan hurried home, deeply shaken. He hadn't realised that the suspension of Charles Bryer meant they'd all be under suspicion. He hadn't realised it might be the end of the company, either.

And what of his future? Was he still Charles's heir? If he could be sure of that, he needn't worry so much. He and Maxine had put enough aside to see them through the next ten to twelve years if they were careful; after that, Charles's money would make them rich for the rest of their lives.

It struck him, then, that he hadn't been nearly supportive enough of Jane Bryer. Better to have her on his side, rather than against him. If there were problems with Charles's will, when the time came, the last thing he'd need was a widow disputing the terms. Not that Charles hadn't provided for her, Declan remembered. Even so . . . He'd get Maxine to invite her round for supper; ask Jane what her plans were and promise to help her in any way he could. The thought made him feel quite self-righteous.

When he got home, he heard Maxine talking to someone in their living room. One of her charity committee friends, he supposed, tempted to go quietly upstairs without being seen, to have a shower. He approved of the way Maxine cultivated the 'right' people: socialites who invited them to dinner parties and so enlarged their circle of acquaintances. Declan used that particular word with precision. Friends, these people weren't. Friends came from the same walk of life, shared the same background and history, talked the same language and aimed for the same goals as oneself. Acquaintances were people who had already arrived, and if they were well disposed towards you, or thought you could be useful, gave you a leg up so you could join the ladder at their level.

'Is that you, Declan?' Maxine called out.

Declan stifled an oath, knowing there was nothing for it but to go and say how-do-you-do.

When he entered their large and over-furnished

living room, he stopped and stared, too horrified even to disguise the shock he felt.

'Hello there, Declan! How are you doing, boy?'

A short rotund woman with brassy hair stood up. She was wearing a turquoise shell-suit and white trainers.

'Surprised to see me? Eh?' she chuckled, amused.

Declan stood stock-still. Only one thought passed through his head. Thank God neither he nor Maxine were entertaining anyone important this evening.

'Mum!' His voice was strangled in his throat. 'What are you doing here?'

The woman's laughter became richer and smokier, and she looked at Maxine as if she expected her to share the joke.

'Nice welcome! And me, coming all the way down from Blackburn to see you,' she said.

'Why didn't you say you were coming?' He looked at Maxine almost accusingly, as if she'd done something behind his back.

'You didn't tell me Charles Bryer had made you his heir,' Maxine countered swiftly.

'I didn't . . . ?' Confused, he looked from his wife to his mother and back again. 'Who told you about that?'

'I told her, boy. I thought she ought to know, seeing as how Charles has scampered off,' his mother said calmly.

For a moment Declan wondered if he was going out of his mind. Bitterly ashamed of his uneducated parents, he'd spent the past twenty years trying to avoid them, and giving the impression to his friends that he had been, in fact, orphaned in his late teens. That stopped any awkward questions. Fortunately Charles had never enquired further into Declan's background, but if his mother had been anywhere near Charles Bryer, he could kiss his inheritance goodbye. Charles was a snob.

'What are you talking about?' he demanded nervously. 'How did *you* know that he was leaving me everything?'

'You don't think I'm good enough for you and your friends, do you?' Her manner was blunt but quite amiable, as if she wasn't too bothered by the situation.

Declan blushed furiously, his eyes watering. 'It's not that ... I ... er...' he stumbled. 'Things are different down here, Mum. You don't get on unless you've been to the right school and all that.'

'It didn't seem to stop you getting what you wanted.' Her large plump hands gestured at the richness of the room.

'I have Charles Bryer to thank for that,' Declan replied defensively.

'Exactly!' His mother removed the cigarette from her mouth, and, reaching forward, stubbed it out in a little ornamental Wedgwood bowl. Declan winced.

'What do you mean, "exactly"?' he asked.

She leaned forward confidentially. 'Just in case he never comes back from Switzerland, or wherever he's gone, I thought I'd better tell you straight.'

Declan felt a sudden nasty jolt in the pit of his stomach.

She smiled cheerfully. 'He's your real father, you see, Declan. No one else knows this, but your Dad thinks *he's* your father, and why not? Don't do no harm. I met Charles when he came up to Blackburn on business, nearly forty years ago. I was a slip of a girl then. Wouldn't believe it to see me now, would you?' Her laugh was even smokier, and ended in a cough.

Maxine was looking at her with something that resembled admiration. In on the secret of their existence from the beginning, she'd always got on with Declan's parents because they were an English version of her own: honest-to-goodness working-class people who had no pretences, but no ambition to better themselves either. Unlike she and Declan who craved the good life.

Both women suddenly realised Declan had gone very pale and very quiet.

'My father? How?' he croaked.

'Usual way, boy!'

The laughter was ever coarser and richer this time. She lit another cigarette and, having inhaled deeply, continued. 'He used to come up and see me whenever he could. He'd been married to Jane, Plain Jane I always called her, for several years, and he was doing so well in Lloyd's he didn't want to rock the boat by leaving her. But he made sure you had a good education, and then it was him who gave you your first job, wasn't it?' Her voice was filled with pride.

Declan sat there, not knowing whether he was horrified or pleased.

'Did he pay for my education?' was all he could think to ask.

'He certainly did. And a lot of your clothes, and money for school trips.'

'My God!' He felt stunned. 'How did you explain all that money to Dad? I mean . . .' He paused, confused and embarrassed suddenly.

'I told him my grandmother had left me a few bob. Now, as soon as Charles drops off the perch, you let me know. We don't want no shyster solicitor messing with that will of his. If there's any trouble, you just tell them I'll sell the story to one of them tabloid newspapers. That'll make Plain Jane shut up soon enough!'

'Melissa phoned earlier. She wants to speak to you,' Liza told Freddy when he came home later that evening.

'Oh?' He raised his eyebrows. 'How was your day? Any news at all?'

She told him about her trip to Bexhill.

'Holy shit! I'd have got off work and gone with you if you'd rung me,' he said, aghast. 'It must have been *awful*.'

'It was hideous. I feel as if a steam-roller has gone over me, first one way and then the other,' Liza admitted.

'Why don't you go to bed? I would if I were you. I'll make scrambled eggs for supper and let's have it upstairs in your room.'

She let herself go limp. 'Oh, Freddy, it sounds bliss.'

'Go on then!'

'Thanks. I will.' As she dragged herself up the steep flight of stairs to the first floor, she felt completely exhausted and drained of all emotion. Today had been the worst day, so far. What more pain could life inflict on her now?

When Freddy appeared with supper, there was only one plate of eggs on the tray.

'Aren't you eating, too?' she asked.

He looked faintly sheepish. 'I phoned Melissa. She wants to see me, so I'm popping round there now. You don't mind do you? I won't be long.'

Liza managed an amused smile. 'I thought Melissa sounded rather contrite on the phone.'

'Really? Well . . . I don't know what's going to happen, but I thought I'd better listen to what she has to say.'

Liza nodded. She hadn't seen Freddy look so cheerful for ages.

'You know what the trouble is?' he said. 'It's her mother! I wouldn't be surprised if she didn't put Melissa up to seeking a divorce.'

'You could be right.' For his sake, she hoped Freddy was right. She'd never been fond of her sister-in-law herself, but it was Freddy who was married to Melissa, not her. Perhaps if he came on stronger? Maybe she was a girl who basically liked being told what to do? Liza smiled up at her brother as she leaned against the pillows, the supper tray on her lap.

'Just don't give in too easily,' she advised him, gently.

'Oh, of course not!'

'She'll have more respect for you if you put your foot

down now and say you don't want any more of her nonsense.'

He nodded. 'I will, sis. I will. Wish me luck.' He leaned over to peck her on the cheek.

'Oh, yes, Freddy. Lots of luck.'

With a wave of his hand he was gone.

Melissa opened the front door slowly, and then stood there looking at Freddy.

'Hello,' he said awkwardly.

She stood to one side to let him in. 'Hello.' She looked pale and subdued and shrunken, and he instantly missed the swell of her stomach that he'd got increasingly used to ... Its flatness now was like a reproach. Sadness for what they'd lost made his eyes prick as he stepped, ahead of her, into the living room.

Automatically he said: 'How are you?'

'OK. Would you like a drink?'

Freddy looked around at the vases of flowers, and felt the strangeness of being treated like a guest in his own house. He tried to seize the initiative.

'No, thanks. What did you want to see me about, Melissa? You made your feelings very clear the other day.'

He thought he detected a shaft of panic in her dark eyes.

'I thought ... perhaps ...' Her face crumpled and she started crying. Then she covered her face with her hands and, turning away from him, dropped on to the sofa.

'Well?' Freddy knew he must not let her tears affect his judgement. He hated to see her cry, but then he remembered that she knew it.

'You got your solicitor to write to me,' he said accusingly. 'You've changed the locks, you're having my clothes sent over to Liza's house, and you want a divorce. Right? What more is there to discuss?'

She looked so young and woebegone that for a moment he had to fight the desire to take her in his arms and comfort her. Instead he sat in his favourite armchair, beside the fireplace, waiting for her to say something.

'It's all been a terrible mistake,' Melissa sobbed. 'Mummy got the solicitor to write to you while I was in hospital. I swear, Freddy, I didn't know anything about it until I got back here.' She wiped her eyes with a sodden handkerchief before continuing.

'The day I came home, I realised Mummy was planning to come and live here with me. She'd decided to sell her house and buy this one from you. She said I'd feel more secure if the house belonged to me. And if we got divorced, I wouldn't be liable for your Lloyd's losses.'

'Your mother has got it all worked out, hasn't she!' Freddy remarked drily. 'So I'm kicked out, with nowhere to go, and losses of hundreds of thousands to pay, while you and your mother stay here, all safe and cosy.' He found it hard to keep the bitterness out of his voice.

For the first time, Melissa looked directly at him.

'I asked her to leave.'

'You . . . ?' Freddy could hardly believe his ears.

'I told her,' Melissa continued, 'that the whole point of my loving this house is because it's mine! Well, ours, actually. It's my way of expressing myself without her interference.'

'What did she say to that?' Freddy wished he could have witnessed the scene. He'd have given anything to have seen Eileen Blagdon getting her comeuppance.

'I also told her we were returning the money she'd given us to pay off our losses for this year,' Melissa continued calmly. After her outburst of tears was over, she seemed to grow in confidence.

'I know it will mean selling this house, Freddy, and getting a little flat somewhere, but as we're not going to have a baby,' her voice faltered for a moment, 'well, having the house is not so important, is it?'

Freddy nodded slowly, more amazed than pleased. 'Are you sure that's what you want?'

For the first time, she smiled. 'Yes, it is, Freddy. I'm going to get a better-paid job, and we'll manage somehow, that is if you want us to?'

'I want to, but I have to make sure you want this, too. Your mother is going to be terribly offended, and probably hurt, too. Are you sure you won't regret returning her cheque and giving up this house? It's quite a big step, you know.'

Her smile was tremulous. 'I know, but I always wanted to get away from her. That's what this house has all been about.'

'And is that why you married me?'

She shook her head vehemently. 'No, of course not. I

love you, Freddy. That hasn't changed at all.' She looked around the pretty room. 'My mother has spoilt all this for me, though. It's not like my own nest any more. I actually want to get away from here and start somewhere fresh. A place just for us where she won't be allowed to intrude.'

Freddy looked at her long and tenderly. Then he went over and put his arms around her and pulled her close. Melissa cupped his face in her hands, and kissed him very gently on the lips.

'Let's put the house on the market tomorrow,' she said softly. 'And then we'll look for a tiny place, just for us.'

In response he kissed her deeply and lovingly. 'I've missed you so much,' he whispered.

'I've missed you too, Freddy.'

The woodman's hut in the middle of the forest hadn't been used for years. Far away from the public pathways that criss-crossed the wooded valley near Fowey, nine people made their way, in ones and twos, through the grim twilight of a rain-sodden day.

One of them was blindfolded, gagged, and with his wrists tied tightly behind his back. Beside him, half pushing, half dragging him as he stepped forward blindly, was the leader of the group, ex-SAS officer Captain Neil Palmer. His face was red and glistening with sweat, making it look as if grease had been smeared over his ruddy skin. His powerfully built body moved as if possessed by a brutal force, strong, nimble-footed, hands balled into fists. When they arrived at the hut, he propelled his prisoner through the open door and shoved him roughly into a corner. Then he kicked the lower part of his spine with a booted foot, and the prisoner spun round, collapsing on to the rotting wooden planks of the floor.

Captain Palmer turned to the others with a mocking smile which never reached his cold staring eyes. The elderly widow and the retired schoolteacher, Hannah Windlesham, stared in horror at the victim as Captain Palmer slung a rope around his ankles before pulling it tightly.

'Oh, please . . .' gasped Hannah beseechingly.

Captain Palmer looked at her. 'What's your problem, lady?' His hand moved slowly to the holster at his waist which contained his revolver. He stood watching the group, watching him. Nobody said anything. The smell of damp and decay hung all around them, and the stench of mould filled their nostrils.

The oldest member of the group, Graham Hayes, arrived at that moment, carrying his bursting briefcase. He seemed oblivious to the tension in the hut, as he sank on to a wooden bench which was thickly encrusted with bird droppings.

'All these tragic letters,' he said, tears lodging in the folds of skin under his eyes. 'All from people who have been ruined, made bankrupt; people I'd so hoped we'd be able to help. It's a tragedy. I don't mind so much for myself because I'm old, but for the—'

'Fuck the letters!' bellowed Captain Palmer. 'Fuck

the others! It's *us* who've been betrayed and swindled. May Malcolm Blackwell rot in hell!' He was becoming excitable and out of control. 'Fuck the whole of Lloyd's for what it's done to us!'

The figure in the corner remained motionless as it lay on the floor, while the others looked at Captain Palmer with watchful fear. They'd all come to the meeting today in the hopes of making Captain Palmer see reason. They'd failed in their crazy scheme; now was the time to release their hostage in a way that would prevent him seeing who they were, but Palmer seemed to have reached a new level of disappointment and rage. They all realised that at this moment he was capable of shooting them. He had the revolver in his hand now, and was waving it at Graham Hayes.

'Put all the letters in the middle of the floor,' he said with sudden, dangerous coldness. He was standing rigidly now, like an animal gathering up its strength before pouncing.

With shaking hands the old man tipped from his case hundreds of letters asking for financial help.

'For fuck's sake, tear them up first!' Palmer exploded, his voice breaking on the edge of hysteria. He'd become jumpy again, nervously glancing through the dirt-blurred window of the hut. Mackenzie and Todd stepped forward to help tear up the letters, while Graham Hayes looked stupefied with fear. The others were too sick with terror to move.

Then Hannah Windlesham spoke in a low voice.

'Are you going to burn the letters?' She knew now that

they were for ever bonded by what had happened, and when Captain Palmer answered her, she realised they were all accomplices to a truly dreadful deed.

'I'll torch the hut when we're all out of here,' he said, and the icy madness in his eyes chilled them to the bone.

'Go!' he commanded, standing with his feet apart, giving each of them a darting look of warning that he intended to be obeyed. 'Go! One at a time. Spread out in different directions. Do not contact each other again. Go!' He pointed the revolver at Mackenzie first. Then Todd. Then Hayes, who was weeping silently, followed by the others. There was only Hannah Windlesham left.

'*GO!*' he screamed. '*NOW!*'

Hannah glanced at the prostrate figure on the floor in the corner. She dared not ask what was going to happen to him. In silence, without looking at Captain Palmer, she scurried out of the hut and disappeared, like the others, into the darkness of the forest.

'Why not come out and have dinner with us?' Emma coaxed Liza the next morning.

'I don't think I will, Em,' Liza replied. 'Thanks all the same.'

'Oh, come on! It will do you good. We needn't be late. I'll book a table at the Belvedere.'

'But suppose someone tries to get hold of me?' Liza queried, worried. She'd become terrified of going anywhere, in case there was news of Toby. Every time the phone rang, she dived for it. If the front door bell rang, she rushed to a window to see who it was, in case it was the police with fresh news and not just another journalist. Every minute of the day she was on the alert, listening, waiting and wondering what the hell was happening to him. She'd lost over a stone since he'd gone, and now she awoke, even after only a few hours' sleep, in a sweat, panicking, her teeth clenched, her fists in a tense clutch.

'Liza?' Emma spoke softly.

'Yes?'

'Nothing is going to happen between eight and ten o'clock at night. If you like, tell the police you'll be at the Belvedere, only do please come out and give yourself a break. I'm worried about you. You're not going to be much use to Toby when he gets back if you're having a nervous breakdown, are you?'

'That's true,' Liza replied, wistfully. 'Oh, Em! Do you think he'll ever come back? I'm so bloody scared. They might easily kill him. They'll know they're not going to get the money now, and he can identify them. Would you let him live, if you were in their shoes?'

There was a long pause before Emma replied.

'I don't suppose they want to add murder to their list of crimes,' she replied carefully. 'As it stands, they've kidnapped Toby and Janet Granville, who managed to escape. I don't suppose, if the extenuating circumstances of financial ruin are put forward by a good lawyer that they'd get a heavy sentence. Murder is something else, though.'

Liza let out a long sigh, but already she felt better, listening to her friend's robust tone.

'You're right,' she said thoughtfully.

'Then you'll come out to dinner?'

'Yeah. OK, thanks.'

'Bring Freddy with you.'

'He's not here.'

'Why ever not?' Emma demanded.

'He went round to see Melissa last night, and they've patched things up.'

'So you're on your own? Then you're most certainly coming out with us. How could Freddy leave you alone?'

'I told him to stay with Melissa, Em. D'you know, I haven't been on my own for ages. I really need a bit of space and peace, and I'm not scared of being alone in this house. Right now I almost prefer it.'

'Well you're not going to be by yourself this evening. We'll pick you up at a quarter to eight. OK?'

'OK, Em.'

By that evening Liza was glad she'd decided to go out with Emma and Anthony. She'd slept on the drawing-room sofa for several hours, and the peace that enveloped the house had been wonderful, but now she felt like being with people again, as a sense of restlessness returned. Dressed in black silk trousers and jacket, with her long blonde hair wound up into a casual knot at the back, she waited for them to pick her up. Wandering around the drawing room, unable to sit still now, she wondered why she felt so uneasy. Perhaps, she concluded, it was because she normally never went out without Toby. When he was away on business trips, she took the opportunity to invite her women friends round for supper, or she read and listened to music, and sometimes allowed Tilly and Thomas to watch TV with her in her bed. She missed having Freddy around, too, although she was glad he'd made it up with Melissa.

When the front door bell rang, Liza, picking up her small silk evening bag, hurried to answer it. Anthony stood there, smiling broadly.

'Hello, Liza! This is great. I'm so glad Emma managed to persuade you to come out tonight.'

She kissed him on both cheeks.

'Thanks, Ant. I felt badly about it at first, you know, going out to dinner when we don't even know what's happening to Toby, but I suppose there's nothing I can do by sitting at home fretting all the time.'

'You're right. I think it's amazing how well you're coping. I suppose you haven't heard anything?'

Liza shook her head. 'Nothing.'

Emma was waiting in the car. As soon as she saw Liza, she jumped out and hugged her.

'Well done, Liza. *And* you're looking great!'

'I wish I could say I feel it, but I'm working at it,' Liza replied with a wry smile.

'Good for you! Come on, let's go. I'm told the food is fabulous at this place and I, for one, am starving.' Emma gently pushed her into the car.

'How's the work going?' Liza asked.

'The Lloyd's feature?' Emma gave a satisfied nod. 'Great! I've got more material than I can ever use. Trust has been abused in the most appalling way, and I heard today that thirty thousand members have been affected! The final losses, taking everything into account, may top twenty-five billion! Can you believe it?'

'God, that's terrible,' Liza looked grave. 'We've lost a packet, you know. Almost everything Toby worked for will go. Have you heard if you're all right?'

'Have we, Ant?' Emma suddenly looked worried.

'I heard this morning, actually,' he replied, braking as the traffic lights changed to red.

'And...?'

'We've got off remarkably lightly. Our losses will only be a few thousand pounds each year for the next three years. In total I don't think it will exceed twenty-five thousand, because Toby arranged a stop-loss policy for me,' Anthony replied with satisfaction. 'Having said that, though, I'm going to get out as soon as I can. My nerves aren't strong enough to withstand these sort of frights again.'

'That's probably wise,' Liza agreed. 'I've no idea what we'll do when Toby comes back—' her voice faltered – 'and I don't really care. A tiny cottage in the country with just Toby and the children sounds like heaven at this moment.'

Emma patted her shoulder. 'It'll happen, and you'll look back at this time and wonder how you ever got through it.'

'I'm doing that already!'

'Well, you're doing all right,' said Anthony as he swung the car into the drive of the Belvedere.

Emma, determined Liza was going to try and relax, got Anthony to order champagne cocktails, smoked salmon, wild duck in a cherry sauce, and then tiny strawberries with cream.

The dinner was exquisitely cooked and prepared, but Liza found it hard to concentrate on her friends. They tried to distract her, talking about the children and the forthcoming summer holidays, but she kept thinking of Toby, her mind straying again and again, so that there were moments when she had no idea what they were saying. Then she'd try hard to pull herself back into the now, but it only lasted a minute or so, before she'd remember things like the deserted petrol station, or the morgue at Bexhill or those dreadful ransom notes. Inevitably that caused her thoughts to race off again into a maelstrom of dark shadows and darker fears.

'Would you excuse me if I went home?' she said at last. It was half past ten and she was, for no particular reason, feeling more uneasy than ever.

Emma understood at once. 'Of course. We could do with an early night ourselves. We'll drop you off.'

'Thanks.'

'Are you sure you want to be on your own?' Anthony asked. 'It's a big house to be alone in; would you like us to stay for the night?'

'That's really nice of you, Ant, but I'm fine.'

'Are you sure?' Emma asked.

Liza nodded, touched by their concern.

Ten minutes later he was driving her back to Holland Park Walk.

They insisted on seeing Liza into the house; as she stood in the doorway, silhouetted against the brightly lit hall, she waved goodbye. It was good to be home again. Locking the front door, she turned off the hall light and was just about to go up the stairs to the bedroom, when she heard the unmistakable sound of heavy footsteps in the basement kitchen. Then they stopped, and the silence was heavy and stifling. With the blood thundering in her ears and her mind paralysed with terror, she stood rigid, hanging on to the banister rail, dancing spots of light flickering before her eyes, although the hall was in darkness.

She decided to try and get out of the house as silently and swiftly as she could. Slipping off her high-heeled shoes, she started to cross the hall on tiptoe. Her keys were still clutched in her hand. All she had to do was turn the three locks, disengage the chain and ... *the footsteps were coming slowly up the stairs from the basement.*

Terror struck her with icy prickles down her spine. For a second she hesitated, too frightened to move, then she charged to the front door, fumbling desperately with her keys. Her hands were shaking so much that the whole bunch slipped through her fingers and crashed on the marble floor.

A figure stepped out of the shadows, there was a stampede of heavy footsteps across the hall, then suddenly strong arms were supporting her, holding her so close she could hardly breathe; then a cheek, rough and unshaven, was brushing hers, and a voice, warm and deep in her ear: 'Oh, Liza, my darling. Oh, God! Liza...'

'Toby!' Her heart was still pounding; she could scarcely believe she wasn't imagining it.

He was crying, clutching her as if he could never bear to let her go, kissing her mouth and her eyes and her cheeks and neck in a frenzy of relief. 'Oh, Jesus, I thought I'd never see you again,' he wept unashamedly.

Dazed, she reached over his shoulder for the light switch. The hall was instantly bathed in the brilliant dazzle of the large crystal chandelier. She stared, unbelieving, but it was Toby. It really was Toby: dirty, in ragged clothes, his hair matted, a wound on his temple and his wrists purple with welts and bruises. But he was back, home, and she held him tightly, afraid to let him go, as if he were an apparition that might vanish, leaving her alone again.

A galaxy of dog-eyed daisies bordered the railway track. As the train shuddered to a squealing halt, the three children waiting on the platform spotted him simultaneously.

'Daddy!'

'It's Daddy!'

'Daddy!'

They raced along the platform, Lottie, jumping with lunatic excitement, at their heels; dodging between people alighting from the train, to where Toby stood, a little thinner, a bit more deeply lined, but with as warm a smile as ever. He waited, motionless, with Liza beside him, bracing himself for the first impact, then the second, and then the third, gentler and somewhere around knee-level. He scooped little Sarah up into his arms, beaming with pleasure as he kissed Thomas and Tilly, asking them how they were as he slowly made his way along the platform to where his mother stood.

Hearing about the death of his father had been a blow, and he still had to come to terms with it, but he knew he had so much to be thankful for.

'Hello, Ma,' he said softly, kissing Nina's cheek.

'Thank God you're home,' she replied, smiling shakily.

'Let's go,' Liza whispered. They had so much catching up to do. All of them. Toby nodded, and took her hand. With the children hanging about his neck and shoulders and arms like extra garments, they made their way to where the car was parked.

Extract from an article which appeared in the Globe

LLOYD'S KIDNAPPERS ARRESTED

Emma Turnbull

Seven people have been arrested in connection with the kidnap and attempted murder of Lloyd's broker, Toby Hamcroft, 46. He was held captive for over two weeks while his abductors attempted to extort fifty million pounds from Lloyd's central fund. The leader of the group, Captain Neil Palmer, 39, was found dead in the garage of his Tiverton house, yesterday morning. He is thought to have shot himself.

Toby Hamcroft narrowly escaped death when an explosive device went off moments after he'd been rescued from an isolated hut in a forest in the Fowey area, where his captors had left him bound and gagged. Hannah Windlesham, 62, a retired schoolmistress, and a member of the group involved, returned to the hut when all the others had left, after she became suspicious of Captain Palmer's intentions. She is at present on remand.

This series of bizarre events highlights the recent troubles at Lloyd's, involving unprecedented syndicate losses. Outside Names, whose investment was subject to an unlimited liability clause, have been the worst affected, leaving thirty thousand people seeking financial recompense.

Mr Charles Bryer, 54, former chairman of the now defunct syndicate and agency, Martin E. L. Hamcroft, recently absconded from the country, after being fined one million pounds and suspended from Lloyd's. Rumour has it he has stolen forty million pounds belonging to Outside Names. Forensic examination of a letter containing a death threat, sent in an effort to prevent details of malpractice being made public, suggests that it was the work of Charles Bryer.

Mr Declan Connolly, 36, a colleague of Mr Bryer and formerly of Toby Hamcroft, has received a warning for using privileged information in order to increase his commission from insurance transactions that he carried out. He may yet be subjected to further interrogation from the Director of Public Prosecution.

Meanwhile, Toby Hamcroft, who is married with three children, has been counting the cost of being the only straight card in the pack. He is thought to have suffered very heavy losses, estimated to reach over six million pounds in the next three years.

In the light of these serious events, and with total losses likely to reach an eventual twenty-five billion pounds, the long-term future of Lloyd's remains in question.

More Enchanting Fiction from Headline

BLISS

CLAUDIA CRAWFORD

As she nears her ninetieth birthday, Rachel Salinko can look back on a life well lived. She has achieved wealth, celebrity and, more important, been the shaping influence on three generations of her family's women. Yet for her daughter and granddaughters coming to terms with Rachel's tyrannical love has been one of the great trials of their lives. And, as Rachel reveals her plans for her great-granddaughter Bliss, a girl whose radiance recalls her own long-past years of innocence, it is clear the emotional power struggles are far from over. For buried deep is a secret that could finally destroy the bonds that unite them all . . .

FICTION / GENERAL 0 7472 4749 8

More Enchanting Fiction from Headline

Seasons of Her Life

Fern Michaels

'You're in the spring of your life, Ruby, the best time of all. Everything is still before you. It's your time to grow, to spread your wings, to turn into the wonderful woman I know you will become . . .'

With these parting words from her beloved grandmother, Ruby Connors leaves her bitter childhood behind, venturing forth into a new world of opportunities.

In her springtime, she falls in love with Marine lieutenant Andrew Blue and Filipino Calvin Santos, but only one can win her heart for ever.

In her summer, she fulfils her grandmother's prophecies of marriage and motherhood and experiences the joy and pain of both.

In her autumn, she realises where her true strengths lie and establishes a business that is successful beyond her wildest dreams.

And right into her winter days, Ruby carries closest to her heart the memory of the man she longs for in her soul . . .

FICTION / SAGA 0 7472 4414 6

More Thrilling Fiction from Headline Feature

TELL ME NO SECRETS

THE TERRIFYING PSYCHOLOGICAL THRILLER

JOY FIELDING

'People who annoy me have a way of . . . disappearing'

Jess Koster thinks she has conquered the crippling panic attacks that have plagued her since the unexplained disappearance of her mother, eight years ago. But they are back with a vengeance. And not without reason. Being a chief prosecutor in the State's Attorney's office exposes Jess to some decidedly lowlife types. Like Rick Ferguson, about to be tried for rape – until his victim goes missing. Another inexplicable disappearance.

If only Jess didn't feel so alone. Her father is about to remarry; her sister is busy being the perfect wife and mother; her ex-husband has a new girlfriend. And besides, he's Rick Ferguson's defence lawyer . . .

Battling with a legal system that all too often judges women by appalling double standards; living under the constant threat of physical danger; fighting to overcome the emotional legacy of her mother's disappearance, Jess is in danger of going under. And it looks as though someone is determined that she should disappear, too . . .

'Joy Fielding tightens suspense like a noose round your neck and keeps one shattering surprise for the very last page. Whew!' *Annabel*

'The story she has to tell this time is a corker that runs rings round Mary Higgins Clark. Don't even think of starting this anywhere near bedtime' *Kirkus Reviews*

FICTION / GENERAL 0 7472 4163 5

More Compelling Fiction from Headline

Martina Cole

GOODNIGHT LADY

SHE KNOWS EVERYONE'S SECRETS . . .

The infamous Briony Cavanagh: quite a beauty in her day, and powerful, too. In the sixties, she ran a string of the most notorious brothels in the East End. Patronised by peers and politicians – even royalty, some said. Only Briony knew what went on behind those thick velvet curtains, those discreet closed doors, and Briony never opened her mouth – unless she stood to benefit.

Only Briony knew the hard and painful road she'd travelled to get there. From an impoverished childhood that ended abruptly with shocking betrayal, she had schemed and manipulated, determined to be mistress of her own fate.

But her flourishing business brought her into contact with the darker side of life at the violent heart of London's gangland. Along with her material success came risk and danger. And the Goodnight Lady had her own secret place, a place in her heart that was always shadowed with loss . . .

'Move over Jackie [Collins]!' *Daily Mirror*

'Sheer escapism . . . gripping . . . will definitely keep you guessing to the end' *Company*

'Graphic realism combined with dramatic flair make this a winner' Netta Martin, *Annabel*

FICTION / GENERAL 0 7472 4429 4